KIANNA ALEXANDER
and
JOY AVERY

Then Came You &
Written with Love

HARLEQUIN® KIMANI™ ROMANCE

ISBN-13: 978-1-335-45841-4

Then Came You & Written with Love

Copyright © 2019 by Harlequin Books S.A.

The publisher acknowledges the copyright holders of the individual works as follows:

Then Came You
Copyright © 2019 by Eboni Manning

Written with Love
Copyright © 2019 by Joy Avery

Recycling programs for this product may not exist in your area.

www.Harlequin.com

Printed in U.S.A.

"You know there was a reason I didn't show up that night, don't you? It was completely out of my control, Robyn. I would never have…"

She held up her hand. "It's ancient history."

He snapped his mouth shut, wondering if Rick had been right. Was this about making him pay for what he'd done all those years ago?

She smiled, but it didn't reach her eyes. "I'm not looking for revenge, either. I've moved on from it." She slid back from the table and stood, grabbing her tray. "We're not kids anymore, Troy. I don't believe in playing those kinds of childish games. And, besides, I wasn't the one who hired you. I didn't even know we'd taken you on until you showed up. So your little ego trip has been wasted. I simply haven't thought that much about you since all those years ago."

"Fair enough." He looked up, meeting her gaze. "But do you believe in second chances?"

She narrowed her eyes as if studying him to test his sincerity. "Only when the situation warrants it." She turned and carried her tray to the return point. Once she'd deposited her dishes in the proper place, she strode out of the café without a single backward glance.

Alon.

Noce.

Kianna Alexander, like any good Southern belle, wears many hats: loving wife, doting mama, advice-dispensing sister and gabbing girlfriend. She's a voracious reader, an amateur seamstress and occasional painter in oils. Chocolate, American history, sweet tea and Idris Elba are a few of her favorite things. A native of the Tar Heel state, Kianna still lives there with her husband, two kids and a collection of well-loved vintage '80s Barbie dolls. You can keep up with Kianna's releases and appearances by signing up for her mailing list at www.authorkiannaalexander.com/sign-up.

Visit the Author Page at Harlequin.com for more titles.

CONTENTS

For Robin B., Anya A., Wendy C., Katie D., Fran C. and all the awesome librarians out there—keepers of our history, purveyors of knowledge and some of the coolest folk to sit with for a chat. Librarians rock!

Acknowledgments

All my love to my readers, both new ones and longtime fans. I appreciate you! Shout-out to the Destin Divas, the absolute best squad a girl could ask for. Special thanks to Kaia Alderson, who's always just a text away and helps me sort through the jumble of ideas in my brain. Love to my online group buddies in BRAN and in Romancelandia.

THEN CAME YOU

Kianna Alexander

Dear Reader,

Thanks for picking up a copy of *Then Came You*. I'm so grateful you've chosen to spend your valuable time with Troy and Robyn in the little town of Grandeza, New Mexico.

Knowing this would be my last Kimani, I wanted to do something I'd never done before in contemporary, something I've been wanting to do for a while. So when my editor asked me what my book would be about, I immediately said, "I want to write a cowboy!" I was also looking for a really beautiful setting, one I hadn't written about before, and the Land of Enchantment fit the bill perfectly. While ranching may not be as prominent there as it was in days past, it still continues to this day.

When our story opens, Robyn is looking for an escape and Troy is looking for a place to call home. How can they build a life together with such opposing goals? You'll have to read on to find out.

While this is my last Kimani, please know it won't be my last book. To keep up with what I'm working on, check out my website at www.authorkiannaalexander.com or follow me on Twitter, @kiannawrites.

All the best,

Kianna

Chapter 1

"That's a girl, Molly. Rest up."

Robyn Chance ran her hand along the top of the heifer's head, then stood from her kneeling position. Molly, deep into her first pregnancy, was lying atop a soft bed of hay in a quiet corner of the main barn. Other than looking after the calf, it had been an uneventful Monday for Robyn.

Robyn got her clipboard from the nail on the nearby post and jotted down her observations on Molly's chart. The animal seemed to be handling the pregnancy as well as could be expected for a first-timer, and Robyn expected the calf to make its appearance soon. Smiling, she returned the clipboard and moved toward the wall-mounted sink to wash up.

She'd just dried her hands when her phone vibrated in her pocket. "Hello?"

"Yes, hello. I'm trying to reach Dr. Robyn Chance?"

Her ears perked. "This is she."

"Dr. Chance, I'm Zachary McMillan, from the San Diego Wildlife Conservatory. How are you today?"

This is the call I've been waiting for! She sat down on the old wooden bench just outside the barn door. "I'm fine. I hope you are as well."

"I am." There was a brief pause. "I'll get right to the reason I'm calling. We'd like to offer you the position of director of veterinary services here at the conservatory if you're still interested. I know it's been a long review process."

She could feel the smile spreading across her face. "Yes, I'm definitely still interested." She could gush about how this was her dream job, how it presented the perfect opportunity for her to finally get off Chance land, out of Grandeza and into the world at large.

"Wonderful! There's only one caveat."

She sucked in a breath. "What's that?"

"We'll need you to be here and ready to start in three weeks. Would that be possible?"

She swallowed. That didn't give her much time to find a replacement. Despite that, she wasn't about to turn down an opportunity like this. "I'll be there."

"Sounds great. There's some intake paperwork we'll need. I'll have my assistant email it to you as an attachment, and you can either send it back, or hand-carry it when you arrive. Either way, it will help to speed the onboarding process along."

"I'll be looking out for it. Thank you for the opportunity."

"We're looking forward to having you on the team."

After the call ended, she leaned against the backrest and sighed. She should be over the moon with happiness. She'd applied for five positions, and out of them all, this was the one she'd wanted most, the one that seemed like a long shot. Snagging this job represented the biggest accomplishment of her veterinary career.

When she received good news, she'd usually go straight to the main house to tell her parents. But this time was different. No matter how much she wanted to, she couldn't tell them about his.

Because Cooper and Thelma Chance, owners of one of the largest cattle ranches still operating in New Mexico, had no idea their daughter had been seeking other employment. *I started my career here, and I'm pretty sure they expect me to stay forever.* She was now the sole heir to Chance Cattle Enterprises, though that had not always been the case.

The old, familiar pain rose in her chest, squeezing her heart like a fist. *Would Lacey have stayed? If she were still here, would she have wanted to live out her whole life on Cooper land?* There was no way to know the answer to that. Tears threatened to well in her eyes, so she pushed away those thoughts. They led only to sorrow.

She stood and headed for her office in the one-story brick structure a few hundred yards away from the main barn. Once she'd shut herself inside, she sat behind her old oak desk and pulled out her planner. Her week was fully loaded with tasks to accomplish, and right at the top of the list was acclimating a newly hired rancher to the Chance operation. One of their best men, Amos, was retiring, and it was critical they had a full staff as a busy time of year was almost on them. He was due to report for his entrance meeting tomorrow, and she hoped to get him started by Wednesday. She hadn't been able to find out much about the rancher so far. Mary Ellen Carter, the ranch manager who'd been working with the Chance family for twenty-plus years, had done the hiring. Since the fall calving season was approaching, all nine existing ranch employees were busy with the thirty-two pregnant cows and heifers in stock. Robyn had been assigned to meet with the new employee and get him situated.

She took a deep breath and shut the planner. *How am I going to help the new guy and find a replacement vet at the same time?* It would have been hard even if she had more time. But being limited to the three weeks before she was to start another job complicated things exponentially.

Her parents would be shocked enough to learn she wanted to leave. Then they'd have to digest that her departure was just around the corner. Any longtime employee leaving on such short notice would surely wound them. And she was their daughter, not just any staff member. She frowned at the thought, cringing at the prospect of breaking the news to them.

A knock sounded at the office door. Robyn's gaze followed the sound. "Come in."

Mary Ellen entered, with that ever-present smile on her lips. "Afternoon, Doc."

"Hey, M.E." Mary Ellen had been calling Robyn "Doc" ever since she'd returned home with her veterinary degree from UC Davis.

Mary Ellen eased farther into the office. She was dressed similarly to Robyn, wearing a green long-sleeved T-shirt emblazoned with the Chance Cattle Enterprises logo, jeans and brown work boots. The only difference in Robyn's attire was the white lab coat she wore over her clothes.

Mary Ellen's wavy brown hair, streaked with silver, surrounded an oval-shaped face that held kind blue eyes. "Wanted to see if you've made your rounds to the southern pasture yet."

She shook her head. "I'm headed there next. Is something wrong?"

"I'm not sure. Amos called me and said one of the older cows is looking a bit sluggish, though." Mary Ellen shrugged. "You know how it is when calving gets near. She may just be worn out, but you never can tell with these things."

Amos was one of their more experienced hands, and everyone knew he possessed good instincts when it came to the herd. "I'd better have a look at her, just to be safe." Robyn stood, tucking her phone into her hip pocket. "I think I know the cow you're talking about. Odds are, she's had her last breeding."

"I'm headed over there, so you can ride with me."

They exited the building and climbed into Big Red,

Mary Ellen's extended-cab pickup. As the truck bumped down the dirt road toward the southern part of the property, Robyn watched the familiar scenery roll by. Autumn had kissed the land, turning the verdant greens of spring and summer into rich golds and reds. Behind the carefully maintained fences, stock wandered, grazed or rested. She knew every tree, every hay bale, every patch of grass like she knew her own name. The glow of the afternoon sun illuminated the land, reflecting off the mountains in the distance and warming the air like an embrace.

There was a whole world beyond those mountains, one she'd never had a chance to explore in her thirty-two years on Earth. She wanted to see it, experience it for herself.

As much as she loved this land, her parents and their extended family of employees, she couldn't remain on Chance land forever. The burdensome pain of the past, combined with her incurable wanderlust, wouldn't allow it.

The wind whipped through the pasture, making the grass dance to its tune.

It's not going to be easy to leave all this behind.

Troy Monroe drove his SUV down US 84, with the New Mexico scenery whizzing by his window. The ride from the airport in Santa Fe to his tiny hometown of Grandeza took around an hour, and he was relieved to be arriving soon.

The view outside his window was familiar yet stood in stark contrast to the island setting he'd just left behind. There, he'd seen crystal-blue waters and towering pines. Here, the grasses were taller, browner. The edge of the road was lined with rubber rabbitbrush and other shrubs. The branches of pinon and juniper trees reached skyward, with the rocky peaks of the Sangre de Cristo Mountains towering over it all.

Grandeza was an unincorporated area of Rio Arriba County, with a population of less than three thousand. Their nearest neighboring community, Abiquiú, sat just southwest of town. Abiquiú was home to the famous Ghost Ranch that had served as a filming location for many Hollywood films. Proximity to Abiquiú was Grandeza's only claim to fame—except among lovers of funk and soul music. Troy's father, bassist Johnny Monroe of the jam band Zell's Midnight Preachers, had been born and raised there.

He'd just flown back from North Carolina, where he'd visited his Uncle Carver, Aunt Viola and his cousins, Campbell, Savion and Hadley. In general, he would have no reason to rush home. But since he'd received that upsetting phone call at the airport, he wanted to get to Grandeza as fast as possible.

Jeannie's sick. She's asking for you.

He thought back on the insistent words of Helene, his grandmother's favorite nurse at Grandeza Acres Retirement Villas. He'd spent the better part of his adulthood drifting around the Midwest, taking temporary jobs as a rancher or farmhand wherever he could find them. The only thing that tied him to Grandeza, and to a life he'd all but forgotten, was his father's mother, Jeannie.

Dad's been gone three years now. Johnny had been

killed with most of the members of his band in a tour-bus crash along Route 66 in Nevada. He had no idea where his mother, Sylvia, was. He hadn't seen or heard from her since he was seventeen.

He passed the faded, hand-painted wooden sign at the town limits and released a pent-up breath. The retirement home, located in the downtown area, came into view a few minutes later. Parking in a free space in the lot, he cut the engine. Taking the small boar bristle hairbrush from his glove box, he viewed his reflection in the rearview mirror and ran the brush through his close-cropped black hair. He used his fingertips to brush a few crumbs from his mustache, left behind by the pastry he'd had earlier. It had been a poor substitute for a real meal, but he'd been in a hurry. His eyes were heavy-lidded, revealing his weariness from a full day of air travel. His grandmother expected to see him "always presentable, never unkempt," and despite her illness, he knew better than to go against her oft-repeated admonishment. After returning the brush, he got out and strode across the grassy lawn toward the building.

He entered and went to the reception desk to check in. A short walk down the tiled corridor and out the rear of the main building took him to his grandmother's private unit. As he raised his hand to knock on the door, Helene opened it. A fair-skinned, green-eyed redhead in baby-pink scrubs, she stood about shoulder height to him.

Her expression conveyed relief. "Come on in, Troy. She's waiting for you."

He stepped inside the too-warm apartment as Helene closed the door behind him. "I see Grandma's still cold-natured."

Helene nodded. "That's why I never wear long sleeves in here." She moved toward the galley kitchen, gesturing him toward the bedroom. "Go on back."

In the cozy room, he found his grandmother propped up in her bed, a wealth of pillows at her back. She wore a blue housedress, her petite frame tucked beneath a large afghan. Her silver hair was wrapped around the pink, spongy curlers she favored, and gold-rimmed glasses sat perched on the end of her nose as she looked over the open newspaper on her lap.

He eased toward her, leaned down and kissed her forehead. "Hey, Mama Jeannie."

She offered a small smile. "Hello, sweetheart."

"Still reading the comic strips, I see."

Her thin shoulders lifted in a shrug. "It's the only part of the paper that's not full of bad news."

Pulling the nearby armchair closer to the bed, he sat down. "Helene called me and said you're not feeling well. That you were asking for me."

"Both true. The doctor says my pressure's up." She paused, took a few shallow breaths. "I've been getting really tired and winded." She reached up to stifle a yawn. "So, they put me on bedrest."

He studied her face, noting the pallor hanging over her. "I got here as fast as I could. Just flew back from North Carolina."

"How are my stepson Carver and his family?"

"They're doing well. All my cousins are married now."

Her eyes widened for a moment. "Really? Isn't that something." She eyed him.

When the scrutiny went on a beat too long, he pursed his lips. "Come on, Mama Jeannie. Don't give me that look. You know I'm not the settling-down type."

"You just haven't met the right woman." She smiled, but it faded as she went into a coughing spell. Covering her mouth with one hand, she gestured toward the glass of water on her nightstand with the other.

He handed her the glass, watching her as she took a few long sips. When the coughing subsided, she handed it back to him and he returned it to its resting spot.

"How long can you stay, Troy?"

He heard the weariness in her voice as she asked the question, and the familiar pangs of guilt wrenched his lower abdomen. "I'll be here for a while, Mama Jeannie. I just took a job here in town."

A bit of the old sparkle returned to her gray eyes. "Really? Where?"

"I'll be working over at the Chance spread as a lead rancher. Great benefits, good pay."

She nodded. "Benefits, you say." She paused. "I'm sure you know Robyn is still there, don't you? Only she's 'Dr. Chance' nowadays."

"I know, Mama Jeannie." Yes, he was well aware that his junior-year girlfriend was still in Grandeza. "In a town as small as Grandeza, there are very few secrets."

"Even for someone who only comes through once in a blue moon, huh?"

He grimaced. *I guess I had that coming.* "What are you getting at?"

"I'm not getting at anything."

He tilted his head, giving her a look.

"I'm serious. Why should I meddle in your life? Fate always takes care of things. You'll see."

He sighed and gave the only acceptable reply. "Yes, ma'am."

She yawned, then snuggled down deeper into the mound of pillows. "I'm tired, Troy. Will you stay around for a while, until I take a little nap?"

He nodded. "I'll be here."

Her droopy eyes slipped shut a moment later. Standing, he leaned over her and placed a soft kiss on her weathered brow. She'd lived eighty-nine years, and in that time, she'd buried her husband and her only biological son, and seen more than her share of hardships. While Mama Jeannie and Uncle Carver got along pretty well, their contact with each other was infrequent at best. Despite his wandering ways, Troy loved his grandmother fiercely. The two of them were the only living members of this branch of the Monroe family tree.

Sitting back down, he watched her sleep as he pondered what fate had in store for him.

Can I finally find what I'm looking for?

A true home?

Chapter 2

Seated behind her desk Tuesday morning, Robyn paged through the online résumé database she'd registered with to help her find a suitable veterinarian for the ranch. While the service promised to help narrow her search to only the most suitable applicants, she'd still received quite a few duds. There were résumés from vet students looking for internships, recent graduates who lacked industry experience and vets who'd only worked with small animals.

She reached for her steaming mug of Earl Grey tea and took a sip. It was still early, and already her eyes were beginning to cross from reading over résumés. *At this rate, I'm going to have to switch to coffee.*

It took nearly an hour to pull three qualified candidates from the batch of résumés she'd been forwarded.

She was in the process of saving them to her account files when she heard someone knocking on the door. She called out without looking up, not wanting to jeopardize the file transfer. "It's open."

Moments later, the door swung open and a large, rather wide shadow appeared over her desk. When the computer dinged to indicate that her résumé files had been saved, she looked up.

Her mouth fell open. *Hot damn!* She made a mental note to smack Mary Ellen for not telling her that *he* was the new ranch hand. *What the hell is M.E. playing at?*

Standing on the other side of her desk was the tall, dark and rugged Troy Monroe. Dressed in a tan button-down work shirt, blue jeans and brown work boots, his broad frame dominated the space.

"Morning, Dr. Chance." He removed the sandstone-colored Stetson from his head and held it in front of him. "Hope I'm not interrupting."

She snapped her mouth shut, swallowing. "I, uh, no, I was just finishing something. Good morning, Troy. It's been ages since I've seen you."

"I haven't been around town much the past few years, Doc." His rich brown eyes met hers.

Their gazes held for a long, silent moment, and she felt sure he could read her mind.

She took a deep inhale and tried to ignore the heady citrus scent, with warm and woodsy notes, that filled her nostrils. She cleared her throat. "Please, call me Robyn. We've known each other too long to be so formal."

"Sure thing." He smiled, showing off two rows of

perfect teeth. Gesturing to her guest chair, he asked, "Should I sit down, or…"

She could feel her cheeks go warm. She'd been knocked off-kilter by his appearance, so much so that she hadn't even thought to ask him to sit down. "Yes, have a seat. Sorry. I'm a bit…scattered this morning."

"I'm going to guess you weren't aware that I'd be your new rancher." He eased into the chair.

She tried not to look at the way his jeans stretched around his powerful thighs as he sat. She failed. "You're correct. I'm sure Mary Ellen is getting a big kick out of this. She knows I hate surprises."

He chuckled. "Hopefully I'm not the worst surprise you've ever gotten."

She met his gaze. "Not by a long shot."

An expression passed over his face, some combination of amusement and wickedness that fired her blood. But it disappeared as quickly as it had come.

"So, do you want to catch up, or get straight to the particulars of the job?" He leaned against the chair back, his forearms resting on his thighs.

He appeared deferential, and she almost didn't know how to respond. That had never been their dynamic in the past. He'd been a brooding young man, watching his parents' marriage dissolve before his eyes. She'd been his balm against the stormy sea of his troubled home. Or so she'd thought.

Breaking the silence, she said, "I think we can spare a moment to catch up. After all this time, it would be a bit strange if we didn't."

"I agree."

"So, why don't you start? What have you been up to these last ten or fifteen years?"

He shifted in his seat. "Let's see. I went to community college in North Carolina, got my associate's in business. Finished out with an animal-science bachelor's from NC State. Spent about a year working in the hog-farm industry there but couldn't really…" He hesitated. "It wasn't my thing. Anyway, after I left North Carolina, I came back out west. I've worked on spreads in Texas, Colorado and Kansas. My last job was up near Durango. Now, here I am."

She nodded as she processed his words, more focused on what he'd left out than what he'd actually said. *He never mentioned a wife, or even a girlfriend for that matter.* "Sounds like you've been busy."

"I have." With a slight narrowing of his eyes, he watched her for a moment. "You know, I can see the gears turning in your mind. No, I haven't had any serious relationships or kids."

Yikes. He'd seen right through her like a freshly scrubbed pane of glass. Then again, he'd always been able to read her, so she shouldn't be surprised. "Insightful as always. That will come in handy once you're out working with the animals."

He pressed his lips together, his dark mustache becoming more prominent. "I hope you're not trying to change the subject before you tell me what you've been up to."

She shook her head. "No, of course not." Stroking her hand over the back of her neck beneath her bun, she began her tale. "I went to school at UC Davis, straight through from my bachelor's in animal science on through my DVM. Came home right after college, and I've been working here on the ranch ever since." She let loose a little laugh. "As you can see, I haven't had nearly as much adventure and travel as you."

"You're loyal to your family. I admire that."

I was loyal to you, too. But you never seemed to notice. "I suppose. But loyalty isn't all it's cracked up to be." She cringed, wishing she hadn't said those last few words aloud.

He leaned forward, rubbed his hands together. "I couldn't help noticing you didn't mention any significant others, same as me."

She closed her eyes, knowing there was no sense in denying it. "True. I've dated here and there, but there was never anyone really special…" *Except you.* She knew better than to finish that sentence aloud.

"Seems like we're both bad at relationships."

She shrugged. "I don't know. I never give it too much thought. When the right man comes along, I'll know."

"Let's hope so." His expression unreadable, he settled against the backrest again. "I think we've probably spilled our guts enough. What do we need to discuss about the job?"

Trying not to let his abrupt change of subject rattle her, she opened the top drawer of her desk and pulled out the standard new-employee paperwork.

I may not get my answers today. But he's going to have to explain why he ran off the way he did back then.

* * *

Troy flipped through the stack of papers Robyn handed him, listening as she listed his many duties and responsibilities as a lead rancher. Every now and then, he'd glance up from the pages, watching her lips move as she read from her copy of the paperwork.

He'd come here today prepared for anything—work-related. But nothing could have prepared him for seeing Robyn again after fifteen years. She'd grown into a stunning woman. Even though she was seated behind a desk, he could tell she was taller than the average woman, though still likely shorter than him. She still had those deep waves of glossy brown hair, now streaked with golden highlights that accentuated her slender oval-shaped face. Her copper-colored eyes glimmered with light, and her soft pink lips matched the color of her button-down top beneath the white lab coat. The coat's upper left chest was embroidered with the phrase *Robyn Chance, DVM* in black script lettering.

"Troy, did you hear what I just said?"

Her words, spoken a little sharper than he would have liked, snapped him back to reality. "I'm sorry, what?"

"I asked if you have any expertise with calving." She pursed her lips. "If you hadn't been staring at my chest you would have heard me."

He swallowed. "I'm sorry. I swear I was admiring the embroidery on your medical coat. Who did it?"

Her lips tightened. "Kramer's Uniforms down on Main Street."

"Ah." He nodded, knowing she probably hadn't bought

his explanation. Her full bosom held its own appeal, but he really had been looking at the embroidery when she called him out. Thinking it best to just move on, he answered her earlier question. "No. In general, I'm not a fan of calving, though I'll help out as much as I can."

She chuckled. "You're kidding, right?"

He shook his head. "It…makes me uncomfortable. I don't want to be around when it's happening, but I'll assist with the mother and calf after the, uh, carnage."

"You're serious?" Her eyes were as wide as if he, himself, had said something outrageous.

"Yes." Perturbed, he folded his arms over his chest. "Haven't I been clear?"

She snorted, then covered her mouth with her hands. "I'm sorry. I don't think I've ever heard a rancher say that before. And coming from a strapping man like you, well…it's a bit of a shock."

He tilted his head to the right. "It is what it is, Robyn." The last thing he needed was another woman making fun of him for something he had no control over. His mother had spent years harping on him to man up, to get over his so-called "girlish sensitivity" to violence, injustice and misfortune. No matter what he did, he was never man enough to please his mother. Fortunately, Troy and his father had finally escaped her tyranny, and he'd no longer had to try to be the kind of son she obviously wanted.

She straightened up then, clearing her throat and disguising her obvious mirth. "Again, I apologize. It's actually not a bad thing that you empathize with the animal's pain."

He said nothing, waiting to see where she would go next.

"Calving is a natural process. You know that—you studied animal science just as I did. Hopefully, over time, you'll be able to handle it better. As for now, consider it our little secret."

He gave her a sidelong glance. "You mean you're not going to share my issue with the other hands around the watercooler?"

She shook her head. "I'm not much for gossip. And even if I was, I wouldn't want to undermine you. Telling the four hands you'll be supervising would probably create problems, and we don't need that right now. We've got more than thirty pregnant cows and heifers due to calve before the year ends."

He swallowed the lump forming in his throat. He'd worked at cattle operations before, but never one as large as the Chance spread. The idea of that many calvings set his teeth on edge. "Sounds like an adventure."

She smiled. "You bet. And we'll have another fifty or sixty calves due before spring."

His stomach clenched at the thought, and his face folded into a grimace. "Uh, is there a water fountain nearby?"

She pointed toward her open office door. "Go out and look to your left in the hallway."

He got up and took a few long strides toward the fountain. As he drank from the cold spray, he admonished himself. *Get it together, Troy. You're a grown man.* Once he felt he'd gotten enough, he stood and turned back toward Robyn's office. To his surprise, she now stood in the doorway, holding his Stetson in one hand.

Seeing her standing confirmed his assumption about her height. His petite former flame had blossomed into a statuesque beauty. He hadn't anticipated the immense appeal of her curvy hips and long legs in the light blue jeans she wore. Not wanting to stare, he jerked his eyes toward his hat.

"I'd like to take you on a tour of the property. Show you where you'll be working, and let you meet some of the guys you'll be supervising."

He walked over to her, taking his hat from her grasp. "Sounds good. I'd like to get familiar with how things go around here." *I'd also like to get more familiar with the woman you've become.* He kept that to himself. As Mama Jeannie had said, fate would take care of it. He imagined she'd be quite tickled to know how fast he'd bought into her philosophy. Something about Robyn and being in her presence again, after all this time, gave him a little more faith. "Lead the way."

Her glossy lips tipped into a smile.

His insides warmed like a summer afternoon in Santa Fe. Offering his arm like a gentleman, he waited for her to loop hers through. Placing his Stetson on his head, he walked her to the front door of the building.

Chapter 3

That afternoon, Robyn drove into town to The White Rabbit to meet her best friend for lunch. The sandwich shop, with its *Alice in Wonderland* theme, served the best lunch in town.

Kima Roberson, an esthetician at a local day spa, waved to her as she walked in. "Over here, Robyn."

She walked over and gave her friend a hug before taking her seat at the small table. Kima, dressed in her spa uniform of black scrubs with hot-pink piping, had pulled her jet-black curls up into a high ponytail. Her lipstick matched the accent shade on her uniform.

They took a moment to order their food. Kima asked for her usual chicken salad on a croissant, while Robyn opted to try the buffalo shrimp salad. It didn't take long for their meals to arrive, and over the food, they caught up on each other's lives.

"How are things at the spa?"

Kima shrugged. "Same ol', same ol'. Had a bridezilla and her eight bridesmaids yesterday. She insisted I didn't steam her face long enough during her facial."

Robyn rolled her eyes. "What did you say to her?"

"I told her if I steamed it any longer, she wouldn't have to worry about how her skin looked at the wedding because she'd be in the hospital."

"Your clients are wild." Chuckling, Robyn took a bite of her salad.

"You know how it is. There are only two spas in Grandeza, and House of Enchantment is the only one with the child-care benefit. The owners letting Leah come there for after-school care has been a lifesaver."

"How is my goddaughter? I feel like I haven't seen her in forever."

"It's only been a few weeks. Leah's fine. You know her. She's seven going on thirty-seven." Kima shook her head, popping a potato chip into her mouth. "She asked me when she can start coming to the spa to get massages. Says second grade is stressing her out."

Robyn snorted. As much as she loved Leah, she wondered if the little girl had "been here before," as the older folks often proclaimed about children who seemed mature beyond their years. "Second-grade stress? I've heard it all."

"I swear she's trying to make my hair go gray."

Kima pushed away her mostly empty plate. "So, what's new back at the ranch?"

She didn't want to talk about her morning, but she knew her friend would work the information out of her, anyway, and decided not to avoid it. "The new rancher came for his entrance meeting today."

"I remember you telling me that. Tell me all about him, girl." She raised her water glass for another sip.

"It's Troy Monroe."

The next sound out of Kima's mouth was coughing. Her eyes widened as if she'd just spotted a two-headed cow. She tipped the water glass in earnest, gulping down a large swallow. Finally, over her coughing fit, she placed her French-manicured hand over her chest. "Girl, did you say *Troy Monroe*? *The* Troy Monroe? The one who broke your heart in high school?"

She nodded. "One and the same."

Kima shook her head, crinkling her nose. "Well, damn. I'm guessing nobody told you this before today?"

"I found out the moment he walked into my office."

"Yikes." Kima sat back in her chair, letting her hand drop to her lap. "Well, now that you know it's him, how do you feel about it?"

She blew out a breath. "I don't know. But we've got a busy year-end calving season and I don't have time to think about how I feel right now."

Kima pursed her lips.

"Don't give me that look."

"So, your first love is back in your life, and working on the ranch, no less."

Robyn felt the lump forming in her throat. Crossing her arms over her chest, she said, "Pipe down, Kima. Everybody in the café can hear you."

"Girl, please. This is Grandeza, where everybody knows everybody else's business." She waved a dismissive hand in the air. "What about the job search? Any developments there?"

Robyn gave her a brief update about the director-of-vet-services job in San Diego. Even as she told her friend, though, a pang of guilt stabbed her. She was telling Kima before anyone else. But she knew Kima would be happy for her, and show an unqualified joy not tinged by regret.

A bright smile spread over Kima's face. "That's the job you really wanted. Congrats, Rob!"

She grinned. "Thanks, Kima."

"And I'm assuming your parents reacted well to the news?"

The grin faded. "Well, I…"

Kima's lip curled into a frown. "Don't tell me they don't know about this."

She remained silent, her eyes trained on the view of the mountains outside the window.

"Robyn, are you serious right now? What are you, fourteen? Why in the world are you hiding things from your parents like a disobedient teen?"

She sighed. "Sometimes that's how I feel when I go against their plans for me." *They have such high hopes for me running the ranch. Besides, I'm all they have now.* For years, she'd felt tied to the ranch because she thought it was her job to make her parents happy after they'd faced a bottomless grief. She was tethered to them and their business by guilt and sadness, and she had to break away. It was the only way she could ever hope to gain the life she truly wanted.

Kima's eyes met hers. "You have to live your life for yourself, Robyn. And the only way you can do that is by being honest. With yourself, and with your parents."

"You sound like an after-school special, Kima."

"Becoming a mother teaches you a thing or two about life." She clasped her hands in front of her. "When Skip ran off and left me to raise Leah on my own, I had to make some decisions. I also had to make some sacrifices."

"That jackass. I'd curse his name if he wasn't half-responsible for my goddaughter." *I remember how devastated Kima was when Skip walked out on her.* Their short-lived romance after meeting at a local bar had yielded only one positive outcome: a beautiful little girl with dark hair and sparkling brown eyes that mirrored her mother's.

"Yeah, but enough about the jackass. You're at a crossroads, Robyn. And as much as I don't want you to move away, I want you to be happy. So, I'm going to ask you to do two things."

Shoulders slumped, Robyn remarked, "I know you want me to talk to Mom and Pop. What's the other thing?"

"Talk to Troy."

She tilted her head. "I'm going to have to talk to him—we'll be working together."

"You know good and well I don't mean talking to him about work."

"What else is there for us to…?" She stopped mid-sentence as she caught a glimpse of Kima's narrow-eyed stare.

"I don't want to hear it. You know exactly what I mean, and you know what you need to do."

"He never took our time together as seriously as I did, Kima. If I bring it up now, after all these years, I'll only make a fool of myself."

"Let me ask you something. Has time been kind to Troy?"

"Extremely." Her mind conjured a vision of him standing in her office door. "He's an Adonis in a cowboy hat."

Kima laughed. "Then, girl, get yourself together and make your move. How many more men like that do you think you're gonna meet?"

"None." Because, if she was honest with herself, she knew no one else would ever measure up to the legend of Troy Monroe in her mind.

As if reading her mind, Kima threw up her hands and announced, "It's fate, girl. You can't do nothing to change fate."

Deep down, she wondered what it would be like to be with Troy again. They were both adults now, free of the angst and uncertainty of their teenage years. What would it be like to have a relationship with him now, or even a fling, for that matter?

She shook her head, hoping to drive away those thoughts.

Nothing good can come of them. He's just gotten to town, and I'm doing my best to get away from here.

No. There can't be anything between us.

Her head had it all figured out.

But her heart was another matter altogether.

Troy grasped the handle of the old broom as he moved it across the cement stoop at his modest house. The bungalow, located in the Juniper Heights neighborhood near the western edge of Grandeza, had once been Mama Jeannie's. She'd passed it down to her son, Troy's father, Johnny, when her doctor had advised her to move to assisted living five years ago. A wanderer at heart, Johnny hadn't wanted any part of the provincial life Grandeza provided, so she'd deeded it to Troy.

The old place held many memories. The hardwood floors throughout were gouged and dented in places, thanks to his childhood love of roughhousing and crashing his toy vehicles at every opportunity. Mama Jeannie had taught him the basics of cooking in the old kitchen, where a soft gray paint job had replaced the yellowed floral wallpaper that used to be there. The furniture in the living room was the same sofa and love seat he'd lounged on in his adolescence, though the pieces had been reupholstered since then. The old screen door still hung slightly off-kilter from the time he'd crashed into it while skateboarding in the house as a boisterous teen.

Mama Jeannie had sent him home with an admonishment to clean up since he hadn't been home in a while. He was still sweeping the leaves and debris off the porch when a familiar car pulled up to the curb.

Troy set aside the broom, a smile stretching his lips as he watched his old friend climb out of the blue sedan, a small toolbox in one hand. "Rick! How the hell are you, man?"

Rick Thompson clad in the overalls he wore to work as a mechanic, grinned as he stepped up on the porch. "I'm all right. How about you, stranger? We haven't seen you around here in a while."

The two shared a hearty hug.

"I just got in a couple of days ago. What brings you over here, Rick?"

"Your busted kitchen faucet." He lifted the toolbox.

He frowned. "The faucet's broken?" He'd only been home a short time and hadn't used the sink yet. "I've been ordering in—you know how I hate to cook."

"It's probably better if you don't. I'm handy, but I don't have the expertise to repair fire damage."

He gave his old buddy a playful punch in the stomach. "Very funny, Rick. But seriously, is there really something wrong with the sink?"

"Yeah, man. That thing is way out of whack. First brown water, then no water at all."

He shook his head. *Damn. What else has happened around here since I was home last?*

"I still have the spare key you gave me. I've been looking after the place for the last four months. Mama Jeannie asked me to."

He tried to fight off the pang of guilt that wrenched his gut. "I know. What can I say?"

"You can say you've been by to see Mama Jeannie."

He ribbed him, annoyed that his friend would ask such a silly question. "Of course I have. That's the first place I went when I arrived in town. I got a call from Helene and cut my trip to North Carolina short to get back here." He paused, thinking Rick would ask him how Mama Jeannie was doing.

"I've been visiting her. Went by there Sunday to see her."

His jaw tightened. Even though he appreciated his friend checking in on his grandmother, he couldn't help feeling somewhat put out. "Fixing things around my house and visiting her? Trying to take my place, Rick?"

"Are you kidding? No one can take your place in Jeannie's heart." Rick's expression turned serious. "I'm glad you went to see her. Whenever I was there, she talked about you nonstop. I could tell she was really missing you."

Troy wanted to sink through the concrete and disappear. He mentally kicked himself for neglecting her for so long. Sure, he'd called her two or three times every week, and sent her postcards. Standing here with Rick, though, it was clear that hadn't been enough.

"Can I come in? I wanna get to work on that sink before it gets too late."

Troy held open the screen door and followed his friend inside.

In the kitchen, Troy hung the broom and dustpan on their respective hooks on the wall and watched his buddy work. Rick sat his toolbox on the floor, opened it and fished out a small flashlight. Then, he opened the cabinet doors underneath the sink and lied down on his back, with his head and shoulders inside the cabinet. A moment later, light flooded the cabinet interior.

"So, how long are you going to stay this time?" Rick's question echoed, bouncing off the wood and pipes.

"A while. I took a job in town, and I want to be close in case Mama J needs me. She's not feeling her best." He sat down at the kitchen table.

"Where are you working?"

"The Chance spread."

A loud "ding" sounded from beneath the sink, and Rick slid out. "Say what now?"

"I took a job as a lead rancher at the Chance spread."

Rick shook his head.

"What's that look for?"

"Robyn's still there, man. As far as I know, she hasn't left Grandeza since she came back from vet school."

"I know that. I had a meeting with her this morning."

Rick sat up, his back straight and his eyes on Troy. "What happened?"

Troy shrugged. "We went over paperwork. She explained the expectations for the job and took me for a tour of the ranch."

"That's it?"

His brow creased. "Yeah, man. What else was supposed to happen?"

"You mean to tell me you went there, sat across from her and she didn't bring up the fact that you stood her up for the prom junior year and disappeared after?"

He shook his head. "No."

Rick looked downright bewildered. "I don't even know what to think about that."

"Do like me. Don't think about it."

Rick shook his head back and forth slowly. "No, man. You'd better think about it. Because I guarantee you, she has."

"Maybe not. Maybe she's forgotten about it?"

"Ha! Fat chance."

He stared at his friend, trying to figure him out. "Rick, what the hell are you getting at?"

"Women don't forget, man. Their memories are longer than Route 66."

He shrugged.

"You'd better be on your guard. Maybe she hired you just so she can get revenge." Rick grabbed a wrench from the toolbox.

"You're crazy, man. Robyn isn't that type. Plus, she didn't know I was the new hand until I showed up for the meeting. She said the woman who hired me never told her my name."

"That's what she said." Rick disappeared beneath the sink again, but his voice flowed through the room.

"You better be prepared. My advice is to apologize to her ASAP. Maybe you can avert disaster."

Troy shook his head. "You on some other shit today, Rick." He couldn't believe for a second that Robyn would be that vindictive. She'd always been a kind, caring person. And while he hadn't shown up to pick her up for prom, he doubted she'd have held that against him all these years.

Has she? It wasn't as if I had a choice in the matter. He'd been a minor then, and subject to the whims of his parents.

Deciding not to let Rick's foolishness get to him, he walked to the fridge to grab a drink. "You want something to drink, man?"

"Yeah. A water will work."

He grabbed two bottles of water and handed one to Rick, who sat up to take a long swig.

"How bad is it under there?" Troy peered into the cabinet at the pipes.

"Can't tell yet, but there's probably something lodged in there. A blockage."

He groaned. "Has Mama Jeannie been paying you for all this?"

"Nah. I wouldn't take her money, anyway. But I will take yours." Rick winked at him.

A laughing Troy reached for his wallet.

Chapter 4

Robyn yawned, resisting the urge to raise her latex-gloved hand to cover it. It was Wednesday morning, and she was facing down a serious case of the midweek doldrums. She'd been in the barn since before dawn, assisting with the first calving of the fall season. The young heifer had just birthed her first calf, a male.

Standing by the stall, Robyn observed the calf for any signs of distress. He seemed to be in fine physical shape, which pleased her. But she had other concerns as she watched his mother, tucked away in the opposite corner of the stall, seemingly uninterested in her newborn.

Amos Tolbert, one of the lead ranchers, who'd been assisting her, stood nearby. Amos had been working on Chance land for as long as Robyn could remember.

He was in his late fifties, and had ruddy, tanned skin, blue eyes and close-cropped gray hair. "Mama doesn't seem too attached to baby."

Robyn frowned. "You're right. I'll have to keep an eye on both of them."

She stripped off the gloves and the paper gown she'd worn over her clothes for the delivery and tossed them into the trash bin.

As she and Amos washed up at the large wall-mounted sink, he asked, "Do you need me to stick around? We've got some fences to mend on the northern end of the ranch."

She shook her head. "No. You can go on ahead. I'll radio if I need anything else." She glanced over her shoulder at the stall. "Looks like I'll be here most of the day."

"Okay." Once he'd dried his hands, he disappeared into the early morning sunlight.

She turned her attention back to Molly and her calf. The calf clumsily made its way over to Molly and attempted to nurse and was quickly denied.

Robyn felt her brow furrowing. *She's not taking to the calf. I'm going to have to bottle-feed him.*

She left the main floor of the barn for the storage room. Moments later, she returned with a large bottle of milk replacer. Taking a seat on a low milking stool inside the stall, she coaxed over the calf and began to feed it the meal its mother had denied.

"My, what a hungry baby." She held the bottle with both hands to meet the calf's enthusiastic demand for

nourishment. This was a part of her job that she loved.
It would be easy enough to pass the unglamorous job
of bottle-feeding on to a hand. But she enjoyed doing
it. It soothed her and made the messy parts of her work
worth it.

A soft smile tilted her lips as she thought back on
Lacey. She'd been so small then, not much taller than
the milking stool. Robyn had been six years old, and
certain she knew everything, most especially when it
came to taking care of her baby sister.

Lacey had loved all the animals, but she'd had a special affinity for the baby animals. As small as she was,
she tried to participate in every bottle-feeding. That had
resulted in a lot of frustration for her parents, as well
as some of the hands, who'd been more interested in
getting things done that letting a preschooler entertain
herself at the expense of efficiency.

Sitting there in the morning silence, with only the
sounds of the calf's suckling and the breathing of
the other animals, she felt a connection to her sister.
So many years had passed, and so many things had
changed in her life. But she didn't think the empty place
in her heart would ever be filled again.

A tear slid down her cheek as the calf backed off the
bottle. "Full for now, buddy?" She stroked his furry
little head.

She heard the soft scratch of footsteps on the hard-
packed floor and shifted her gaze toward the barn door.

Troy stood in the opening, with the sunlight streaming in around his broad frame. He wore black jeans, a

red-and-black-plaid shirt and tall black boots embossed with flames. The brim of his black Stetson obscured his eyes.

She brushed away her tears. "Good morning, Troy."

"Morning, Robyn." He entered the barn, using his curved forefinger to bump up the brim of his hat. His brown eyes held concern. "You all right?"

She used her sleeve to wipe away the remaining moisture clinging to her cheeks. "I'm fine. I just get a little emotional sometimes during calving. The beginning of a new life and all that." She didn't relish lying to him, but she preferred a small fib to a very big, uncomfortable truth.

He nodded, his long strides bringing him closer to the stall she sat in. "First calf of the season?"

"Yes. You missed it by just over an hour."

"I'm not going to say I'm disappointed." He stooped down next to her, giving the calf's head a quick rub.

She took a breath, amazed at how the refreshing, masculine scent of his cologne could overcome the stench that hung in the air inside the barn. *He smells so good.*

He spoke, breaking the silence. "He's a good-looking boy."

"That he is. I just wish Molly had taken to him better." She gestured to his mother, still tucked into her corner of the stall.

"It's still early. Maybe she'll come around."

She shrugged. "It's possible. If not, one of the other

cows may take him on and let him nurse. And if that doesn't work, we'll just bottle-feed him."

She watched him lift the calf's hooves and inspect them. "I already examined him. He looks very healthy."

"I agree." He smiled at her.

She felt her insides melt down into her boots like hot butter. Troy's smile had always done that to her. It was so open and sincere. It made her feel as if she was in on a secret, a special something shared just between the two of them.

His expression changed then, the earlier concern returning. "Are you sure you're okay, Robyn?"

She nodded hastily, rising from the low stool. "Yes, I'm sure. I appreciate your concern, though."

"I'm always going to look out for you, Robyn. In that respect, nothing has changed between us."

She blinked a few times. "What do you mean?"

He chuckled. "Don't you remember? In sophomore year, when that guy smacked you on the butt with a ruler as a prank?"

She thought back, and it took a moment to dredge up the memory. She snapped her fingers. "Oh, yes. Trevor Umstead. Class clown and all-around jerk. He thought snapping girls' bras and that sort of thing was so hilarious. He spent that whole class period skipping class, so he could stand outside the girls' bathroom and pop them on the behind as they passed him."

"I remember. But do you remember what Rick and I did to him after that?"

She frowned, her gaze shifting up toward the hay-loft. "Um, refresh my memory."

"We pretended to buddy up with him, just so we could make sure he got caught."

She laughed as the memory returned. "Right, I remember now! You guys left a confession note pinned to the back of his jacket, and he got a week of detention and had to write all the girls apology letters."

"See? And that was before we dated." He stood then, towering over her at his full height. "I've always looked out for you, and I don't plan on stopping anytime soon."

She swallowed, feeling her heart pounding in her chest. Sure, he'd had his moments of chivalry. But was his memory really that selective? Or was he teasing her? *He can't think I've forgotten about prom.* "I don't know if I'd say always, but you've had your moments."

He frowned. "I'm not perfect, never have been."

She shook her head. *I'm not getting into this with him. Not now.* "I'm going out to see how the fence mending is going."

Without waiting for him to respond, she turned and walked out of the barn.

Troy spent the next few hours traveling between the main barn and the southern section of the ranch, which was to be his domain. Mary Ellen, the ranch manager who'd hired him, had given him the keys to a company golf cart for getting around the property. There had been stock to weigh and evaluate, feed stations to monitor and fill and many more tasks to attend to. By lunchtime, he was both tired and hungry. Making his way to the main office building, which housed a small café for ranch employees, he heard his stomach rumble. Once he'd parked the golf cart among the row of them on the side of the building, he climbed out and joined the other employees headed inside.

He'd just entered the lobby when he heard the buzz of conversation increase in volume. He glanced around, looking for the source of the commotion, and his eyes landed on the man himself.

Dressed in black slacks, a blue button-down CCE shirt and black boots, Cooper Chance paused to straighten his silver-tipped bolo tie as he smiled and shook hands with his employees. Troy watched the cattle baron move through the tangle of men and women, headed in his direction. He brushed a hand over his jeans, loosening some of the hay and bramble he'd attracted over the course of the morning.

Cooper approached him and stopped, grinning broadly. His dark skin, twinkling gray eyes and thick black mustache remained unchanged from years ago, save for a few gray hairs. "Well, Troy. Welcome to the Chance family. Good to see you again."

He returned his new boss's hearty handshake. "Likewise, Mr. Chance. Thanks for the opportunity."

He grinned. "Don't mention it. You're a son of this town, and you came highly recommended from the Roberts spread up in Durango."

"I'm glad to hear that." He'd worked on the Roberts

family dairy farm for about eighteen months prior to applying for the job here at Chance.

"I usually sit in on initial meetings, but I was all booked up during yours. My apologies." He gave him a hearty slap on the shoulder. "You're still welcome to come by my office if you have any problems that Mary Ellen or my daughter can't handle."

Troy thought on that. He didn't know much about Mary Ellen, but from what he knew of Robyn, she was capable of just about anything she set her mind on doing. "Thank you. I'll keep that in mind."

"Well, I've got a lunch meeting, so I'm headed out. We'll talk more soon, Troy."

"Great. Have a good day, sir."

Cooper shook his head. "None of that 'sir' stuff, now. Call me Coop. Everybody does around these parts." He put on his dark blue Resistol felt hat, tipped it and disappeared outside through the glass doors.

Troy moved into the café and got in line. After he'd helped himself to the buffet lunch of fajitas, rice and beans, he got a paper cup of lemonade and took his plate to an empty table near the windows.

As he went to take his seat, he saw Robyn walk by with a tray of her own.

He called her name, taking care to be heard, but not being too loud.

Her head swiveled his way, and she stopped midstride.

He gestured to the empty chair across from him. "Care to join me?"

A soft smile lifted her lips and she nodded while walking toward him. Once at the table, she set down her tray and slid into the chair. "Thanks."

"So, how are Molly and the calf? Has she warmed up to him yet?"

She shook her head. "No. Right now, we just wait and see." She picked up the fork from her tray and began mixing the steak, onions, peppers and rice in her bowl. "How have things gone for you so far?"

"Good, but busy. There's a lot to do around here."

She chuckled. "Now you know why we hired you on. There's never a shortage of things that need to get done."

They began eating and as he watched her, he noted the delicate way she filled her fork and lifted it to her lips. She seemed a little more relaxed than she did earlier. He wasn't one to press a person about their personal business, but he could have sworn she'd been crying when he'd come into the barn this morning. She'd covered nicely with that story about being moved by calving, but even though she was a vet, he wasn't buying it. Something was definitely on her mind, though he saw no trace of it at the moment.

"Oh, I meant to ask you. How is your grandmother? I heard she wasn't feeling well."

Small-town life strikes again. He wasn't at all surprised that Robyn had heard about his grandmother's health issues. "She's stable. I'm going over to see her when I get off work today."

"Mrs. Monroe is such a sweetheart. Tell her I said hi, and that I hope she feels better."

"I will." He thought about asking her to come with him to visit and give Mama Jeannie the message in person. But knowing Mama Jeannie, she'd declare them a couple and start naming her great-grandchildren before they even sat down.

They spent a short time consuming their lunch in friendly silence, and he wondered what she was thinking about. Finally, he said, "Rick came by yesterday to look at the faucet." They'd all been schoolmates years ago, and Rick had always been Troy's main running partner.

"Oh? I haven't seen him in a while. How's he doing?"

"He's good. His handyman business is thriving, especially since he doesn't have any real competition here in Grandeza." He chuckled then, thinking back on the declarations Rick had made while wedged inside the kitchen cabinet. "Rick's still crazy. You know he said you hired me on here to make me pay for standing you up for junior prom? I don't know where he gets this stuff."

She set down her fork, and something flashed in her eyes, something he couldn't read. "Rick's always been like that, hasn't he?"

"Yes. I just shook my head."

"He's half-right. I remember being stood up. I don't know any girl who wouldn't remember such a thing."

He paused, watching her.

Her expression, flat and unreadable, revealed nothing.

"You know there was a reason I didn't show up that

night, don't you? It was completely out of my control, Robyn. I would never have…"

She held up her hand. "It's ancient history."

He snapped his mouth shut, wondering if Rick had been right. Was this about making him pay for what he'd done all those years ago?

She smiled, but it didn't reach her eyes. "I'm not looking for revenge, either. I've moved on from it." She slid back from the table and stood, grabbing her tray. "We're not kids anymore, Troy. I don't believe in playing those kinds of childish games. And, besides, I wasn't the one who hired you. I didn't even know we'd taken you on until you showed up. So your little ego trip has been wasted. I simply haven't thought that much about you since all those years ago."

"Fair enough." He looked up, meeting her gaze. "But do you believe in second chances?"

She narrowed her eyes as if studying him to test his sincerity. "Only when the situation warrants it." She turned and carried her tray to the return point. Once she'd deposited her dishes in the proper place, she strode out of the café without a single backward glance.

Alone at the table, Troy slid his tray away from him.

Now, the question is whether I warrant a second chance.

True, he'd returned home to look after his grandmother. But being here in Grandeza seemed to hold another benefit, one he hadn't expected. Robyn was still here, and they would be working together. Perhaps fate was giving him the second chance Robyn seemed hesitant to give herself. A chance to right the wrongs of his past, and to prove to her how much he'd grown.

He wasn't the type of man who ran away from a good woman. And if she'd let him, he planned on showing her that.

Chapter 5

Robyn entered the café that evening and looked around, taking in all the decorations the office staff had hung. Amos had given thirty years of service to Chance Cattle Enterprises, and now that he was taking his well-earned retirement, everyone had agreed the occasion called for a party. Amos, being the practical person he was, would probably never have agreed to anyone making a fuss over him, so they'd worked on the party without his knowledge. Tonight, they'd finally get to see if their efforts had paid off. She walked to the buffet, where Mary Ellen stood. Wearing a knee-length black dress and matching boots, she was busy arranging paper plates and utensils for the partygoers.

Mary Ellen glanced up from her task and smiled as she approached. "Hey, Robyn. How are ya?"

She pursed her lips. "Don't even try it, M.E. What do you mean by hiring Troy Monroe and keeping it from me?"

"Remember how you said you were swamped dealing with the cows getting ready to calve, and not to bother you with stuff unless it was really important?"

She rolled her eyes. "You know what I meant."

She shrugged. "It didn't seem all that important to me, so I decided not to bother you with it." A gleam of mischief flashed in her eyes.

"I'm going to get you, M.E. When you least expect it."

She chuckled. "If you say so. Anyway, you look nice, Doc."

She looked down at the dark blue maxi dress she'd chosen for the party. "You know me. I'm not one for dressing up, but I do all right."

"You're early, so why don't you help us finish setting up?"

"That's why I'm here. What needs to be done?"

She listened as Mary Ellen rattled off a few tasks. Stashing her purse and denim jacket by the reception desk, she got busy helping with the remaining setup.

With that done, she eased into a seat at one of the tables by the window to await Amos's arrival. Her father had been given the task of getting him there, because no one in Grandeza turned down a request from Cooper Chance. No one but her, she thought, once again feeling a pang of unease about the news she'd yet to share with her father and mother—that she was leaving. Soon, she reminded herself. Very soon. After a few hours' work culling through résumés and reaching out to applicants, she had a good candidate on the hook now to be her replacement, and she knew there was money in the budget to bring him on, even with her still on the payroll.

While she sat, watching the door, Troy walked in. He wore dark blue jeans, a bright red button-down shirt and black boots emblazoned with flames. Her gaze swept over his tall, broad frame. She appreciated the way the fabric of his clothes stretched to accommodate his muscles.

He's grown so much since high school. When she'd known him, he'd still been a boy in many ways. Not now. He was, most assuredly, a man. He had a confidence about him, and he wasn't ashamed of the sensitive side she'd always admired. He didn't rely on machismo and empty displays of so-called masculinity. He just strode into a space and owned it. Parts of her wanted to explore all the ways in which he'd grown…but she set aside those desires for now. Or at least she would try to, she thought, as he strode in her direction.

She stood, and he entered her space, grasping her hand. "Evenin', Robyn."

"Hey, Troy."

"You look really lovely."

She smiled, feeling the warmth touch her cheeks. "You're not too shabby yourself, cowboy."

He grinned. "Thanks for inviting me to the party."

"It will be a great way for you to get to know the other folks who work here on the ranch."

He nodded. "I suppose it would—if I were interested."

Tilting her head to one side, she gave him a sidelong glance. "Pardon me?"

"I'm just being honest. I'm sure they're great folks. I'll get to know them in time, I'm sure." He squeezed her hand. "But right now, my interest is on you."

She swallowed. "You already know me, Troy."

He shook his head. "I know who you were, who you used to be. I don't know much about who you are now."

She looked down then, studying the toes of her low-heeled brown leather ankle boots. "People don't change that much."

"You'd be surprised." Using his free hand, he curled one long finger beneath her chin, raising it so their gazes could connect. "I'm not going to press you. But I'm making you aware. I want to know the woman you've become, Robyn."

She swallowed again, overcome by the masculine scent of his cologne, and by the seriousness she sensed in his words.

"He's coming!" someone shouted.

The lights in the café flicked off, and she felt Troy step away from her in the darkness.

Grateful for the reprieve, she held on to the table's edge and crouched low.

Moments later, the lights came back on, and she jumped up, joining the rest of those assembled as they all shouted, "Surprise!"

Standing in the doorway with Cooper, Amos placed his hand over his chest. "Good gracious!"

Laughter filled the room as the old rancher entered and began shaking hands and thanking the folks who'd come out to wish him a happy retirement.

Robyn left her table and met up with the man of the hour, giving him a hearty hug. "Congratulations, Amos."

He chuckled as he returned her embrace. "I thought I told y'all I just wanted to go nice and quiet into retirement."

She laughed. "Come on, Amos. After thirty years? You know we couldn't allow that."

Shaking his head, he thanked her and walked away to greet the other partygoers.

The atmosphere was so festive, with Amos's favorite bluegrass flowing from the speakers, she almost forgot about her encounter with Troy. Occasionally, she would glance around the room and spot him. Every time she saw him, she would find him watching her.

"Robyn!"

She swiveled her head, looking at Mary Ellen. "What is it?"

"Didn't you hear me calling you? What in the world are you thinking about so hard that you can't hear?"

"Sorry. What do you need?"

She shook her head. "Go into the storage room and grab some more cups and plastic utensils? We're almost out."

"Yeah, I'll get some." Robyn navigated through the tangle of bodies toward the hallway, then turned toward the storage room at the end of the hall. The music thumped, vibrating the floors, though the sound lessened a bit as she got farther away from the café.

She found the storage room door propped open and nearly tripped over a brick near the door frame. Using the toe of her boot to edge the brick out of the way, she entered the room and flipped on the light.

"Robyn."

She turned at the sound of the deep voice calling her name.

Troy stood in the doorway.

"What is it?"

"Do you have a minute to talk?"

Her brow hitched up. "About what? I came to get some more supplies for the party."

He stepped inside the room.

"Troy, wait…"

The words escaped her lips a moment too late, and the door snapped shut. "Crap. That door's been busted for a while, and it doesn't seem like anyone's gotten around to fixing it yet."

He turned around, tried the knob. It wobbled from side to side worthlessly. A groan escaped his lips. "Sorry about that."

She shook her head. "Don't worry about it. I shouldn't have moved the brick."

"How long before they notice we're missing?"

She shrugged. "I don't know. M.E. did send me for something. But with the music as loud as it is, screaming for help is out of the picture."

"My phone's on the table."

She sighed. "Mine is in my purse."

He laughed. "Dumb luck, huh?"

"Well, what do you want to talk about?" She leaned back against the shelf. "Looks like we've got plenty of time now."

Troy moved farther into the storage room but left a good amount of distance between himself and Robyn. He didn't want to make her feel uncomfortable, especially in such close quarters.

She shifted a bit to face him, letting her left shoulder rest against the wooden shelf. Hands clasped in front of her, she looked his way. "What do you want to talk about, Troy?"

Fate had chosen a funny way of giving him the chance to explain himself, and he wouldn't pass that up. "First, I want to explain what happened back then. Why I didn't show up to take you to prom junior year."

Her face creased into a slight frown. "Honestly, Troy. You don't actually believe what Rick said. That I'd hire you to subject you to some sort of juvenile torture plot?"

He shook his head. "No, I don't believe that. I could tell from the look on your face when I walked into your office—you were genuinely surprised to see me." He chuckled. "I've known Rick for years and he's always been a little crazy. I've learned when to ignore him."

The tightness seemed to melt away from her face. "Okay. I'm listening."

He took a deep breath. "I'm sure you remember how bad things were back then between my parents."

She offered a small nod.

"Well, two days before prom, things really boiled over." He sat down on the concrete floor, feeling as if the weight of the memories pressed him into that position. "It was after eleven at night when I woke up to the sound of them screaming at each other. Dad was railing at my mother about not being discreet with her boyfriends. She yelled back about how he wasn't man enough for her, and how he was raising me to be as weak as he was."

Her eyes widened and she covered her mouth with her hand.

He didn't elaborate on how his mother's words made him feel, how she'd been berating his sensitivity and lack of unfounded aggression since he could walk. He'd felt such pain and confusion because she couldn't accept him just the way he was. But that wasn't a factor in this tale, so he kept it to himself. "I overheard most of the shouting match. But the worst part was when she screamed these exact words—'Get out, Johnny! And take that weak-ass boy with you!'"

"Oh, no." Her eyes were damp now.

He hadn't wanted to make her cry, but he wanted her to know the truth—that he'd never purposefully abandoned her. Part of him thought he was saying too much, but now that he'd begun the telling, he couldn't stop the words flowing from his lips. "Then I heard my dad's footsteps coming down the hallway. He flung open my bedroom door and said, 'Troy, we're leaving.'

We spent about fifteen minutes packing as much as we could take, and then we left."

"In the middle of the night?" She closed the distance between them, lowering herself to the floor beside him. "Where did you go?"

"Dad drove us to the airport and called his brother. Uncle Carver booked us on a first-class flight to Raleigh that morning, and we stayed with his family a few months. After Dad got us a place in Wilmington, I finished high school there."

A tear escaped and ran down her cheek. "Troy. I'm so sorry."

He shrugged. "Not your fault. Not my fault, either. At least, that's what the therapist said." He released a humorless laugh, hoping to soften the mood.

"I thought being stood up was rough." She brushed away her tear. "And it was. But what you went through that night was so much worse. Just...horrible."

He looked her way, finally asking her the question that had been on his mind since he'd boarded that flight all those years ago. "When you realized I wasn't coming, did you stay home?"

She shook her head. "No. Actually, once you were an hour late, Kima and some of the girls came over and we all went together in a limo. It turned out to be a great night, considering."

Hearing that made him smile, despite the sadness lingering inside him. "I'm really glad to hear that. I was worried you'd stay home and miss out on the experience because of me."

A soft smile lit her face. "That's really sweet, Troy."

Silence fell between them for a moment, marred only by the semidistant sound of the music being played in the café, along with the muffled din of conversations and laughter.

To break the silence, he said, "Seems like they're having too much fun to notice we're missing."

She giggled. "I appreciate you telling me all this, Troy. But can I ask you one more question?"

"Sure."

"Why didn't you contact me? You could have reached out after you were settled in North Carolina, but I never heard from you until you appeared in my office the other day. Why?"

I should have seen that question coming. "Honestly? I don't know. I can tell you that seventeen-year-old me had no desire to explain what had happened. I just don't think I had the capacity, or even the vocabulary, to explain it then. And I wasn't sure I should. My dad didn't want anything to do with my mom then. He didn't even want her to know where we were. Contacting you might have meant Mom would find us, Grandeza being as small and close-knit as it is. That was a convenient excuse for me not to face the music with you."

"And what about all the time that's passed in the interim?" She gave him a pointed look.

He sighed, knowing he'd have to continue to be honest, and the truth wasn't glamorous or profound. "So much time had passed, I just figured you'd moved on. Once I allowed myself to believe that, it was easy to let myself off the hook, and not reach out." He ran a hand over his face. "I will say that part of me is glad I waited. It feels right to be able to do this in person."

She let her gaze drop to the floor.

"After Dad died in that bus crash a few years back, I waited for her to reach out to me. To send a card, or somehow acknowledge his death." He rested his head against the cool, painted cinderblock wall behind him. "She never did. I haven't seen or spoken to her since the night we left Grandeza."

"I'm sure she must have heard about it. Everyone in town knew." Robyn shook her head. "I know she'd sold her house and moved by then, but that crash made national news."

"I did get a card from you and your family. I remember that." He leaned closer to her, looked into her eyes. "I remember how I felt when I saw your handwriting. The same handwriting from those love notes you used to slip me in class."

Her cheeks bloomed with color.

"How did you even find me?"

She shrugged. "I think my dad's assistant found your address…through the funeral home listed in the obituary. All I did was write in the card."

"Just seeing the note you'd written inside really helped to soothe my grief, Robyn."

"You've always had a kind heart. It's what made you different from all the other guys I knew. Honestly, it's what drew me to you." Emotion sparkled in her eyes. "I'm glad I could comfort you, Troy. In a way, that's all

I ever wanted to do. Shelter your heart." She reached up and put her warm palm against his cheek.

"I know. And I could use that comfort again."

She leaned up, and a moment later, their lips touched. His were eager, seeking. Hers were as soft and lush as the petals of a rain-dampened rose. She looped her arms around his neck, and he circled his around her waist, pulling her against his body, against his heart.

Where she belonged.

Chapter 6

Holding her phone against her ear, Robyn walked up the driveway to her childhood home Thursday afternoon. Located near the geographic center of the ranch, the sprawling single-level brick house hadn't changed much since she'd gone off to UC Davis.

"Geez, Kima. Quit yelling."

"I'm not yelling, I'm shouting—there's a difference."

She rolled her eyes. "What were you expecting me to do? Call you that night and check in with you? Last I checked, my mama's name was Thelma Chance."

Kima sighed. "Girl, I know I'm not your mama. But I can't believe you didn't tell me right away that you kissed Troy! That's headline news and you know it."

Stepping up onto the wide cement porch, she groaned. "Fine. I'm sorry I made you wait twenty-four hours to find out this earth-shattering news."

"Apology accepted. Just make sure you keep me up-to-date on what happens next."

"There is no *next*, Kima. It was just a little kiss."

"Mmm-hmm." Kima sounded unconvinced. "If you say so."

"I'm at my parents' for dinner, so can we continue this little inquisition later?"

"Have you told them yet you're leaving?"

"No. But I will. Soon, I promise. When the time is right."

"Is the time ever going to be right?"

Robyn didn't answer. She would do it soon, just as she'd told Kima. Really.

"All right, girl. 'Bye."

She ended the call and tucked her phone into the hip pocket of her jeans. Kima had been her best friend since forever, but sometimes Robyn found her nosiness exhausting.

Moving closer to the door, she pulled open the screen door and used her key to enter the house.

Inside, she left her shoes on the tray by the door and hung up her denim jacket and black leather purse, then headed through the living room toward the kitchen. The smell of garlic, basil and oregano permeating the air made her stomach rumble with hungry anticipation of her mother's home cooking.

On a side table between the living and dining rooms, her mother had arranged a group of silver framed pictures. Pausing by the table, Robyn picked up one of the photos, examining it. The image was of her and Lacey, sitting on the front porch eating ice cream. She'd been about five, meaning Lacey had been about two. Sitting there with their pigtails, tiny overalls and little faces smudged with chocolate, they were the embodiment of youthful innocence.

If only things hadn't gone so wrong.

It's almost her birthday. She doubted she would ever get over the questions, the wondering what her sister would have been like as an adult. Would they still be so inseparable?

Now, she would never know. The old pain rose again, threatening to bring the tears to her eyes. She returned the framed photo to its proper place and continued into the kitchen.

There, she found her mother, sprinkling fresh herbs over her famous lasagna. Thelma King Chance looked up at her daughter's entrance and offered her a bright smile. "Hi, baby. You're just in time—I just took this out of the oven."

She placed a soft kiss on her mother's cheek. "Is it half-veggie and half-traditional?"

Thelma nodded. "Yes. You know your father. The more I try to get him to eat healthfully, the more he resists. So, I make compromise lasagna."

Robyn giggled. At the age of fifty-four, Thelma looked at least a decade younger. Her copper-colored skin, brown eyes and wavy dark hair were glossy and youthful, giving no hint to her true age. She was dressed in a green A-line dress, covered with a white floral print apron bursting with pink-and-yellow blooms.

"Can I help out?" Robyn moved to the sink to wash her hands.

"Sure. You can grab the salad and the dressing out of the refrigerator and bring it to the table." Thelma slipped her small hands into the burgundy oven mitts she kept hanging on pegs near the stove.

They worked together to get the food on the table, where the three places had already been set. As she put down the still smoking pan of lasagna, Thelma cupped her hands around her mouth. "Cooper! Dinner!"

Robyn chuckled inwardly. Her mother had been calling her father to dinner that way for as long as she could remember. She'd asked her mother about that one time. The response had been "I already cooked. I'm not chasing after him, too."

Cooper called back, "Here I come!"

They took their seats on opposite sides of the table, with Thelma to the right and Robyn to the left. Cooper entered a few moments later. Dressed in tan slacks and a gray polo shirt, he stopped to kiss his wife and daughter on the forehead before slipping into his chair at the head of the table.

Eyeing the lasagna, he frowned. "Aw, honey-bun. Don't tell me you made that half-and-half stuff again."

Thelma chuckled. "Don't worry, dearest. I turned the side with all the meat and cholesterol toward you, so you won't have to reach too far."

Robyn dropped her head, covering her smile with her hands. The way they carried on tickled her. She supposed that after nearly thirty years together, there was little room for pretense in a marriage. At some point, you just said what you had to say and dealt with the fallout.

Cooper rolled his eyes. "Whatever. We live on a cattle ranch, so you're not about to get me to give up beef."

"I only want you to cut back, not give it up." Thelma shook her head. "You're going to do what you want, anyway, so be my guest, you old mule."

Despite the harshness of her words, there was a smile in her eyes.

Cooper winked at his wife. "Nice to know you still care, sweetheart."

Thelma pursed her lips. "You are such a mess."

After the plates were fixed, they all dug in. Robyn took a small piece from each side of the lasagna pan, savoring the lightness of the vegetarian slice and the richness of the meat-and-cheese-laden one. The dichotomy reflected her parents' relationship; despite their differences, they went together very well.

The conversation around the table was mostly about town gossip, since Thelma forbade discussing ranch business at her dinner table. Robyn listened as her parents traded tales of the dramatic goings-on in Grandeza, the most shocking being an electrical fire at Martinez Building Supply.

"Anything exciting happening in your world, Robyn?"

She met her mother's expectant gaze and felt the tightening in her stomach. She loved her parents, and there would always be a part of her that longed to share her good news with them. She wanted them to be proud of her, to share her joy at landing the position. She knew she had to tell them soon, and the longer she put it off, the harder it would be for them to take. She couldn't face it now, though. *I'm pretty sure my leaving counts as "ranch business," not to be discussed at the table. So, I'll just set it aside for now.* She certainly couldn't tell them she'd kissed Troy while locked in the administrative-building storage room. Keeping secrets from them bothered her, and she promised herself she'd tell them, right after she'd settled on a replacement. Then she could present them both pieces of news at once: her leaving, and how she'd secured someone to take her place. At least then she'd be taking some worry off their shoulders about how they'd get along without her, since she wouldn't be leaving them in the lurch without a ranch vet.

So, she gave the only answer she could. "Not really."

"I expected you'd be a little more…affected by Troy being back in town." Thelma sipped from a glass of ice water.

Robyn's eyes widened. "So, you knew, too? Why didn't anyone tell me?"

Her question was met with silence.

Finally, Cooper answered. "With Amos retiring, we needed someone with the right skill set to replace him, and we needed them fast. There wasn't time for a lot of back-and-forth."

"And you thought what, exactly? That I would interfere with his hiring, because of something that happened in high school?" Ever since Troy had stood her up, her parents and friends had danced around the subject, acting as if she'd been scarred for life. It irked her to no end. *Do they really think I'm that fragile? I'm no china doll.*

She stood, tamping down her frustration in favor of being respectful of her parents. "Mama, it was delicious. I'm tired, so I'm going on home. Thanks for having me." Her cottage, just outside the western border of the Cooper spread, was just a short drive away. That had proven to be both a good and a bad thing at various points in her life. Right now, she wished she could escape a bit farther away from this uncomfortable situation.

She turned and left the room, and no one called after her or followed her.

And that was just fine with her.

Troy walked down the corridor inside the main building of Grandeza Acres, with Rick trailing behind him.

Helene paused as she passed them. "I was just coming to meet you two. She's out in the courtyard."

Troy frowned. "Is she well enough for that?"

Helene nodded. "Dr. Johnson was okay with it. She said she wanted some fresh air." Gesturing for them to follow her, she led them to the glass doors on the interior side of the hallway.

As Helene went on about her work, Troy and Rick stepped out onto the brick patio.

Jeannie reclined on a lounge chair, a magazine spread across her lap.

His first instinct was to admonish her about straining her eyes by reading in the fading light, but he knew better than that. "Hi, Mama J. How are you feeling?"

"Better."

Rick stepped forward. "Hey there, Mama J. It's good to see you up and about."

She chuckled. "Hey, Rick." She waved them forward. "Sit down, you two. Take a load off."

After they'd each grabbed chairs and pulled them near, they joined her. The setting sun still cast its yellow light over the patio, but he could feel the chill of the evening coming on.

"How much longer are you going to stay out here? You know it gets pretty cold at night."

"Pshaw, Troy." She gestured to the thick afghan thrown over the foot of her lounger. "I've got that in case I get a chill. You worry too much."

"It's all out of love."

She reached up, her withered hand stroking over his jaw for a moment. "I know. And I love you right back."

Rick said, "I fixed the sink. It's working just like new."

"Thank you, Rick."

"No problem. Troy's money is thanks enough." He grinned.

Troy elbowed his friend. "You're a regular saint, Rick."

She laughed. "Well, he's always entertaining."

While Rick cracked jokes with his grandmother, his mind wandered to thoughts of Robyn. The kiss he'd shared with her had been an unexpected joy. He'd opened up to her in a way that he hadn't in years, and on a level he never had with anyone else. Something about her called to him, promised him a safe haven against the storms raging inside him. Back when they were younger, she'd played that role well. He'd had no shortage of teen angst, considering his home life, and she'd always been there to provide a soft place to land.

He'd been unable to stop talking once he started. She'd listened to him, and while she'd held him accountable for his actions, she hadn't belittled or disrespected him.

In many ways, sitting close to her on the cold concrete floor hadn't been very different from sitting next to her on the couch when they were teenagers. He vented, she listened. She asked questions, he gave answers. It was the same dynamic that had always existed between them.

He'd been so lonely back then. Sure, he'd had his friends, the guys he played basketball and pulled pranks with. But none of them wanted to listen to his problems. He'd made every effort to keep them from learning just how screwed-up his home life really was, because he knew they'd never understand.

But Robyn was different. She gave him the gift of a listening ear, of a caring heart and open arms. He'd kept some of the more upsetting details to himself during their talks, not wanting to overburden her. Still, her presence in his life had been a balm to the pain of his teen years, and he would never forget how much she'd meant to him.

After all these years, we still fit together.

He remembered the feeling of her lips touching his, of her embrace, of her lithe body pressed against him. That brief contact had awakened a yearning in him, one he'd thought had been extinguished long ago.

Mama J cleared her throat. "Are you with us, Troy?"

Snapped back to reality by her question, he straightened up in his chair. "Sorry about that, Mama J. Just a little distracted."

She gave him a knowing look. "I just bet you are."

Rick shook his head. "As I was saying, do you remember that time we toilet-papered the school?"

"You mean freshman year after we won the homecoming game against Phillips Academy? Of course I remember."

"Man, the next day, it looked like a snowstorm had hit." Rick leaned back in his chair, looking off into the distance as if seeing the scene in his mind's eye. "I just wish it hadn't rained. It was a pain in the ass to clean it up."

Mama J cut him a sharp look. "Language, Rick."

"Sorry. But what about sophomore year, when we plastic-wrapped the principal's car? That was epic. Do you remember the look on Dr. Byrd's face when he came out to the parking lot?"

Troy cringed.

Mama J appeared displeased.

"What?" Rick looked back and forth between them.

"So, you participated in that mess, Troy?"

Troy sighed, cutting his eyes at his friend. "Thanks for dropping a dime on me, Rick." Up until this little story time, Mama J hadn't known Troy was in on that prank.

Rick winced. "Sorry, man."

"You two." Mama J's tone was sharp. "If I wasn't so tired, I'd go upside both your heads."

"I wouldn't blame you." Helene appeared next to them. "Are you about ready to go in, Jeannie?"

She nodded. "Yes. I'm about ready to fall asleep."

The men stood and helped her to her feet. Helene handed her the old carved walking stick she used and draped an arm around her. "I'll get her tucked in. Have a good night, guys."

"Thanks, Helene." Troy leaned in to kiss his grandmother's brow. "I'll be back to see you in a few days."

Jeannie yawned. "Okay. 'Bye, darling."

He watched as Helene escorted her inside, then turned to Rick. "Man, I can't take you anywhere."

"My bad, dude. I thought she knew. I thought everybody knew. Grandeza's roughly the size of a postage stamp."

Walking through the courtyard toward the breezeway that connected the rear parking lot to the front lot, he fished around in his jeans pocket for his keys.

"So, what's happening at the job, with you and Robyn? Has she sprung the trap yet?"

He shook his head. "Rick, you're tripping."

"Am I?"

"Listen. If she's trying to mess with me, she's got a funny way of doing it." He gave his friend a brief recap of the storage-room incident.

Rick's eyes widened. "Wow. Y'all kissed, huh?"

"Yes. So, I think that effectively puts your revenge theory to bed."

He emerged from the breezeway and crossed the grass in front of the building. "I don't know, man.

Maybe she's just biding her time. Maybe she wants a shot at standing you up, the way you did her."

"You're such a conspiracy theorist."

"Can't help it. I watch a lot of those crime documentaries." He scratched his chin. "Think about it. If she seduces you, gets your feelings caught up in her web of deception, then it'll hurt that much more when she finally gets you."

He shook his head as he walked up to his car and unlocked the door. "Rick, she's not out to get me. And even if she was, it would be worth the risk."

A few spaces over, Rick climbed into his truck, leaving the door open. "The kiss was that good, huh?"

"Hell, yeah." There was chemistry between them, an undeniable attraction that hadn't been dampened by time or distance. "And I intend to see just how far this thing between us is gonna go."

Rick yanked his door closed, then buckled up and fired up his truck. "Good luck, my man. Keep me posted. I might need to identify your body." With a wink and a laugh, he pulled out of the space and motored away.

Troy laughed as he got into his own car. Everybody needed a crazy friend, and Rick definitely had him covered in that respect.

Chapter 7

Friday morning, Robyn pulled into a spot at The Caffeine Connection and cut the engine. The coffee shop was part of a strip of stores that had been in downtown Grandeza ever since she could remember. Many of the current tenants were new, but the building had been there for decades. A hair salon, a clothing boutique, a drop-in child-care place and a post office rounded out the small shopping center.

When she entered the coffee shop, she inhaled the heavenly aroma of roasting beans. It was just after eight, but still a little earlier than she'd normally be out before work. Only Troy's invitation could have drawn her from the comfort of her bed, out into the early morning air. She'd dressed in a pair of dark denim jeans, a white turtleneck and sneakers. To keep things simple, she'd pulled her hair into a low bun, brushed on a little makeup and placed a pair of small gold hoops in her ears. She was presentable, yet comfortable.

She went up to the counter and placed her order for a small blond roast coffee and a croissant. Leaning against the end of the bar, she waited for her order, while watching for Troy's arrival. The windows lining the front of the shop gave her a great view of the parking lot and the road beyond it.

She'd just gotten her drink and pastry when the door swung open, causing the bell above it to jingle. She looked toward the sound and let her gaze sweep over Troy. It seemed no matter how many times she saw him enter a space, the novelty would never wear off. He wore a black sweater, brown slacks and black loafers. It was the first time she'd ever seen him without boots on, but the black Stetson was still perched on his head.

He took off the hat as their gazes connected, and a smile that could only be described as sexy stretched across his handsome face.

He generated such a heat inside her, she marveled that the coffee in her cup didn't come to a boil.

Physical attraction was just the beginning. There was no ignoring his drool-worthy handsomeness. But the things she'd always found attractive about him, like his gentle heart and his honesty, remained. Time had been good to him in many ways. He'd grown into his looks and matured emotionally as well.

"Morning, Robyn." His deep voice broke into her thoughts.

"Good morning." There were other people in the shop, and the sounds of their conversations reminded her of their presence. But when she looked at him, she felt as if they were the only two people in the world.

What is he doing to me?

"Go ahead and sit. You don't have to wait for me to order." He approached the counter.

She nodded. "Okay." She prided herself on being put together but being around Troy left her on the verge of swooning. Taking her drink and pastry in hand, she moved toward one of the two empty tables in the back and sat down. A short time later, Troy joined her. As he raised his mug of hot chocolate to his lips and formed an O shape to blow away some of the steam, she swallowed. The scent of the chocolate wafted toward her. Mixed with that fresh, masculine scent that followed wherever he went, it was almost her undoing.

"So, how long has this place been a coffee shop?"

She thought about his question, grateful for a diversion. "About a year and a half, maybe? I know the Sullys retired and moved down to Nevada."

"That sounds about right. I know the last time I was here, about two years ago, it was still Sully's Ice Cream."

She smiled. "We spent a lot of time here back in the day."

"We sure did. After school and on weekends, this was the hangout spot."

She looked around the space as she sipped from her mug. The new owners had changed a lot, which made sense considering the differences between an ice-cream parlor and a coffee shop. Still, a few pieces of the original decor remained.

"The walls are still the same color, I see." Troy pointed behind her. "They kept the same tables, just repainted them. And they kept one of those framed drawings of an ice-cream cone."

"I guess it's sort of an homage to what used to be here."

He chuckled. "Good memories here."

"Yeah."

"Do you remember that we had our first kiss here?"

She squinted. "Are you sure?"

"Yes, I'm sure. It was at the table behind us."

She turned and glanced that way.

"Remember? The table used to be bright blue. I brought you here after a football game for a dish of cookies and cream—your favorite."

She looked at him, wondering why and how he remembered so many details of that night. "You remember all that?" It touched her that he could still recall something so sweet, a remnant of her youthful eagerness.

"Yes." He reached across the table and took her hand in his. "When we kissed the other night, it brought back a lot of great memories, Robyn."

She drew a deep breath. "We should really talk about that. It didn't mean…"

He squeezed her hand, and she stopped in midsentence.

"I don't want to talk about what it didn't mean. Do you remember what you told me that first day, in your office?"

She blinked a few times. "I'm not sure what you mean."

"You told me you only gave second chances where you felt they were warranted."

She nodded, recalling what she'd said. "Yes. I remember now."

"So, the real question is, do you think what we once shared warrants a second chance?"

Her mouth fell open, and she snapped it shut.

"I've told you what happened, why I didn't come for you on prom night. I was honest with you—now I'm asking you to be honest with me."

She swallowed.

"I still care about you, Robyn. And I'm pretty sure you still have feelings for me." He tilted his head to the right. "If I'm wrong, and you don't want to pursue this, I promise to respect that. But I can't help sensing that there's something special between us."

She looked down at the table, where his hand was wrapped around hers. Maneuvering around until their fingers were laced together, she met his eyes. "You're not wrong, Troy. I do still care about you." How could she not? Didn't he know he was her first love? That she'd measured every other man she encountered by the feelings he inspired in her, and that no one could ever match him in her heart?

He smiled. "Then let's do this, Robyn. Let's just see where things go."

She felt her chest tighten. "I don't know if I can offer you any type of commitment right now. It's...complicated."

"I'm fine with that. I'm not asking for a commitment, or for any labels. I'm just asking for a chance to spend time with you and get to know you for who you are now."

She inhaled, then exhaled slowly. *What would be the harm in spending time with him?* They were both adults now, and there was no peer pressure, no societal expectations or disapproving parents standing in their way. They were free to do as they pleased. And when she looked at him, she had a feeling pleasure would play a major part in this arrangement. *There's nothing stopping me from walking away if things go bad. Hell, I've even got a job offer in another state waiting for me.*

Finally, she nodded. "I'm in."

"Great." He moved forward in his seat, leaned in.

She met him halfway, savoring his kiss. He tasted of chocolate and whipped cream. And when her lips touched his, any semblance of hesitation she might have harbored melted away.

When the kiss ended, Troy could feel himself grinning. "I'm glad we've come to this agreement."

Robyn's shy answering smile warmed him nearly as much as the heated kiss. "So am I."

He was still holding her hand, and he didn't want

to let go. But if he was going to finish the last of his drink before it got cold, he couldn't simply hold on to her forever.

She seemed to be thinking the same thing, and they unlocked their interlaced fingers almost simultaneously.

"You know, there's no reason folks on the ranch need to know we're seeing each other," she remarked, brushing the crumbs from her croissant off the table.

"I agree. Mixing romance and work can get a little sticky."

"Eventually they will probably know, with Grandeza being as small and dull as it is. There's not much to do around here besides gossip." She gave a little chuckle, one that held both amusement and resignation. He watched her, trying to gauge her mood. "I'm not too worried about that. I'm more concerned with discovering you."

The soft smile she'd had earlier returned. "Well, what do you want to know?"

He led with the biggest question on his mind. "Have you dated much during the time I was gone?"

Her eyes widened. "Wow. Right to the point, eh?"

He shrugged. "I shoot from the hip, as they say."

Shaking her head, she answered, "Not really. I've had three or four boyfriends. There's always so much going on at the ranch that I really haven't felt like there was time for dating."

"Were any of those boyfriends serious?"

"I'm not sure what you mean by serious, Troy." She pressed her lips together into a thin line before speaking again. "Are you asking if I was ever engaged? If I discussed marriage with any of them? Or are you asking me if I slept with them?"

His jaw tightened. He leaned back, realizing why she'd reacted that way. "I'm sorry. I don't want you to think I'm grilling you, and you can feel free to reveal whatever you're comfortable with and keep the rest to yourself."

She narrowed her eyes but remained silent.

He shoved his hands into his pockets. "Well, crap. We were off to such a good start and now I've ruined it." *Damn it, Troy. Keep that up and you'll screw up your second chance before it gets off the runway.*

"It's all right, Troy." She blew out a breath. "I'm not a virgin but that's all I'm saying on that."

He felt a twinge inside but did his best to brush it off. They'd been young when they were together, and neither of them had been ready for sex back then. Still, knowing another man had been the one to introduce her to the pleasures of physical intimacy didn't sit right with him. *Had whoever it was been good to her? Did he take his time and make it as memorable as I would have?* He knew better than to raise those questions aloud; she'd made it clear she'd cut him off at the knees if he delved too much into the topic.

"That's a fair answer, Robyn." He removed his hands from his pockets, flexing his fingers. "And I'm willing to answer your questions, too. I'm not out to hide anything from you."

"Good to know." Her gaze shifted then, as if she was looking past him.

He turned to see what had her attention.

There was an older lady approaching the counter, holding the hand of a small child. The little girl, wearing a pink dress and four pigtails festooned with a matching ribbon, had to be about two or three years old.

"Look at her. She's precious." Robyn's eyes sparkled as she spoke.

"She is a little cutie." He couldn't help smiling as the older woman stooped down to hand the tot a sugar cookie, which she immediately bit into.

Suddenly, the little girl noticed them. Tugging her hand away from her guardian, she ran over to their table and went right to Robyn.

"Sophia, what are you doing? Don't bother these nice people." The older woman was close on her heels.

He smiled. "It's not a problem, ma'am."

"I'm Cora, by the way. My apologies—my grand-daughter is quite the little social butterfly."

"She's no bother." Robyn held out her hand. "Hello, sweetheart."

The grinning little girl reached out to take Robyn's hand, but in the process, dropped her sugar cookie. Tears welled in her eyes, and she opened her mouth to release a plaintive wail.

The older woman frowned. "Oh, goodness."

Robyn stood. "I'll get her another cookie."

The older woman started to protest, but Robyn insisted. Moments later, Troy watched as Robyn paid for the new cookie, handed it off to little Sophia, then bid the pair farewell as they left the coffee shop.

She's amazing. He didn't know a lot about her life since he'd been away. But he could tell some things about her hadn't changed. He'd known her since middle school. She'd been extraordinarily caring as a young girl, and now, she still cared about others just as much as she had then. Having grown up with a selfish mother, who thought only of herself and seemed to take pleasure in insulting him and his father, Troy admired the innate kindness Robyn possessed.

Returning to her seat, she met his gaze. "What's that look on your face?"

"Amazement," he admitted. "You're just…such a good person."

Her expression changed then, and she looked away from him. "I'm glad you think so highly of me, Troy."

He frowned, wondering what she meant by that. It seemed he believed in her goodness more than she did. *Why would she react that way?* Curiosity rose up inside him, but he knew now wasn't the time to ask.

Breaking into his thoughts, she asked, "How is Mama Jeannie? Does she need anything?"

"I don't think so. She's very well taken care of."

"I know. But what does she like to do with her spare time?"

"She takes Spanish classes, goes to bible study." He snapped his fingers, remembering something she'd said to him. "She does like those adult coloring books and the crossword puzzles."

"Then I'll send her some."

The amazement grew. "You don't have to—"

"I know I don't have to. I want to." She offered him a smile. "Both my grannies are gone now, so consider Mama Jeannie adopted. She could use a granddaughter—right now it's just you."

"And Rick. Don't forget Rick. He's her honorary grandson now."

She giggled. "Can't leave her to that fate."

"All right. I don't think she'll turn down your generous offer." He pushed aside the mug that held the remains of his tepid cocoa. "Listen, I know I just asked you to meet me here for coffee. I don't want to monopolize your time, but I also don't want to let you go just yet."

Her eyes glittered. "I…I'm enjoying your company as well."

"What do you have planned after work?"

"Not much."

He rubbed his hands together. "Then what do you say to doing something fun?"

She cut her eyes at him.

He chuckled. "Not that. I was thinking we could play some games."

"Oh. I was about to say." Her expression softened. "What do you have in mind?"

"I know just the place."

Chapter 8

Robyn couldn't help smiling as she stepped into Way Back When Gaming Center. "This was a really cool idea. There isn't anything else like this in Grandeza, or anywhere nearby, honestly."

Troy grinned. "Rick told me about it, and I knew I had to come here. I'm just glad you agreed to come with me."

Moving farther into the brightly colored space, she turned slowly to get a full view of the interior. The walls, painted a lemon yellow, were covered with full-color images of beloved video-game characters. To the left, there was a whole wall full of cabinet-style arcade games. The rear wall featured a basketball-shooter game, Whac-A-Mole and a target-practice game, and along the right wall there were tables stocked with over-size decks of playing cards, as well as chess, checkers and other classic board games. In the center of the space there were an assortment of gaming tables, including foosball, air hockey, pool and table tennis. In an alcove behind the Whac-a-Mole game, there was a service window that sold food and beverages.

"Somehow, they still managed to give this place a really adult vibe." She moved toward the wall of arcade games.

"Well, according to the guy at the door, you have to be twenty-one to get in. But they don't have many teenagers showing up, anyway. Too retro for them." Troy walked up beside her and draped his arm over her shoulder. "What do you want to play first?"

She set her gaze on the stand-up zombie shooter game. "Care to take on a horde of the undead with me?"

He laughed. "Sure. Show me what you've got."

They took up positions in front of the game. She took the red plastic shotgun in hand while he grabbed the blue one.

She fed tokens into the game with her free hand, then stepped on the start button on the mat. "Let's do this."

Seven hundred and fifty-six zombie kills later, Robyn danced around a flabbergasted Troy.

"Wow! I never would have thought you had the killer instinct. At least not on that level." He returned his plastic weapon to its holder and stepped back from the machine. "Obviously it was a mistake to let you pick the first game."

Laughing, she gave him a playful punch in the shoulder. "Okay, champ. You pick the next game."

"Let's try foosball. You any good at that?"

She shrugged. "I haven't played in years."

"Let's give it a go then."

At the table, they manned the handles for their respective teams, and he dropped the white ball onto the playing field. And when the game ended, her kickers were still spinning on their shiny silver axis when she sank the winning shot.

He smacked a hand against his forehead. "Savage, Robyn. You're truly savage."

Unable to hold back her chuckles, she asked, "Have you been letting me win?"

He gestured to the room, teeming with other people. "Look at all these folks in here. You think I'm gonna *let* you embarrass me like that, in front of half of Grandeza's population? Nah."

That only made her laugh harder. When she finally recovered, she wiped the tears of mirth from her eyes. "I haven't laughed like this in a while. Thanks, Troy."

He crossed his arms over his chest.

"Sorry, sorry." She sobered up. "Listen. You can pick something else. How's that?"

He took a deep breath. "Table tennis."

Her brow hitched. "You wanna play Ping-Pong?"

"Yes, I want to play table tennis."

"Okay. I'm down."

They walked the short distance to the vibrant green tables, then took sides at the last available one. She grabbed the paddle, which was affixed to the side of the table with a hook and loop strip.

He took a ball from the bucket, grabbed his paddle and stood poised to serve. "You ready, Robyn?"

She raised her paddle, giving him a nod.

Half a second later, she heard a crack at the same time the little white ball whizzed past her right ear.

She jerked her head around to look for it and spotted it on the floor near the Whac-A-Mole game. Turning back to Troy with wide eyes, she found him smiling.

She jogged over to get the ball, then tossed it to him.

He caught it in midair.

"Okay, now. Don't take my head off with this serve." She returned to her place and lifted her paddle again.

He bounced the ball on the table and launched it toward her.

She swiped at it a moment before it would have hit her in the chest.

He returned it.

She swiped again but missed. This time the ball sailed by her on the left side.

He grinned at her while she went, again, to fetch the ball.

Well, he looks mighty pleased with himself.

The rest of the game continued much the same way, with the tiny white sphere sailing past her like a comet, and her swatting at it uselessly, then fetching it.

When it was over, she returned the paddle. "Looks like we should have started with table tennis, Troy."

He laughed. "Nah. The despair of those earlier defeats only helped my game."

She shook her head. "I'm never playing you in this game again."

"Sure, you will, when the sting of losing wears off."
He winked.

Later, they sat at a table outside the arcade, sharing
an enormous plate of nachos.

Sipping from her lemon-lime soda, she asked, "When
and how did you get so good at table tennis? What, did
you train for the Olympic team or something?"

He released a deep, rumbling laugh. "Nah, I played
a lot with Dad."

"Do tell." She settled into the padded seat, eager to
hear the tale.

"Back in the day, after I graduated high school, Dad
got a gig to go on tour with Zell's Midnight Preachers.
I didn't have any plans for the summer before college,
so I went with him."

She leaned forward in her seat. "What was that like?
The Preachers seem like a pretty wild bunch, based off
their music." The funk-soul band was known for elaborate stage costumes and racy lyrics.

He scoffed. "It's not an image, trust me. They really
are like that. Anyway, I rode the tour bus that whole
summer with Dad, the band and Zell himself. They kept
a folding tennis table in the back of the bus. Whenever
the band had a stopover, and Dad wasn't in rehearsals
or on stage, we'd pull it out and play."

She smiled, imagining a teenaged Troy playing Ping-
Pong with Mr. Monroe. "I bet you saw a lot of things
that year."

"I did. But Dad was serious about shielding me from
the band members' lifestyle. I wasn't in school, and I was

technically an adult, but he made it clear that I wasn't to indulge in any of their vices." He leaned back, looking up at the darkened sky. "We set that table up in parking lots, hotel suites, dressing rooms—wherever we could find space. Zell saw how much we loved the game, so he gave the folding table set to my dad after the tour."

"It seems you've kept your skills sharp since then."

He nodded. "I'd play with Dad whenever we were together. After he passed, I started playing racquetball—the skill set is pretty much the same. Every now and again, when I was in town, I'd play with Rick."

She reached out to him, grabbing his hand. "You're a very complex man, Troy."

"I guess that's true."

"I'm learning a lot about you."

A ghost of a smile crossed his face. "And do you like what you've learned so far?"

She nodded, meeting his smile with one of her own. "Yes, I do."

Maybe even a little more than I should.

After leaving the arcade, Troy drove Robyn home. Her modest cottage sat on a half acre of land just outside the ranch's borders. The parcel had been a gift from her parents on her twenty-first birthday.

Standing on her front porch, she looked up at Troy. His hat was in his hands again, and the soft yellow glow of the porchlight illuminated his rugged handsomeness.

"I had a great time tonight, Troy."

"Really? I'm glad to hear that." He grabbed her hand, held it gently within his own.

"I really enjoyed myself. So much so, I'm half-tempted to let you inside."

His dark eyes flickered with interest.

She swallowed, feeling the heat rise to her face as she realized the double meaning in her words. "Inside... the house, I mean."

"Whatever you meant, I'm sure you know I would accept your invite."

She cleared her throat, trying to shake off the tightness gathering there. *Why did he have to come back into my life now? I finally landed my dream job, and a shot at getting out of this little town, and along comes my first love to screw up the plan.* "I think we both know that's a step we're not ready to take yet."

He looked thoughtful for a moment. "I suppose you're right." He tugged her close to him, draped his arms around her waist. "You're made of temptation, Robyn Chance. But I'll always respect your boundaries." He fixed her with a penetrating look. "Always."

Moments later, their lips touched, and her insides turned to ash from the searing heat of his kiss.

He released her, then stepped back to put on his hat.

She stood there, her mouth agape while he took her key and unlocked her door. He pushed the door open, then moved away and gestured her inside.

With a tip of his hat, he said, "Good night, Robyn."

"Good night."

He stepped off the porch and walked away.

She was still standing in the doorway watching when he drove away.

That man is going to be my undoing.

* * *

Creeeaaakkk.

The old wooden stairs groaned their protest beneath the weight of Troy's boots as he climbed up to the attic. As he entered the room, he scrunched his head and shoulders forward since the low ceiling couldn't accommodate his full height.

While he moved over the dust-shrouded wooden floors, he shined the beam of his flashlight around the space. The beam was no match for the inky blackness of this rarely visited space, which had only one small porthole-shaped window. The small sliver of pale moonlight hit the floor like a dim spotlight but provided no help in navigating the room.

He stifled a yawn with his free hand, but it morphed into a sneeze as the thick dust coating everything invaded his nostrils. Sniffling, he moved toward the far end of the attic.

Finding the large mahogany wardrobe, the only thing in the space that wasn't coated in dust, he pressed the lever-style handle and opened the door.

Inside were his two most prized possessions. He kneeled on the floor, to give his neck and shoulders a break from his awkward positioning and reached inside the wardrobe. Moments later, he carefully slid out the folding tennis table and set it aside.

Stretching until he touched the cool, smooth curves of the object he sought, he finally pulled out his father's bass.

The main body of the '87 Music Man StingRay was a shimmering jet-black, embellished with red, orange and yellow paint that formed flickering flames along the bottom. Sitting down on the floor, he pulled the instrument into his lap and cradled it close to his chest.

Just the same as he'd done in his dream—the dream that had awakened him and sent him up here to seek out the comfort of his father's treasured instrument. He needed to touch it, needed to feel the solid weight of it in his hands. It reminded him of his father, of the music he'd loved so much, and of the bond they'd shared.

Johnny "J-Rock" Monroe had taken this bass with him all over the world, laying down basslines for the legends of funk, soul and R&B. Johnny had been a wanderer at heart, just like Troy. But he'd always returned home to his son.

The years that stretched between the present moment and the moment when he'd learned of his father's death seemed at once instantaneous and eternal.

I can't hold Dad. But I can hold his bass.

He would take his comfort where he could get it.

Robyn's face entered his mind. He thought back on the day he'd spent with her. Even when he'd spoken with her about his father, he hadn't felt the pangs of grief that normally accompanied such conversation. Something about being with her changed the way he felt, let the pain melt away to reveal the humor and happiness of his memories.

She's probably asleep. If he had any say in the matter, he'd be asleep, too.

Maybe it was because her life was so stable. Was it her solid, two-parent upbringing that made her such a buoy on the storm-tossed sea of his life? His own raising had been so different from hers—messy, imperfect and held together with masking tape. His father had spent a lot of time on the road, and his mother had spent a lot of time complaining. His dad was an explorer, ever-curious; she was a shrew, never satisfied with anything. And here he was, a combination of the two of them, and in many ways, just as broken.

He'd been traveling from city to city for the better part of his adulthood, searching for the right place to settle. On the surface of things, he wanted what most people did: stable employment, a nice home, a sense of community. Deep down, he knew what he was really seeking: a place to call home. A place where he'd get the acceptance denied to him by his mother, and the predictability made impossible by his father's lifestyle and career. His craving for a real home had been the most intense longing in his life...

Up until the moment he'd laid eyes on Robyn.

More than anything, he wanted to break away from that the brokenness of his past. Somewhere out there was the place he belonged. He only hoped he'd find his true home before this life ended.

A faint sound drew his attention. It was coming from beneath him, somewhere in the main house.

My phone.

Who would be calling me at this hour?

Panic set in as he realized something must be happening with Mama Jeannie. He stood, the bass still in his grasp, and quickly but carefully picked his way down the stairs and to his bedroom. Grabbing the ringing phone from the nightstand, he sat down on the bed.

"Hello? Is something wrong with Mama Jeannie? Do I need to—"

"Troy, everything's fine. It's me, Robyn."

A sigh of relief escaped his lips. "Thank goodness." Setting the bass on the bed next to him, he asked, "Why are you calling me at this hour? I didn't expect you to be up."

"I was raised on a ranch, Troy. Up with the chickens and all."

He glanced at the digital clock on the nightstand. Four forty-nine. "Hell, I don't even know if the chickens are up yet."

She giggled.

"What's up?"

"I know it's kind of an odd request, especially at this hour, but…would you like to go hiking with me today?"

His brow furrowed. "It's kind of short notice."

"I know, sorry about that. I should have asked you before you left my house, but I was, um, distracted."

He thought back to their heated kiss. "So was I, so I guess I can't really blame you."

She giggled. "So, what do you think? Wanna come along?"

"I'm game. Where do you usually hike?"

"The state parks around here and Santa Fe. Either Hyde Memorial or Heron Lake."

"I'll go. Let's do Heron Lake." He rubbed his chin. "Ever been out on a canoe?"

"Not recently."

"Then let's make a day of it. We'll hike early, then canoe the lake at sunset. How's that?"

"Sounds like a pretty awesome day."

He detected an undertone in her voice, one he couldn't quite place. Considering the hour and the newness of their relationship, he decided to take her agreement at face value.

"Great," she said. "I've got a whole list of stuff you should bring with you. Got a pen?"

"Give me a sec, I'll grab one." He snatched a pen and a small notebook from the drawer of his bedside table. "Okay. I'm ready." While she rattled off the list, he jotted down the items.

After confirming that he'd taken good notes, she yawned. "Now I've got to decide whether to get dressed or lie back down for a bit."

He chuckled. "Don't get back in bed, it's a trap. You'll oversleep for sure."

Another soft giggle met that remark. "See you in a few hours, Troy."

"I'll be there."

After he disconnected the call, he sat on the edge of the bed for a moment. It was as if she'd known he was thinking of her.

Amazing.

Placing the bass on a safer position on the bed, he went to take a shower and get ready for the day.

Chapter 9

"I can't believe you're ditching me for a man."

Robyn sighed in response to Kima's complaint. "Oh, come on, Kima. You've gone hiking with me every year since forever, and this is the first time I've ever gone with someone else."

"That someone else is a *man*." Kima placed terse emphasis on the last word.

Robyn put the phone on her bed, then sat down and pulled on the heavy brown boots that would protect her feet and ankles from the uneven, rocky terrain. "You've been on me to give Troy a real second chance, haven't you? This is part of that."

"Girl, I meant go on regular dates. You know, like regular people? I thought y'all would do the dinner-and-movie thing." Kima blew out a breath. "I never thought it would mean getting left behind for the hike."

"I'm going on a Saturday this time, and you know how hard it is for you to get Saturdays off at the spa."

"That's beside the point, Robyn."

"I'm sorry, Kima. I just…feel like this will be good for us. Out there in the wilderness, there are no distractions, no pretenses." She needed to get away from the ranch, away from the watchful eyes and listening ears of the townsfolk. If she was going to make the right decisions about her future, she needed to clear her head. She finished lacing her boots and let her feet dangle off the side of the bed. "If there's anything hidden between us, it's going to come out."

"Remember you said that."

She felt a twinge.

"Does he know about her? That she's the whole reason you go on this trip every year?"

She swallowed. "No."

"I'm just worried about you, Robyn. If you need support up there…"

"He hasn't given me any reason to think he wouldn't be supportive."

Kima's tone softened. "If you need me, call me, girl. Because if he gives you any trouble at all, you know I'm flipping tables."

She smiled. "I love you, too, Kima. 'Bye, girl."

"Later."

She disconnected the call and went to toss the rest of her gear in the brown backpack she always took with her on these trips. She'd be meeting Troy at Heron Lake State Park in an hour or so, and as she rifled through the pack, she made a mental inventory of everything inside. First-aid kit. Snacks. Bottled water. Multitool. Ponchos. Flashlight. Lighter. As an experienced hiker, putting together her kit had become second nature.

She slung the backpack over her shoulder, tucking her phone, driver's license and a bit of money into one of the pockets on her cargo pants. Then she grabbed her sunglasses and hat and left the house.

When she pulled into the parking lot at the park a little while later, she saw Troy waiting for her. He'd parked his SUV, and was leaning his back against it, his attention trained on the screen of his phone. She cut the engine, grabbed her backpack, got out of her vehicle and walked toward him.

He was dressed in thick olive-green cargo pants, black hiking boots and a fitted, long-sleeve black shirt. Beneath the brim of his straw cowboy hat, a pair of dark sunglasses obscured his eyes. There was nothing to obscure the smile he wore when he saw her, though.

"Morning, Robyn."

She moved next to him, gave him a peck on the lips. "Good morning, Troy."

"You look nice."

She looked down at her layered long-sleeve T-shirt, tan cargo pants and boots. "Thanks. My mind was more on preparedness than fashion today, though." She gestured at the canoe tied to his roof rack. "Nice vessel."

He grinned, reaching up to pat the canoe's bright green hull. "Saranac 160. Smooth ride and easy to paddle. Perfect for a quiet evening on the water."

She swallowed the lump that formed in her throat when he mentioned the water. Hiking had been her suggestion, and it seemed only fair to let him choose something for them to do as well.

I'm not afraid of the water. It will be fine.

"So, what can I expect on this hiking adventure?" His voice cut into her thoughts.

She returned her attention to him. "The Salmon Run trail here is really great. It's five and a half miles of natural beauty. It's got some gorgeous views, and there's a suspension bridge that'll take us over the Rio Chama River."

He appeared impressed. "Sounds nice. And how long does it normally take you to hike it?"

"I can do the whole thing in about five hours."

His thick eyebrows rose, and he stared at her with wide eyes. "Say what now?"

She chuckled. "Since you're not a hiker, I thought we'd take the East Meadow trail. It's a little over two miles and the terrain isn't as rough. So, about three hours."

He placed his hand over his chest and exhaled dramatically. "I appreciate you."

Giggling, she shook her head. "Do you have all the stuff I told you to bring?"

"Yep." He turned around to show her the green pack on his back. "I'm ready."

"Then let's hit the trail." She grabbed his hand, and they got underway.

It was well past the height of the busy season, so there weren't any other hikers on the trail. The temperature hovered near sixty-five degrees, and along with partly sunny skies and a light breeze, it made for a pleasant hike. She inhaled deeply, filling her lungs with the sweet, fresh air, scented by the towering pines above them. He kept pace with her over the hilly terrain, holding her hand in his.

The only sounds were the birds and wildlife, and the loose gravel crunching beneath their boots.

"Doing okay, Troy?"

He nodded. "I can hang."

"Be on the lookout. There're all kinds of animals out here. Deer, turkeys, elk and the occasional mountain lion."

He coughed. "Very funny, Robyn."

"It's not a joke, but okay."

He groaned, running a hand over his face. "Lord. What did I let you talk me into?"

She laughed. *He's obviously a little uncomfortable, but at least he was willing to try it.*

"Guess I didn't ask the right questions before we came up here." He shook his head. "How many times have you hiked here?"

"I've been coming here to hike every year since I was seventeen."

"Alone?"

She shook her head. "Usually, Kima comes with me. I think I've done it alone three times, but those were all times she couldn't make it. She's got my goddaughter to take care of."

"Okay, and in all the times you've been up here, how many times have you actually seen a mountain lion?"

"Only once, and that was from a distance." She met his eyes. "Are you really nervous about it?"

He maintained eye contact. "No, just cautious."

She nodded, understanding where he was coming from. She could appreciate a man that leaned on reason rather than bravado and bluster in a situation like this.

They rounded a bend in the trail, coming within sight of the trail terminus, situated above the Willow Creek arm of Heron Lake. "It's not too much farther. The trail ends at the overlook just ahead."

He reached into his hip pocket, extracted a handkerchief and wiped it over his brow. "All right."

A sound caught her attention. She stopped, pointing to a grove of bushes just off the trail. "I hear something."

He halted, his gaze swinging in the direction she indicated. While they watched and waited, the rustling sound increased as the branches began to shake and buckle.

She took a step back, and he moved as well, inserting himself between her and the bush.

Her gaze darted to his face, and she saw the determined set of his jaw. "Troy?"

He held up his hand. "Something's coming," he whispered, never taking his eyes off the dancing bush.

Troy kept a wary eye on the wall of leaves, waiting for whatever might leap out. The muscles in his shoulders were coiled tighter than a spring. The foliage was dense enough that he couldn't even guess what might be rolling around in there, and part of him didn't want to.

It would be just my luck if Robyn has her second

mountain-lion sighting today. As ridiculous as it was, he thought about Rick's insistence that she had been planning his downfall. Rick would probably pass out if he heard Troy had gone hiking with Robyn, only to be eaten by a wild animal.

The moment seemed to drag on into eternity as he stood between her and the unknown entity troubling the bushes.

Finally, two squirrels darted out of the foliage, one in hot pursuit of the other. As they scurried by and disappeared into the brush on the opposite side of the trail, his tension finally dissipated.

She laughed "Dang. I thought we were gonna see a fawn or something."

He blew out a breath, crossing his arms over his body so he could work some of the knots out of his shoulders. "If it's all the same to you, I think I'll wait a while before I come hiking with you again."

She giggled, starting to move again, and gestured him forward. "Come on. Wait until you see the view at the overlook."

They came to a stop at the trailhead. Standing next to her, he draped an arm around her waist as they gazed out over the glassy surface of Heron Lake. The breeze created ripples on the water's surface, though there were no vessels in sight. In the distance, the shimmering gray of the water seemed to reflect the bluish-gray sky. Around the lake, the pines and other tall trees seemed to stretch on forever.

"Wow. It's beautiful up here."

"Told ya."

He eased her against him. "A sight like this makes me want to…" He curled his finger beneath her chin.

She smiled as she leaned up for his kiss. After a few humid moments, she pulled back. "Maybe we should eat something before we head back."

"That's probably wise. So, I'm gonna fight off the urge to neck with you like a hormonal teenager."

She put her hand to her mouth, but not soon enough to cover her peals of laughter.

Sitting on the ground, they ate in companionable silence. While he ate his turkey sandwich, chips and banana, she munched on a protein bar, chips and hummus, and a crisp red apple. It wasn't the most comfortable seat he'd ever been in, but he felt some of his tiredness melt away just the same. By the time they'd each finished eating and drained two bottles of water, he was ready to head back.

She asked, "We're going to use the main access to the water, right?"

He nodded. "Yeah. It'll be a lot easier to get my craft on the water from there."

Returning to the parking lot was easier and faster, since he felt more familiar with the terrain of the trail. While Robyn tucked her backpack into the trunk of her car, he changed out of his boots into a pair of neoprene water shoes.

"Did you bring water shoes or sandals?"

She held up a pair of black sandals. "I'm about to put them on. Do you need help getting the canoe down?"

He nodded. "Thanks." A short time later, they were walking toward the lake's edge, each of them carrying an end of the sixteen-foot-long vessel.

With the canoe settled on the ground near the edge of the lake, they slipped into their life jackets on the shore. Then, he gestured for her to sit down in the forward seat.

She hesitated, coming to a halt next to the vessel.

Tilting his head, he observed her. She seemed to be conflicted about whether or not she should get in. Up until now, she'd never given him any indication she was nervous about going out on the water. "Is something wrong?"

She closed her eyes momentarily, and when she reopened them, she seemed to have recovered from whatever bothered her. "I'm fine." She slipped into the seat, reaching down to grab the paddle propped against the bow.

He gave the canoe a strong push, then quickly climbed into the stern seat behind her. He wrapped his hand around the handle of his paddle as the current pulled the canoe out onto the water.

Once they'd been afloat for a few minutes, he asked, "Doing okay up there?"

"Yeah." She glanced over her shoulder, giving him a small smile.

They rowed out a bit, and he purposefully steered in a way that kept them close to the shore. The cliffs overhead were alive with the echoing sounds of the ospreys nesting on their undersides. Moving them forward until he thought he'd found a good spot, he lifted his paddle out of the water and placed it across his lap. "Let's just hang out here for a while."

She pulled in her paddle, resting it against her. The setting sun cast a yellow-orange glow over the water, making the surface shimmer. The tableau reminded him of the dancing flames of a campfire.

He heard her sigh. "This is gorgeous."

"You said you come here every year to hike. You never come out on the lake?"

She shook her head, her gaze focused on some far-away point.

He narrowed his eyes. "I'm confused. Are you afraid? You seem a little…uncomfortable right now."

"I'm not afraid of water. I'm a strong swimmer."

He waited, sensing she had something more to say.

"Do you know why I come out here, every year, on the same day?"

"I haven't got a clue."

She took a deep breath. "It's my way of remembering someone I loved, of connecting to their spirit by being out in the quiet of nature."

He frowned, grateful she couldn't see his expression at the moment. *Who is she talking about?* Was it one of the boyfriends she'd been so reluctant to discuss at the coffee shop?

"I had a younger sister, Troy. Today is her birthday."

He felt his mouth fall open. While he was partly relieved that she wasn't grieving another man, he was also shocked by what she'd said. "A sister? But I've known you since middle school, and you've never…"

He closed his mouth, giving her the opportunity to fill in the numerous blanks.

"By the time we met, she was already gone." She dropped her gaze to the water then, her shoulders slumping. "It happened when Lacey was three and I was six, almost seven. There used to be a pond on the southern edge of the ranch."

He leaned back, scratching his chin. Then he remembered. The fenced-off garden near the southwest pastures. It was planted with beautiful flowers, but he'd never seen anyone go over there to enjoy them.

"We were playing hide-and-seek. I couldn't find her, and I told the hands. They got my parents, and everyone combed the property near where we'd been playing." Her voice cracked. "And then they found her…in the pond. She'd drowned."

His heart flexed in his chest. "Oh, no."

"They tried to shield me from it, but I saw her." She was shaking now, her voice soft with emotion. "After that, my parents drained the pond, and my mother had the garden planted there in her memory."

Dear lord. She'd never told him. He supposed it was too deep a grief to share, and she'd kept it to herself. "I need to get you back to shore."

She picked up her paddle as he picked up his own, and slowly moved it beneath the water's surface while he steered them the short distance back to the shore.

And as soon as they were on land again, he took her into his arms and held her as she wept.

Chapter 10

When she recovered enough to speak again, Robyn looked up into Troy's eyes. "I'm sorry. I didn't mean to put a damper on our day together."

"Don't worry about it." He gave her a squeeze. "I'm glad you felt safe enough with me to tell me about her."

She stepped out of his embrace, and immediately missed the warmth of it. Using her hands, she swiped away her tears. "I don't really know what to do now. I mean, I feel like I ruined the vibe."

He gave her an easy smile. "No, you didn't." He gestured to their gear, still sitting on the shore. "Wanna help me haul this crap back to my car?"

She nodded, feeling her mood lighten just a little.

They took the canoe and paddles back to the parking

lot, and he retied it to the roof rack. With that done, he asked, "Are you in a hurry to leave?"

She looked back toward the water, now glistening as twilight rose on the horizon. The surrounding mountains reached up, seeming to touch the bands of the golden skyline. "We can stay a little longer. Let's go sit by the shore." She got the flashlight out of her pack and tucked it into her pocket.

Hand in hand, they returned to the edge of the water. He found a spot in the soft grass and sat down. Once he was settled, he opened his arms and she joined him, sitting between his parted thighs and resting her back against the steadying strength of his chest.

Cool night evening caressed her face, drying the places dampened by her tears. A sense of peace washed over her, her soul feeling just as cozy as her physical body did.

He ran a hand over her hair. "Why don't we tell each other our most embarrassing moments?"

She giggled. "Why would I want to do that?"

"Come on, it'll be fun, and I'll go first." He cleared his throat. "Okay. How's this? When I was in my twenties, I was hanging out in North Carolina with my cousins. They live on an island, and my older cousin Savion is big on fishing. He's got an awesome fishing boat now, but back then, we were still just fishing off the pier."

She swiveled her head, so she could look at him. "Go on."

"One day, I was at the pier with Savion. We're standing on the pier, casting our lines. He goes first, and since he's been fishing since he was a kid, his hook goes like a thousand yards out. Then he asks me if I want him to help me with my cast. Of course, I said yeah. He tells me to put my arms up, like this." Troy raised both arms above his head, making his right hand into a fist. "I'm holding the rod over my head now. He tells me to stretch back for the cast…and I sneezed."

Her brow creased. "What happened then?"

"I sneezed so hard I got a cramp in my back. When my back locked up, I dropped my rod. Then Savion tripped over the rod while trying to help me, bumped into me and I fell off the damn pier."

She covered her mouth. "Well, damn."

"I'm a decent swimmer, normally. But with my back jacked up like that, all I could do was float. Savion had to jump in and rescue me. Ever since then, he's called me a landlubber."

She threw her head back and laughed. Wiping away tears, she asked, "Oh, so your cousin thinks he's a pirate now?"

"I don't know, maybe. He's got a pretty sweet ship now, so I guess he can call himself whatever he likes when he's on the *Queen of Zamunda*."

She tilted her head. "That's the name of his boat?"

He nodded. "Yes. My cousin may be a blowhard, but he has good enough taste in movies to know that *Coming to America* is a stellar film."

She made a show of rolling her eyes, hoping he could see her in the growing darkness. She flicked on the flashlight and stood it on the ground next to them. "I wouldn't say stellar, but that's a conversation for another day."

He frowned slightly, but then his expression softened. "Your turn. Time to tell your most embarrassing story."

She drew a breath, looking up at the sky as she thought back on the many mortifying moments in her life. "Oh, I know. During my graduation ceremony from UC Davis, my heel got caught in the top step as I was going up to get my degree. To avoid the face-plant I saw coming, I grabbed the dean's arm...and we both fell."

His laughter rumbled through the darkness. "Wow, is this on video somewhere?"

She chuckled. "My parents probably have footage. Anyway, at least we both landed on our butts. The dean was totally cool about it and laughed it off as she handed me my degree."

"Still, yikes. I've seen the crowds that show up for college graduations. That's a lot of people, and they all saw you bust your ass."

By now they were both laughing. She laughed until tears spilled down her face for the second time. Only now, they were the happy tears of amusement. And when the laughter finally subsided, she felt the change in her mood. A lightness came over her, and as she looked into his eyes, she knew where this night would end.

She raised her hands, cupping his face and feeling the subtle scratch of the day's stubble against her palms. "Thank you for this, Troy."

"You're welcome."

Their gazes connected, held for a long, silent moment.

"I don't want this to be over." She moved one hand, placed soft kisses along the line of his jaw.

"It doesn't have to," he replied.

She leaned in then, kissing him in earnest. When their lips touched, she felt the sparks lighting up her soul. His arms encircling her, his tongue moving against her own and the softness of his lips drew a low moan from her.

He leaned back. "Too much?"

She shook her head. "No. Just right."

He watched her in the darkness, his desire evident.

"Come home with me, Troy."

"Is there any particular reason?"

She heard the teasing in his tone, but she was well past playing coy. Her body was calling out for his touch, and she would not deny that. "I want you to make love to me."

"You're sure?"

"Yes. Absolutely." She pecked him on the lips again, knowing that if she leaned into the kiss, they'd be here all night.

He eased away from her and stood up. Extending his hand, he said, "Let's go."

Grabbing her flashlight, she took his hand and let him pull her to her feet. Then they walked together through the grass.

Later, as they kissed their way into Robyn's house, Troy fought to keep his raging desire in check. He'd had no idea that their physically active day would lead to this. Despite the slight soreness he felt coming on from the hike, he had no complaints.

She asked me to make love to her, and I'm damn sure going to give her what she wants.

He'd deal with the fallout from all the exertion later. Now, the only thing on his mind was making her moan.

She pulled away from him then. "I need a minute to lock up."

He obliged her, watching as she shut the door and flipped on a floor lamp nearby. The illumination showed the interior of a modest one-story home. She had polished hardwood floors, lots of colorful throws tossed over the backs of her beige sofa and love seat and a large Oriental rug centering the room.

"So, this is your place?"

She smiled. "Yes. It's nothing fancy but that's just the way I like it."

"I think it's nice."

"Thanks." She walked past him, opened a small closet in the hall beyond the living room and stored her backpack and purse inside.

The sway of her hips reminded him of what she'd asked him to do. "You'll have to give me a tour—"

"Tomorrow," she said, finishing the sentence. She beckoned to him from her spot in the hallway as she moved deeper into the house.

Heeding her invitation, he followed her.

At the end of the hall, she led him into a large bedroom. She clapped her hands, and two lamps, one on either side of the bed, illuminated.

He looked at the bed, dressed in a frilly white comforter and throw pillows, then back to her. "Damn shame what's about to happen to those throw pillows."

With a sexy smile, she drew him close. Pressing her lips against his, she gave him a quick kiss, then pushed him down so he sat on the edge of the bed.

In the soft glow of the lamplight, she slowly undressed, baring herself to his hungry eyes. First, she kicked off her boots and dragged off her socks.

He did the same, which wasn't easy since he couldn't tear his eyes away from her. He finally got his footwear off as her top went flying. She peeled the cargo pants down her legs, then kicked them off. With only her bronze-colored bra and black panties on, she turned her back to him.

Taking her cue, he stood and unhooked her bra as she shimmied out of it. When she hooked her thumbs in the waistband of her panties, he gasped. She worked them down slowly, with a tantalizing bend in her waist that put her luscious ass on full display.

Unable to resist, he pulled her against him. "See what you do to me, Robyn? See how ready you make me?"

"Mmm." She glanced back at him over her shoulder. "I think you're overdressed, Troy."

"I couldn't agree more." He breathed the words into the side of her neck, then stepped back to strip away his clothes. Once he was nude, he returned to his seat on the edge of the bed. "Come here, baby."

She joined him, and they lay down together, their naked limbs entangling. The warmth of her body and the fragrance of her skin drove him insane with want. She'd awakened a craving in him that dated back to their days in high school. Back then, his desire for her had been little more than hormone-fueled lust. But they were grown now, and he felt very much capable of pleasing her in all the ways she deserved.

Rolling her onto her back, he kissed her parted lips, the hollow of her throat, the curve of her shoulders. He kissed his way down her body, pausing to take the dark tips of her full breasts into his mouth. He savored them until she moaned, then moved to flick his tongue over the whorl of her navel. His hands moved over the plane of her belly, then lower, seeking the treasure she offered him.

"So perfect, baby. Better than I could have dreamed."

Sighing, she parted her thighs.

He kneeled before her and nuzzled between her open legs, kissing her there, and she trembled. When he began to pleasure her in earnest, he gripped her hips in his hands and swept his tongue through her womanly folds. He kept up his gentle assault, tasting every bit of the sweetness flowing from her until her screams of ecstasy echoed in the darkness.

"You're so sweet." He leaned over, grabbing his pants and getting his wallet from his back pocket. Sheathing himself with protection, he rejoined her on the bed.

She was still trembling, and when she opened her eyes, they were damp. "That was so…"

"Shhh." He placed a gentle finger against her lips. "We're just getting started." Moving atop her, he centered himself between her legs.

She mewled as his hardness bumped against her sex. "Troy…"

"Are you ready?"

"Yes…" She wove her arms around his waist, pulling him in.

Moments later, he slipped inside her, and both of them gasped. The tight grip of her body cradling his manhood almost sent him over the edge. He kept his strokes slow, even, measured, as he wanted to prolong the pleasure.

Her moans and cries rose on the air, sounding like a song of passion written just for him. Gathering her hips in his hands, he cupped them and lifted her, enabling himself to reach new depths. The pitch and tempo of her moans climbed, and his body tensed with the immense joy of it all. She wrapped her legs around him, held on tight as their bodies moved together in a passionate dance.

He increased his pace, matching the fervor his body demanded. She rose to meet him, stroke for stroke. He leaned down to kiss her eyes, her cheeks, her lips. She was giving him her most precious possession, and he would give no less than everything he had in return.

The pleasure rose and swelled, and when she came this time, she called out his name. The sweet sound of his name on her lips drove him over the edge, and as he growled his release, she pulled him close against her chest.

Lying on top of her, listening to the pounding of their hearts, he felt something inside of him coming to life. A part of him he'd locked away long ago had now been awakened, and it was all because of the beautiful, passionate woman lying in his arms.

I love her. It wasn't even a question anymore. Honestly, it never had been. When they were high-school sweethearts, he'd told her he loved her and had meant it. What he felt now was deeper, strengthened by time, forged in the fires of separation and grief. She'd been a more stable figure in his life than his own mother had.

So much for the casual, no-strings fling. He'd been a fool to think he could be with her and not get his heart involved.

Her soft snores ruffled the silence, breaking into his thoughts. Rolling off her so he wouldn't crush her, he maneuvered her around until he could pull back the covers. Then, he drew her into his arms and covered them both.

She sighed and snuggled closer to him, her eyes still closed.

And he knew, at that moment, that she'd taken his heart, for keeps.

Chapter 11

The first thing Robyn felt the next morning was a gentle caress against her cheek. Opening her eyes, she smiled when she saw Troy lying next to her. The morning sunlight streaming into the room illuminated his handsome face, and she was nearly overwhelmed with a giddy sensation.

"Happy Sunday." He propped himself up on his elbow, offering her a smile.

"Hey, you." She leaned up for his kiss, running her hand over the muscled plane of his bare chest. "What time is it?"

"It's almost noon."

Her eyes widened. "Oh, wow. I slept hard, didn't I?"

"You were practically in a coma." He laughed. "It's all good. That just means I did my job."

She gave him a peck on the lips. "Oh, yes. You did your job very, very well."

"I aim to please."

She sat up, stifling a yawn. "I'm hungry."

"Makes sense, seeing as how you slept through breakfast." He chuckled. "Want to go out and grab lunch?"

She nodded as she yawned again. "Sounds great. I don't feel like cooking anything."

"Well, I'll wait while you shower. I already did—I didn't think you'd mind."

She inhaled, smelling the distinct scent of her lemon verbena body wash. "Why would I mind, when you smell so yummy."

He got up then, and she could see that he'd put on a pair of boxers. "When you come out, you can give me a tour of your place before we go eat."

She laughed. "Okay, but it will be short. This is only a two-bedroom, two-bathroom house." That said, she climbed out of bed and stretched.

He made no effort to hide his admiration for her nudity. "You're beautiful, do you know that?"

Winking at him, she disappeared into the bathroom and closed the door behind her.

When she emerged from her room in black jeans, a yellow T-shirt and a tan cardigan, she found him sitting on the sofa with his phone in hand. He'd dressed, too, in jeans, a blue plaid shirt and the hiking boots he'd worn yesterday.

She gave him the "grand tour" of her home. She

took him to her spare bedroom, which she used as her home office-slash-library. The gray-white-and-yellow-striped wallpaper was barely visible behind the three bookcases she kept there.

"Wow, you've got a ton of books here." He walked over to the nearest shelf and picked up a book on botany. "And on so many different topics."

She smiled. "I love to read and indulge my curiosities, especially about the natural and social sciences. Archaeology, anthropology, biology…"

"Chemistry." He gave her a soft kiss on her lips as he replaced the tome. "That's funny, because I'm interested in anatomy myself." He made an obvious show of ogling her hips.

She gave him a playful tap on the arm. "Behave, Troy, or you won't get the rest of the tour."

After showing him her bathrooms, her citrus-fruit-themed kitchen decor and her collections of snow globes and crystal animal figurines, she brought him back to the living room. "Now you've seen it all. My little place, my weird obsession with the color yellow and my tendency to collect useless knickknacks."

"I like your decor. It's very…you." He draped his arm around her shoulder, kissed her on the cheek. "Now that we're both dressed, let's go eat."

She gave him a long look, studying his face. *What's happening between us?*

Then, she asked, "Listen…after lunch, would you be up for one more adventure with me?"

"I'm not hiking near any more mountain lions, Robyn."

She snorted. "No, nothing like that. Have you ever been down to the Ghost Ranch in Abiquiú?"

He shook his head. "Can't say I have."

"I really want to go there. They have an awesome library in an adobe building and two museums."

"Wow. So, you're into that sort of thing?" He scratched his chin. "I thought you'd be more into the movie-filming stuff."

"I'm into both, honestly. I'm a woman of many interests."

"Okay. As long as I'm not in danger of being mauled, I'm down."

She grabbed her keys from the bowl by the door. "Great. I'll drive."

They left her house, stopping off at a fast-food place for burgers and fries before taking US 84 south to Abiquiú.

Later, she held his hand as they explored the grounds of the Ghost Ranch. According to the tour guide in the welcome center, the whole place encompassed about twenty-one thousand acres. "It's so beautiful here."

"It is. I've never seen anything like it." He pointed off in the distance. "I mean, we've always seen mountains, growing up around here. But look at those rock formations. Really remarkable."

She followed his gesture, inhaling sharply as she took in the sight. The huge red-rock shelves, with their jagged faces bearing variegated lines of grays, browns and tans, reached heavenward to embrace the endless blue sky. The sheer beauty of the scenery stole her breath.

When she finally tore her eyes away from the natural beauty of the surroundings, she started walking again, with Troy following her. She stopped near the entrance of the Florence Hawley Ellis Museum of Anthropology. Tugging his hand, she said, "We've got to go in here."

He obliged her, following her inside.

The interior of the museum featured exhibits that gave insight into Native American culture dating back ten thousand years. Hand in hand with Troy, she marveled over the displays of tools, handmade pottery and more. After leaving there, she tugged him into the neighboring Ruth Hall Museum of Paleontology. The exhibits on the many fossils found in the quarries of the Ghost Ranch were fascinating and enlightening.

"Look at this, Troy." She pointed to a display. "'The Coelophysis graveyard discovered here in 1947 yielded numerous intact, well-preserved specimens, one of which is now considered the type specimen for the entire genus.'"

He tilted his head to the side. "In other words, the one they measure all the other fossils against was found here."

"Right. I'm impressed. I thought you were tuning me out."

"Why would I do that?"

She shrugged. "Not everyone is interested in archaeology, anthropology, all the 'ology's' I enjoy. Hell, Kima's my best friend, and even she refused to come here with me. Said she didn't want to spend all day looking at some old dusty bones."

He let his fingertips graze over her jawline. "How

can I not pay attention to something you're so passionate about? Watching your eyes light up is enough to get me into it."

His words were both surprising and pleasing, so she rewarded his sweetness with a soft kiss on the lips.

As they exited the second museum, he asked, "What else do you want to see, while we're here? I know there's something else."

"What makes you say that?"

"Watching you. I can tell you have an almost boundless curiosity. You're not just wrapped up in your own life and problems, unlike some of the other women I've known."

She turned his words over in her mind. *He thinks so highly of me. And here I am, keeping things from him.* She opened her mouth, preparing to tell him about the job in San Diego. But she couldn't do it, let him know she was leaving. That would mean another person would know her plans before she'd told her parents. "That's really sweet of you to say, Troy…"

"I love that about you. There are so many things about you to love."

Her breath caught in her throat. *Where is he going with this?*

Are we about to exceed the boundaries of this casual, no-strings arrangement?

He turned her way, fixing her with a look that seemed to penetrate her very soul. "I—"

She quickly spoke over him. "You know what? I really want to see the cabin they used in *City Slickers*.

We'll have to drive there, but I really don't want to miss it. Would you be up to that?" She hated interrupting him, but she couldn't let him finish that sentence. She sensed he'd been about to say something profound, something that would change things between them in a way that couldn't be reversed.

Things are happening too fast between us. I can't let myself get swept up in this, not with that job waiting for me in California. Even as she told herself that, she knew leaving Grandeza would be more difficult that she'd anticipated. *I'm not so sure I want to leave anymore.*

His eyes narrowed for a moment, as if he could read her thoughts.

She squirmed.

Then his expression softened. "I'm game. But after that, we're going back to Grandeza. We do have to work tomorrow, and Mondays are rough enough without being completely exhausted."

"Deal." She sighed, relieved that he didn't try to change the direction of the conversation back to what he'd originally wanted to say.

She had to steel herself for the future, for the break that would inevitably come when—if—she left. And that was part of the problem with dwelling on her feelings for him. It made her want to stay, when just a few days ago, no one could have convinced her that was a good idea. Why'd he have to show up in her life now, when she was about to step off into a different world, one away from her parents, her small town, the ranch, into a new freedom she desperately craved?

I know it's going to come back up again. But I don't want to deal with it now.

After they returned to Grandeza late that afternoon, Troy drove his SUV home. Stashing his canoe and gear in the shed behind the house, he went inside and started a load of laundry.

As evening came on, he fixed himself a steak and a baked potato. After he ate, he sat down in the living room and flipped on the thirty-two-inch wall-mounted flat-screen television. The local sportscaster was delivering the results of the weekend's high school and college football games, as well as the stats on the professional matchups, some of which were still underway.

Folding the pile of clean laundry, he thought about the day…and the night he'd spent with Robyn. He'd wanted to stay longer this evening, but practicality demanded he come home. He needed clean clothes for work this week, and no matter how much he'd wanted to hole up with her and explore every inch of her body with his tongue, adulthood equaled responsibility.

He mused on that moment outside the museum, when he'd been ready to pour his heart out to her, and she'd abruptly changed the subject. *Did she sense what I was about to say?* He didn't know. Still, he hoped she wasn't afraid of the growing connection between them because as far as he could tell, there was no stopping it.

The many bumps and bruises he'd faced in life had taught him to accept and enjoy the blessings that came his way. He wasn't about to say no to this one. He wanted to embrace it, and her, as forcefully and happily as he could.

In a way, he understood her nervousness. They'd set out to keep things casual between them, after all. But now that they'd made love, he doubted there was any going back. Things were likely to escalate from here.

A knock at the door sounded, and he set aside his clothes to see who it was. He checked the peephole, expecting to see Rick there, coming over to share his latest conspiracy theories.

To his surprise, he saw Robyn standing on his front porch.

Opening the door, he said, "Hey, Robyn. What are you doing here?" She'd changed clothes and was now wearing a maxi dress, similar to the one she'd worn to Amos's party. This one was yellow and had three small heart-shaped cutouts just below the high neckline. Her glossy hair was down now, framing her face in just the way he liked.

She sucked her bottom lip into her mouth for a moment. "I…missed you."

He leaned against the door frame. A smile tilted his lips, accompanying the sense of satisfaction and peace that filled him at the knowledge that she'd sought him out. "I missed you. But I didn't expect to see you again until tomorrow at work."

"I didn't plan on coming over here. Something just… came over me." Her expression turned serious for a moment. "Earlier, at the museum… I think there was something you wanted to say."

"There was."

"I've been thinking a lot about us. Not just today, but ever since we decided to spend time together."

He listened, keeping quiet until she could get out what she wanted to say.

"I know we were supposed to keep things casual, but... I don't think I can anymore." She reached up, caressing his jaw. "I...feel like I'm falling for you."

His heart clenched in his chest, and he placed his hand atop hers. "I'm here to catch you. You know that, don't you, Robyn?"

"Then you'd better brace yourself. Because I'm pretty sure I've fallen in love with you, and I don't think I can get up."

Rubbing his face against the softness of her palm, he smiled. "Great. Because I love you, too, and I don't know how to turn it off. Frankly, I don't think I want to."

She smiled up at him. "Are you going to invite me in?"

He rested his hand on his chin, making a show of considering the notion. "Well, you do look good enough to eat."

"I'm assuming you've had dinner." There was a sly look in her brown eyes.

"I have." He placed a possessive hand on her hip. "But I could go for dessert."

She giggled as he pulled her inside the house and shut the door behind them.

Chapter 12

Rubbing her bleary eyes, Robyn sat up in bed and blinked a few times to allow them to adjust to the blinding sunlight streaming through the vertical blinds.

She checked the time on her phone and groaned. *I've got to call into the ranch. I should have been there an hour ago. That's what I get for having Friday-night sex on a Sunday.*

Troy emerged from the attached bathroom. Aside from a smile, he wore only a towel draped around his hips.

The same strong hips she'd wrapped her legs around only hours ago.

She sucked her bottom lip into her mouth, pinning it between her teeth.

"Good morning." His deep, velvety voice seemed to fill the space.

"Very good," she commented, not bothering to hide her admiration of his body.

He chuckled. "Oh, so you like what you see?"

"You already know I do." She dragged away her gaze, turning toward the window instead. "As a matter of fact, I think you better get dressed, or neither of us is gonna make it to work today."

"That was my plan. After that, I'll make a quick breakfast."

Her brow hitched as she looked his way. "You cook?"

He shrugged. "I dabble. A man's gotta eat. Bacon and eggs?"

"Sounds great."

"Shower's free if you want to use it." He flipped on the light in his closet and walked in.

She nodded, glad she brought an extra set of clothes. "My clothes are in my overnight bag, in the car."

He poked his head out of the closet. "I'll grab it for you. Just pop the trunk."

She grabbed her keys from the nightstand. Moments later, he emerged from the closet in a CCE blue shirt and a pair of medium-wash blue jeans that molded to his powerful thighs like a second skin. Still sitting in bed, she watched him stride out, then return with her bag. "Here you go."

"Thank you." She opened the bag, taking out the fresh underclothes, black slacks and long-sleeved red top.

"I'm headed to the kitchen." He disappeared into the hall.

When she joined him in the kitchen later, showered and dressed, he steered her to the small table. Then he set a plate in front of her, heaped with fluffy eggs and four slices of bacon. She smiled as he added a glass of orange juice. "Wow. Trying to spoil me?"

"Maybe." He winked. "Is there going to be a problem with me going in late today?"

She shook her head. "Should be okay. As far as I know, nothing big is on tap. Besides, it's the herd that determines schedule. We just go with the flow."

"Mary Ellen told me as much when she hired me, but I just wanted to be sure." He forked up a helping of eggs. "I can stay late if need be."

"That's reasonable. There are always at least three ranch hands on duty, even overnight. You might meet some of the night staff if you decide to stay long enough."

He finished off his eggs. "So, what do you like to do, when you're not working?"

"Well, you already know I love hiking. There are so many great state parks around here—just that one hobby could fill all my free time."

"Does it?"

"No. I've done some exploring in the Carlsbad Caverns, and I go down to Ruidoso now and again to tour the wineries. There are also some great spas in Santa Fe." She thought of Kima. "Whenever I go out of town to a spa, Kima complains—she works at the only Black-owned one in town."

"Wow. Your hobbies make me feel pretty lazy."

Her eyebrows shot up. "Oh, really? What do you like?"

"Other than table tennis, I play checkers and poker. Occasionally I go to the gym for racquetball." He blew out a breath. "Don't you have any less strenuous things you like to do?"

"I love watching old comedies. Eddie Murphy is a favorite of mine."

He snapped his fingers. "Comedy films. There's a hobby I can share with you without pulling something. What's your favorite Eddie Murphy movie?"

She didn't hesitate. "*Trading Places*, hands down."

He pursed his lips. "Are you serious? You'd choose *Trading Places* over *Coming to America*?"

"Yes. What's wrong with that?"

"*Trading Places* was funny but *Coming to America* is a cultural phenomenon."

She gave him her "unimpressed" face.

He countered, "How many people do you hear quoting lines from *Trading Places* in everyday speech?"

She thought about that. "Point taken, but I stand by my choice." She folded a crisp slice of bacon into her mouth.

"Think about this. You remember that big wedding at the end? How Akeem ends up marrying Lisa in the end, even though it looked like he had screwed things up with her?"

She nodded, chewing a mouthful of food.

"That's one of the first examples I ever saw of the triumph of true love. I know it's fictional and all, but that was sorely lacking in my life. My parents' marriage being as imperfect as it was, I needed images like that, you know? Just so I could see that marriage could be something beautiful and special."

A soft smile came over her face. "I'm not gonna lie. I loved Lisa's sparkly pink wedding dress. For a long time, I though I wanted one just like it." She picked up her last slice of bacon.

"Do you think you'll ever get married, Robyn?"

She nearly choked on the bacon. Grabbing up her orange juice, she took a few sips. Finally recovered from the random question, she said, "Why would you ask me that?"

He tilted his head to the right. "Why not? I'm just interested in your take."

She looked down at her empty plate, not wanting to meet his scrutinizing gaze. "I…can't say I've thought much about it." Small-town life in Grandeza meant a tragically small dating pool, and an even slimmer chance at privacy. So, instead of dating, she'd thrown most of her time and energy into her work on the ranch, putting aside any further thoughts of cotton-candy wedding gowns and ten-tiered cakes.

"Really?" The raised pitch of his voice indicated his surprise. "I wouldn't have expected you to say that."

"It's not every woman's goal to be married, Troy."

He frowned, his lips thinning. "I didn't say it was. I

merely asked you a question. But you don't have to answer it if it makes you uncomfortable."

She placed a hand to her temple. "That question came out of left field, so forgive me if I didn't have a prepared answer."

"Never mind, Robyn." He stood, gathered his empty plate and hers, and stalked to the sink to put the dishes away.

She cursed inwardly. *Very smooth, Robyn. You handled that like a champ.* She imagined most women would be pleased if a man they cared about asked them how they felt about marriage. Yet, she wasn't most women. There were too many variables to consider, too many issues to resolve before her new job. She had to keep her focus on those things, and she couldn't let herself be distracted by these emotions, no matter how enticing they were.

She'd already done that once when she'd let cravings for his masterful loving guide her to his doorstep. While she had no regrets about making love with Troy, she also didn't want him getting too attached.

Tell him about the job, her inner voice admonished her. But she couldn't. If she told him now, it would sap the enjoyment out of the short time she had to spend with him before she left. Besides, she'd not yet told her parents. She shouldn't tell a single other person until she informed them. Why did the thought of that make her sick to her stomach?

Attachment is a burden. It means giving up my dreams in favor of his. Her mother had spoken to her years ago about that dynamic of marriage. How could she give in to that now, when she was finally on the verge of starting her dream job?

He returned to the table. "I'm going to head out to work. Do you want to wait a few minutes, so we don't show up at the same moment?"

She swallowed because she could hear the hurt in his voice, though his face remained neutral. "That would probably be best."

"Fine. Lock the door behind you." He left her his house key and strode out, and a short while later, she heard him fire his engine and drive away.

Sitting alone at the table, she groaned. So much for enjoying the afterglow. Last night, he'd taken her body to heights of passion she'd never experienced. Now, mere hours later, they were at odds.

What is this thing between us? And where is it going?

Not wanting to spend too much time dwelling on that loaded question, she got up and got her things to head for work.

Troy left the ranch after lunch on that afternoon, headed for Grandeza Acres. Mama Jeannie had back-to-back appointments with her doctors, and he'd agreed to go with her. The retirement home provided transportation for residents to get to their appointments, but she'd asked Troy to take her, so he could get the report from her doctors, firsthand.

As he drove her toward the hospital, Mama Jeannie asked, "What's going on with you and Robyn?"

He hazarded a quick glance her way before returning his eyes to the road. It was just long enough to see the expectant expression she wore. "Honestly? Your guess is as good as mine."

"Troy, what in the world do you mean by that?"

He pulled up to a red light. "Mama J, I really care about Robyn. I always have. I've tried to be open with her, I've explained what happened between us in the past, and she seemed satisfied with that."

"That's good."

The light changed, and he drove across the intersection. "That's the problem. I'm opening up to her, but I feel like there's something else she's not saying."

"Like what?"

He shook his head. "I don't know." He paused, remembering the bombshell she'd dropped on him that evening on the lake. "Did you know she had a younger sister?"

She released a deep sigh. "Yes. I remember when she passed. Such a tragedy."

He felt his brow fold in on itself. "Why didn't anyone tell me about all this?"

"Why should we? What point would there have been in telling you?" She folded her arms over her chest. "That poor sweet girl died long before your parents moved to Grandeza. Thelma and Cooper suffered so much. Why would we dredge up their pain?"

He turned onto Martin Road. *I hadn't thought of that.* "I guess that makes sense. I just feel like it was this big secret that everybody in town knew, but I was left out of it."

"That's not what's bothering you, Troy. You said so yourself. You want Robyn to open up to you about her life, and she has. I'm sure it wasn't easy for her to tell you about her sister."

"It wasn't." He recalled the way she'd collapsed into his arms by the lake, the way her entire body had shaken with the force of her sobs.

"She and her family have carried that pain for a long time now."

He pulled into the parking lot of the hospital and took the first available space near the entrance.

She hung her handicap placard on the mirror, then looked him in the eye. "You need to give her time, Troy. You haven't even been in town that long. Don't press her."

He exhaled through parted lips. "I just want to be there for her."

"Show her that."

"How?"

"Certainly not by making demands on her, but by giving her space and the grace she needs to open up on her own."

Now that he wasn't driving anymore, he watched her. He noted how tired and pale she looked, and how heavy her breaths were. "Mama J, did I upset you?"

She shook her head. "No. I'm just tired, Troy."

That seemed like an understatement. He'd always known her as a formidable woman. Looking at her now, she appeared small, frail. His heart clenched in his chest. "Let's get you inside."

He went around to the passenger side and helped her out of the car. Keeping his arm around her, he braced her with support as they entered the hospital, headed for the cardiology clinic.

During her appointment with the cardiologist, Troy listened as the doctor described his findings. "The echocardiogram gave us some good information. We're seeing some light swelling, indicating an increase in pressure on the right side of her heart. I think you'll find more answers in pulmonology."

After a series of tests, the pulmonologist, Dr. Mertz, did have answers. She gathered Mama Jeannie and Troy around the large computer monitor in her examination suite to show them the images displayed there. "Mrs. Monroe, we're seeing a lot of scarring and thickening here, around your air sacs." She used a stylus to highlight the area. "I suspect you have a rather advanced case of interstitial lung disease."

He frowned. "How serious is that?"

"It's chronic and could become very dangerous under certain circumstances."

Mama Jeannie's expression remained flat. After a short inhale, she asked, "How did I get it?"

"There are many environmental factors and medicines that can cause it. Based on your medical history, I believe it's a two-fold cause. First, your first house had asbestos insulation, and second, you've been taking a certain class of medication to treat arthritis in your hands and wrists. Over time those medications can lead to or aggravate lung problems."

"Isn't that something?" Mama Jeannie shook her head. "Take medicine for one problem and it gives you another."

"What kind of treatment will she need?" Troy sat forward in his chair, awaiting the answer.

"None, yet. I'll have to perform a lung biopsy to be sure of the diagnosis and to try to pinpoint the cause. We'll make an appointment for you before you leave." Dr. Mertz swiveled on her stool, closing the image window and making notes in the chart displayed on the screen.

"Surgery?" His grandmother was already in a weakened state, and now they wanted her to go under the knife? "Isn't there another less invasive way to diagnose this?"

Dr. Mertz appeared sympathetic but shook her head. "I wish there was. In a less advanced case, I would start with an outpatient bronchoscopy. But in your grandmother's case, considering how much scarring I can see in the imaging, I think we need to move straight to surgical biopsy. It's the only way to be sure I can get a large enough tissue sample for accurate diagnosis."

Mama Jeannie, her face showing a mixture of worry and resignation, nodded.

He'd never known his grandmother to be afraid of anything. From the stories his father told, she'd faced down fire hoses and racist neighbors in the Jim Crow south, held her head high when gossips called her a home wrecker for marrying a divorced man and held down a household in Grandeza, where she knew no one and had little support.

But when he looked into her eyes now, he saw the fear. Just a faint glimmer, but enough to set off alarm bells inside him.

Dr. Mertz laid a hand on her shoulder. "Jeannie, we're going to take very good care of you. So, don't you worry."

"I expect nothing less." She gave the doctor a thin-lipped, watery smile.

Troy's heart clenched as he watched his grandmother talking with the doctor. If only he could fix this for her, the way Rick had fixed the shoddy plumbing beneath the kitchen sink. *I'd give anything to be able to make this go away.* She was the last member of this branch of the family. Everyone else was gone. His grandfather Horace had passed away over a decade ago. *Three years since Dad died. And my mother is so distant, it's as if she doesn't exist.*

Between here and North Carolina, Mama Jeannie and I are the last ones left.

He couldn't even entertain the thought of losing her; it was too painful to fathom.

Once the paperwork was complete and the date set for the biopsy, Troy took his grandmother's hand and escorted her outside.

"It's going to be all right, Mama J."

She patted his hand gently. "I know, sugar. I know."

Chapter 13

Inside the welcoming interior of The Caffeine Connection Tuesday afternoon, Robyn sipped from a ceramic mug of blond roast coffee. She was waiting for Dr. Victor Rockford to show up for his second interview. If everything worked out well today, she would finally be able to have the conversation with her parents about her new job.

She knew it was risky setting up the job hunt for her replacement. There was always the chance that word would get back to her parents, that the ranch had been advertising for a new veterinarian. She had to take care of this quickly so at least they'd know she'd done her duty to them and the ranch before leaving. She sighed. *I know they're not going to be happy about this.* Still, she hoped that by already having a qualified, capable replacement lined up, she could soften the blow.

This is something I need to do. I can't spend my whole life on the ranch, never seeing anything outside of Grandeza.

She sat down her mug as her thoughts strayed to Troy. *Last time I was here, I was with him.* She thought about the connection between them, and how it had been growing ever since they'd been trapped in the storage room during Amos's retirement party. If she was honest with herself, the magic between them had really started the moment he'd walked into her office that first day. Or maybe—maybe it was just a continuation of what they'd shared years ago in high school.

How would Troy react to news that she was leaving New Mexico? She had no way of knowing, though she assumed he wouldn't be happy about it. But they'd agreed to a casual, laid-back arrangement. No ties and no expectations. It could barely be called a relationship. Surely, he wouldn't be selfish enough to try to stop her from going after her dream job.

Would he?

Dr. Rockford walked into the coffee shop then, and she pushed aside the thoughts. Her main focus now had to be on making sure he was the right fit for the vet position at Chance.

He was a tall man with a thin, athletic build, and was draped in a dark blue suit. He had tan skin, dark hair and green eyes. Overall, he was a good-looking man, though she was more interested in his credentials and skills as a medical practitioner, not his physical appearance.

She stood, smiling as he came near the table. "Dr. Rockford. It's so good to see you."

While they shook hands, he said, "Please, call me Victor."

"Certainly." She gestured toward the counter. "Would you like to grab a drink?"

"I'm good. I already had my caffeine this morning. Don't want to overdo it."

"Great. So, let's get started." She opened the folder on the table, containing his file. "When we video-chatted before, we spoke a lot about your experience and credentials, which are impressive. Now, I'd like to get a better perspective on whether you'll be a good fit for the job, personality-wise."

"That makes sense."

"Tell me a little more about yourself. What made you decide to seek other employment?"

He nodded, a sparkle coming to his eyes. "I've been married to my wife, Hannah, for twelve years. She stays home with our three-year-old daughter, Isabella, and we've got a Saint Bernard named Captain Kirk."

"Ah, Trekkies, I see." She chuckled. *It's so endearing how much he loves his family.*

"Hannah and I are looking for a change of scenery." Victor leaned back in his chair. "Santa Fe is great, but we're looking for something—"

Her phone, which she'd placed facedown on the table, buzzed loudly.

She gave him an apologetic smile. "Excuse me." Turning the phone faceup, she brought it under the edge of the table and read the display. It was Troy. If she'd been at her desk, she'd take the call. *Hell, if I was at my desk, he'd probably just show up at my office.* But she didn't want to be rude to Victor, so she swiped the screen, sending the call to voice mail. Leaving the phone facedown on her thigh, she looked to Victor. "I'm sorry about that. Please, go on."

"Sure. I was just saying my wife and I want something a little more spacious and rustic. More acreage, less traffic."

"Well, you'll certainly find that here in Grandeza."

"Yes. This town is really very charming. I've already brought Hannah and Izzy here for a walking tour, and they loved it."

"I'm really glad to hear that." She knew that for a man like Victor, having his family hate the place would have probably been a deal-breaker in terms of him taking the job. "Do you have some extra time today?"

"I took the day off from work, so, yes."

"Great. I'd like to invite…" Her phone buzzed again, the vibration rattling through her thigh and straight through to the wooden seat of her chair. Sighing, she said, "One second." Another look at the screen showed Troy calling her. Again. For Pete's sake, that was the second time in five minutes. She swiped the screen again, this time adding a short text.

Can't talk now. Call u later.

After she sent the text, she put the phone on silent mode. "Again, excuse me."

If he was bothered by the interruptions, he did a great job concealing it. With an easy smile, he said, "No problem."

"I'd like to invite you out to the ranch, so you can get a brief tour, meet a few people and see how we operate." Tossing the phone into her purse, she asked, "How does that sound?"

"I'd love that."

"You can follow me there. It's about ten miles outside the town limits."

He stood. "Okay. Let me grab a bottle of water for the road, and then we can go."

After Victor got his drink, they went to their respective cars. On the road, she maintained an even speed, so he could follow her without getting left behind. When they arrived at the ranch, she led him up the long dirt road to the main building and parked in the gravel lot.

They met at the door.

"This is our operations center." She gestured toward the glass doors. "All the offices are inside here, including the one that will be yours if you decide to work with us."

Inside, she briefly introduced Victor to the receptionist, then took him down to Mary Ellen's office.

Mary Ellen, standing by her office window with an inventory sheet in hand, greeted them when they entered. "Hey there. You must be Doc Rockford."

He gave her a hearty handshake. "Please, call me Victor. It's nice to meet you."

"Likewise." Mary Ellen shifted her gaze to Robyn, looking at her pointedly.

Robyn shook her head and mouthed the words *not now*.

A loud ringing sound echoed through the office, and Victor pulled out his phone. "I've got to take this, it's my wife." He headed for the door. "Please excuse me, I'll be right back."

As soon as Victor left the room, Mary Ellen laid into her. "You brought him here and you still haven't told Cooper and Thelma what you're planning?"

"How did you know?" Robyn asked her. She'd only told Kima so far.

"I'm ranch manager. I saw the vet advertisement. And I also pulled some papers from the printer you'd downloaded about a San Diego job. I wasn't snooping, but I put two and two together. I knew what it meant."

Robyn nodded and sighed. "I don't see any reason to tell them until he's hired. If he doesn't work out, there's no reason my parents need to know about him."

Shaking her head, Mary Ellen placed the inventory sheet on her desk. "Robyn, it's bad enough for you to keep this from them. But asking me to participate in this? It's not right." She rubbed a hand over her face. "Your parents hired me on when I was desperate for work, and they've always done right by me. I can't do this."

Her shoulders slumped. "M.E., I'm sorry I put you in

this position. I promise I'll have that conversation with them very, very soon."

"You'd better." Mary Ellen leaned against the edge of her desk. "Because come Monday, I'm telling them myself."

Victor returned then. "Sorry about that. Is there anything else you'll need from me?"

Robyn shook her head. "I'm pretty sure we covered everything already."

Mary Ellen added, "You're free to wander around and have a look at the ranch, if you like."

He smiled. "Sounds good. I think I'll do that." Moments later, he disappeared again.

Mary Ellen looked Robyn's way again. "I meant what I said, Robyn. You've got until Monday." She gave her a pointed look as she slipped from the room.

Robyn nodded grimly, then rested her forehead on the top of her desk.

Around four, Troy got into his golf cart and left the pasture in the capable hands of his team as he headed for the operations center.

His attempts to contact Robyn had been rebuffed all day long, and now that the workday was winding down, he hoped to catch her in her office, before she left for the day.

I know she's busy. We both are. But I miss her. He'd spent much of the day fantasizing about her. In between watching over the herd on his section of the ranch, checking the water levels in the tanks and troughs and refilling the hay stations, his mind had been occupied by memories of her, naked in his arms.

He was both enamored and conflicted, because of what he'd seen earlier.

He'd driven into town during his coffee break, and pulled into a spot at The Caffeine Connection, hoping to grab a cup of coffee to fight off the afternoon blahs. He'd cut the engine, slipped his keys from the ignition and took off his seat belt.

Just as he reached to grab the door handle, he glanced into the front window of the coffee shop.

There, he'd seen Robyn.

And she hadn't been alone, nor with her friend Kima.

She'd sat at a small table for two, across from a man he'd never seen before. The man, dressed in a business suit, said something to her, and her face lit up as she burst out laughing.

Troy's jaw tightened as he thought back on that moment. *Who the hell is that guy?*

When I called her earlier and asked her to meet me, she said she couldn't talk. At the time, he'd assumed she was referring to something work-related. Sitting there, watching her with the other man, he felt like a fool. He didn't even want to think about what she might actually have been busy doing.

Making love to her had been a magnificent experience. She'd captured his soul in a way no other woman had, and he doubted another woman could. Yet, ever since she'd shared his bed, she'd become standoffish, distant. *What's going on with her?*

He left the cart among the others on the side of the building, climbed out and headed for the door. Hopefully, she'd be there, and he could get some clarity on the situation. He knocked on her door, and smiled when she opened it.

"Hey, Troy. Come on in." She stepped back, allowing him space to enter.

Once he was inside, she returned to her seat behind the desk.

He closed the door and sat down across from her. "How has the day been for you?"

"Busy. You?"

He felt his brow crease. Remembering his grandmother's advice, he decided not to press her. If there were things she wanted him to know, she'd tell him on her own. "Same. The cows on my section seem awfully thirsty for this time of the year, so I spent a lot of time at the tanks today."

"We only get an average of three days of rain in October, and we still haven't gotten any rain even though the month's half over. Maybe that's why." She paused. "You haven't had any issues with the stock, have you?"

He shook his head. "Not really. One of the new calves is a bit of a wanderer, but we've been able to keep him pretty well wrangled."

"Good. I purposefully had the hands move some of the stock around a bit, so you wouldn't have to deal with the pregnant animals."

He frowned. "Why would you do that?"

She looked surprised. "Don't you remember? You

told me you're not comfortable with calving. I was simply trying to keep things less stressful for you, at least until you get settled into the job."

So, she literally rearranged the herd, to protect me from my own irrational fear? The prideful part of him puffed up. "You didn't have to do that."

"I know. I just felt it would be helpful."

He steepled his fingers. "Have you ever made accommodations like that for anyone else on staff?"

"Honestly, no. I've never had to."

He heard what she said, but he also heard what she didn't say. No one else who'd worked on the spread had ever complained about this aspect of ranch work. *She must think I'm pretty weak.*

"You took Mama Jeannie to the doctor yesterday, didn't you? How's she doing?"

He noted the abrupt change in topic and tried to adjust his expression, in case his face had revealed his inner turmoil. He answered her question by giving her a brief recap of the doctor's findings. "Basically, she's going to need surgery. Her biopsy is scheduled for Thursday morning."

She gave a solemn nod. "Keep me posted on how she's doing, or if she needs anything."

"I will." He thought about how long they'd been talking, and how matter-of-fact her manner was. "I came by earlier, and you weren't here. When I called you, you didn't pick up."

"As I said, it was a crazy day. I was off-site, but still handling ranch business."

He drew a deep breath, disappointed when she hadn't taken his opening to tell him the truth, how she'd been having coffee with another man. Had that been ranch business, or just something she didn't want him to know about? *Is she keeping secrets from me?*

He pushed aside those thoughts, not wanting to become that guy. They were embarking on a new journey together, one that had to begin from a pure place, a place of trust. Up until now, she'd given him no reason not to believe in her. Maybe she just needed another shot at it. "What do you think about going to dinner tonight?"

She grimaced. "I'd like to, but I can't. We've got two cows we expect to go into labor over the next few hours, so I'm not sure how long I'll have to stay tonight."

He nodded. "Okay. Why don't I go into town, pick something up and bring it back? The café's not open for dinner, and you've gotta eat."

"That's really thoughtful. Thanks, Troy." She offered a soft smile. "How about Mexican? Tacos, maybe?"

"I'm down."

"Tell you what. I'll call into The Red Sombrero downtown and make an order. By the time you get there, it should probably be ready." She scooted her chair back, grabbed her purse and fished around until she pulled out her wallet. "And since you're so graciously going to pick it up, I'll cover the food."

"You don't have to…"

She waved him off, her phone in hand. "No worries. It's quicker to pay over the phone. That way they'll start assembling the order right away."

Standing, he gave her a curt nod. "All right, then. I should be back in less than an hour."

She waved, already on her phone with the restaurant.

He turned, shaking his head as he left.

He felt…dismissed.

This whole situation had him perplexed, and he didn't care for that out-of-sorts feeling at all.

They'd been so close, yet today he felt worlds apart from her. She wasn't telling him something—something important. He could feel it. Maybe it had been a mistake to let his emotions deepen for her so quickly. Maybe this was just a fling, after all, and he was kidding himself that it could be something bigger.

Chapter 14

After she placed her order with The Red Sombrero, Robyn began looking over reports from the hands. So far, eight of the expectant animals had calved, with one being a stillbirth.

That leaves a little over twenty more to go in all, and two more before this month is out. Just thinking about it exhausted her. The animals had been bred in a way that would hopefully give the staff some recovery time between births. Nature, however, often had other plans.

Her rumbling stomach reminded her how much she anticipated Troy's return with the tacos.

A knock sounded. "Come in."

Mary Ellen opened the door. "We've got a live one over in the northeast pasture."

Robyn got to her feet. "Is she in active labor?"

"She's got all the classic signs."

Mary Ellen's walkie-talkie beeped, and a voice crackled over the frequency.

"We've got a backward entry here."

Mary Ellen announced, "Based on that transmission, it looks like the calf is breech."

Robyn sighed. "So much for tacos. I may need some assistance. Is Victor still here?"

She nodded. "He's in the main barn, talking to a few of the hands. That's where he headed after he spoke to his wife."

Already on her feet, Robyn said, "Get him down to the northeast pasture. And make sure we have the pulley, and the calving ropes set up."

"I'm on it."

Outside the building, the two of them climbed into Big Red. Mary Ellen motored off, stopping for a few minutes by the main barn. "Can you help us out, Doc?" she called out. "We've got a breech calf."

"Sure thing." Victor stopped conversing with the others, and joined Mary Ellen and Robyn in the truck's cab, as the hands brought the proper equipment out of the barn and loaded it onto the truck bed. After they climbed in the back to assist, Mary Ellen got them underway again.

"What kind of breech are we dealing with?" Victor asked, looking to Robyn.

Wedged between M.E. and the new would-be ranch doctor, Robyn shook her head. "I don't know."

Mary Ellen's two-way crackled again. "M.E., it's getting serious out here. What's your location?"

She radioed back. "We're right on top of you."

They came to a screeching halt next to the pasture's supply shed. The distressed cow stood near the main water tank, her mournful moos indicating her discomfort. As everyone hopped out, Robyn ran toward the cow and the two hands attending to her.

"Take over, Doc." One of the hands, Sam, threw his gloved hands up in the air. "There's one hoof in the canal, along with her tail."

Victor kneeled near the cow. "Thank God it's only hip flexion. The full breech position is far worse."

The hands who'd come along with the equipment started setting up the pulley and calving ropes, while Mary Ellen helped the two vets don the long, transparent gloves typically worn for this type of work. She then applied the proper lubricant.

Tying on her face shield, Robyn flipped a five-gallon bucket and sat near the cow's tail. "We're going to have to turn it. Victor, give me a hand here."

"I'm with you."

Reaching into the cow's birth canal, she eased the calf's leg back inside for better positioning. Then, working in tandem with Victor, she got a grip on the calf's hock, rotating and lifting until better positioning was achieved.

"We're doing good, but we need to get it out before its airways are cut off." Victor stood braced and ready, with the ends of the calving ropes in his hands.

She nodded but maintained her focus. Suffocation was a common problem during breech births, but she was determined to deliver this baby intact and alive. She maneuvered her hands a bit more, finally catching hold of a hoof. "I'm ready for the rope." As soon as Victor handed it to her, she looped the end of the rope around the hoof.

"All right, get ready. Victor, you lead. All hands on deck to pull the rope while I raise his hock. Let's see if we can get her out without the pulley." She saw the machinery as a last resort because there was potential for injury to both mother and baby when it was used. "Ready?"

She saw the hands lined up along the rope, with Mary Ellen nearest to the pulley. Everyone on the line nodded.

"Pull!" Robyn lifted the calf's hock, bringing it forward in the birth canal while the team worked the rope. Slowing, the tension increased, and she had just enough time to kick aside the bucket and scramble out of the way before the calf's body slipped out and onto the grass. She landed on her bottom a few inches away.

The calf, though safely out, was lying motionless on the ground.

Robyn's heart thudded in her chest.

Victor dropped the rope and squatted to examine the calf. Placing his hand behind the animal's front left leg, he checked for a pulse.

The pasture was silent. Robyn held her breath.

Victor nodded. "She's still with us."

She exhaled.

"She's a bit bluer than I'd like, and not breathing well." Victor's voice held concern.

Robyn moved closer, watching, in case he needed help. Breech births put a lot of stress on both mother and baby, and calves born breech often had trouble breathing. "Mary Ellen, a piece of hay."

With the straw in hand, Robyn placed it gently into one of the calf's nostrils, then moved it from side to side.

Moments later, the calf's head popped up, and it began coughing.

The cow ambled over then and began licking her baby clean.

Robyn smiled. "She's going to be fine." Not only was the calf breathing well, but her mother was also showing signs of good bonding.

A cheer went up among the group.

Turning to Victor, she said, "Looks like you'll do fine here. I'd shake your hand but…"

He laughed. "Don't worry, I think it can wait."

She stood, and let the hands unroll her messy gloves. Once free of them, she headed into the shed to scrub her hands.

Emerging a few moments later, she looked to her right, past Mary Ellen's truck.

There was Troy.

He stood near the road, just beyond the pasture fence, with his SUV behind him.

She wasn't sure what to make of his expression; it was unclear whether he was shocked, or physically ill, but he didn't look happy. She felt certain he'd been standing there long enough to have seen the calving, based upon his presentation.

Damn. I'm still hungry, but I'd forgotten about the tacos with all this going on. She started walking toward him.

"Who's that?" The question came from Victor, who was drying his hands on a clean shop towel as he walked alongside her.

She sighed. "That's Troy, one of my lead ranchers."

Just as they neared the fence, he added, "Doesn't seem like he's got the stomach for the job." Victor walked away, chuckling.

Troy's expression changed then. Shoulders slumped, he bowed his head and turned away.

Oh, no. He heard what Victor said. She quickened her pace. But before she could reach him, he turned and bolted for his truck.

"Troy!"

Ignoring her as she called out to him, he got into the driver's seat and slammed the door. Moments later, everyone on the pasture watched as he drove off.

"Look, I'm sorry. Maybe I shouldn't have been so loud," Victor called.

Robyn ignored him as she turned toward Mary Ellen's truck. "I need to get back to the office."

"Sure thing." Mary Ellen followed her, and they were soon headed back to the operations center.

Driving toward the ranch's main gate at top speed, Troy struggled to put what had just happened behind him. He'd stopped by the operations building and left the bag of tacos on Robyn's desk.

Just because I lost my appetite, that doesn't mean she can't eat. Hell, she paid.

When he'd returned from The Red Sombrero, the receptionist had told him where Robyn was. She had not, however, informed him that she was engaged in calving. Had he known that, he would have simply waited at the office.

Turning out onto the main road, he left the ranch behind, determined to make it home as quickly as he could. All he wanted to do right now was put distance between him and the ranch.

It had been bad enough to have to witness the difficult calving, his least favorite part of ranching. But watching her work with that man, the same one he'd seen her with earlier, really set his teeth on edge.

His phone rang. He knew without looking who it was.

Engaging the hands-free calling option in his SUV, he answered. "Hello."

The sound of her familiar voice filled the vehicle. "Troy, it's Robyn."

"I know. What do you need?" The words came out a little gruffer than he'd intended, but he let that go. "I left the food you paid for on your desk, if that's why you called."

"I got the tacos, Troy. That's not why I'm calling."

"Well?"

"Why'd you rush off like that?"

"I think you know the answer to that." What kind of game was she playing here? "Didn't you hear your friend? He was right. I don't have the stomach to be there."

She sighed deeply. "He's not my friend."

"You seemed pretty chummy back there from where I was standing."

"What are you getting at, Troy?"

His eyes locked on the road ahead, illuminated by his headlights, he said, "I saw you with him."

"I know. So, did everybody else who helped deliver that calf, so I'm not seeing your point."

"No, Robyn. I mean, I saw you with him earlier, at the coffee shop. You know, when you were just so busy that you couldn't be bothered to take my call?"

She gasped. "Troy, have you been following me or something?"

"Oh, please. I wanted a latte. I stopped by your office to see if you wanted anything, and you weren't there. So, I called. And imagine how surprised I was to pull up and see you sitting there, laughing and joking…with him. You seemed to be enjoying yourself immensely while texting me that you couldn't talk."

"Hmph." She paused. "I was calling to make sure you were all right because I know you don't like calving. And *this* is what's bothering you?"

"Both things are bothering me. I can multitask."

A bitter laugh followed that statement. "Troy, you have no idea how crazy you sound right now."

He felt weak, emasculated, and it ate him up inside. His mother had spoken to him that way, too, as she reminded him why he'd never be man enough. She'd also been a cheater, not staying true to his father. He knew not all women were like that, but his mother's behavior had given him a suspicious nature. He tried to fight it, but sometimes failed. Like now. "Then there's no reason to keep talking to me, is there?" Without waiting for a response, he ended the call and turned his focus back to driving.

She called again, but he ignored it.

When he finally made it back home, he shed his clothes and took a hot shower. With the hot water cascading over his body and the steam filling the stall, he dropped his head into his hands.

When he'd first returned to town, his mind had been on his grandmother and making sure she was okay. Now, Robyn had him so stressed out, he risked losing focus on Mama Jeannie. That had to change.

He emerged from the shower clean, but not refreshed. Throwing on his boxers and a T-shirt, he fell into bed.

He closed his eyes, but sleep eluded him.

He lay there for three hours, alternating between scrolling through social media on his phone, tossing and turning, and staring at the ceiling.

Tired of flopping around in bed like a fish out of water, he grabbed his phone from the nightstand and punched in the number of someone he hoped could shed some like on this whole mess.

Mary Ellen answered on the second ring. "Hello?"

"It's Troy. Do you have a minute?"

"It's awfully late at night for you to be calling me." She yawned. "Let me guess. Taking a sick day?"

If he'd been in a less stormy mood, he might have laughed. "No. I just wanted to ask you a question."

"Shoot."

"Who is that guy I keep seeing with Robyn?"

"You mean Victor? He's a veterinarian."

"Oh." He thought about that for a minute. *Maybe she really was doing something work-related when I saw them together the first time.* He mentally kicked himself for the way he'd spoken to Robyn earlier. She'd called him out of concern, and he'd snapped at her. *How could I have been so mistrustful? I shouldn't have let my suspicions get the better of me.* "He must be new."

"Technically he hasn't started yet." She yawned again. "You don't think we just let any geek off the street help us deliver calves now, do you?"

"No."

"I mean, you saw what went down out there. First breech we've had in a while. Your average Joe couldn't have handled that."

He swallowed, not wanting to think about what he'd seen. "Listen, I get that he's a vet. The next question is, why is he here?"

"Oh, no. I'm not getting in the middle of this." A third yawn. "Look, I'm tired. You said you're not taking a sick day, right? So just come in tomorrow and talk with Robyn about it yourself."

"I will. Thanks."

"Thank me by letting me sleep."

"Good night."

He set aside the phone and stared up into the darkness, wondering why the ranch would be hiring a new vet when they already had a top-notch one.

What in the world is Robyn up to?

Chapter 15

Wednesday morning, Robyn sat down on the right side of the conference-room table. She'd been up since before dawn, going over what she would say to them, over and over. Even now, her plans were still running through her mind.

Accentuate the positive, downplay the negative.

Remind them you love them.

Validate their feelings.

Across from her, her parents sat, side by side. Thelma, in her favorite blue jogging suit festooned with crystals around the sleeves and neckline, sat quietly flipping through a magazine. Cooper, dressed in his normal uniform for working on the ranch, was far less relaxed. He sat forward in his seat, with one elbow resting on the table, and drummed his fingers there, indicating his impatience. He also hadn't taken off his hat, which meant he didn't plan on being here long.

"Robyn, what is this all about? Your mother's retired, but I still have things to take care of." Cooper leaned back in his chair, eyeing his daughter expectantly.

"Go on and say what you have to say, before your father's head explodes," Thelma remarked, barely looking up from her magazine. "You know how impatient he can be."

She swallowed the nervous lump sitting in her throat, then drew a deep, calming breath. "Mom, Pop. I'm leaving the ranch."

Thelma looked up, appearing confused. "What do you mean?"

"I mean, I'm leaving the ranch. I'm taking a job at the wildlife conservatory in San Diego, and—"

Cooper slammed his hand down on the table, his brown eyes blazing. *"What?"*

She cringed. "Pop, look. I just feel like I need to do this. It's a dream job. I'd get to work with large animals from all over the world and lead a team that's making new discoveries and—"

"And what are we supposed to do for the herd?" Cooper steepled his fingers. "We can't go without a vet, Robyn. Not with the number of animals we have. The local vet in Grandeza can't handle the herd, plus all the dogs and cats of the townsfolk."

She offered a pensive smile. "That's the great part. I already found and hired a replacement."

"And you didn't think we'd want to have any say

in that process?" Cooper shook his head. "Robyn. I'm surprised at you."

"There wasn't time, Pop. I'm due to start my job in San Diego at the beginning of November. And I didn't want to leave you without a replacement lined up. So I acted as quickly as I could…and quietly, so you wouldn't be upset."

Thelma blinked back tears. "You're leaving so soon?"

Cooper raised his hands, using his fingertips to massage his temples. "Let me see if I have this right. You decided, without saying anything to us, that you are going to leave your job, hire your own replacement and take a job in San Diego, all within the course of a month. Is that right?"

She nodded, sensing it would be better to stay quiet in her response.

Her father released a bitter chuckle. "I always thought I'd leave a legacy here when I was gone. Something for you and your sister to share." He folded his arms over his chest. "Lacey's been gone a long time. But apparently, so have you."

A small sob erupted from Thelma's mouth at the mention of Lacey's name.

"That's not fair, Pop." She shook her head, the tears collecting in her eyes. "I'm over thirty and I've never really lived anywhere else. I stayed way longer than I ever thought I would, partially out of guilt. But it's not fair for you to bring her into this."

"Not fair? You hide things from us, you sneak around behind our backs and now you want to tell me what isn't fair?" He groaned. "This was such an immature thing to do. So deceitful and selfish. If you didn't work for family, do you think another outfit would tolerate this behavior?"

"Pop, it's not like that. Sometimes I just feel so stifled, so trapped here. I just need to see what lies beyond the ranch. Can't you understand?" She bit her lip, hating to say these things, but they'd been bottled up inside for so long. She loved her parents, loved the ranch, but she needed to explore what she wanted, to feel liberated. Shouldn't they want those things for her, too?

"I guess I could understand that you would want to leave us someday, Robyn." He stood, turning toward the door. "But like this? I never would have thought it would happen this way."

Brushing away her tears, Thelma joined her husband. "I can't believe you would do something like this, Robyn. The dishonesty—we raised you better than that."

Cooper took Thelma's hand and swung open the door.

He nearly walked right into someone standing in the hallway.

Robyn's gaze followed their departure.

Her heart stopped when she saw Troy standing there, his face a mask of pain and confusion.

"So, that's what's going on, Robyn? You're leaving, just like that?"

Oh, no. He must have overheard. Could this get any worse? And she'd tried so hard to do the right thing—

hiring her replacement before notifying her parents, telling Troy she was okay with a casual relationship. She'd tried to be decent, and now she felt anything but.

Cooper said gruffly, "Excuse me. Thelma and I are leaving."

Robyn got up and headed for the hallway, where all the people she cared about were gathered, but were quickly moving away from her.

Mom and Pop aren't going to listen to me anymore, at least not now. She turned to Troy. "Can you just give me a chance to explain?"

While Cooper and Thelma walked out the door, Troy stood in front of her in the lobby, arms folded over his chest. "I'm listening."

She glanced around the space. The receptionist was behind her desk, and there were a few staff members hanging out near the café on the other side of the lobby. "Do we have to do this here? Let's go to my office." She went in first and held the door open for him to enter behind her.

"Make it quick. I have work to take care of."

She heard the ire in his voice. *I deserve that.* "How much did you hear?"

"Not much. I just heard your mother say you were leaving soon, and everything that came after that."

"Troy, I never meant for any of this to happen. I accepted a job at the San Diego Wildlife Conservatory. It's a dream job for me, and I applied more than six months ago. I'd given up on it, but then they called. The only catch was the three-week time line."

His expression remained flat. "I spoke to Mary Ellen. I called her after I left last night, to find out who that man was. She told me he was the vet, but that I'd have to ask you if I wanted to know more."

She nodded, unsure how she felt about him talking to M.E. to find out who Victor was. She knew he was upset about her leaving, though, so she let that pass.

"Mary Ellen has been a great friend to me through this, but I imagine she's upset as well."

"Robyn, you think people are upset because you took a job, but that's not the problem here. What you've done is give people the impression you were committed to them, when all the while you were planning on leaving. That's not fair."

She dropped her head. "I know." His words stung like a hundred tiny paper cuts. But he hadn't said anything untrue. She knew he was talking about him as much as the ranch.

"I opened my heart to you. I thought you were doing the same. But you weren't. You were hiding things from me this whole time. I can't do this, Robyn, no matter how much I...love you."

She looked up, feeling the tears gather in her eyes. "Troy, please."

"It's pretty clear there's nowhere for this relationship to go now, Robyn. Now I understand why you didn't want to take things beyond the casual level. It's just a shame that I'd started thinking of us in more serious terms."

She cringed, squeezing her eyes shut. "Troy, please..."

"With everything that's happened, I think it's better if we just end this now. I can't invest any more of my heart into this. You said you'd shelter me, Robyn. Yet somehow, I feel like I've been left out in the cold." With a shake of his head, he turned and walked out of her office.

Through watery eyes, she watched him cross the lobby, swing open the glass doors and walk out into the sunshine.

Once he was gone, she fell back in her chair and let the tears fall freely.

Troy crawled out of bed at an ungodly hour on Thursday to drive Mama Jeannie to the hospital for her procedure. From the moment he helped her into the passenger seat of his SUV, she rested quietly there, in and out of sleep. He kept quiet, so as not to disturb her. She was usually much chattier, but he was somewhat grateful for the reprieve. After a sleepless night, mostly spent trying not to think about Robyn, he wasn't much for conversation.

The rigmarole of getting Mama J out of the car, into the hospital and properly checked in seemed to wake her up. Once they finally got her into the preop suite, the staff dressed her in a hospital gown and tucked her into a bed to await her trip to the operating room. He took up a seat in the plastic chair next to her bed.

"Troy, tell them to bring me another blanket. I'm freezing in this drafty gown."

He summoned a nurse and got the blanket, draping it over her small form. "Better?"

She nodded. "Yes. Thank you, sugar."

He returned to his seat next to her bed.

"Before they take me back there, what's wrong with you?" She looked at him pointedly. "There's something weighing on your mind, and it's not just me."

He blew out a breath. "Things have blown up between Robyn and me. But I don't want you to worry about that. You just rest."

She frowned. "That's too bad. You going to be okay?"

He nodded. "I'll be fine. It's better that I found out now, before things got any more serious."

"What happened?"

He gave her a brief recap of what had transpired between them.

"That doesn't sound like her at all. She's not one to keep secrets, especially from her parents." She yawned. "I'm sure you'll figure out what you need to do, Troy."

His brow hitched in surprise. "You mean you're not going to tell me what you think I should do?"

She shook her head. "No, I'm not. You've got good sense, Troy. I trust you to make the right decisions for your own life." She paused. "And that's why I have something important to tell you."

"What is it, Mama J?"

She took a breath. "You have an inheritance."

He frowned, confused. "What do you mean? Dad

left me something else besides his accounts and the bass guitar?"

"No, sugar. This is an inheritance from your grandfather."

"Grandpa left me something?" This came as news to him since it had been more than a decade since his grandfather's death. "I'm really confused, so can you explain?"

"Back in the sixties, your grandfather Horace helped a friend build a hotel, up in the Sangre de Cristo Mountains. It's called the Heaven's Edge Resort. Have you heard of it?"

He shook his head. "I haven't."

She smiled as if remembering. "Beautiful place. Built to look like an old Spanish fort. Anyway, after the building was done and the place opened up, Horace's friend lost most of his money in the casinos down in Vegas. In order to get liquid again, he sold his interest in the hotel to us back in '72. Took most of his savings, but your grandfather bought the place, so he could help his friend get back on his feet."

"Wow. I can't believe I'm just now hearing all this."

"Hush up, there's more!" She coughed. "Horace tried to groom Johnny for business so he could pass it on to him, but you know your daddy wasn't trying to be anybody's innkeeper. He didn't want anything to do with the place. That's why he left with Sylvia after they married, and she got pregnant with you."

"That's why we lived in North Carolina when I was little? Because Dad was running from an inheritance?"

"He thought to own the place meant being stuck there, bless his heart. He was a wanderer. Couldn't stand being tied down." She raised her hand to cover another cough. "Horace held on to the hotel but put it in his will that the place would be deeded to you at his death."

He stared at her in the silence of the car. "You mean I've owned this place for over a decade? Why didn't you tell me before now?"

"Are you raising your voice at me, Troy Gregory Monroe?"

He straightened. "I'm sorry, Mama J. I don't mean to disrespect you. I'm just shocked and confused by all this."

She put a frail hand on his shoulder. "That's understandable. The reason I never told you is that I know you. You're so much like Johnny. I didn't want you to feel obligated to come back to Grandeza. I wanted you to take your time and figure out what you want and where you want to be, on your own terms. I'm part owner, but Horace always wanted it to go to you."

"Mama J, I…"

"I trust you, Troy." She was quiet for a moment. "If anything should happen, go to my place and tell Helene to give you my hatbox. All the documents are in there."

He could see the lines of her face changing before his eyes. "Everything is going to be fine. It's just a little biopsy."

She gave him a weak smile. "I know, sugar."

A moment passed, and he felt a sense of dread rising. But he refused to let her see it. *I won't burden her with my fears at a time like this.*

The nurse returned then. "Mrs. Monroe, we're going to get your IV started. Dr. Mertz is almost ready for you."

Troy moved aside to give the nurse space to work. Once the IV was hooked up, the doctor came in to give her a preprocedure speech. Troy remained by his grandmother's side throughout all of it.

The sedatives started to take effect, and her eyes grew heavy. "I'm so tired, Troy."

What if I lose her? What if she's too tired to keep fighting?

He cradled her hand in his own. "It's okay, Mama J. You just rest, and I'll see you after it's done."

"Okay, sugar." Her eyes closed briefly, then reopened. "I love you, Troy."

He leaned over, kissed her forehead. "I love you, too."

She drifted off to sleep then, and a few minutes later, the medical team came and wheeled her off to the OR.

Gathering her purse and the bag containing her clothes, he followed the yellow line out of preop and made his way to the waiting room.

Mama J trusts me. She did everything she could to leave me free to make my own choices.

Yet Robyn couldn't trust me enough to share her hopes and dreams with me.

Two women, both of whom had withheld information from him, for different reasons.

The question is, what am I going to do now? A few days ago, he'd been imagining a future with Robyn. Now, he didn't know what to do. All he knew was that he couldn't simply turn off the love he felt for her.

He shook his head, not wanting to figure this out now, under the scrutiny of the dozen or so other people occupying the vinyl chairs in the waiting area.

For now, his main concern was Mama Jeannie.

Chapter 16

Thursday, Robyn stayed in bed well past noon.

The last time I stayed in be past ten was when Troy was here.

Then, she'd been sleeping off the effects of his love-making. Now, she was trying to hide from the world, and from the pain of losing him and disappointing her parents, all in the same day.

That pain was so crushing, she'd taken a rare personal day off from work. Burrowed beneath her soft bedding, she didn't know if she'd ever get up.

She had the right to be independent, but had she handled things the right way? Maybe it was selfish to think she could just arrange things and skip off to her future. She should have talked to them first, told her she was discontent. Maybe they would have listened to her concerns and been more willing to work with her to find a solution.

And as for Troy… She went back and forth between feeling awful she'd kept this from him and being angry at his reaction. He had no hold on her, no commitment. Even if they had been falling for each other, he had no right to think she shouldn't pursue a future of her own choosing. Yes, they'd declared their love for one another, and yes, they'd shared some toe-curling encounters in the bedroom. But what did they have beyond that? They hadn't yet established any parameters for their relationship. It was all still so new.

And now, it may be shattered beyond repair.

Eventually, she was forced out of bed by nature. So, she moved from the bed to the couch. All she wanted to do was sit by the television, binge her favorite comedies and eat junk food.

Her phone rang, snapping her out of the trancelike state she'd fallen into. "Hello?"

"Robyn, it's Kima. What's going on with you?"

She sighed. "Let's see. My parents have probably disowned me, and Troy hates me. Other than that, just your typical Thursday."

Kima gasped. "What happened?"

She gave her the rundown of yesterday's disastrous beginnings. "I managed to alienate almost everyone I care about, in one fell swoop."

"You haven't lost me, although you know I'm about to hit you with a giant-sized 'I told you so.'"

She cringed. "I know, I know. I should have seen this coming."

"You've made a big ol' mess for yourself. Now, you're gonna have to woman up, and fix it."

"I don't even know where to start." She groaned, pressing herself into the sofa cushions as if they could swallow her up.

Kima popped her lips. "You're going to have to make a decision about that job."

Robyn nodded to herself. "I know. I was so sure of myself. I felt so positive I wanted to leave this town." She paused, searching for the right explanation. "I felt trapped here, as if I couldn't breathe free. I needed to get away to some place new. Now, I don't know..."

"If maybe the something new just needs to be a new attitude, not a new place?" Kima said softly. "I get what you're saying. I think you need to ask yourself, though, is it really worth everything you stand to lose if you take the job?"

At one time, she thought it was. Now she wasn't so sure. "Probably not."

"Then handle that. Aren't they expecting you in like, a week?"

"Yes. And if I rescind now, I'm probably giving up any shot of ever working there in the future, because of the short notice."

"You know what? Maybe they're not the best employer in the world asking you to come out there on such short notice. You could at least ask for an extension. If they can't do that for you, I'd rethink whether they are a good fit. I'd say you call them, see what you can find out about starting later and then move on to making things right with your parents. They did birth you, you know. You owe them."

She ran a hand over her face, knowing her friend was right. "Fine. When I get off the phone with you, I'll call the folks in San Diego. What are you doing when you get off work?"

"Nothing, after I pick Leah up from school."

"I feel like I haven't seen her in ages."

"Tell you what. I'll bring her over later with some ice cream, and we'll just hang with you for a while. How's that?"

She smiled, grateful to have such a true friend. "Thank you, Kima. I don't know what I'd do without you."

She chuckled. "Finally! If I'd known that was all it would take to get you to admit that, I'd have offered you ice cream a long time ago."

After she hung up with Kima, she placed a call to the San Diego Wildlife Conservatory. First, she asked about an extension on the offer, telling them it was proving too difficult to meet the deadline. She explained that this was her parents' ranch, and she couldn't just abandon them so quickly. She said she thought the earliest she could arrive would be in the New Year.

As Kima suspected, they didn't respond well.

"I'm sorry, Dr. Chance, but when we made the offer, it was on the condition you come right away. You'd seemed eager to start, and we need someone far sooner than the New Year," said Dr. McMillan, the same man who'd originally called to offer her the job.

"Does that mean you're no longer interested in me? If I can't be there in…a week?"

"I'm afraid so. We're disappointed that you won't be joining us, Dr. Chance."

"So am I and let me again offer my apologies for the inconvenience. I was so gratified with your invitation, I accepted the position too quickly, without fully considering my circumstances." Although she was polite, inside she seethed. Kima had been right. She didn't want to work at a place that was so cold, so unreasonable. They'd kept her dangling for months, and wouldn't even budge on an arrival date? She suspected working there would be unpleasant.

"I see. I appreciate you letting us know, and I respect your honesty."

"There are just some personal matters here in New Mexico that I must attend to, and I can't take the position in good conscience, at least not at this time." There, she was rejecting them, not the other way around. It felt good.

"I understand, Dr. Chance. We wish you the best of luck in your professional endeavors."

She knew that was corporate speak for "Don't ever call us again," but she had to accept the consequences of her actions. "Thank you."

She blew out a breath, relieved that she'd handled at least one of the tasks on her list.

A different kind of relief washed over her, though— something deeper than the satisfaction of taking care of a distasteful job.

She felt…free. She felt at peace. With the worry about the job in San Diego no longer hanging over her, she could handle things the right way. She suddenly realized she was glad to be staying at the ranch, happy not to leave. Another thing Kima was right about—feeling free was a state of mind, not a location.

Now, I just need to see if I can get Mom and Dad to talk to me. So, shifting positions on the couch, she pulled the throw up around her pajama-clad body and dialed her mother.

"What is it, Robyn?" Her mother's tone was flat.

"Mom, I really need to talk to you and Dad. Can I come by the house tomorrow? I'll bring Chadwick's doughnuts." They were her parents' favorite, from a local baker with a shop in downtown Grandeza.

"Nice use of bribery, honey."

"I'll use whatever I have in the toolbox."

Her mother released a long-suffering sigh. "Fine. Come on over, around nine."

"I'll be there. I love you, Mom."

"I love you, too," she replied softly before hanging up.

Hours later, she'd showered and dressed, feeling no need for her friend and goddaughter to see her looking like a hot mess. She'd also straightened up so that when Kima and Leah arrived, all the evidence of her earlier tear-fueled snack binge had been thrown away.

Leah skipped in after her mother, with that ever-present smile on her face. "Hey, Auntie Rob."

"Hi, sweetheart." She bent down to kiss the top of Leah's curly head.

Leah immediately reached up to adjust her hair. "Don't flatten out my 'fro, Auntie."

She laughed. "I wouldn't dream of it."

Kima, already emptying the grocery bags she'd carried in, said, "What flavor do you want?" She gestured to the containers on the dining-room table. "I've got cookies and cream, strawberry and chocolate fudge."

"I want strawberry, Mommy!" Leah stood by the table, her little legs doing a happy, anticipatory dance.

"I'll take a scoop of each." Robyn pulled down bowls from the kitchen cabinet and brought them, along with the ice-cream scoop and three spoons, to Kima.

Soon, the three of them were in the living room, enjoying the cold, creamy treat. Kima and Robyn were on the sofa, while Leah sat on the floor with her bowl. To entertain her, the television was on a kids channel.

"So," Kima began around a mouthful of ice cream, "have you started handling things?"

She nodded. "I already called the conservatory and told them I can't take the job. Then I called my mom, and asked if I can come by tomorrow, with Chadwick's doughnuts."

She looked impressed. "Nice idea. Those doughnuts are a nice bribe."

"Mom said the same thing."

"I think you're forgetting something, though."

She shook her head. "No. I know I have to deal with Troy. I just don't know what to say to him."

"I can't tell you what to say, except that you should start with an apology." She spooned up more ice cream.

"You'll have to figure out the best way to let him know you mean it, and that you're never going to be dishonest with him again."

"Auntie?"

"Yes, Leah?" She turned toward the sound of her goddaughter's voice.

"Why don't you just take him to your talking place, and then you can make up?"

Her brow furrowed. "Talking place?"

Kima shook her head. "At her school, they have a little alcove in the classroom—the teacher calls it the 'talking place.' Whenever two students are having conflict, they go there and sit until they work it out."

Leah nodded. "When kids go in, they're mad. But when they come out, they're friends again."

If only things were that simple between adults. But maybe there was a way to apply that same logic to her situation. "Thanks, Leah."

"Anytime, Auntie."

Troy walked into his grandmother's closet at her apartment Friday, pulling the cord to illuminate the space.

"It's on the shelf to the right," she called. "It's pink."

His gaze finally landed on the hatbox. "I see it." Reaching up, he took it down and turned off the light.

Back in the front room, he brought the box to his grandmother and placed it on her lap.

"Are you sure you're up to this right now, Mama J? You just had surgery yesterday."

"I'm fine," she insisted, taking the lid off the box.

"Now that I've got a solid diagnosis, the right meds and some oxygen, I'm right as rain."

He looked at her, noting how she didn't seem bothered by the nasal cannula she wore. The clear plastic tubing was barely visible, and Dr. Mertz had instructed her to wear it for a few hours every day to help with her shortness of breath.

She shuffled through the papers, then lifted out a set of stapled pages. "Here it is." Handing it to him, she said, "That's the deed to the Heaven's Edge Resort."

He looked it over, and from what he could see, the document was legit. "If I'm the owner, who's been running the place for the last ten years?"

"Your grandfather hired some very loyal, capable people to manage the hotel. They're a local family from the area, and they keep in regular contact with me."

"And the money?"

"Some goes into an account that pays for my care here. Your grandfather made sure to set that aside for me." She pointed to the pages. "The rest is in a trust, being held for you. If you look on the last page, you'll see the lawyer's name that's in charge of the account. Go see him, and he can get you access to the funds."

He sat back, taking in all this new information. "This is all so crazy. How much is in there?"

She shrugged. "I don't know. All I know is, my portion will be enough for me to live on, comfortably, until I turn one hundred and five."

His eyes bulged. "Wow."

"Ask the lawyer. I'm sure he has all the details." She

raised her hand, stifling a yawn. "As a matter of fact, go ask him now, so I can take a nap."

He laughed, then went over to give her a kiss on the cheek. "Promise me you'll hang around until you're a hundred and five, Mama J."

She grinned. "I'll do my best, sugar."

He left the retirement village and drove downtown. Within the hour, he sat across the desk from Gilbert Rojas, the attorney in charge of his grandfather's assets.

Mr. Rojas placed a pair of reading glasses on the end of his nose as his paralegal handed him a printout. "Mr. Monroe, I've run a check on your trust account. The current balance is—"

He glanced at the printout and named a number well north of seven figures.

Troy nearly fell out of his chair. "That much?"

"Yes. After payroll and other expenditures of the hotel are met, a percentage of the profits go into this account. That's been the case since your grandfather gained ownership in 1972. Mr. Monroe was also very fastidious about sticking to a budget. He was a very smart man, securing his family's future this way. Very few of my clients have that kind of discipline and foresight."

Troy couldn't but help smile, not only at learning the size of his newfound wealth, but also at hearing someone speak so highly of Grandpa Horace. "Thank you, Mr. Rojas."

"No problem, Mr. Monroe. Now that I've verified your identity, I'll contact the bank, to let them know you've come forward to claim the account. You should be getting a call from them soon about accessing the funds."

Troy left the lawyer's office feeling like his entire life had changed. The next order of business was to get up the mountain to see the hotel he now owned, but that could wait until tomorrow.

He knew he should celebrate, but there was a cloud of darkness hanging over his otherwise sunny mood.

Robyn.

She'd wronged him, crushing his heart. She'd been ready to leave him behind, without telling him. Just as he'd done to her the night of their junior prom. Maybe Rick had been right about her setting him up for a fall.

Still, he couldn't seem to quell his love for her. *What am I gonna do when she leaves town? I can't go on pining after her forever.* How could he trust her again, after the way she'd behaved?

Knowing she was wrong was one thing. Forgetting how she'd made him feel was another.

The papers in his pocket constituted a new life for himself, one of relative ease. He no longer needed his job at the ranch, but he wasn't sure how he wanted to move forward just yet.

Fortunately, thanks to his grandfather, he could take as much time as he needed to figure things out.

Chapter 17

When Robyn walked into the dining room at her parents' house on Saturday morning, they were already waiting for her. She felt their gazes on her as soon as she entered.

Much like the last time, her father was dressed for work, and her mother, for leisure. Today's tracksuit was green with gold trim.

She set the box of doughnuts on the table, then sat down two seats away from her mother.

Her father, at the head of the table, watched her intently.

"Good morning, Mom, Pop."

They each responded in kind, her father grumbling, her mother murmuring.

To break through the awkwardness, she flipped open

the doughnut box. "I got a dozen, assorted. I hope that's okay."

"It's fine." Cooper reached in, taking a cruller. "We're more interested in what you have to say than we are in the doughnuts."

"Your father's right about that." Thelma folded her hands, resting them on the table.

Drawing a deep breath, she began. "I want to start out by saying I'm very sorry for my behavior. There are no good excuses for what I did, and I'm not going to try to make any. But, if you'll let me, I'd like to try to explain."

Cooper gave her a solemn nod.

"Earlier in the year, I started looking at veterinary jobs on the West Coast. I applied for four jobs, one of them at the San Diego Wildlife Conservatory. It was my dream job—a chance to work with exotic animals and be a part of the discussion on conservation. I knew it was a long shot, but I applied, anyway." She shifted in her chair. "Months went by. Two of the jobs rejected me, and one was announced as filled. Only the San Diego job was left, but I never expected to get a call. But then, a couple of weeks ago, I got the call. I was so excited, I said yes right away."

"Sounds like you got a little ahead of yourself." Thelma's voice was soft.

"I did, in the worst way. I can't believe I thought I could fill my position, move my household and make it there in three weeks." She shook her head, thinking back on that day. "Anyway, it was a bad decision. A bad decision to hide my search from you. A bad decision to tell the conservatory I could be there in three weeks. A bad decision to think I could just replace myself without telling you about a new hire. Who knows? Maybe I'll work at a place like the conservatory one day, but if they can't wait for when I'm ready, they're not for me now."

Cooper asked, "Does that mean you're not taking the job?"

She shook her head. "No. I called them yesterday and backed out. I just couldn't leave, especially knowing how much I'd upset you."

Thelma reached out, took her hand. "You've made a very mature decision, Robyn. And I want you to know, you should never feel you have to hide your dreams from us. Never. Sure, we want you to stay here. But we're proud to have raised a smart, independent woman. We don't want you to feel tied to us by duty, but only by love. I know it must have been hard to give up that position."

"It was." She squeezed her hand. "But it would have been even harder going through life feeling like I betrayed you and Pop. I love you two so much, and I promise never to do anything like this again."

Her mother stood, held out her arms. "Come here, Robyn."

She hugged her mother tight. "I'm so, so sorry. Please forgive me."

"We love you, and we'll always be here for you, no matter what, sweetie." Thelma kissed her cheek, leaving behind traces of her shimmery brown lipstick.

When her mother sat back down and reached for a doughnut, Robyn cast a pensive gaze on her father.

He was still seated and appeared to be considering what she'd said.

"Pop? Do you think you can forgive me?"

Finally, he nodded. "Of course. How could I not? You know how much I love you. What your mother said, that goes for me, too."

She went to him, leaning down to kiss him on the cheek. "Thanks, Pop. And do you think it would be okay if Dr. Rockford stayed on? The money's in the budget. I'd checked on that. That way, I can step back a bit, and actually use some of my vacation time."

"I'm fine with that."

He chuckled. "All right, enough of that mushy stuff." He stood, brushing crumbs from his work shirt. "I need to get out there and make sure the ranch is still running. You two can stay here with the doughnuts." Plucking one more cruller from the box, he walked out. The sound of the front door opening and closing indicated he'd left.

Alone with her mother, she asked, "Do you think Pop has really forgiven me?"

"Yes, I do. You know he's not one for emotional displays." She munched on a chocolate-covered doughnut. "I think a part of his heart was lost when Lacey died."

"I miss her." She felt the tears gathering in her eyes.

"We all do. No matter how many years go by, we're never going to forget her." Thelma turned toward the photograph of her daughters sitting on the sideboard. "She's always in our hearts."

She exhaled. "I think part of me was trying to run from her memory, you know? Sometimes, remembering her is just too painful." She ran a hand over her hair. "I guess I thought if I wasn't on the ranch anymore, it wouldn't hurt so much."

"Remember the therapist we took you to after it happened? Dr. Moore?"

She nodded.

"Do you remember what she told us, about grief?"

"Yes. Grief is the product of immense love."

Thelma squeezed her shoulder. "Don't you see? We all loved her, and we all miss her. It's okay to feel sad about it sometimes, but never let go of those happy memories of her."

She felt a lightness come over her then. "You're right, Mom. Thanks for the reminder."

"That's what I'm here for." She smiled, pushing a lock of Robyn's hair out of her face. "One more thing, sweetheart."

"What is it, Mom?"

"Have you talked to Troy?"

She shook her head. "I'm pretty sure he doesn't want to talk to me."

Thelma frowned. "But since you love him, you're just going to have to try, now, aren't you?"

"Mom, how did you know that…?"

She waved her hand. "Oh, come on. I'm your mother. I know you better than anybody. Of course I know when my daughter's in love." She paused. "I also know a good man when I see one, and Troy is a good man. You'd better come up with some way to make him understand."

She nodded. "Kima told me the same thing. Actually, I have something in mind, but I might need some help."

"What are you going to do?"

"I'm going to take Leah's advice, and make us a 'talking place.'"

Thelma frowned. "You mean Leah, Kima's little girl? You're taking advice from a second grader?"

"Kids are very perceptive."

She looked unconvinced.

"Don't worry, Mom. It's a solid plan. You'll see."

Walking into the operations center on the ranch, Troy removed his hat and let the glass door swing shut behind him. It was late evening, just after six.

He'd spent the better part of the day up at the Heaven's Edge Resort, touring the facilities. As his grandmother had said, the hotel was modeled after an old Spanish fort, with the exterior looking like a cluster of adobe buildings. The interior, with its brightly colored decor, had all the modern amenities of a five-star resort. Beyond everything he'd seen, he'd gotten a chance to meet the Riveras, the family that ran the resort. They were very happy to meet him and seemed like hardworking, dedicated people. He could see why the place had been so profitable.

He'd been on the way home when he got a text from Robyn, asking him to meet her here. He had no idea what she wanted, but he figured there was only one way to find out.

Standing in the lobby, he looked to the reception desk. Tina wasn't there, and neither was most of the staff. Most people, except the weekend skeleton crew, were gone by four thirty on Friday and didn't return until Monday.

Walking past the desk, he went to Robyn's office

and found the door open. Taped to the door was a hand-written note.

Troy, please come to the storage room.

He frowned. *What in the world?* Shaking his head, he took the note and went down the hall, past the darkened offices and the empty café. Approaching the storage room, he could see the door propped open with a cinderblock. A faint, flickering light emanated from the room.

When he made it to the door, he saw the source of the light.

There, in the center of the storage room, stood Robyn. She wore a flowing strapless dress, the soft white material falling from her waist down to the floor in a swirl of fabric. On the floor near her feet were two large, fluffy cushions. All around her, on the edges of shelves and the tops of file cabinets, were dozens of lit candles.

She looked like an angel. He'd thought of her that way before, but not so much now.

She smiled when he came into view. "Troy. You came."

He nodded. "What's all this?"

She gestured around. "This is our talking place."

Confusion knit his brow. "Pardon me?"

She took a few steps closer to him. "My little goddaughter, Leah, told me about the way her classmates solve their arguments. They go to a talking place in the classroom. I thought I'd create something like that for us."

He couldn't help smiling. "It's a cute idea."

"She's a cute kid. A regular little second-grade philosopher."

He noticed how she left a little distance between them, and the pensive way she watched him. He blew out a breath. "I'm assuming those cushions are for us to sit on?"

She nodded. "If you're willing to stay, and work this out with me."

He entered the room then and sat down on one of the cushions.

Brushing the dress beneath her, she sat next to him. "Would you rather speak first, or listen first?"

He adjusted himself on the cushion. "I'd like to talk."

"I'm listening."

"I just want you to understand that I would never step on your dreams, Robyn. I would have thought you knew that, but I guess not. More than anything, it hurt me to think you didn't trust me enough to share those things with me. Were you really just going to pick up and leave like that?"

She dropped her head. "I don't know what I was thinking...except how much I wanted to move on. I couldn't possibly relocate that quickly, and any employer who asked that of me isn't one I want to work for. I should have known better."

He remained quiet, letting her speak her piece.

"Aside from that, Troy, I never expected to fall in love with you." She looked up, meeting his eyes, with the tears in hers. "Being with you again changed everything. At first, this was all about spreading my wings, leaving the ranch and seeing the world. Now I realize, you're my world."

Her words touched him. "Do you mean that, Robyn?"

"I really do. I mean it so much that I called and told them I'm not taking that job."

"You gave it up?"

She nodded, wiped her tears. "There was no way I could take it and leave things as they were. Not with my parents, and not with you."

He absorbed the weight of her words. *She's not leaving anymore. And it looks like I'm not leaving, either.*

"I can't make you stay with me, Troy, and I won't try. After what I've done, I would understand if you want to break things off." Her shoulders drooped, and she seemed to be focused on the cushion beneath her. Another round of silent tears followed her words, and he could see the resignation in her face.

He slipped his arm around her shoulders.

She jerked her head up, with a glimmer of hope and surprise in her eyes.

"It's okay, Robyn. I'm okay. Right here, with you. With us."

Her lips quivered. "Really?"

"Yes. I love you, and there's no changing that. But I want you to promise me something."

"Anything."

He took her hand in his. "Never hide your heart's desires from me again. Because I'm going to want to give them to you. Okay?"

A sob escaped her as she fell into his arms.

There, in the dimly lit room, he held her close against

him, feeling his heart swell with affection. When she finally calmed down, he stroked his hand through her hair. "I have something to tell you."

Smiling up at him, she asked, "What is it?"

"I'm a millionaire."

She gave him a playful punch in the arm. "Come on, Troy. Don't joke with me, I'm still fragile."

He smiled, taking the card he'd gotten from the hotel from his pocket and handing it to her. It displayed the logo of the Heaven's Edge Resort and listed him as the owner.

Shifting her gaze to him, her eyes grew wide. "What does this mean?"

"My grandfather left me that hotel, along with a sizable trust."

"Oh!" Her scream of surprise echoed through the building.

He laughed. "Let's get out of here. Come with me, and I'll make you scream for a whole different reason."

Another wave of tears came as he drew her close and kissed her.

Chapter 18

Balancing a platter of her mother's famous cranberry sauce, Robyn sidestepped through the kitchen and into the dining room to set it down. With the platter safely placed on the table, she stepped back to admire the rest of the Thanksgiving feast laid out there. There was roast turkey and ham, yams, green beans, macaroni and cheese and so much more food that the table was probably groaning under the weight of it all.

In many ways, this was a typical Chance family holiday. Her maternal aunts and uncles, along with her cousins, and a few of her father's buddies from town, had all descended on the ranch house. But this time, there were two more very special guests.

She watched with a smile as Troy waited on Mama Jeannie, bringing her drinks and whatever else she needed. Seeing the way he cared for his grandmother demonstrated what a kind heart he possessed. If they had kids one day, she knew he'd make a wonderful father.

"Robyn! Come and get the rest of these pies!"

No time for fantasizing. She shook her head and returned to the kitchen.

Later, as they all sat down to the meal, Cooper said a brief blessing over the food. "We'd go around, have everyone say what they're thankful for, but with thirty people, that'll take all day."

Laughter filled the room.

Soon, the din of silverware striking dishes and a myriad of unrelated conversations filled the space. Seated between Mama Jeannie and Troy, Robyn sampled the yams and moaned when the sweetness hit her tongue.

"You eat like a bird," Mama Jeannie joked, helping herself to a piece of turkey.

She chuckled. "Don't worry. Once the sweets come out, you'll see what a pig I can be."

Troy shook his head. "What am I gonna do with you two?"

While they ate, Robyn listened to Mama Jeannie's tales of her childhood in Birmingham, her days as a student at Auburn University and meeting and falling in love with Troy's grandfather, Horace. Troy listened as well, his expression conveying his interest even though he'd probably heard these anecdotes before. Jeannie was a great storyteller, and Robyn knew she was going to enjoy spending more time with her.

As the meal ended and desserts were shared, Robyn gave into her sweet tooth and devoured two slices of apple pie. She was eying the peach cobbler when Troy stood, striking his glass with a fork.

All eyes turned to him, including hers.

"Happy Thanksgiving, everyone. I just wanted to thank Mr. and Mrs. Chance for welcoming me and my grandmother into their home and making us feel like family."

Robyn smiled, noting the unfiltered approval on the faces of her aunts. *Isn't that sweet?*

"In fact, I'd like to make that family tie official." He reached into the pocket of his sport coat and withdrew a ring box.

"Oh!" Robyn gasped, her hand flying to cover her open mouth.

Squeals went up among Robyn's female relations as he dropped to one knee beside her. Popping open the box, he said, "Robyn, I've loved you since I was seventeen. Back then I didn't know what I wanted. You've taken me on so many adventures these past few months, but I want our life together to be the biggest and best adventure. Will you marry me?"

Tears filled her eyes, blurring the image of the round cut yellow diamond ring. Overcome with emotion, she half sobbed, half shouted her answer. "Yes, Troy."

The whole gathering broke out in cheers and applause as he slipped the ring onto her finger.

Behind her, Mama Jeannie squeezed her shoulder. "You two are going to do well together."

"I agree." Rising on his knees, he leaned in and kissed her soundly. "I love you, Robyn Chance."

"I love you, too." She held him close, soaking in the immense joy of being in the arms of the man she loved.

For so long, they'd both been searching for the place they belonged.

As it turns out, where we belong...is together.

* * * * *

Zahra was sure surprise showed on her face. Seemed someone had experienced a change of heart toward her. Wait. Something occurred to her. *We'll*. He'd said *we'll* make it work. "You're staying, too?" flew out before she could catch it.

"Do you have a problem with that?" he asked.

No, but she should have. "I was never the one with the problem, remember?"

"That's arguable," he said.

"Shall we argue it?" she shot back.

One corner of his mouth curved into a sexy smile that drew Zahra's full attention. Yep, she definitely should have a problem with him staying. Oh, the delicious trouble she could get into with this man.

"I think we already have, and I'm pretty sure I lost," he said.

Zahra laughed and so did Gregor, each returning to their task.

"What's up with the camera?" Gregor asked.

She eyed the black camera bag sitting on the counter. "I don't plan on snapping pictures of you and selling them, if that's what you're thinking."

"It had crossed my mind."

And with good reason, she thought. "I love capturing pictures anywhere I go. I have a small studio in NoDa. North Davidson and Thirty-Sixth," she said for clarification, but was sure he was familiar with Charlotte's popular art district. "You should swing by sometime. I'll give you a free head shot."

"Thanks, but no, thanks. Cameras and I aren't on the best of terms right now."

"Because of the scar?"

Joy Avery works as a customer service assistant. By night, the North Carolina native travels to imaginary worlds, creating characters whose romantic journeys invariably end happily-ever-after.

Since she was a young girl growing up in Garner, Joy knew she wanted to write. Stumbling onto romance novels, she discovered her passion for love stories; instantly, she knew these were the type of stories she wanted to pen.

Joy is married with one child. When not writing, she enjoys reading, cake decorating, pretending to expertly play the piano, driving her husband insane and playing with her two dogs.

Books by Joy Avery

Harlequin Kimani Romance

In the Market for Love
Soaring on Love
Campaign for His Heart
The Sweet Taste of Seduction
Written with Love

Visit the Author Page at Harlequin.com for more titles.

WRITTEN WITH LOVE

Joy Avery

Dedicated to the dream.

Acknowledgments

To everyone who has supported me on this glorious and beautiful journey, I acknowledge you.

Dear Reader,

I'm not sure where to begin, but I'll start by saying THANK YOU for joyriding with me on this journey of love. I'm forever grateful for the support you've shown me from my very first Kimani Romance to now, my last. You've made this one heck of a ride.

What are the odds Zahra would end up at the same secluded estate as her celebrity crush? Pretty darn good, obviously! Unfortunately, she's in for one well-packaged *rude* awakening.

Despite Gregor's status, Zahra doesn't take any mess from him. And truth be told, he likes it! I absolutely love the banter between these two. Watching their animosity turn to sparks and then flames tickled my heart. When stubborn and strong willed collide, it makes for one heck of an interesting journey. I hope you enjoy the ride!

Oh, did I mention Waterspout, the most adorable dog ever?

Stay in the know about all things #joyaveryromance by subscribing to my Wings of Love newsletter: www.eepurl.com/KkLkL.

Feel free to drop me a line or two at www.joyavery.com or via email at authorjoyavery@gmail.com. I love hearing from readers!

As always, I wish you light, love, laughter and a HAPPILY-EVER-AFTER!

Joy

Let's connect:

Facebook.com/AuthorJoyAvery
Twitter.com/AuthorJoyAvery
Instagram.com/AuthorJoyAvery
Follow me on Amazon: Amazon.com/author/joyavery
Follow me on BookBub: BookBub.com/authors/joy-avery

Chapter 1

No distractions.

These were the words that had instantly sold Zahra Hart on the idea of spending the next two weeks at her literary agent's summer home in Lake Lamont, North Carolina. No interruptions were precisely what she needed to put the finishing touches on her romance novel. Hopefully, her next *bestselling* romance novel. After the last two duds, she needed a winner.

This seclusion would be good for her. Quiet time to just write. No sister blowing up her phone to discuss her latest relationship drama or barging in at the most inopportune moments to siphon off hours of her valuable writing time to discuss her inability to understand men. As if anyone did. And definitely not Braswell,

continuously attempting to justify sleeping with another woman and ruining their three-year relationship.

The latter caused a ping of pain to ripple through
her chest. After six months, his betrayal still stung like
hell, which was a prime reason why she had yet to finish the novel that should have been done weeks ago.
She groaned, regretting the pressure her procrastina-
tion would place on her.

She had no one to blame but herself. But in her defense, who could write about love when the despicable
emotion was the last thing on her mind? Though she'd
said it several times before, this time she meant it. She
was done with love.

Maybe.

Definitely for the foreseeable future.

Ugh. Why did she still have to believe in happily-
ever-after?

It wasn't like she needed the distraction of love. The
exact opposite, in fact. With writer's block jamming her
creativity, she needed to shift her focus elsewhere. With
her writing in limbo, her focus was needed elsewhere.

Her mother's words drifted into her head. *The right
one is out there and searching for you at this very moment.* Well, apparently, her supposedly *right one* was
directionally challenged because at thirty-five, she
hadn't been found yet. It wasn't like she'd been hiding
all these years.

Okay, maybe she wasn't *completely* done with love,
but Mr. Right One was taking a long time to locate her,
so he'd better make one hell of an entrance into her life

when he finally showed up. She was talking firework-level sparks that ignited her entire soul. She wouldn't settle for anything less. An average Joe who was capable of seeing past his own damn ego. Yeah, that was the type of man she needed.

"Right one." She scoffed. "Yeah, *right*." Was there even such a thing? She was poised to say no until she recalled her parents' relationship. They'd been happily married for decades. Considering those two, true love definitely had to exist. Maybe just not for her.

"If it's meant to be, it'll be," she mumbled to herself.

"You say something, darlin'?"

Zahra eyed Captain Skip—the gentleman at the helm of the boat and the person responsible for getting her to her destination—and gave a lazy smile before shaking her head. "No, sir." Her smile turned into inward laughter when she considered how much Captain Skip resembled an older, rounder, tanner version of the Skipper from *Gilligan's Island*. Was that how he'd gotten the name?

Even though she wore a thick coat and huddled inside the partially enclosed structure, the icy wind still penetrated to her bones. Now she understood why Leona and her family made this trip only in warmer weather.

Captain Skip inhaled a deep breath. "Storm's coming through."

Zahra's brow shot up. Had he gotten that from a mere whiff? She tilted her head toward the clearest sky she'd ever seen. Not a gray cloud swirling. For kicks, she drew a breath. The chilly, crisp late-January air stung her nostrils. All she took in was the freshness of Lake Lamont. No hint of precipitation.

She appreciated the clear atmosphere. Unlike the air back in Charlotte, which was most often—thick and unpleasant. Still, she loved living in the Queen City.

"Won't be able to get back up here till after it passes. Could be three or four days if it's severe. Think you'll be okay?"

Yes, she would be. Perfect, actually. Stormy weather was when she did her best writing. "I'll be fine." She appreciated the older man's grandfatherly concern.

Initially, the only-accessible-by-boat thing had given her pause. But for only a couple of moments. All the time it had taken to research the crime rate in Lake Lamont and discover it to be practically nonexistent. A damaged fence here, a smashed mailbox there.

"Good thing you won't be—"

Captain Skip paused at the sound of her cell phone ringing.

"Ooo, I have a signal." The last time she'd checked, there hadn't been any bars. She fished the device from her purse and smiled when the name and face of her fabulous agent for the past five years filled the screen. Making the call active, she held the phone to her ear. "Hey, Leo."

Leona Landen's voice crackled on the opposite end. Zahra stood in hopes of acquiring a stronger signal. Swaying, she grabbed hold of one of the metal railings supporting the canopy. "Leona, are you still there?"

"I'm—"

The call dropped before Leona could finish her sentence. *"Shoot."*

The bars flatlined again, so Zahra stuffed the cell phone back into her purse. Leona had probably just wanted to make sure she'd arrived safely. So far, so good.

"Those devices don't work all that well around here. It's hit or miss. Mostly miss. That's why I rely on this trusty gadget." Captain Skip held up what resembled a CB microphone. "Dual band. Seven hundred and fifty channels. Excellent frequency range."

"Sounds useful. But it seems a little too daunting to carry around in my purse."

Captain Skip bellowed with laugher, slapping his thick thigh several times like she'd told the best joke he'd ever heard. When his amusement dried up, he said, "Yeah, I reckon that would be a bit difficult," then experienced another fit of laughter. It clearly didn't take much to tickle the jolly man.

Several minutes later, they rounded a bend and Landen House came into view. Leona's description of the structure, made of beautiful light and dark cobblestone, hadn't done it justice. She'd labeled it a cozy getaway. The large home was more like a secluded paradise, dotted with what seemed like a thousand windows, great for natural light. Her favorite. Yep, she was going to absolutely love it here.

Three equally impressive homes shared the island, the closest two or three miles away. Good. She wouldn't have to worry about prying neighbors. Assuming the houses were even occupied this time of year. Places like this were mostly used as summer homes, not permanent residences.

A short time later, Zahra stood in the foyer of the contemporary-styled home. Obviously, someone had been there to prep for her arrival because it was warm and cozy inside. A set of stairs leading to the upper level was to her right, while an office slash library rested to her left, connecting to a large family room. She ventured that way, removing her coat and tossing it over a chair. The open space was decorated in a teal, gray, white and taupe color scheme. It was absolutely gorgeous. Pictures of sailboats and seashells hung on the walls.

Veering into the adjoining kitchen, she took in every inch of her surroundings. The room resembled something plucked from the pages of a luxury kitchens magazine spread. Stainless steel and expensive wood decorated the sterile space. Oh, she was going to enjoy preparing meals in here. It was twice the size of the kitchen in her condo.

And speaking of cooking, she moved to the fridge and peered inside. Just as Leona had promised, the woman had it stocked to the brim with everything she could possibly need. Along with tons of fresh produce.

"Gold Peak Green Tea. Hmm." She usually preferred hot tea, but she'd give it a go. Removing a bottle, she twisted the top and took a long swig. The masculine voice that rang out in the room nearly caused her to drown in the liquid. Coughing ferociously, the bottle slipped from her hands. Wide-eyed, she ogled the hooded man filling the doorway, her wobbling legs threatening to betray her.

Despite just downing a few ounces of liquid, her mouth went dry, her stomach churned and her pulse rate tripled. Her heart pounded so ferociously against her rib cage, she was surprised it couldn't be seen thumping through her clothing.

In hindsight, she wished she'd taken the self-defense class her sister had suggested some months back. Eyeballing the guy, Zahra doubted the techniques would have been beneficial now. It would take a skilled professional to take down this mass of a man. While she could barely see his face under cover of the hoodie, she could feel his eyes boring a hole through her.

Bile rose and burned the back of her throat, but she forced herself into self-preservation mode. Dying today was not an option. She hadn't even seen *The Lion King Live* yet. It was on her bucket list, so she couldn't kick it.

When he thought he heard the hum of a boat, Gregor Carter's eyes rose from the twenty or so pills he held in his hand. Spilling the opioids back into their bottle, he sat it on top of the nightstand and stood. He winced at the dull pain that radiated through his ankle. While his joint felt much better than it had several weeks ago, it still wasn't where it needed to be. Where it had been prior to the accident.

After rotating his foot in a circular motion several times to loosen the stiffness, he crossed the room. At the window, he realized his hearing hadn't deceived him, spotting the same vessel he'd arrived on two weeks ago pulling away from the dock. While he hadn't seen anyone disembark from the watercraft, he knew someone had entered the house by the chime of the alarm.

Thad?

His agent hadn't said anything about coming. Was he here to check on him? Had Thad noted the hint of desperation in his voice when they'd spoken earlier? If anyone knew Gregor was not himself, it would have been Thad. Not only was he one hell of an agent, but he was also a damn good friend. Loyal.

He moved back to the bed and stashed the pill bottle inside the nightstand drawer. It would have been so easy to swallow the pills and dull it all—the hate mail, negative commentary by broadcasters, messages from so-called fans calling him everything from selfish and irresponsible to reckless and the worst quarterback in the league—but he wasn't going out like that. He wasn't going out like his father. *Coward.*

It hurt like hell that even some of his teammates regarded him as the enemy and had turned their backs on him, but he knew most of their animosity stemmed from the fact that they'd wanted so badly to head to the Super Bowl. Hell, so had he.

If he hadn't known any better, he would have sworn he wasn't the one in jeopardy of losing everything. But he did know better, and his career—along with countless endorsement deals—was in limbo. The only thing the world seemed to care about was the fact that he'd missed one of the most important playoff games of the season, which—by their assertions—had caused the Carolina Thoroughbreds their shot at the Super Bowl.

It irked him that no one cared he'd suffered an ankle sprain that had sidelined him and threatened his livelihood. Nor had they considered the fact that he'd already brought them four Super Bowl wins.

And they'd had the nerve to call me the ungrateful bastard.

He recalled some of the social media posts he'd read. Fans felt let down? How in the hell did they think he felt? This was supposed to be his opportunity to earn a fifth championship for his beloved Thoroughbreds. And he'd blown it. Over a woman. The recollection angered him. *Never again.*

Everyone had assumed he'd been horsing around the night of the accident, up to his usual antics. But it hadn't been the daredevil in him that had forced him to barrel down the road on his Harley at a stupid speed. It had been the scorch of betrayal.

Walking in to see his ex bouncing up and down in another man's lap, in the bed Gregor had purchased, in the condo he paid for... Well, that had been enough to make any man irrational. Instead of a confrontation that would have surely led to bad press, he'd left in a rage.

Too bad that had yielded the same result he'd been trying to avoid. He should have just smashed the bastard's face in and spared himself weeks of physical therapy.

That night had changed him. Not his ex's treachery—

of course, that had affected him, too—but the accident. Seeing his life flash before his eyes had forced him to reevaluate things. Since that night, nothing in his life felt…adequate. A link was missing.

Gregor released a heavy sigh. Maybe this was all his fault. Maybe he should have had better control over his emotions. Maybe he had been selfish and reckless for driving too fast and getting into the accident. *Maybe, maybe, maybe.* None of it mattered much now. The damage had been done.

Pulling on a black hoodie that cloaked his head and hid the scar that was a continuous reminder of that night he'd hit the asphalt, he moved from the downstairs master bedroom to greet Thad.

To Gregor's surprise, it wasn't Thad he found as he followed the rustling into the kitchen. His eyes fixed on the jean-clad round rump sticking out from between the refrigerator door. Something unmistakable gripped him. Lust. Even in a state of utter despair, his sexual appetite was still as ferocious as ever.

Ms. Round Rump hummed a tune similar to something one might perform to lull a fussy baby. Who was she? And what was she doing here? When she came up with a bottle of *his* green tea, he scowled but remained silent. *Apparently, a thief.*

Growing up in foster care had taught him to be keenly aware of his surroundings at all times. A lesson Ms. Round Rump clearly hadn't been taught. He could have been a serial killer readying to make her his next victim. Luckily for her, he would never dream of hurting a woman.

His eyes washed over her profile. She was…cute, in an average sort of way. Nothing about her really stood out to him. In fact, if they were in a room filled with a dozen other women, he doubted he would have even noticed her. Well, maybe from behind. His gaze flowed the curve of her butt. As an ass man, hers garnered his attention.

When she tilted her head back, her brownish-red hair—pulled into a ponytail—swayed back and forth. Again, while she was…cute—in an average sort of way—she wasn't his type. Obviously, his body disagreed, because he stirred below the waist. Probably just a reaction to the fact that it had been over a month since he'd enjoyed his second favorite pastime. Sex.

If he was as good as he thought he was when it came to assessing a woman's body, she was a curvy size sixteen. He couldn't recall the last time he'd been with a woman who wasn't a size six or smaller. Despite the lean dishes he'd grown accustomed to, this full plate was tempting as hell.

"That belongs to me," he said, alerting her to his presence.

The scene that unfolded would have gone viral on the internet. Ms. Round Rump choked. The plastic bottle fell from her hand and made a *thunk* when it hit the floor. Liquid pooled at her feet. When she attempted to flee, she slipped and went down. Hard.

Apparently, her butt did more than just tempt because she practically sprung back up as if she had hydraulics attached to her behind. On her feet again, she stumbled backward and slammed against the refrigerator. A mix of fright and shock danced in her wide, dark brown eyes. She frantically scanned her surroundings, he assumed for a weapon.

Honestly, he would have laughed had he been in a humorous mood.

"Wh-who are you? Wh-what do you want? I don't have any money," she said.

Money? Her money was definitely the last thing he needed. He had far more than enough of his own. And he would trade every dime to go back in time to a point when he wasn't considered public enemy number one through ten.

Gregor crossed his arms over his chest. "I think I should be asking the questions here. Seeing how you're standing in *my* kitchen."

Well, not exactly his kitchen, but she didn't know that. Or at least he hoped she didn't.

With a full-on, frontal view, Gregor got an opportunity to see the whole of Ms. Round Rump's body. She had an hourglass shape, with a few extra minutes in the hip region. In addition to being an ass man, he was a breast man, too, and hers were magnificent. But were they real? Something told him yes. It had been a long time since he'd cupped breasts that weren't man altered.

Finding her face again, his brow furrowed slightly. He was sure he'd never met her before, but oddly, she looked familiar. Then again, being an athlete, he encountered so many women that they eventually all started to resemble each other. But her... Her low, cautious tone drew him back to their confrontation.

"*Your* kitchen?" she questioned.

"That's right," he said. The kitchen had been his for the past two weeks, so he wasn't sure it could be viewed as an outright lie.

Some of the apprehension she'd displayed moments earlier faded, and she seemed surer of things now, more relaxed.

"And you are?" she asked. Her tone no longer shaky; instead, confident.

Obviously, the hoodie did a great job of masking his identity, which was perfect. No one needed to know he was here, especially the media. Another reason why getting rid of her was urgently necessary. The second she discovered who he was, she'd sell him out to the highest bidder. Just like his ex. He'd learned the hard way; women couldn't be trusted.

"A friend of Thad's." It was all she needed to know.

Keeping her distance, she eyed him as if trying to decide whether or not to believe him. "I'm Zahra Hart. A friend of Leona's."

Zahra. A friend of Thad's wife. Was that why she looked so familiar? Had he seen her at one of Thad's functions? He bet that was it. Why was he wasting his time trying to figure it out? It didn't matter who she was or how he recognized her. The only thing of importance was how to get her gone. Having her here was too risky.

"Leona offered me the place for the next couple of

weeks. However, she'd stated I would have the place to myself," she said.

The same thing Thad had told him. Had this been some kind of setup? *No.* Thad would have never done this to him, especially with everything he was going through *because* of a woman. In a hard tone, he said, "Thad gave *me* exclusive use of the house."

Her full, glossy lips curled into a smile. "Welp, it seems as if we have a problem."

"No, we don't, since you're leaving," he said. "Problem solved."

Her expression turned to a look of disbelief. "Excuse me?"

"I was here first," he said.

She gave a single humorless laugh. "*Really?* What are you, five?"

Gregor's jaw tightened, but he didn't respond. Mainly because he *had* sounded a bit childish. But he didn't care. He just wanted to be left alone to wallow in self-pity for the remainder of his time here.

With all pleasantries clearly exhausted between them, Zahra pulled her hands to her hips and eyed him sternly. "I have just as much right to be here as you, Thad's friend. And I'm staying." Her arms spread wide. "This house is large enough that we never have to lay eyes on each other again. And you can't even begin to fathom how grateful that makes me."

Well, he could say one thing about her. She had balls. "I don't have time for this. I'll leave," he said, turning to walk away.

She snickered. "Good luck at that," she muttered.

The statement felt like impending doom. Facing her again, he grumbled, "What is that supposed to mean?"

Zahra scowled at him in silence as if debating whether or not to offer him an explanation. "Captain Skip says there's a storm coming," she finally said.

"Well, it's not here now, is it?"

As if he'd wronged the universe in some severe manner, and it chose this very moment to seek revenge, rumbling sounded in the distance.

Not passing up the opportunity to rub it in his face, she said, "Hmm, did you hear that? Sounded a lot like thunder. Must be a storm rolling in."

That condescending smirk she flashed before turning and heading toward the back door revealed just how much pleasure she'd gotten out of this moment. Anger didn't bar him from copping another look at her butt. *Damn.* Another time, another place. The sound of her voice snapped him from his appraisal.

Over her shoulder, she said, "You could always swim. It's only, what, ten miles to the mainland? Give or take. I'm confident you'd make it. I'm sure your swollen ego will act as the perfect flotation device."

That mischievous glint in her eyes suggested she rooted less for him and more for the lake to open up and swallow him whole.

Chapter 2

Zahra was determined to get a cell phone signal. She desperately needed to talk to Leona and straighten this debacle out. How had she and the cloaked bandit both been granted access to the lake house at the same time? Especially when she was supposed to have the entire place to herself. But according to Mr. Crabby, so was he.

No, we don't, since you're leaving. "Arrogant bastard." Who did he think he was? And what the heck was up with the hoodie? *Creepy.* It was like he hadn't wanted her to see his face. *Mission accomplished.* Then it dawned on her. If he was a friend of Thad's, maybe he was an athlete or something. An A-lister, if he hadn't wanted her to recognize him. Her brain raked over the possibility.

The gray clouds that now filled the sky had gobbled

up the sun, noticeably dropping the temperature several degrees. Pacing the backyard in nothing but a thin sweater made her wish she'd bothered to grab the coat she'd left inside. Too bad she'd been more concerned with putting distance between her and Mr. Crabby than with warmth.

Three bars popped up on the screen, and she hurriedly dialed Leona. Zahra folded her arms across her body to generate more heat, shivering when a gusty wind kicked up.

"Zahra, I've been—"

"There's a man—a rather rude and arrogant man—wearing a creepy, oversize hoodie to hide his face standing in the kitchen," Zahra said in a whisper, as if he were within earshot.

"Oh, God, Zah, I'm so sorry. I tried to call and warn you. I had no idea my husband had offered up the place to one of his clients, as well. I'm so sorry."

So, did that make Mr. Crabby an athlete? Basketball, she'd bet. While she hadn't seen his face—other than the thick beard jutting from the hoodie—his body had been quite impressive and built for dunking a ball. Tall, solid—she dissolved the thoughts abruptly. *No, no, no, no, no.* She was not lusting over this rude, obnoxious stranger. A really delicious smelling stranger, but a stranger nonetheless. *Ugh.* She was stuck on an island with an arrogant athlete. *Just great.*

There was only one professional athlete she would even entertain being stranded with. And her luck was definitely not that good. The roar of thunder snagged

Zahra from her fantasies. It sounded much closer now. Her eyes moved heavenward. Judging by the nasty rain clouds, it wouldn't be long before the sky opened up.

"It's not your fault. Your heart was in the right place." Zahra sighed. "He's right. He was here first. I should be the one who leaves," she said, more to herself than to Leona.

"Clearly, there's just one *teeny-weeny, itsy-bitsy* additional thing I should tell you," Leona said.

"I know already."

"You do?"

Zahra ignored the hint of surprise in Leona's tone. "Yes."

"So why aren't you freaking out?"

"I mean, is that even necessary at this point? There's nothing I can do about it. Captain Skip said he wouldn't be able to get back until it passes. I think I can tolerate Mr. Crabby for twenty-four hours." Surely, she could ignore him for that long. She chose not to accept the fact that the storm could linger three to four days as Captain Skip had mentioned was a possibility.

Zahra glanced out over the water. She'd actually been looking forward to settling in here for a while. Something about the place felt right. That was, of course, before encountering Mr. Crabby. *Oh, well*. She'd just have to get as much writing done as she could before the boat returned to take her back to the mainland. Maybe she'd check into the cute lavender B&B she'd admired.

Zahra felt the first raindrop and cringed. "Leo, it's starting to rain, and I'm standing outside. Can you contact Captain Skip and let him know I'd like to be picked up as soon as safely possible?"

"Your housemate is Gregor Carter," Leona rattled off. "*Your* Gregor Carter."

Zahra went corpse still. Had Leona just said what she thought she'd said? The man she'd sparred with was Gregor *freaking* Carter. She shook her head in disbelief. *Nope.* The man she'd encountered couldn't have been *her* Gregor Carter. Her ultimate fantasy.

Heat coursed through her at the mention of the bad-boy quarterback who played for her favorite team, the Carolina Thoroughbreds. The man who'd been character inspiration for many of her books—including the one she was currently penning. The heartthrob who'd held real estate in her fantasies since Leona had arranged for him to grace the cover of her very first novel several years ago. Four-time Super Bowl champion. The best quarterback in the league. And of late, Thoroughbred fans' number one enemy.

No. Whomever she'd come toe to toe with in the house wasn't *her* Gregor. While he did have a reputation for being rash, the Gregor she'd fashioned in her head was kind, gentle, loving. Nothing like the grump she'd encountered.

She had questions, like a thousand and one of them, but her brain wouldn't send the command to speak. Instead, she turned and eyed the house. The curtains in one of the lower-level windows swayed as if Gregor had been peering out at her.

Well, at least now she understood the hoodie thing.

He really hadn't wanted to reveal his identity. After that horrible motorcycle accident, a month or so ago, he'd vanished from the public eye. Since his disappearance, the media had made all kinds of speculations concerning his whereabouts: rehab, on sabbatical, in hiding. The list went on.

In a million years they never would have guessed Lake Lamont, which was probably why he was here. In another million years, she never would have imagined winding up here with him. What were the odds? At least now she understood why he'd seemed so eager to get rid of her. He probably thought she would expose him. There was no need to worry about that. His secret location was safe with her.

Zahra couldn't believe she hadn't realized she'd been bickering with Gregor *freaking* Carter. Even without seeing his face, she should have recognized him by his body alone. God knows she'd fantasized about it enough.

Leona's garbled voice sounded over the line, drawing Zahra's attention back to the conversation. Zahra returned to her original position in hopes of regaining a stronger signal.

It worked.

"Zahra, are you there?"

"I'm here. What were you saying?"

"According to the forecast, it'll be storming for at least the next couple of days. But this could still work."

Still work?

Was Leona serious? What the woman wasn't taking

into consideration was the fact that there was a huge difference between avoiding someone for a couple of days and steering clear of them for two weeks. And not only that. The real-life Gregor had completely shattered the beautiful image she'd painted in her head of fantasy Gregor. That made her even less compelled to be near the man for *any* length of time.

Gregor stabbed Thad's telephone number into his cell phone and waited. Pulling back the curtain in his bedroom, he glared out at Zahra, chatting away on her phone. He didn't trust her. Narrowing his eyes, he pinned her with a glare. Who was she on the phone with?

When Thad's gleeful voice danced over the line, Gregor skipped a customary greeting. "Who is she?"

Several seconds of silence lingered before Thad spoke. "*Ahhh*, who is whom?"

Gregor gave it to him, he sounded genuinely confused. "The woman I found standing in my kitchen—your kitchen, the kitchen—guzzling my tea."

"I...don't know anything about any woman. Did she say who she was?"

Gregor released a heavy sigh. "Zahra something. Hoggard, Holden. Something with an H."

"Hart," Thad said plainly.

Why hadn't the man sounded surprised? "So, you do know her?" Gregor's face scrunched. "Wait. Did you—"

Thad cut in before Gregor could finish his thought. "No. Hell, no. I didn't set you up."

"Good. So, what's she doing here, man? You know my situation. If she—"

"Don't worry. I'll handle it," Thad said. "There's absolutely nothing to worry about."

That was all Gregor needed to hear. He'd worked with Thad long enough to know if he said he would handle it, he would. And in a speedy and thorough manner. The notion put Gregor at slight ease.

"No one can know I'm here. I just need room to breathe," Gregor said more to himself than to Thad.

The men chatted a couple minutes more before ending the call. Gregor tossed the device aside. He needed a drink. Hazarding another glance out the window to make sure Zahra was still there—lessening his chances of running into her again—he headed back to the kitchen. He was stuck there with her, but it didn't mean they had to interact. As long as they stayed in their respective corners, avoiding each other shouldn't be a problem.

Removing the bottle of Silver Swan Vodka from the freezer and a shot glass from the cabinet, he poured himself two fingers, downed it in one gulp and winced at the burn as the smooth liquid went down. Waiting for it to settle, the black camera bag sitting on the table caught his eye. His jaw tightened at the possible threat it posed. There were some sites that would pay thousands for a photo of him right now.

The door creaked behind him. Without bothering to acknowledge her, he poured himself another drink.

"Look… I know we got off to a rocky start, but we're kind of stuck together whether either of us like it or not."

"Not," he muttered to himself and poured another shot.

Apparently, she had the hearing of a moth because she said, "Trust me, I don't want to be here any more than you do. But we are here. Can we just please…?" Her words trailed. "Maybe we can just pretend to like each other for the next two weeks."

Next two weeks? Oh, he didn't plan to stay here a day longer than he had to. With his back still to her, he said, "I'm too old to pretend I like you. But do whatever works for you."

Zahra sighed heavily behind him. Why wasn't she tearing into him? Before she'd gone outside, she'd been poised to sever his jugular with her teeth. So why was she being so cordial now? What was she up to? He lifted his glass.

"I don't like all of this animosity," she said. "We're both—"

Gregor slammed the glass onto the counter before it reached his lips. Finally turning to face her, he said, "I have an idea. I'll *pretend* you don't exist, and you can do the same."

Chapter 3

Zahra was determined day two at the lake house would go far better than the day before had gone. If she encountered Gregor, she would just kill him with kindness. She had this. No way would she let a man, especially this man, get under her skin. Oh, she wasn't unsympathetic to him. She knew of his recent troubles, the accident, and she had a soft spot for those kicked in the gut by life. But she wouldn't let pity shift her equilibrium.

A boom of thunder shook the house, causing her to yelp. Staring out of the window, she shivered at the sight of the dark skies. Torrential rain had started to fall yesterday, and hadn't let up one bit. Now she understood why no boats could operate during this mess. And it was only supposed to get worse, according to the news report she'd watched that morning.

Before heading downstairs, she checked her cell phone to see if she had any bars. *Nothing.* Releasing a heavy sigh, she tossed the device onto the bed and made a mental note to look into switching carriers. It made no sense that she had to trek around the yard in a hundred different directions just to locate a signal.

She recalled Captain Skip saying reception was spotty, but this was ridiculous. Especially when she desperately needed to call her sister and vent. *Wow.* How the tables had turned.

Zahra came to a screeching halt when she entered the kitchen. Gregor was there, the entire jug of milk pressed to his lips. While he wore the same creepy hoodie as the day before, it was no longer cloaking his face.

On television she'd only ever seen him with close-cropped hair. Now, he sported a head full of glossy, dark curls. The kind you wanted to run your fingers through. Gathering her common sense—and jaw off the floor from his display of poor etiquette—she said, "Oh, my God. What are you doing?"

Gregor pulled the milk jug from his full lips. Turning his back on her, he snapped the hood over his head. "Tending to my business. You should try it. It works well if you do it right."

Asshole. "You're drinking from the *entire* jug of milk?" Her face scrunched. "That's disgusting. You do know there are plenty of glasses in the cabinet, right? I can get you one, if you'd like."

As if for spite, Gregor tipped the jug to his lips again and took a long swig, lowered it, dragged the back of his large hand across his mouth and released a satisfying, *"Ahhh."*

"No need," he said, returning the container to the fridge. "I'm done."

Kill him with kindness. Kill him with… Just kill him. "What if at some point I'd wanted to drink milk?"

"There's plenty left." He brushed past her. "Knock yourself out."

More like, knock you out. She swung around. "I don't want any of it now. I have no idea where your mouth's been."

Gregor backtracked, moving dangerously too close for comfort, but she didn't let it rattle her. Dang, he smelled good. *Ugh.* No, he didn't. He smelled horrible…in the best way imaginable. This proved it. She was insane.

"I'll tell you where my mouth's been if you really want to know."

All kinds of mischief danced in his eyes, causing her cheeks to heat. "Spare me the raunchy details. I'm pretty sure I couldn't stomach them."

Gregor eyed her long and hard. Still, she didn't waver. His eyes glinted with what she translated as distaste. A moment later, he smirked, rolled his eyes and moved away.

Self-absorbed bastard. With an apparent obsession with hoodies.

Zahra questioned if it was possible to go from absolutely adoring someone to completely loathing them in a matter of days. She hard-stared at Gregor's back. *Yes!* Yes, it was.

Assessing the situation, her lips ticked up into a cunning smile as she recalled how her mother had handled things when she'd caught her father drinking from the milk carton once. They still laughed about it to this day. Maybe Gregor Carter needed a similar lesson.

Gregor didn't usually partake in midnight snacking, but the chocolate chip cookies and ice-cold milk were calling his name. At the mention of the milk, he laughed at how bent out of shape his house pest had gotten when she'd caught him drinking from the jug. If she'd wanted milk, she should have brought her own. "This is all mine," he said, pushing aside the bag of jalapeño peppers to remove the milk from the fridge.

Forgoing the use of a glass, he popped the top and tossed the container back. The instant he lowered it away from his mouth, he knew something was wrong.

"What the...?"

His lips were on fire. Two long strides carried him to the sink, where he turned the water on full blast and positioned his mouth underneath the stream of cold water. After several minutes, he experienced relief. But his lips still tingled. She did this. He growled to himself, certain Zahra was responsible for his lava lips.

After drying his mouth and beard, he placed the jug under his nose and took a whiff. The pungent smell caused him to draw back and cringe. "What is that?"

Whatever it was, it was hot as hell. Then it hit him. The jalapeño peppers he'd moved to get to the milk. Since his stomach wasn't burning, she must have only rubbed the pepper along the rim of the jug. Gregor snarled toward the stairs. Who the hell was this devious woman?

Making haste up the steps, he banged on Zahra's bedroom door like the law. If it scared her, it would serve her right for such vicious—yet stellar—payback. The prankster in him had to appreciate and commend her efforts, because this was something he would have done to one of his teammates—or something one of them would have done to him.

But the fun-loving Prankster Gregor was just Irritated Gregor now. She didn't know him well enough to pull such antics anyway.

The door flung open, and Zahra stood wild-eyed in front of him. Judging by her disheveled appearance— clothing backward, hair flying in several different directions, bewildered expression—he had startled her. Good.

"What's wrong? Is there a tornado?"

When he saw genuine fear in her eyes, he almost felt sorry for the way he'd hammered on her door. Almost. "What the hell did you do to my milk?"

Her face scrunched into a tight ball. "Your milk?" She was either attempting to play dumb, or she was still a bit disconcerted by his visit.

"Does jalapeño peppers ring a bell?" he asked.

Obviously, recollection set in, because she had the

audacity to snicker, then smirk. "Did things get a little hot in here?" Laughter followed her statement.

Oh, so she thought it was funny? Well, this meant war.

Unable to return to sleep again after Gregor had pounded on her door like a madman, Zahra popped open her laptop and finished typing a new chapter. With her creativity fueled by the grouch downstairs, her words flowed. At least he served one good purpose. He gave her great fodder to work with. At this rate, she'd finish this book ahead of schedule.

But not tonight. Well, this morning since it was already after one o'clock. Her eyelids felt as if they weighed a thousand pounds apiece. It was time to call it. Plus, she needed all of her energy to deal with her nemesis.

Clearly, he hadn't thought the jalapeño thing had been funny. That was okay. It had been meant as more of a lesson than a prank. The look in his eyes as he left her door suggested his payback was imminent. She wasn't worried. She could handle whatever he tossed at her.

Undressing, she climbed into bed and hoped to resume the good sleep she'd been getting before the rude awakening. *"Yes,"* she moaned, snuggling under the layers of warmth. This was exactly what her body needed.

The second her head hit the pillow, she was out. At first, she thought the sound of Tupac's voice was in her dreams. As she gradually became more lucid, she realized the blaring music came from downstairs.

Frazzled, she eyed the clock. *Three eighteen.* She growled. *Gregor.* Clearly, this was his payback. No way would she give him the satisfaction of believing he'd defeated her. She slammed back down onto the mattress and covered her head with a pillow. She'd show him.

After an hour of Tupac's greatest hits, Zahra couldn't take another lyric. Dragging herself from the bed, she slid into her pants, pulled her shirt over her head, then padded across the icy floor and out of the room.

It wasn't until she was standing in front of Gregor's door did she realize she'd put her shirt on backward. Her first thought was to ignore it, but if she was to appear stern, she couldn't confront him looking disheveled.

As fate would have it, the second the fabric was off her body, the gateway to hell opened. Zahra screeched, then turned. "Close your eyes," she said, scrambling to get the shirt over her head. Of all times for her to have forgone wearing a bra. Fate really did hate her.

Finally pulling it together, she took a deep breath and turned. The air in her lungs came out like a puff when her eyes slammed into Gregor's bare, glistening chest. Forgetting she loathed him, her eyes homed in on his impressive torso.

An intricately designed tattoo covered his entire right pec, connected to more ink on his shoulder and extended halfway down his arm. His left pec held a roaring lion's head. The artwork was phenomenal. And so was the canvas. Her eyes locked on to the single bead of sweat that ran down the center of his chest. Had he been dancing or working out?

As if they had a mind of their own, her eyes trailed to the thin line of fine black hairs that disappeared beyond his designer boxers. She swallowed hard.

Snapping from her stupor, her gaze shot up to meet his. All she could do was stare stupidly. His hair was pulled back into a man bun. And damn, did it look sexy as hell on him. Though most of it was covered by his beard, the scar he'd been rumored to have acquired in the accident was visible. Had this been the reason for the hoodie? Was he self-conscious? A cunning expression played on his face like he knew she was checking him out. Heck, it wasn't like she'd done a good job of masking her admiration. Kind of hard to appear unyielding when you were drooling.

Gregor propped himself against the doorjamb, folded his sculpted arms across his chest and studied her hard. The longer he eyed her with that assessing stare, the more anxious she grew.

"Are you here to apologize?" he said.

"*Apologize?* I'm not the one blaring music at three in the morning when someone is trying to sleep. So, what would I have to apologize about?"

"Spiking my milk."

His milk? Arrogant *and* selfish. Why wasn't she surprised that he felt solely entitled to it? "I'm assuming you'll be apologizing for contaminating *our* milk."

Gregor's eyes narrowed. A beat later, he backed into the room and slammed the door in her face. A millisecond later, he cranked up the volume. "Hail Mary" rumbled the walls. She typically loved Tupac, but not at this moment.

"Asshole," she muttered, retreating back to her room. "Asshole," she repeated in a yell this time. Stomping up the stairs, she ground her teeth. "I've got your 'Hail Mary.'"

Inside her bedroom, she paced. God, she couldn't wait to be rid of him. The man was unbearable. If only she could do something to—a mischievous grin curled one side of her mouth. The way the music vibrated the entire house, it definitely wasn't coming from a computer or a cell phone.

Sliding into her shoes and shrugging into her coat, she grabbed her phone and crept back downstairs. Exiting the back door, Zahra used the light of her cell phone to guide her. She hoped the device truly was waterproof as the manufacturer had claimed. The wind swayed her steps and rain pelted her body. She could have really used an umbrella and lead feet—to anchor her to the ground—but didn't allow the lack of either to stop her.

It seemed like forever before she found the breaker box. Popping it open, she dried her hands best she could and prayed she didn't electrocute herself. Locating the circuit associated with Gregor's bedroom, she switched it off. The music stopped instantly.

Score.

Chapter 4

Zahra's fingers moved a mile a minute across her keyboard. She channeled all the frustration Gregor had drawn to the surface into a scene where her heroine was ripping the hero a new one for being the most obnoxious bastard she'd ever met.

This story was starting to mimic her current situation. Instead of her hero and heroine being housemates, they were new neighbors. It wasn't Tupac that had awakened the heroine, it was Otis Redding. And instead of shutting off the power, she'd called the police.

Speaking of malicious acts, why hadn't Gregor confronted her about the breaker? No doubt it had probably pissed him off. She seemed good at doing that. Maybe he'd been too angry to confront her. Then again, he was most likely just biding his time. Plotting the ultimate revenge. It was probably wise to keep an eye open.

Zahra's stomach growled, reminding her she hadn't eaten anything since breakfast, when she'd gone downstairs just long enough to grab a piece of fruit. Playing nice, she'd chosen to give Gregor "McCrabby" the run of the house. Plus, she didn't have the energy to spar with him.

She turned her head to one side to eye the clock. *Eight.* Starving, she decided to take a chance that the coast was clear now. Swinging her legs over the side of the bed, she planted her feet onto the floor. Even through her socks, the icy hardwood assaulted her. The thermostat definitely needed to be adjusted.

On the steps a few seconds later, Zahra almost turned around and retreated back up the stairs when the glow of the television radiating from the family room suggested Gregor was there. Why was she in hiding like some coward, anyway?

Highlights of the Thoroughbreds' playoff game showed on the screen. Man, that had been a hard loss. How could Gregor bear to watch it? Because of his accident and missing the important game, everyone had blamed him for squandering their chance at the Super Bowl Championship. To villainize him had been unfair. As was to blame him for his teammates not bringing their A-game. To put it nicely, they'd sucked.

Zahra recalled the countless fumbles and interceptions. It was like they hadn't even tried without Gregor. None of that had been his fault. One man shouldn't be tasked or expected to carry an entire team—despite how good said man was. And Gregor was good. Great, even. Her father's voice played in her head. *That boy was born to carry a football.* She agreed.

Continuing down, she assumed Gregor was stretched out on the sofa because she didn't see him. Rolling her eyes away from the room, she veered toward the thermostat. *Sixty-two!* No wonder she was freezing. She glared toward the family room. He was behind this. Obviously, the devil needed a cooldown.

Bumping it up several degrees, she turned to walk away but slammed into a wall of rock-hard muscle. Zahra was sure Gregor hadn't meant to touch her, let alone wrap one of his strong arms around her waist and pull her close to his solid frame. His action wasn't one she felt violated her. It actually seemed more like a protective instinct to keep her from falling. The move had taken her so much by surprise that she froze in place. Admittedly, it wasn't such a bad position to be in.

Even without the mask of the hoodie, Zahra wasn't sure she would have recognized him still. The full beard—also new—made him appear distinguished. And good Lord, why did he have to smell so damn good all the time?

Even with the scar on his face, he was still one of the most handsome men she'd ever laid eyes on.

The heat generated from their closeness melted away some of her disdain for him. His light brown gaze held her captive as they stood and stared in silence. His expression was soft, gentle, yielding. It confused her.

No man's touch had ever felt so good. Especially a man who, she would gamble to say, hated her. A tingling sensation started in the palm of the hand that rested on his chestnut-brown skin, moved up her arm, over her shoulders, through her chest, down to the junction between her thighs and exploded, sending a surge of pulsating desire racing through her entire body.

Snapping out of the trance induced by Gregor's touch, scent and presence, she pulled out of his hold, confused by the reaction she'd had to him. There had definitely been a spark. Then again, what woman wouldn't have had a response to being in Gregor Carter's strong arms? He was all physically-fit, hard-bodied man.

His kind expression hardened slightly. Obviously, the old Gregor had returned.

"What are you doing?" he asked.

It took Zahra a moment to find her words. "Adjusting the thermostat."

"Why?"

"Because it's cold in here."

"It's comfortable."

"It's cold."

Gregor's eyes scanned over the thin pajama pants and matching spaghetti-strap top she wore. "Maybe you should put on some more clothes."

"Yeah? Well, maybe you should take yours off." It took Zahra only a second to realize the implication of what she'd said. That had definitely not come out as intended. Needing to distract from her blunder, she said, "You know what? Fine, I apologize. I apologize for the milk. I apologize for crashing your pity party. I apologize for inhaling the same air as the almighty Gregor freaking Carter." She did some crazy zigzag with her arms.

Instead of responding, he eyed the thermostat. "Seventy-eight. Are you trying to commit murder by heat-stroke?"

Was that a hint of a smile on his face? So, he did have a sense of humor. "Yes," she said with a fair amount of humor in her tone.

Gregor folded his arms across his chest, tightening the muscles at his biceps and causing them to swell like melons. "Can we compromise?" he asked.

Compromise? Wait. What was happening here? Was Gregor, dare she say it, being cordial to her? Apparently, someone had been dipping into the vodka bottle she'd placed in the freezer earlier after it had been left sitting out. However, she hadn't smelled any alcohol on his breath. And they had been pretty close. Temptingly, tantalizingly, torturously close.

Never being one to bite her tongue, she mimicked his stance and narrowed her eyes at him. "Why are you being nice to me? Are you trying to knock me off guard, then exact your revenge for the power thing?"

"It had crossed my mind," he said. Gregor shrugged one sculpted shoulder. "I'm being nice because I'm a nice guy."

To that, Zahra tilted her head to the side and arched her brows before barking a single, humorless laugh. Yeah, he had to be wasted on something to have forgotten the way he'd treated her the past couple of days. "You're going to have to do better than that. And make it believable this time." She held up her hand when Gregor's lips parted. "On second thought, never mind. I'm really not interested in whatever lie you're about to tell." She turned to walk away.

"Chamomile tea," he said.

She stopped. What did her favorite tea have to do with anything? Facing him, she said, "What?"

"Several years ago, you gave me a cup of chamomile tea when I was nervous about taking my shirt off in a room full of people for a photo shoot."

Instantly, the memory filtered into her head. The very first time they'd met. How could she have forgotten that? He'd been so quiet, so humble. A far cry from who he was now. Or should she say whom she felt he pretended to be for the public. She wasn't wholly convinced that meek man she'd photographed several years ago didn't still exist under all the layers of arrogance Gregor now wore. Then again, fame had a way of ruining people. But there was an understated gentleness about him that suggested it hadn't completely consumed him.

She flashed a lazy smile. "You remember that, huh?"

"Actually, Thad helped to jog my memory when we spoke earlier today."

The oddest question popped into her head. "Did the tea work?" Because she recalled him working the camera like a pro.

"No, but your kindness did. I wasn't used to peo-ple…" His words trailed. "It helped a lot."

Her gaze slid away briefly, unsure how to handle this far-more-pleasant Gregor. This could all be some kind of ploy. "You weren't the only nervous one that day. My hands were shaking so bad, I'm surprised we got any usable shots." Tea hadn't helped her either. With the combination of her inexperience behind the camera and Gregor's presence, she'd been a bundle of nerves.

"Why were you nervous?" he asked.

The question took her by surprise. She certainly couldn't reveal that the sight of him shirtless had sent her system spiraling out of control. Back then, all he would have had to do was blow on her and her clothes would have fallen off. Now… Well, now, she wanted to believe she was less *impressionable* than she had been at twenty-seven.

"I was fairly new to photography. Leona somehow convinced my publisher to let me do the shoot." She shrugged. "Probably because it saved them money. It didn't hurt that you were a swiftly rising star."

"You wanted me."

Zahra jolted. "Wh-what? Wanted you? I…I didn't want you."

Gregor pushed his brows together. "Thad told me you were responsible for me getting the gig. That you specifically requested me."

Understanding set in. "Oh. *Ohhh*. You meant…" A nervous laugh slid past her lips. "Um, yes. Yes, I did request you. Since it was a football romance, I thought having you on the cover would be a nice touch."

"That cover landed me several endorsement deals. I suppose I should thank you."

"You're welcome. Though I'm not sure I should take credit for your ability to work the hell out of a camera."

A beat of less-daunting silence played between them. Gregor's eyes trailed to her lips, causing a wave of anxiousness to wash over her.

"What did you think I meant?" he asked.

Playing dumb, she said, "About?" Knowing full well he was referring to her response to his *you wanted me* comment.

He chuckled. Thankfully, he didn't push the issue. She was certain he knew exactly what she'd been thinking.

Gregor slid his hands into his jeans pocket. "About that compromise."

"Seventy-seven point five," she said.

"Seventy-four," he countered.

"Seventy-six."

"Seventy-five. And I'll keep my clothes on."

Fifty and you take them all off. Of course, she kept that to herself. She pretended to consider the offer for a moment before jutting out her hand. "Deal."

The second they touched, a familiar sensation blossomed in her palm. While she hadn't been able to read Gregor's expression before, it translated loud and clear now. Ambiguity crinkled his features. Yep, he'd felt it, too. And like her was probably trying to figure out what it meant. Energy this intense had to represent something, right? She wasn't sure she liked the list of possibilities.

Reclaiming her hand, she pointed over her shoulder. "I should—"

Gregor's eyes lowered to her mouth again. This was so confusing. Was the same man who she was sure would have dropped-kicked her off the island mere hours ago fantasizing about kissing her?

Yes, he was. And the idea thrilled her.

Gregor eyed the clock again—the tenth time in the past hour—and groaned. Why in the hell was he still wide-awake at three in the morning? That was easily answered. *Zahra*. Ever since he'd learned of the past he and Zahra shared, his attitude toward her had changed. Why couldn't he stop thinking about her?

How could he have not instantly recognized her? Her hair was different now—much longer than the short style she'd once sported—and she'd gained a few pounds, but still… The woman had played a huge part in his success. That book cover had single-handedly made him a sex symbol. He'd become a fantasy for women all over the world.

How could he have forgotten all about that day? Ah, he remembered. Zahra had rejected him. That had never happened before and hadn't happened since. It still puzzled him why she'd flat-out said no to his dinner invitation. Like she'd said earlier, he'd been a rising star. Women flocked to him. Then and still.

The attraction he'd had to the kindhearted woman came rushing back. She'd done everything she could to make him feel comfortable in such an awkward situation. Back in those days, he wasn't as comfortable as he was now with taking off his clothes in front of a crowd of people.

What would have happened had she said yes?

I would have ruined her.

Back then, he hadn't been the man a mother would have been proud of. Fidelity hadn't been too high on his list of priorities. He hadn't been the man he was now. But while he'd changed considerably, his playboy label still haunted him. It had caused a lot of problems in his relationship with Selene.

An image of his ex popped into his head. She'd stabbed him in the heart with the heel of one of those red-bottom shoes she coveted. His thoughts drifted to the night he'd found her in bed with her ex. One minute he'd been all smiles and excitement about surprising Selene for her birthday, the next he was laid up in the hospital, waiting to learn if he'd ever play football again.

That night still gave him chills. Until that night, he hadn't given much thought to mortality, especially his own. He did now, along with the fact that he would probably die alone. No wife, no kids, no family. There were his foster brothers, but he hadn't done a good job of staying in contact with them. Roth had his growing family. Lauder had his, plus life as a senator. And his own hectic lifestyle.

Zahra's face flashed into his head.

A relationship and love were the furthest things from his mind right now, but he had to admit that the accident had him thinking about things he hadn't thought much about before. He recalled staring around the empty hospital room after the accident, no one there to hold his hand and comfort him. It had saddened him.

Honestly, he could marry tomorrow, if he wanted that. He didn't. A bought marriage didn't appeal to him. A union should be built on love and trust. *Got to have trust.* Admittedly, it would be nice to meet a woman who didn't care about his fame and cared even less about his fortune. Someone who saw Gregor Carter— foster kid, mentor, average guy—not Gregor Carter, pro-baller, money machine or career booster. Beneath all the lights, the action, he just wanted a normal life.

He laughed to himself. Who the hell was he kidding? He'd kissed a normal life goodbye the day he signed his first multimillion-dollar contract. He bet Zahra had a life close to perfect. Family who cared. Friends who expected nothing from her but loyalty.

Did she have someone waiting at home for her? If so, what would they think about her being here with him? Well, she wasn't exactly there with him like that, on some secret rendezvous. And it wasn't like he even wanted to be here with her.

So why had he told Thad he would ride out the remaining two weeks?

Chapter 5

The howling wind drew Zahra away from the memory of the dirtiest, freakiest, most beautifully exhilarating dream she'd ever had. The one that had forced her out of bed and downstairs to write at four that morning. The head-flick had starred her and none other than Gregor freaking Carter.

She groaned at the fact that the dream of his making love to her had actually brought her to an orgasm. This hadn't been the first time he'd invaded her sleep; however, it had been the first time it had felt so real that she'd bolted up in bed and eyed the space beside her, convinced he was there.

While the entire ordeal had irked her, it had provided fodder for one of the best chapters and love scenes she'd written, thus far. She eyed the clock illuminating on the microwave. 7:00 a.m. Had she really been at it for three hours? Her stiff neck and tired fingers told her she had.

Pushing away from the table where she'd set up shop, she stood to stretch. Her legs instantly confirmed the amount of time she'd sat there. Making her way across the room, she filled the Keurig machine with fresh water, popped in a pod and pressed brew.

As she waited, her eyes were trained on the doorway leading into the room, almost expecting Gregor to be there. Maybe even hoping.

In her fantasies, Gregor was harmless. In real life he was anything but. Over the years, she'd watched his antics—oftentimes outlandish—play out on TV. Another immature man should be the least of her desires. However, the Gregor in the bedroom down the hall was in stark contrast to the flashy, boisterous man who mocked referees and danced in the end zone.

Unfortunately, the more she tried not to think about Gregor, the more ferocious his presence became. Why did she always do this? Why was she always drawn to men who were no good for her? Maybe her sister, Ava, had been right when she'd stated Zahra was a magnet for assholes.

Laughing at the ridiculous accusation, she grabbed her cup of coffee, strolled to the back door and glanced out at the angry water. Would she ever get to leave this place? The windstorm they'd been experiencing since yesterday had the lake in an uproar. Rough waves slammed into the dock, causing it to sway erratically.

Something in the distance caught her eye. She squinted to bring it into better focus. She gasped. "Oh, no." The coffee sloshed from the cup when she slammed it onto the counter. The hot liquid burned her fingers, but that didn't faze her. Dashing out the back door, she rushed toward the water, determined to save him.

"Ninety-six...97..."

Gregor stopped mid-push-up when he thought he heard yelling. Blaming it on the wind that had howled all night, he started again, only to be interrupted a second time. Coming to his feet, he peeked out the window to see Zahra wading through the water.

"What the hell is she doing?" he whispered to himself.

The angry waves thrashed her from side to side. It stunned him that she remained upright. Despite the water's rage, she kept moving farther into the lake. A beat later, an upsurge toppled her over, her body disappearing under the rough waters.

He sprinted from the room, down the hall and out the back door, pushing his ankle to the limit. He didn't allow the discomfort to sway him. By the time he made it to the water's edge, Zahra had resurfaced, giving him an uncanny degree of relief. The water should have jarred him when he entered it wearing nothing but a sleeveless undershirt, jogging pants and limited-edition sneakers he'd paid close to four hundred dollars for, but it didn't. *Adrenaline*, he told himself.

When he reached a listless Zahra, he pulled her into his arms and held her as snuggly to his chest as an intercepted football. The sensations that zapped through him electrified his entire body. He was stunned that the current hadn't fried them both.

"I got you," he said in a voice he barely recognized.

"Save…" She drew in a deep breath. "Save him, please."

Save him? Was there someone else out there? Gregor's eyes swept the lake's surface so fast it took his brain a moment to catch up and inform him he'd seen something. He narrowed his eyes and scrutinized something bobbing in the distance.

Was that…a dog? It was, and it was fighting to stay afloat.

"Can you make it to shore?" he asked.

Coughing, she nodded. "Yes."

"Go, now," he ordered, then took off toward the distressed animal without giving much thought to his own safety.

Even with his strong swimming skills, the treacherous waters proved to be a challenge. Thankfully, he reached the animal. The dog didn't put up a fuss when he cradled it in his arms. Utilizing what he'd learned as a lifeguard, he got them both to safety.

Zahra bound into the water again, this time wrapping an arm around his waist in an effort to assist him out of the water. Instinctively, he draped an arm around her shoulders. On shore, he wanted to drop to his knees and recoup for a moment, but he refused to show that level of weakness.

Zahra stood directly in front of him, her hair soaked and dripping, her clothes clinging to her trembling body. This was so not the time to imagine stripping her out of them.

"Are you okay?" she asked, concern gleaming in her cautious eyes.

He nodded, then lowered his gaze to the dog, not wanting to get sucked in by her show of compassion. The wet, shivering animal tilted its brown head upward and eyed him. The creature seemed to be expressing gratitude through its wary-eyed gaze.

"You're okay, boy," he said. It whimpered, then rested its tiny head against his chest. "You're safe now." The dog had to be no more than fifteen pounds. How in the world had this little thing survived out there? When he glanced up, Zahra was looking at him in a weird manner. "What?"

"Nothing. I think he likes you," she said.

There was something, but he didn't press it. "It seems *she* does. I tend to have that effect on women. All this natural charm." Zahra scoffed, leading him to believe she didn't recognize his magnetism at all. Well, she would be the first woman in years unfazed by him. "What were you thinking about risking your life like that?" he said, addressing the danger she'd placed herself in. "You could have died out there."

"I didn't know you cared."

"I don't. Your death would have just given the media something else to hound me about," he said with a decent amount of humor present in his tone.

"I'm glad to see you value human life over your own discomfort."

Her lips ticked up into a delectable smile, and his

eyes fixed on her mouth. For some reason, he felt an insatiable need to taste her.

"Um, we should get inside and out of these wet clothes before we both catch pneumonia," Zahra said, breaking his concentration.

At the mention of removing clothes, his eyes lowered to her soaked shirt. The muscles in his stomach clenched tight when he realized she wasn't wearing a bra. Her dark areolae glowed from beneath the fabric and her hardened nipples beamed bright with blinding temptation. "There you go again trying to get me out of my clothes," he said.

"Ha! You wish."

Yes, he did. "What are we going to do with her?"

"Well, we can't leave her out here." She shrugged. "I guess we'll just have to bring her inside. Warm her up. Feed her."

He nodded in agreement, and they sloshed toward the back door.

Zahra ironed her hands up and down her arms. Her teeth chattered when she spoke. "Y-you're limping. Y-your ankle, is it o-okay?"

"It's been better," he said. "But I'll live."

"Good."

Good? That surprised him. He was sure she would have preferred he froze to death.

Inside, the bundle of wet fur went easily to Zahra. Oddly, he missed her in his arms. What in the hell was happening to him? Since coming into contact with Zahra, he'd been experiencing things that made little sense to him. Like what had transpired between them in the water. Had she felt the surge of electricity, too?

"I'll tend to her while you go and change," Zahra said.

"What about you?" he asked. "You're wet, too." He fought against the erotic images attempting to barge their way into his psyche. The struggle to not lower his eyes to her chest again proved just as difficult.

"I want to get her settled first. You've had a traumatic episode, isn't that right?" she asked the dog in an animated voice.

Why was she so invested in this animal? And why on God's green earth would she risk her life to save it? Then again, why had he?

"Do you like hot chocolate?" Zahra asked.

Gregor thought she was addressing the dog until she glanced up at him. Did he like hot chocolate? That was like asking him if he loved playing football. The answer would always be hell yes. For him, drinking the beverage always brought back good memories of his childhood. The few he had.

"Yeah, I do, actually."

"Good. I'll make us some. That's if you're not opposed to drinking hot chocolate with me. I don't want to force you into anything."

"I think I'll survive." He flashed a half smile, then headed out of the room.

"For the record, you're not that bad after all, Gregor Carter. Arrogant, yes. Obnoxious, absolutely. But you're okay."

Appreciating her words, he tossed a "Thank you," over his shoulder.

"You're welcome. See, pretending we like each other's not that hard after all, right?"

"Who's pretending?" he said, disappearing around the corner. He did like her. Who wouldn't? She risked her life for a drowning dog.

Inside the bedroom, Gregor stripped out of everything except his underwear, then shivered at the chill that kissed his bones. Tossing the drenched clothing aside, he headed toward the bathroom, but stopped at the sound of scratching at the door. When he opened it, dark, innocent eyes stared up at him. "Hey, girl." He knelt and tussled the dog's damp fur. "What are you doing here? Couldn't live without me, huh?"

Gregor lifted his new buddy into his arms and moved back into the room, chatting with the animal as if it understood every single word he was saying. He would have never classified himself as a dog lover, but this one was growing on him. Maybe they now had a connection. He had saved her life.

Sensing someone behind him, Gregor's eyes rose to the mirror to see Zahra, lips parted, standing in the doorway. Instead of turning, he watched as her eyes roamed over his body: legs, butt, back, shoulders. She assessed him so thoroughly, it warmed his damp, chilly skin.

When their gazes collided in the reflection of the mirror, they held for a long, intense, sexually charged moment. He turned to face her because, again, he was no longer that bashful man he'd been years ago. Her eyes performed a slow perusal down his body, stopping at his crotch.

"Did you need something?" he asked.

"Yes."

A second later, she jerked as if she'd realized just how sensual her tone had been. Her eyes darted up to meet his. "N-no. No. Absolutely not. I don't want anything from you. Why would you ask something so ridiculous?"

Gregor's brow furrowed. "I didn't. I asked if you *needed* something, since you're standing in my doorway staring at me. I'm not sure why you heard *want*. Unless, of course—"

"I neither need nor want anything from you. I simply came in search of Waterspout. I turned my back for only a second and she was gone."

His brows bunched in confusion. "Waterspout?"

"The dog. The name seemed fitting."

"You do know she probably belongs to someone on the island and already has a name."

"I do. But since she doesn't have a collar on to tell us said name, she's Waterspout for now."

"She wandered in here." As he passed *Waterspout* to her, their hands grazed. Zahra flinched. They eyed each other for what felt like an eternity. Needing to break free of her hold and the thick veil of sexual tension, he said, "Was there anything else? I'm kind of freezing. I need to take a hot shower."

Which was a lie, because just the sight of Zahra in the snug-fitting top and curve-hugging jeans she now wore raised his temperature dangerously high. And if he didn't push away the image of her naked and underneath him, she'd really get a show.

"I'm about to whip something up for breakfast. Are you hungry?"

Hot chocolate *and* breakfast? He folded his arms across his chest. Zahra's eyes lowered briefly to his biceps, then found his gaze again. "Depends," he said.

"On?"

"Whether or not you can cook."

A slow smile curled her lips. "My sister and I spent summers with our old-school, Southern grandmother who cooked like every day was Thanksgiving. I was raised by traditionally Southern parents who rarely allowed us to eat fast food. I can handle myself in the kitchen quite well, Mr. Carter."

For a moment, Gregor envied Zahra. The mention of a sibling, grandmother, parents, reminded him of what he'd craved growing up. A family. "We'll see," he said. "I don't play when it comes to my food."

"We shall." Her eyes lowered to his mouth for only a second, before she turned to leave. "I'll let you get that shower."

Gregor peered out into the hallway and ogled Zahra as she glided down the hall. He didn't retreat when she tossed a half glance over her shoulder, presumably to see if he was watching her walk away. Yes, he was. Unapologetically, at that. Her hips swayed as if they were moving to some unheard melody.

While he doubted she would ever admit it, there was something Zahra Hart wanted. Him. He wanted her, too.

Chapter 6

Those back muscles.

The chest.

That bulge.

That imprint against Gregor's black boxers gave Zahra heart palpitations. By the looks of things—and she'd looked hard—the man was heavenly endowed. And she'd never thought of herself as a tattoo person, but the sight of them on him did something to her.

She eyed Waterspout stretched out at her feet. "This is all your fault."

Waterspout's head rose. She tilted it to one side and perked her ears as if to say, "My fault?"

"Yes, your fault," Zahra said in response. "Had you not wandered off, I would have never been exposed to Gregor's hard, firm, delicious body," she said in a whisper. "I saved your life. Kind of." Gregor had done most of the heavy lifting.

In those tantalizing moments she'd stood toe to toe with him, she's most certainly had wanted him. And he'd known it.

Ugh.

Nope, nope, nope, nope, nope. She would not allow that man to get to or inside her. Still, heat pooled between her legs at the thought of making love to Gregor. If he handled the female body the way he handled a football— and something told her he did—he could ruin a woman for other men.

The idea of being ruined by Gregor was far too appealing. "*Legs closed*, Zahra."

"Do you always do that?"

Zahra's attention snapped to Gregor. The burgundy sleeveless T-shirt he wore, displaying those cannonball arms of his, yanked her good sense for a moment. "Do what?"

"Talk to yourself."

Her breath hitched for a moment. Had he heard her lusting over him? "Sometimes I need expert advice," she said. To deviate from the subject, she pointed to a mug. "Your hot chocolate is ready."

Gregor retrieved the mug, took a whiff, then a sip. Then another. "Damn. This is the best hot chocolate I've ever tasted." He brought the mug to his lips again. "I hope there's more."

"Plenty." After Gregor finished a second serving

of hot chocolate, she slid an onion toward him, then a knife. "Here you go."

He stood beside her. "What am I supposed to do with this?"

"Chop the onion."

He barked a laugh. "I don't cook. I have people for that."

Zahra rested a hand on her hip. "Well, unless you can pull said *people* from those black sweatpants, you chop."

"Has anyone ever told you that you're a little bit on the bossy side?"

She shrugged. "Once or twice. But I like to think of it as having keen leadership skills. Let me guess, you're used to a submissive woman?"

"I'm used to a woman who prefers to shop rather than cook."

"I'm sorry to hear that. I'm also guessing she didn't feel she had to cook. You've got people for that, remember?"

Gregor chuckled, then commenced chopping the onion. Clearly, he'd had some experience in the kitchen, because he handled the onion like a pro. Zahra tried her best to ignore the way his forearm muscles flexed each time he cut into the onion. God, his arms were beautiful. His entire body was beautiful, in a drive-a-woman-a-fool type of way.

"What?"

Gregor's voice brought Zahra back to reality. "Nothing. Just admiring your…chopping skills. They're impressive."

"I haven't always had people. At The Cardinal House…"

Gregor's words dried up as if he'd realized he was

about to say too much. His eyes slid back to the onion. Too late. He'd stirred her curiosity.

"The Cardinal House?"

He studied her a second or two before finally saying, "A group home. I grew up in foster care."

When he turned away, Zahra assumed this was a subject he didn't particularly like to talk about, so, she didn't push. Focusing on the potato in front of her, she said, "Sooo, I may have mentioned to Leona that I would be staying for the next two weeks."

"You were offered the place, too, which means you have just as much right to be here as I do. We'll make it work."

Zahra was sure surprise showed on her face. Seemed someone had experienced a change of heart toward her. Wait. Something occurred to her. *We'll.* He'd said *we'll* make it work. "You're staying, too?" flew out before she could catch it.

"Do you have a problem with that?" he asked.

No, but she should have. "I was never the one with the problem, remember?"

"That's arguable," he said.

"Shall we argue it?" she shot back.

One corner of his mouth curved into a sexy smile that drew Zahra's full attention. Yep, she definitely should have a problem with him staying. Oh, the delicious trouble she could get into with this man.

"I think we already have, and I'm pretty sure I lost," he said.

Zahra laughed and so did Gregor, each returning to their task.

"What's up with the camera?" Gregor asked.

She eyed the black camera bag sitting on the counter. "I don't plan on snapping pictures of you and selling them, if that's what you're thinking."

"It had crossed my mind."

And with good reason, she thought. "I love capturing pictures anywhere I go. I have a small studio in NoDa. North Davidson and Thirty-Sixth," she said for clarification, but was sure he was familiar with Charlotte's popular art district. "You should swing by sometimes. I'll give you a free head shot."

"Thanks, but no thanks. Cameras and I aren't on the best of terms right now."

"Because of the scar?"

Gregor's eyes met hers. When he didn't respond, simply pinned her with a hard stare, she wondered what raced through his head. The poker face he donned was unreadable, but somehow, she knew she'd touched on a delicate subject for him. "I only ask because you constantly shift that side of your face away from me. But at least you're no longer wearing that creepy-ass hoodie," she said for comic relief.

He chuckled but remained silent.

Zahra dried her hands and shifted toward Gregor, resting her hip against the island. "There's no reason to be self-conscious, Gregor. You're still an extremely attractive man." Before she realized what was happening, she rested her hand against his cheek and turned his head to face her. "It's your battle wound. Wear it with pride." Her index finger glided along the raised tissue. "A little coconut oil, and in a few weeks you'll never even know it was ever there."

Realizing she was caressing his cheek, she allowed her hand to fall. Shifting back to the potatoes, she could feel Gregor's gaze on her. When she glanced up, something gentle swam in his eyes. No man had ever scrutinized her so intensely. "Chop, chop," she said. Turning away, she took a moment to catch her breath and pretend he hadn't electrified her soul.

"Yes, ma'am."

"You know, I'm surprised you didn't let me drown this morning."

It took Gregor a moment to respond. "I'm not a monster. Despite what the media is saying about me."

"They are going in pretty hard on you, huh?"

"Hard is an understatement. Who knows, maybe I deserve it."

Zahra whipped her head toward him. "No, you don't. No one deserves that type of treatment. They're bullies, and bullying is *never* okay. Especially by so-called adults. That kind of behavior teaches children it's okay to make someone feel like crap. It's not."

"You seem…passionate about bullying."

"I had a heroine who was a child psychiatrist. Sure, you hear about it, but in my research, I discovered how truly devastating bullying can be. The toll it has on lives. And not just the lives of the individuals being bullied. It's horrifying."

"I have conversations with my boys all the time about bullying," he said.

Zahra arched a brow. "I didn't know you had kids." He'd done a fantastic job of keeping that out of the news.

Gregor held up his hands in a defensive manner. "I don't. I'm referring to the boys who participate in my Cultivating Men Foundation."

"You have your own foundation?" Zahra was impressed.

"You sound surprised."

Admittedly, she was. "What does your foundation do?"

"We provide mentorship for young men in foster care."

"Nice. How long have you been doing this?"

"We're coming up on our third anniversary."

"Okay. I see you. Using your superpowers for good." She smiled. "Something tells me there's far more to Gregor Carter than you allow the world to see."

"Even if I showed them, the world would only see what they wanted to see."

"True," she said.

A wave of comfortable silence played between them.

"I asked you out," Gregor said.

Zahra pushed her brows together. "What?"

"The day of the photo shoot. I asked you out to dinner. You said no."

So, he did remember that. When he hadn't mentioned it earlier, she assumed he'd forgotten. Unfortunately, he didn't remember the day clearly. "Your henchman asked me out, not you. *My man Gregor wants to take you out for steaks and shrimps*," she said, mimicking the raspy-voiced, three-hundred-pound man who'd approached her.

Gregor laughed. "Tiny."

Zahra's brows shot up. "Tiny! The man was at least seven feet tall and as wide as the front of my SUV."

They shared a laugh.

"That tactic usually worked," Gregor said. "But not on you."

"I can't believe any woman in her right mind would think that was an acceptable way to be asked out."

"You'd be surprised."

"Actually, I doubt I would be. I imagine most women would have jumped at the opportunity to be wined and dined by Gregor freaking Carter."

"And yet, you flat-out turned me down."

"I'm not most women."

"No, you're not," he said.

Something about the way he eyed her caused heat to swirl in the pit of her stomach. Their gazes held a long and paralyzing moment.

"If I had approached you, would you have said yes?" he asked.

"No," she said without hesitation.

"Ouch. Mind if I ask why?"

"Are you sure you can handle my answer?"

"Try me."

For a moment, Gregor wasn't sure Zahra would answer his question. She eyed him as if trying to discern whether or not *she* thought he really could handle her response. Trust him, he could.

When Zahra burst into laughter, he eyed her like she was crazy. "What's so funny?"

"You should see your face right now."

She laughed some more.

"What's wrong with my face?"

"You look like you're waiting for someone to reveal whether or not you're the father."

And she laughed some more.

Her amusement was so contagious, he found himself laughing right along with her.

"You can be so intense," she said, tossing a piece of potato at him. Sobering, she said, "There were a few reasons I said no."

A few? He couldn't wait to hear them. "Such as?"

"For one, I thought I was worth more than a second-hand invite to *steaks and shrimps*," she said, using the same raspy voice as before.

He nodded. "You're right."

"For two, I was already seeing someone."

Back then, that would have only been a hiccup, not a complication. In his skewed manner of thinking, no woman had been off-limits. If he wanted her, he usually got her. All except this one.

She continued, "For three…"

Her words trailed, leading Gregor to believe whatever hedged on her tongue wouldn't be pleasant. And since he had an idea about what it was, he continued for her.

"My reputation." It hadn't been a secret that he'd… enjoyed an active social life.

"Yes. I usually form my own opinions about people, but it was kind of hard to discount your reputation when you constantly highlighted the fact that you loved women. *Lots* of women."

He wouldn't deny that. "You were right to say no. I was an asshole back then."

"Back then?" She smirked.

"Damn, woman. You really don't pull any punches, do you?"

"Not my style, *playboy*."

"*Ex*-playboy. Are you forgetting that for the past year and some change I'd been in a committed relationship?"

Zahra's forehead crinkled. "Yeah, that stunned me."

"You make me sound like a monster." And maybe he had been. "People change."

"I won't dispute that. But the more people change, the more they stay the same."

"Maybe." But not in his case.

An hour or so later, Gregor pushed away from the table after enjoying one of the best breakfasts he'd ever consumed. Zahra had clearly wanted to prove a point—that she could throw down in the kitchen—and she'd succeeded. Herb and garlic steak and onion potatoes. Buttered grits seasoned to perfection. The most mouthwatering biscuits he'd ever tasted. The woman could cook. Waterspout apparently thought so, too.

Gregor eyed the dog, lapping at the last of the grits Zahra had placed in her bowl—minus the salt and butter, of course. But Waterspout didn't seem to mind. The dog cleaned her bowl, glanced toward Zahra and whined.

"No more," Zahra said, wagging her finger at Waterspout.

Obviously, the K-9 knew better than to protest, because she flashed one of the most pitiful faces he'd ever seen on any animal, then curled up next to her empty bowl. Probably hoping Zahra would feel sorry for her. Good luck with that. The woman was a hard case.

Gregor reared back in the chair, crossed an ankle over his thigh and eyed Zahra. "So, do you normally go around risking your life for drowning dogs?"

"Not usually, no. But I had a heroine in another book who was an animal rights activist. I guess her love for animals sort of wore off on me."

"You could have died."

"I could die crossing the street. Plus, I wasn't worried. Our ancestors had me covered."

"What does that mean?"

"Apparently, you don't know the history of Lake Lamont or Hinnetville."

Gregor shook his head.

"Let me school you. Hinnetville was established by free slaves after the Civil War. It was incorporated in 1885. Rumor has it the water of Lake Lamont is sacred. So many were baptized here that the waters contain the spirits of our ancestors."

He laughed. "How in the world do you know all of that?"

"Research. I'm a romance writer. Everything is a potential love story," she said.

"Maybe I should start writing romance novels. It obviously exposes you to interesting facts."

"Do you believe in happily-ever-after?"

"No," he said without hesitation.

"Wouldn't you consider being a number-one draft pick, signing one of the largest contracts in history and playing for your dream team a happily-ever-after?"

"That's all career stuff. I thought we were talking personal. The L-word."

"The L-word." She laughed. "Gregor Carter, are you afraid to say love?"

"No."

"Then say it. Say it three times and it just might come true."

"You say it."

"Love, love, love, love, love, love," she said, poking him playfully. "See, I didn't even turn to stone."

Obviously, she wasn't apprehensive when it came to love. "If you'd been through what I've been through, you'd understand why the word doesn't interest me." His jaw clenched at the memory of his ex's betrayal.

"How do you know I haven't gone through something similar?"

He chuckled. "I doubt there's a man out there stupid enough to have cheated on you."

"There is. My ex."

"What happened?"

By her expression, she contemplated whether or not

to share something so personal with him. He understood her hesitation. Talking about what had gone down with him and Selene wasn't easy either.

"Several months ago, I learned he'd slept with his assistant. Of course, he went through the whole spiel about how it hadn't meant anything, and how much he loved me and how he should be allowed to make one mistake. The nerve of him," she said more to herself than to Gregor.

While she laughed, he knew she really found no humor in the situation. Sometimes, laughter was a coping mechanism.

"When I refused to forgive him, he had the audacity to blame me for his infidelity."

Zahra's situation mirrored his own with Selene. At least Zahra's ex hadn't sold her out to the tabloids, exposing intimate and personal details about their relationship.

"So, now you know all my sordid details. What happened between you and your ex?"

Until this moment, he hadn't considered the door he'd be opening with his inquiry. Zahra walked right through it.

"Similar to your situation. I learned she was cheating." He neglected to mention the fact that he'd walked in on them in the act.

Zahra's brows furrowed, signaling possibly confusion. Was she recalling the many gossip blogs' accounts that had painted him as the unfaithful one? With his past, no question she'd believed them like so many others had.

"There were always circulating rumors, but I never cheated on her," he said. "Not once."

"There were images of you in a threesome," she said matter-of-factly.

That damn photo again. "Selene initiated that encounter and was a part of it." The image had been so distorted, he could have claimed it wasn't him, but with change comes opting for the truth, rather than maintaining lies.

"Who initiated it is irrelevant. You brought another woman into your bed, Gregor. Regardless if your girlfriend was there or not, sanctioned it or not, it's still cheating." Zahra stood and collected their dirty dishes. "God, you athletes and your reckless and dangerous lifestyles."

Her reaction stumped him for a moment. Was she angry? He doubted it would matter if he told her that the incident happened when he and Selene first started dating and hadn't happened since? Or the fact that, while he'd willingly participated, afterward he'd told Selene he was done with that kind of thing, that he only wanted their relationship to include the two of them, no one else. And why should he have to explain himself to her anyway?

Alongside Zahra, he cleared the table. "It's easy for people to judge when they're on the outside looking in."

"When you leave the blinds up and curtains wide-open for the whole world to peer inside, you have to accept that someone is bound to judge."

He captured her wrist in a gentle, nonabrasive manner. "Are you judging me for the man I used to be?"

Gregor wasn't sure why, but he grew anxious waiting for her response. Again, why did her opinion of him matter? After their time here was up, they would never see each other again.

Zahra's eyes darted to where his hand rested as if his touch offended her in some way. Finally locking gazes with him, something gentle sparkled in her eyes, replacing the hint of coldness he'd seen several moments prior.

"No, I'm not," she said in a tender tone. "Trust me, I'm not without fault."

He doubted she had any skeletons stuffed in her closest.

Pure and undeniably sexual tension swelled between them. Zahra's breathing became visibly shaky. His own was unsteady, too. Lowering his eyes to her mouth, his stomach knotted with need, ultimate desire. He needed to kiss her, dammit. But before he could align his lips to hers, she backed away.

"Um, I should… I should clean up."

"Wait." The word came out so urgently it stunned him. Caution, anxiousness or fear danced in her eyes. He couldn't tell which. Clearly, she, too, had experienced the draw between them but chose to run from it. Instead of seizing the unspoken invitation her eyes extended, he said, "Thank you for not judging me."

She nodded, then moved away. Yep, she definitely wanted him, too. So, who would make the first move?

Chapter 7

On his way into the kitchen, Gregor peered through the glass that gave a direct view of the sunporch. Zahra was still there. Standing just out of view, his appreciating eyes roamed over the contours of her body in the light gray jogging suit she wore. Her hair was pulled up into a ponytail, and she wore glasses. When she bit at her lower lip, he couldn't help but think how sexy she looked. A naughty schoolteacher came to mind.

Frequently, he found himself thinking about her. Pondering her likes and dislikes. Speculating on what made her tick. It was so exhausting. *What in the hell are you doing to me, woman?*

It had been several hours since he'd passed by earlier that morning, and he couldn't believe she was still at it. As long as Zahra had been typing away at that keyboard, he was surprised her fingers hadn't fallen off.

His gaze lowered to Waterspout, curled into a ball at her feet. Since the bad weather had finally tapered off and the sun was actually starting to peep through the clouds, he was surprised no one had come looking for her. While he'd originally been the dog's object of affection, she'd put him down for Zahra. Probably because she was the one who fed her.

And speaking of food. It was three in the afternoon, and he hadn't even seen Zahra stop for a glass of water. Which meant she probably hadn't eaten. How was she still functioning? He would have shut down a long time ago. Well, she did strike him as a fighter. *Resilient.* That was so attractive to him.

The thought of her starving spawned the wildest idea he'd had thus far. He continued into the kitchen, removed sliced meat and fixings from the fridge, washed his hands and made Zahra a sandwich: layers of salami, ham, roast beef, turkey, cheese, lettuce, tomato, spices and mayo. On a plate, he cut the massive sandwich in half, framed it with chips and a pickle, grabbed a bottle of water from the fridge, then delivered the meal.

Zahra never glanced up when he entered the room, but her fingers stopped midstroke when he slid the dish in front of her. Her question-filled eyes rose to him, then lowered back to his offering. A slow smile curled her lips, forcing him to mimic the response.

"What's this?" she asked.

"Fuel. You've been at it all day. You need to eat." As if the universe deemed it necessary to cement his claim, her stomach roared rather loudly. "I think your body agrees."

Zahra laughed. "I think you're right. Thank you, Gregor. This was extremely kind and thoughtful of you." She eyed him with playful suspicion. "You didn't poison it, did you?"

"Of course not." Since their first encounter, he'd witnessed a lot of looks in her eyes, but none as tender as the one on display now. "And you're welcome. I'll let you get back to work," he said, backing away.

"Where do you think you're going?"

Confused by the question, he spoke a hesitant, "Back inside."

"I know you don't expect me to eat this massive sandwich all by myself, do you?"

"Are you inviting me to have lunch with you?"

"I guess I am."

"Well, I guess I accept."

Gregor eased down into the chair next to her. He discounted the comfort he experienced being near her. Over the next couple of hours, they ate, laughed, talked, shared moments of refreshing silence. He couldn't believe how easy it was to talk to her. It was like having a conversation with a close friend he'd known for decades. That should have been a warning sign.

Zahra circled a hand over her stomach. "Oh, my God, that was so good. I'm stuffed. I feel like I need several hours of physical activity after eating that sandwich."

He could think of one or two activities he would have liked to participate in with her. He shook the naughty imagery away. "You didn't finish your half."

"It's not from lack of trying."

True. She had put a decent dent in it. Watching her savor the sandwich had been a welcoming sight. His ex hadn't been much of an eater. And when she did, it was like observing a bird peck at a seed. Zahra definitely wasn't shy around food.

Zahra picked up a small piece of meat and popped it into her mouth. "What?" she asked.

Gregor grinned. "Nothing."

"You're not used to women doing anything other than nibbling around you, huh?"

"Something like that," he admitted.

"You really do live a life shrouded in pretense, don't you?"

Not everything in his life was a sham. Deciding he'd kept her distracted long enough, he stood. "I'll let you get back to work."

"You don't have to go," she said.

Oh, yes, he did. The longer he stayed near her, the more ferociously he wanted her. "I have some things to take care of," he lied. As he moved away, Zahra snagged the hem of his shirt, stopping him in his tracks.

"Thank you for lunch," she said.

Staring down into her face, he lost himself in those dark brown eyes. Something powerful grabbed hold of him and refused to let go. The harder he fought it, the more potent it became, until he just couldn't resist the urge to taste her mouth a minute longer.

Inching the plate back onto the table, he braced a hand on the table's edge and the other on the back of Zahra's chair. Dipping low, he allowed his mouth to hover inches from hers.

"What are you waiting for?" she asked in a wanting tone.

Her boldness stunned him. *What exactly was he waiting for?* Something was holding him back. What? That tiny voice in the back of his head warning him against Zahra. *Walk away*, it ordered. *She's not like the other women you've encountered. This one could damage you. Save yourself.*

Didn't the tiny voice see that kissing her was saving himself? If their lips didn't touch, he would die of need. His lips grazed hers gently, then reared back and sought permission to continue. What Zahra didn't say with her mouth, she said with her eyes. The passion dancing in them told him she wanted as much from him as he wanted from her.

His kiss deepened, hungrily searching every inch of her warm wetness with his tongue, savoring it thoroughly. Her moans of satisfaction rang out in the room, mixing with his. He'd never tasted a mouth so sweet. Had never desired to consume a woman whole with a kiss until now. Had never felt energy so highly concentrated it altered him in some glorious way.

The voice in his head grew louder, more demanding. *Stop this now. You're reaching the point of no return.*

Too late. There was no way he could turn back now if he wanted to. This journey would undoubtedly lead to extreme pleasure. Didn't he deserve that? Didn't he deserve this? To be so consumed with passion that he couldn't think straight? Yes, he did.

But even so, he ended their kiss. Pulling away from Zahra's mouth had to be what it felt like trying to free yourself from quicksand that's swallowing you whole. Somehow, he managed to escape her hold, but the effects of the ordeal still lingered.

A worry line creased Zahra's forehead. "What's wrong?"

That was a loaded question, but before he could fire off his answer, the doorbell rang, startling them both. Waterspout released a barrage of barks, then jetted toward the front of the house like a trained guard dog.

"Who could that be?" she asked, still gripping the fabric of his shirt.

"I'll check."

"No!"

He eyed her curiously.

"Whoever it is might recognize you. I'll go," she said.

She was out of the chair before he could say more. The fact that she'd willingly opted to protect him spoke volumes. And he'd heard every syllable. He stayed out of sight, but close by in case she needed him to come to her aid.

The kiss they'd shared replayed in his head. Hell, that wasn't just a kiss. It was more like an electrifying, soul-stirring, brain-scrambling undeniably electrifying connection. One he'd been foolish enough to break. But it had been necessary. What they'd shared had felt so good, so right, so necessary that it had spooked him. No woman had ever intimidated him before. Usually, it was the other way around. By any account, he didn't like it. Not one little bit.

His gaze fell to the notebook next to Zahra's laptop. Angling it for a better look, he scanned the scribblings on the page, stopping at one particular section.

Though things had started off rocking with them, they'd smoothed out nicely. Still, there was a level of discomfort. Mainly because Tyana had never wanted a man as strongly as she wanted this one. But they were from different worlds, saw things through opposing lenses.

Money and fame allowed him comforts and pleasures most would never enjoy. Such privilege made him reckless, as it would most men, so she didn't much hold that against him. His environment had molded him. Gabriel was a risk-taker; she was not. Yet, he'd been the only man to ever make her wish she could be. She wanted him, but only for one night.

She wasn't ready for a relationship. Her heart had suffered the blows of betrayal one too many times. Plus, Gabriel couldn't offer the kind of relationship she wanted, the only kind she would entertain—one filled with trust and steeped in love. No, anything with him would be just sex, because he wasn't the type of man who could commit to just one woman.

Gregor pushed his brows together, then sent a hard stare toward the front of the house. Was this about him? Rich, famous and reckless. It sounded like him. All but the reckless bit. That was the old Gregor. Still, he had to ask the question again, was this about him?

Nah.

It was about some dude named Gabriel. A character in her story.

Yep, this was all about the book, right? So why did it feel so personal?

Zahra wasn't sure how she'd made it to the door when her world was still spinning after that dizzying kiss. The way she'd devoured Gregor's mouth had been downright shameful. Instead of being appalled at herself, she was satisfied. She'd been the aggressor for once. *What are you waiting for?*

Boy, had he delivered one hell of a delicious feast. The way his tongue had claimed the inside of her mouth—swiping, licking, searching—had her to the point of sexual delirium. No man had ever kissed her that way. And she wanted more.

If other parts of him worked as efficiently as his mouth, she couldn't wait to experience them. Did she want to experience more of him than just a kiss? Could she abandon inhibition and allow herself one noncommittal night with Gregor?

Would she allow it?

Should she allow it?

These were tricky questions. The only thing she knew for certain was she couldn't wait to get back to the sunroom and finish what they'd started.

"Shh, Waterspout," she said.

The dog seemed determined to let the entire Lake Lamont community know just how fierce she was. When Zahra opened the door, Waterspout barreled toward the older black gentleman standing there in weathered boots, brown coveralls and a worn ball cap. Her tail wagged so hard, her entire body shook.

Waterspout wasn't alone in her excitement. The man scooped her into his arms like a child. There was no need to question who he was; because of the way Waterspout clung to the man, there was no doubt in Zahra's mind she belonged to him.

"Thank you, sweet Jesus, you are alive. I've been so worried about you, girl. Don't you ever scare me like that again."

The two were all over one another like long-lost lovers reunited after decades of searching for each other. "Hello," Zahra said, breaking up their reunion.

"Oh. Pardon my manners, or lack of them. I'm just so happy to see my Brownie."

Brownie? So that was Waterspout's real name. She liked Waterspout better.

The man's voice quavered and eyes glistened. Instantly, Zahra felt a great deal of compassion for him. Clearly, he loved *Brownie* very much.

"I'm Bernard Buchanan. I live several miles up the lake. This little adventurer—" he jostled Water… Brownie "—decided she'd sneak out of the house and take a dip. The rough waters carried her farther and farther down the lake. I couldn't get to her. I prayed and prayed she'd be okay. I've checked every residence. From my house—several miles up the lake—to here. In my heart, I didn't think my Brownie could have survived in the water this far down the lake, but I held out hope." He glanced down at the dog. In a shaky voice, he said, "My prayers were answered."

"I spotted her drifting and immediately rushed in after her. Those waters were treacherous. I'm just glad I was able to save her, and we both came out okay. A little shaken and stirred, but okay." Zahra took credit rightfully due to Gregor, but she couldn't actually give it to him at the moment.

"How can I ever repay you for what you've done for her, for us both?"

"No payment necessary."

Mr. Buchanan thanked Zahra profusely and offered her a reward that she refused several times. When he shared with her that Brownie had belonged to his late wife, who'd passed a little over a year ago, and how devastated he'd been when he thought he'd lost Brownie, too, a tear trickled from her eye. She could feel the love he held for them both.

Several moments later, Zahra said her goodbyes to Brownie and made her doggie-promise she wouldn't jump into raging waters anymore. Brownie covered her in countless doggie kisses, but it was clear her heart belonged to Mr. Buchanan.

Sadness filled Zahra as Mr. Buchanan and Brownie strolled away. While she'd known someone would likely come to claim Brownie, she still hated to see her go. Gregor would hate he didn't get a chance to say goodbye.

Gregor.

The thought of picking up where they left off cheered her up.

Chapter 8

When Zahra returned to the sunroom, it was empty. Confused, she peered through the glass that gave an unobstructed view of the backyard. No Gregor. Where was he? The bedroom? The notion made her stomach flutter.

Considering what had happened between them in the sunroom, his bedroom was probably the last place she needed to be. Still, she found her feet moving in that direction. Standing at his closed door, she lifted her hand to knock, but froze.

What if he'd retreated to his bedroom *because* of what had happened between them? What if he regretted kissing her? What if he were intentionally avoiding her? With all those things in mind, her hand fell to her side and she shied away.

Before she could make a clean escape, the door

creaked open and she stopped. Taking a moment to get her thoughts together, she plastered on a smile, despite feeling anything but jovial. However, jubilation came the second she turned to see Gregor. Eyeing him caused an unexpected soothing effect.

He stood propped against the doorjamb, arms folded across his chest, gawking at her as if he were waiting for her to spark their conversation. "Hey," she said. Gregor flashed a half smile but remained tight-lipped. *Okay.* She pointed over her shoulder. "That was Waterspout's owner. Turns out, her name is actually Brownie. I like Waterspout better."

"You okay?" he asked.

He speaks. "I'm good. Kinda have doggie-fever now, though."

Another bout of silence cloaked them. Gregor scrutinized her as if he were attempting to read her thoughts. What in the heck was up with him? The man was like a maze that veered in a thousand different directions. She doubted anyone ever made their way out.

Obviously, he regretted what had happened between them. Unsure how to handle that, she said, "I guess I should let you get back to whatever it is you were doing before I—"

"Am I Gabriel?"

Zahra's brows bunched. "Are you—" She stopped abruptly, awareness setting in. He'd read her notes.

"Rich, famous, reckless. He's based on me, right?"

Nervous tension flooded her. *You've got this. Just*

play it smoothly. "All of my books are loosely based on people I've come in contact with. It's—"

Gregor pushed away from the door frame and stood tall, his commanding presence withering some of her confidence.

"I'm not asking about all of them. I'm asking about the one you're writing now." He neared her like a gorgeous, stealthy jaguar closing in on its prey. "Is it based on me?"

"Loosely."

"Loosely," he echoed, but more to himself. "And the woman, the one who's never wanted a man the way she wants me—"

Zahra parted her lips to point out his error, but he corrected himself before she could.

"My bad. I meant to say *him*." A small smile curled his praise-worthy lips.

Smug bastard. A sexy-as-hell smug bastard. But a smug bastard nonetheless.

"So, is she based on you?"

"All of my heroines are a small reflection of…" Her words dried up when she noted the spare-me-the-BS look on his face.

"Loosely," they said in unison.

When Gregor's dark and daunting eyes blazed a scorching hot path down the length of her body and back up, she thought for sure she would melt.

"I'm going to take a cold shower," he said, turning away from her. "You can join me if you want," he casually tossed over his shoulder.

Zahra gasped at his bold proposition. The nerve of him to assume such a thing would even appeal to her. It did, but that wasn't the point. Gregor disappeared into the bathroom, leaving her standing there slack-jawed. Finally recovering, she eased into the bedroom, but stopped several feet from the bathroom entrance.

"I am not one your groupies," she called out.

Gregor reappeared. Only this time, he was shirtless. Zahra's breath hitched. His chest was terrain she could spend days exploring. His abs were like beautiful rock formations, and her desire to climb him grew with every passing second.

"I never said that you were. Just admit you want to join me."

Her gaze snapped upward, colliding with his. "I most certainly do." *Oh, God.* "Do *not.* I most certainly *do not* want to shower with you. I've showered already but thank you for the offer."

Jeez. Could she have sounded any more ridiculous? *I've showered already. Really, Zahra? That was the best you could come up with? You're a writer, for goodness' sakes. Now the man probably thinks you would have accepted his invitation had you not showered already. And then you thank him for the offer? Wow.*

Gregor closed the distance between them, and Zahra fought to maintain some semblance of strength, despite feeling like a helpless bird with a broken wing.

"So, I guess you don't want to spend one night with me either, huh?"

She barked a laugh. "All we did was kiss, Gregor. People kiss every day. It doesn't mean—"

Before she could form another syllable, Gregor's lips pressed against hers hard and fast. The way he claimed her mouth defied description. How could he paralyze, arouse and frighten her all at once?

Just a kiss?

Her arms snaked around his neck, pulling him closer to her. In a million years, she would have never imagined anything could have topped the kiss they'd shared earlier. This one did. But calling this sweet and delectable torture just a kiss was an insult. This was anything but ordinary.

More power, more energy, more determination lingered in his exploration. He claimed her mouth as if he had something to prove. But to whom? Her or himself? She allowed her trembling hands to roam over the contours of his warm, firm body. He moaned into her mouth when she used just her fingertips to trail down his back. Apparently, he liked it.

Everything about this moment was perfect, and scared the hell out of her. Breaking the kiss, she stared into his eyes and swore she saw disappointment. "What are we doing, Gregor?" she asked, her hands planted against his chest to keep her body from involuntarily leaning forward to lock lips with him again.

"Getting what we both want," he said.

"And what makes you think *you* are what I want?"

Without skipping a beat, he said, "The way your breath hitches when I get close to you."

"What?" she asked in a shaky tone. "That is ridiculous. My breathing is just fine." Which was a lie because her heart was about to pound out of her chest.

Gregor didn't refute her claim, simply added to the list. "The way you tense when I touch you."

Did she? Clearly, her brain knew the dangers of being too close to him; unfortunately, her body didn't seem to much care about them. "I, um, don't like to be touched. I have a…touch allergy." *Sweet Jesus*. What was wrong with her? Why did she keep saying stupid stuff? *Self-preservation*.

"A touch allergy, huh?"

"Yes. It's a thing. Google it."

Gregor chuckled, a sound so damn tantalizing, her toes curled in her shoes. All types of caution bells and verbal warnings went off in her head: DANGER AHEAD. But it was too late. Her fate was sealed.

This may have been her body, but Gregor was piloting it, taking her higher and higher to the point of no return. Admittedly, she was enjoying the ride. She just prayed they didn't crash and burn.

On the outside, Gregor appeared unfazed by the woman in his arms; however, on the inside, a beast raged to break free. Tomorrow, they may both have regrets, but today…today was theirs. Taking a chance, he placed his hands behind Zahra's thighs and hoisted her up. When she cradled his face and crashed her mouth to his, it proved what he'd known all along.

Moving to the bed, he laid her down gently and blanketed her body with his, their mouths never breaking apart. His heart thumped with anticipation. Had he ever wanted a woman as desperately as he wanted Zahra? Desperately, because this woman was really that critical.

He'd dreamed about this moment, burying himself so deep inside her she would feel him in her chest. That fantasy was about to become a reality. The thought sent fire blazing through his veins and straight to his dick.

"Wait," Zahra said, against their joined mouths.

Gregor's heartbeat kicked up a notch. Only this time it was fueled by fear that Zahra had changed her mind. Respecting her objection just as much as if it had been the word *no* that had crept past her lips, he drew back and glanced down into her troubled face.

"Do you want me to stop?" he asked.

"No."

The urgency in her tone made him smile. But he was confused. If she didn't want this to end, what was the problem? "What's wrong?"

Her eyes moved away, but only briefly. "I don't… We can't… I'm not looking for a relationship, Gregor."

She had nothing to worry about, because he didn't want a commitment either. Tonight would be about nothing but sex. The physical was all he had to offer her—or anyone else, for that matter. "I know."

"I just want…" Her words trailed a third time.

"You just want my body."

Her eyes widened—out of shock, he assumed—then returned to normal size.

"Yes," she said.

His one brow shot upward, her frankness surprising him. "You have it," he said, grinding his painful erection against her hot core. His mouth hovered a scant inch from hers. "You have it," he repeated.

"Take off your clothes."

Damn. It seemed Zahra was just as take-charge in the bedroom. He liked it. But right now, he was in control. "Ladies first."

She made a motion to remove her top, but he stopped her. Damn she was eager, which translated to one thing: it had probably been a while since she'd had sex, or at least a while since she'd been satisfied with it. Either way, her drought and/or displeasure would end tonight.

Zahra closed her eyes and allowed herself to just feel. Gregor worked in silence, removing her shirt, then her bra. She sucked in a deep breath when his lips closed over her taut nipple. It had been so long, too long since she'd been teased or touched this way. It felt good. So, so good.

After giving her opposite breast equal attention, Gregor planted slow, delicate kisses down the center of her torso. Each time his lips grazed her skin, her breathing caught. Tiny bolts of pleasure penetrated to her soul when his warm mouth claimed her throbbing core. Unable to control herself, she cried out as the sensations overtook her.

Gregor worked his tongue like a seasoned pro. It wasn't long before he had her strangling the sheets between her fingers, the blaze of an orgasm burning its way to the surface. Then it hit her like a meteor, knocking her off her axis.

Her back arched off the bed as another guttural cry thundered through the room. Gregor didn't stop. He continued to feast on her, the overload of pleasure making her dizzy. It seemed like forever before the intense wave passed. When it did, she fell flat against the mattress, her chest rising and falling in rapid succession.

As satisfying as the release had been, she wanted more. And by the naughty twinkle in Gregor's eye, he was about to give it to her.

Gregor left her briefly and journeyed across the room. When he returned, he carried a box of condoms—magnums, judging by the gold packaging—and placed them on the nightstand. Did he always travel with protection? Being Gregor freaking Carter, it was probably necessary.

Eager didn't begin to describe how she felt watching Gregor roll the condom down the length of his swollen member. "Amazing," she said absently, then laughed at herself once she realized it had slipped out.

Gregor flashed one of those sexy-ass half smiles she'd grown overly fond of. Damn him for being so freaking debonair.

"Thank you," he said, blanketing her body with his.

Zahra actually experienced a brief moment of discomfort when Gregor inched inside her. Did it stem from the fact that it had been a while since she'd had sex or the fact that she'd never been with a man as well-endowed as Gregor? While both were true, she went with the latter. He must have felt her flinch, because he kissed his way to her ear and whispered, "Relax." Apparently, she hadn't been his first bed partner who'd needed soothing while welcoming him inside. Thankfully, he was a considerate lover, filling her slowly and allowing her body time to adjust to him.

And it did.

Her canal stretched to accommodate every glorious inch. With varying speeds and depths, Gregor thoroughly satisfied the greedy beast inside her. "Faster," she moaned, getting into perfect rhythm and harmony with him.

"No," he countered, slowing his movement even more.

"Please?"

Please? When had she ever been okay with begging, especially in the bedroom? When a man possessed the ability to make your entire body sing such a beautiful melody, she answered.

"I can't," Gregor said.

Zahra opened her eyes to see him staring down at her. "Why?"

"You feel too good."

His admission and a slight show of vulnerability brought a reserved smile to her face. "It's okay. We have all night, right?" Her elation faded. "Unless you only want me once," she said. "Which is totally acceptable if—"

He cut her off. "I want you all night long."

"Good answer." She pushed her mouth to his.

Her frantic hands explored his body, loving the feel of his warmth and hardness against her fingertips. Not wanting their connection to end, she fought hard to deaden the orgasm building inside her. But with each delicious stroke, Gregor rotated his hips, grinding against her sensitive clitoris. It contributed to her undoing. Lava-hot heat pooled in her stomach, and the muscles between her legs contracted. Several seconds later, she exploded with a release far more potent than the first. Her nails dug into Gregor's damp flesh.

"Shit." He forced the word through clenched teeth.

For a second, she thought it had been because of the potential pain she was inflicting, but when he released a grunt that vibrated the walls and slapped an open hand against the headboard as if to balance himself, she knew the real culprit. He pulsed inside her. No, pulse wasn't a strong enough term. Gregor quaked through her, causing her to shatter a second time from the force of his release.

After his last unsteady delivery, he collapsed onto his back, his chest heaving up and down. In a stunning move, his arms curled around her and guided her against his chest. She didn't protest, because what was a casual embrace between two people who'd just swopped energies? Besides, they both clearly knew where they stood.

Chapter 9

Zahra hadn't anticipated spending every night in Gregor's bed, but for the past several, it's exactly what she'd done. No objection. No regret. Mainly because he was such a complete lover. Gentle and patient when needed. Rough and intense when wanted. Somehow, her body seemed to silently communicate with him; he proved to be an attentive listener, fulfilling every unspoken request and never taking one inch of her body for granted. If he thought it would bring pleasure, he explored it. And she'd allowed it. All of it. All of him. She hadn't anticipated their…fling, for lack of a better word, to span beyond one night—possibly two. Yet, neither had seemed able to get enough of the other.

She dragged her hand across the empty space beside her. This was the first time she'd awakened in bed alone.

Usually, she was greeted by the warmth of Gregor's body hugging her close to him. That was one of the things she missed most about being in a relationship. The intimacy. While she knew none of this affection was real, she was enjoying it just the same. Regardless of how it appeared, their dynamics hadn't changed. They were still just two people enjoying each other's company in the most divine manner imaginable. Two people who would soon go their separate ways.

Zahra ignored the ping of discontent the knowledge of the future brought forth. When it was time, she'd walk away from Gregor. That was the plan, and she intended to stick to it. Shuffling out of bed, she dressed and headed into the kitchen. By the time she left Lake Lamont, she would be ten pounds heavier. Gregor knew how to work up an appetite.

Through the back door, she spotted him standing outside, puffing on a cigar. She took several minutes to appreciate his body in the wide-leg stance. She knew firsthand just how powerful and effective his lower extremities were. On a whim, she retrieved her camera and snapped several shots of him from behind. Something about the olive-green sweater, dark jeans and boots begged for exposure. Not to mention Gregor's impressive silhouette.

After capturing several great shots, she slid the camera back into its case and decided to join him. "Can I hit that?" she asked.

He smirked at her. "Can you handle it?"

"Well, I can't imagine it's headier than you, and I seem to handle it just fine, wouldn't you say?"

"I would," he said, offering her the cigar.

She took a drag, then released the smoke in perfectly formed Os. "Mmm. That's good."

"It better be. It cost fifteen hundred dollars."

Her eyes widened. "For one cigar." Actually, it wouldn't have mattered if it had been an entire case.

Gregor nodded.

Zahra shook her head. "Can't mess with money."

He chuckled. "You seem comfortable with cigars. Most women aren't. Did your ex smoke them?"

Braswell? The idea of him putting anything he deemed impure into his body would have appalled him. A health nut to the umpteenth power. "No. My dad does. When my mom lets him, that is."

They laughed.

"So, your dad's whipped, huh?"

"He would be the first to say yes, without any hesitation and my mom would agree to the same." *He's the love of my life*, her mother often said. A smile curled her lips thinking about them.

"Your parents sound great."

Staring off at the dancing waves, she said, "They're amazing. If it wasn't for those two, I wouldn't believe true love actually existed. Best friends since the stroller, two kids and still in love after all of these years. That's rare."

"It must have been nice growing up surrounded by so much love and family."

"The best." Sadness flashed in Gregor's eyes, and he turned away. Her heart went out to him. Growing up in foster care had to be difficult. "Are you game for a little fun?" she asked to lighten the mood.

Gregor's sorrow faded, and mischief danced in his darkened eyes. "Absolutely."

"Great. Give me a few minutes to dress, and I'll meet you inside."

His roguish grin dimmed, and he cocked a brow. "We'll need clothes?"

Zahra barked a laugh. The man's libido seemed to be permanently channeled to overdrive. "Yes, we'll need clothes."

The idea of a quickie was tempting, but she knew if they climbed into bed, they would stay there all day. Gregor wasn't a one-hit-and-quit man. He went on and on.

An hour later, Zahra and Gregor trekked into the woods behind the house. She needed to gather nature shots for the upcoming charity event at her studio. She'd gotten great pictures by the lake: the water, dock, houses in the distance and a colorful horizon.

"Tell me again why I'm following you into the woods. I've seen enough horror movies to know that this is probably not a good idea."

"You agreed to be my bodyguard while I capture some amazing pics for the silent auction at my studio. It's for charity."

"I agreed under duress."

She tossed her head back in laughter. "Duress?"

"Yes. You were looking at me with suggestive eyes. It made me weak and vulnerable."

Zahra bumped him playfully. "You're full of it." Gregor gave her one of those sexy chuckles. *Ugh!* Why did she like that sound so much?

"What charity are you raising funds for?" he asked.

"Operation Warming Souls Foundation." By Gregor's expression, he was unfamiliar with the group. Unfortunately, many were. "OWS assists homeless women vets."

"Ah. Sounds like a very worthy cause. How'd you get involved with them?"

"I discovered the organization while doing research for a book. My heroine was a single mother and vet who'd fallen on hard times. She couldn't keep a job because she suffered from PTSD. Had no family to turn to. I met a woman whose life mimicked my heroine's. She was a single mother, a vet and homeless."

"Wow," he said.

"She and her daughter slept in their vehicle, because it was unsafe for her to be in a shelter with a young child." Zahra's voice cracked, and she swallowed hard to remove the lump of emotions lodged in her throat. "Could you imagine being in such a horrible situation? And with a child."

"Unfortunately, I can."

Zahra stopped abruptly and eyed him. When she parted her lips to speak, he paused her with a flash of his hand.

"I prefer not to talk about it," he said.

She nodded. They continued moving. "I witnessed how prevalent the homeless vet problem is and wanted to help. OWS helped this young woman reestablish herself. Give her life meaning again. I donated 50 percent of the first month's proceeds from the book to OWS and the other fifty to Joleena and her daughter."

Gregor's expression registered surprise. "That was generous of you."

"Joleena's feedback brought the book to life. Readers absolutely loved it and wanted to know how they could help, too. Shortly after, I started the event at my studio. It's a huge success and has grown every year. People really show up for the cause. You are more than welcome to attend. Friends support friends, right?"

Gregor looked away. "We'll see."

"You should stop hiding."

Gregor stopped. "Excuse me?"

Zahra waved her hand through the air. "Never mind. Your personal life is none of my business."

"You're right. It's not."

While he was clearly trying to be respectful, Zahra knew she'd touched a nerve. She should have stopped there, but Zahra being Zahra, she continued. "But if it were my business, I'd tell you to stop hiding. I'd tell you to let the world see that the accident, the bashing, your ex… I'd tell you to let them see that none of those things have broken you."

"How do you know they haven't broken me?"

Zahra noted a hint of agitation in his tone but didn't allow it to distract her. "I know because there is still so much brilliant light dancing behind your eyes. You're lost, Gregor, but you're not broken. You're built to last."

Gregor pinned her with one of the most powerful stares she'd ever witnessed from him or anyone else. The warmth of it heated her skin. Something shifted between them at that moment.

His eyes narrowed on her in a quizzical manner, then he inched closer. "You have something in your hair."

Lost in his allure, she said, "What?"

"There's something crawling in your hair."

He lifted his hand toward her head, but before he could assist, she was moving her fingers like tiny tornados through her locks. "What is it? Get it out!" She squealed and hopped around as if squashing grapes. The camera dangling around her neck thrashed back and forth pounding into her chest. *"Eek."*

"It's gone. It's gone," Gregor said through rolling laughter. He captured her hands and held them to his chest. "Calm down. You're going to knock yourself unconscious."

"Some bodyguard you are. Letting me get attacked by insects." His touch soothed her frayed nerves.

"Thank you for what you said earlier. I appreciated it."

"You're welcome."

A moment of necessary silence fell between them. Something rustling in the brush caught Zahra's attention. A flock of cardinals sat perched on a tree limb. She knew from watching a nature show on TV that cardinals were territorial and usually traveled solo. Except in winter, when they dropped their guard and hunted for food together.

"Aren't they beautiful?" she said, lifting her camera and snapping several pictures.

Gregor nodded. "Every time I see a cardinal, it makes me think of my time at The Cardinal House."

His expression gave nothing away, so Zahra asked, "Good memories?" If not, she would regret opening up old wounds. A smile touched his lips, signaling they were.

"The best. Life was simple then. On occasion, I actually miss it." He chuckled. "It's crazy. Sometimes I wish I was back at the ranch. Granted, my life is far more bountiful now, but at the ranch, I never had to wonder who was genuinely in my corner."

"I can't imagine walking in your shoes, Gregor. Cameras constantly flashing in your face. Reporters hounding you. People continuously hurling negativity at you. You must really have tough skin. I would need therapy to get through it all."

Gregor parted his lips to say something, but obviously had a change of heart.

"Come on," she said, leading them deeper into the woods.

"My skin's not as tough as you think. I feel things probably too deeply sometimes. All I ever wanted to do was play football. Unfortunately, the unpleasantries come with the territory." He shrugged. "Gotta take the good with the bad."

"You seem awfully comfortable in the spotlight to me."

"I'm a brand. Standing out builds that brand. Endorsement deals, movie roles, romance novel covers." He bumped her playfully.

"Yeah, but it also gets you scrutinized."

"Zahra, I've been scrutinized my entire life. At least now the scrutiny comes with a shitload of zeros."

"You would prefer money over the peace of mind?"

"Honestly, I prefer them both. But since I've never known true peace, I guess I'm not really missing out on anything."

So many emotions rushed through Zahra as she listened to Gregor. Sad ones mostly. He truly was a man lost. But the good thing about it, being lost was usually when people found themselves. And once he discovered who he truly was, he'd find peace.

Gregor hurried into he kitchen to retrieve the bottle of honey he'd seen in one of the cabinets. He and Zahra were about to be in a sticky situation. Snatching the jar off the shelf and a spoon from the drawer, he started out of the kitchen, but his vibrating cell phone on the counter stopped him.

"Not now, Thad."

Allowing the call to roll into voice mail, he continued out of the room. Halfway down the hall, the phone vibrated a second time. The apparent urgency troubled him. Backtracking, he grabbed the phone off the island and slid his thumb across the screen, making the call active. What bad news did Thad have for him now? "Thad?"

"Man, I've been trying to reach you for like an hour."

"We—I dozed off. What's up?"

"I know I said I wouldn't bother you, but this couldn't wait. I need you on a plane to Indianapolis tomorrow morning. I've already arranged for Captain Skip to come for you first thing and a helicopter to get you to the airport."

It took a second or two for Thad's words to penetrate. "Indianapolis? Why am going to Indianapolis?"

"The manufacturer of the motorcycle suit you were wearing the night of your accident wants to talk with you about being the face of their motorcycle gear product line. Talk about blessings. This is huge. And a clear sign that your storm is blowing over."

Thad went on and on, but Gregor tuned him out, his attention gliding in the direction of a waiting Zahra. The idea of cutting his time short with her made his stomach knot. He could tell Thad no, that he wasn't up for meeting with them, but that would only open a line of questioning he didn't want to deal with. And should he even be considering blowing off what could be a lucrative partnership for a fling? Which in true essence was all he and Zahra were. Two consenting adults who'd agreed to walk away once their time at Lake Lamont was done.

"Earth to Gregor. Man, are you there?"

Thad's elevated voice brought Gregor back to the conversation. "Yeah. Yeah, I'm here. This is um…good news. Great news. I'll be there."

Thad was silent for a moment. "What's going on with you?" he finally said. "Usually, you loudly and annoy-

ingly tell me how you're the man when a potential endorsement deal comes into play."

Gregor turned away from the force drawing him toward the bedroom, shook off whatever this was that had
a hold on him and got into character. "I am the man. You
already know this. So, let's get this money. Just make
sure you bring your A-game to Indianapolis tomorrow."

"There's the G I know. Welcome back. You had me
scared for a minute. And don't play me. I always bring
my A-game. Just ask my wife."

Both men laughed.

"Nah, I wouldn't want her to have to lie and jeopardize her chances of getting into heaven," Gregor said,
which brought on more laughter.

Sobering, Thad said, "Speaking of literary agents,
how's it going with you and Zahra?"

Gregor glanced at the jar of honey he was still holding. "We barely see each other. She mentioned something about finishing a book." Apparently, he'd sounded
convincing because Thad didn't give him the usual
there's-something-you're-not-telling-me response: a sar-
castic *uh-huh*, followed by, *Man, I wasn't born under a
hay bale in the middle of last night.*

The two men chatted a while longer. Gregor ended
the call with "See you in Indianapolis tomorrow," the
words reminding him tonight would be his last with
Zahra. Tossing the phone aside, he sat the honey on the
counter, pressed his palms against the cold stone and
leaned forward, dropping his head.

"You're leaving?"

Gregor flinched. Damn, Zahra had overheard his conversation. More like eavesdropped. Of course, he kept the accusation to himself. Turning, every cell in his body sparked with awareness. Zahra stood completely bare in front of him.

Dragging his eyes away from the swell of her breasts, he locked gazes with her. By the evil twinkle in her eyes, she knew exactly what she was doing to him. As if his tented underwear wasn't revealing enough. "Yes." It was faint, but he swore he caught a glimpse of disappointment on her face.

Closing the distance between them, she pressed a finger into his bare chest. "Good. Maybe now I can finish my book without you as a distraction."

She smiled, but to Gregor, it didn't appear genuine. Did the idea of walking away seem just as daunting to her as it did to him? "A distraction, huh?"

"Yes."

Zahra yelped when he scooped her into his arms. "Woman, I'm about to distract the hell out of you." His eyes roamed over her body. "I'm going to distract you over and over again."

"Well, I guess one more night without writing won't hurt. Plus, I could use the inspiration."

"In that case, I'm going to inspire the hell out of you, too."

When they entered the bedroom, Gregor tossed her onto the mattress, then pretended like he was going to collapse onto her, but actually gently covered her body with his. "What's wrong?" he asked, noting the serious expression that came over her face.

"I've enjoyed every second with you," she said. "Not one single regret."

"So have I," he admitted. And only one regret—that they didn't have more time together.

"I wish things could be different…"

Gregor parted his lips to foolishly say they could, but Zahra continued before he could get the words out.

"…but they can't. For good reason. We're both healing."

True. But instead of responding, he captured her mouth in a savage kiss. If this was their last night together, he wouldn't waste it.

Chapter 10

Zahra didn't want to think about the fact that tonight would be her last night with Gregor. All she wanted to consider was how good he was making her feel at this very moment. He'd brought her to amazing sexual heights. It would take a long time for her body to recover from him when it crash-landed from his absence.

She moaned into his mouth when he ground his erection against her already eager core.

"You like that?" he asked against their joined mouths.

"Mmm-hmm," was all she could manage.

"Good. Then you're going to love this."

Seconds later, he snaked down her body, peppering delicate kisses all over her skin. Between her legs, he teased her hardened sex with the tip of his tongue. Her back arched slightly from the intense sensations shooting through her like tiny rockets. He greedily devoured her. But when he inched two long fingers inside her and worked them with the same vigor as his tongue and mouth, her body twisted, turned and thrashed.

"I can't… I can't hold it," she said.

"Then don't," he said.

Zahra cried out, then her body seized. Coming down off the high, she said, "I need to feel you inside me."

She liked how instinctively bold she was with him. She'd never been what one would call sexually assertive until now. Gregor seemed to thrive off it, and that gave her more and more confidence to tell him exactly what she wanted.

After removing his underwear and placing on a condom, he flipped her onto her stomach in one swift motion, hiked her hips and gave her exactly what she wanted, hard and fast. Eager to receive, she met each of his powerful thrusts. The slapping sounds of great sex wreaked havoc on her concentration.

"More, Gregor. More. Please."

As always, he delivered.

"I love it when you beg," he said through what sounded like clenched teeth.

A beat later, he exploded inside her, his primal-sounding growls mixing with her moans, whimpers and cries from the delight she experienced from her own release. Unable to maintain an upright position, she dropped onto the bed. Gregor collapsed, too—half on the mattress, half on her. She loved the feel of his hot, slick flesh. The only thing that could be heard in the room was the sounds of heavy breathing and her soft pleasure hums.

Maybe this thing between them didn't have to end. Maybe they could maintain this casual connection. Wasn't it benefiting them both? He was on one side of Charlotte, she another. They could easily meet in the middle, then go their separate ways after they'd both gotten what they wanted. Just maybe—

Her cell phone vibrated, derailing her train of thought. Her service was so spotty inside the house, she was surprised a call had gotten through. Lifting it off the nightstand, she grimaced. *Braswell.* What did he want now? She'd said all she needed to say to him the last time he'd called her to plead his weak case, which was a couple of days before she'd arrived at Lake Lamont.

Dragging her thumb across the screen, she sent the call to voice mail. Though he was a continuous nuisance, his call had helped to bring her back to her senses, reminding her why continuing this thing with Gregor was a bad idea. She couldn't risk her feelings getting involved. Truth be told, she was already start-ing to feel…*something* for him. Yeah, it was a good thing he was leaving.

"Who's Braswell?"

Damn. He'd seen the name on the screen. Her first instinct had been to lie, but she decided against it. She had nothing to hide. "My ex."

"Ah." A second later he said, "Are you two still close?"

Was he slyly asking if they were still intimate? "Heck, no. We're good and over. He just can't seem to grasp it."

"I know why," he said, pinching her butt.

"Ow." She swatted him playfully. "For the record, I offer far more than just good sex."

"Great sex," Gregor said.

Zahra smiled into her pillow. "Great sex."

His arms tightened around her, and he kissed her earlobe before whispering, "I'm sorry for what he did to you. It sucks being betrayed by someone you never would have expected to deceive you," he said.

Zahra found it strange that he hadn't said *by someone you loved*. Had he not been in love with his ex? Had it only been a relationship of convenience? "Yes, it does," she said.

Gregor sighed. "It makes you question being in a monogamous relationship at all."

Those words caused Zahra to shimmy her body free so that she could face him. "Really?"

"Don't tell me you've never considered that," he said.

"No. There is something breathtakingly beautiful about two people truly committed to one another. Loving each other unconditionally. Voluntarily devoting their lives to each other. Building a life together. Something divine and soothing and amazing in having that one special person to protect, love, cherish, respect you. At all costs." She paused a moment. "I've never had that, but I do believe it exists. And while I may have been dumped on by love, I'm still not against the sanctity of monogamy, because my parents show me every day that it's possible."

Gregor eyed her for a moment before saying, "Damn."

Zahra laughed. "Too much?"

He pushed a wet strand of hair from her forehead with the tip of his index finger. "I wouldn't have expected anything less from you."

Gregor pulled her into his arms, and she rested her head against his chest. The thump of his heartbeat—strong, powerful—had become a soothing lullaby to her. Too bad she would have to get used to falling asleep without it.

Chapter 11

Gregor smiled at the familiar baritone voice behind him. Hogan Reed. Dr. Reed, as most people addressed him. Not Gregor. To him, the man with a strong resemblance to Richard Roundtree was affectionately known as "Old School." Gregor stood and greeted him with an embrace reserved for close friends.

Parting, Dr. Reed surveyed their secluded surroundings, a park several miles out of town. "What's up with this clandestine location? And why couldn't we have met in my office as usual?" He tightened the trench-style coat around him. "It's a little nippy out here."

"A few bloodsuckers are still hounding me. I couldn't take the chance of them following me to your office," Gregor said in regard to the gossip tabloids.

He thought by now that he would have been old news.

At least social media had moved on to the next scandal—an actress headed to rehab for the fourth time.

Dr. Reed eased down onto the wrought-iron-and-wood bench. "I wish black men would squash the stigma associated with therapy. We'd live longer, have more fathers in the home, more wealth in the family, more peace in our communities." He tossed his hand up. "But hey, what do I know?"

Gregor didn't see that happening anytime soon. He, himself, had only ended up in therapy by accident. One day he'd struck up a conversation in his favorite coffee shop with an older brother reading *Invisible Man* by Ralph Ellison.

The serious man had been so easy to talk to that Gregor had revealed a good portion of his life story to a complete stranger. When they said their goodbyes, he'd given Gregor his card. Gregor had been shocked to learn that the man he'd spent close to four hours talking to had been a psychologist.

Instantly, Gregor had gone on the defensive, stating he didn't need a shrink. Dr. Reed had simply said: *Everyone needs someone to talk to.* Turned out, he'd been right. Over the years, they'd grown close, with Dr. Reed being more like a father figure than his unconventional therapist. They talked real, open and personal to each other.

"You know a lot," Gregor said. "But for the record, this isn't therapy. We're just two old friends chatting."

"How you holding up, young'un?"

Gregor shrugged. "I'm holding. Signed another endorsement deal. The company whose apparel I was wearing when I wrecked. How ironic is that? Ten mil." For some reason, the money aspect didn't bring him the usual joy.

"Congratulations. And the other stuff?"

Gregor sighed. "I'm used to being a target. This won't break me. I'm built to last." Had he just quoted what Zahra had said to him?

Dr. Reed clapped him on the shoulder. "Damn straight. How was the lake?"

A lazy smile curled Gregor's lips. "Good. Rejuvenating. I met someone."

He thought about the morning he'd left Lake Lamont; Zahra had kissed him goodbye like he was heading off to war. In a way, he had been. Leaving her had been like fighting a battle.

"Weren't you on a secluded island? Is she a mermaid? She must be mystical to have snagged your attention. Last time we talked, I recall you saying to hell with women, relationships and love."

The two men shared a laugh.

"I thought I was, but this woman…" Gregor filled Dr. Reed in on everything, including the no-strings arrangement he and Zahra had shared.

"No strings attached can be a tricky thing," Dr. Reed said.

Gregor gave a humorless laugh. "You're telling me." He fell back against the bench. "I can't stop thinking about her, but I know I should. Somehow, she got to me."

Gregor wanted to pretend he'd never met Zahra, pretend they'd never made love, pretend she hadn't gotten to him. He'd wanted to believe he could pretend they'd never met. But he was wise enough to know it wouldn't be that simple. Nothing in his life ever was or ever had been. Not only did he *want* to pretend all of those things, he also *needed* to. There was no room for romance in his life. He didn't need the distraction or the risk.

It had been a week since he'd left Lake Lamont, but he'd thought about Zahra every single day. How ridiculous was that? He barely—he was about to say he barely knew her, but to be honest, it felt as if he'd known her a lifetime. Like he was more familiar with her than some of the guys on the team he'd known for years. How was that possible?

"Tell me about her," Dr. Reed said.

Gregor gave a relaxed smile as an image of Zahra filled his thoughts. "She has a fire inside her, that's for sure. She's bold, honest, outspoken. Beautiful. This woman is drop-dead gorgeous. Inside and out. Her heart's the size of the sun."

"Sounds like an amazing woman."

The image of her standing on the dock waving goodbye to him as the boat sailed away played in his head. They'd watched one another until the boat disappeared around the bend, leaving him with nothing but memories.

"She is. Can you believe she jumped into raging waters just to rescue a dog? A dog," he said as if he still couldn't believe she'd done it, despite being right there. "She didn't care about messing up her hair, ruining her nails or even dying. All that mattered was saving Waterspout." He faced Dr. Reed. "That's what she named her, Waterspout. Turned out her name was actually Brownie."

"I like Waterspout better," Dr. Reed said.

"So did she."

Things were quiet between them for a moment.

"She's different from any woman I've ever known," Gregor said, breaking the silence.

"Clearly. In three years, I've never once heard you speak so passionately about a woman. Not even your ex. Now the question is, what are you going to do about it?"

"Nothing. Zahra made it clear she wasn't looking for a commitment. Honestly, I'm not sure I am either."

Dr. Reed barked a laugh. "Young'un, it seems to me you're already committed or at the very least dedicated to the possibility of what could be. You're scared."

"*Pssh*. I'm not—" Gregor paused at the sight of Dr. Reed's don't-even-try-to-play-me expression. "Maybe I am. Other than you, I've never truly been able to open up to anyone. She has the ability to short-circuit my defenses, exposing me. What if she doesn't like what she sees?"

"Then she's not the one for you. Love doesn't come with stipulations. *I'll love you if you have no flaws*. Or, *I'll love you if you never make mistakes*. That's dumb love. True love is smart. It knows no one is perfect. Yet, it grows and blooms anyway."

Gregor nodded.

"You've been through a lot, young brother. Known

enough heartache for two lifetimes. Yet, you haven't let it break you. If this woman means something to you, don't let her get away. Maybe she will tell you to get lost and never contact her again, or maybe you mean something to her, too. Don't you think you owe it to yourself to find out?"

Maybe.

This wasn't like him, denying himself something he wanted. And he damn sure wanted Zahra. In every way. He yearned for her. Those sweet kisses. That warm touch. Her delicious scent. The feel of her in his arms. The idea of any other man enjoying her in the ways he had ripped at his insides and angered him. What in the hell had this woman done to him?

Actually, the question should have been, what in the hell had he done to himself? He was fully to blame for this. After the first time making love to Zahra, he should have ended it there. Being inside her had felt too damn good and too damn right. He didn't want to admit it, but she'd left her mark on him.

Chapter 12

Zahra walked arm in arm with her sister at the Spirit and Mindfulness Expo. They'd made the four-hour drive from Charlotte to Raleigh to attend the popular event. The crystals, gems, stones, palm readers and such were right up Ava's alley. Zahra, however, didn't much believe in any of it.

But coming meant she got to spend time with Ava. Plus, she needed a distraction to take her mind off Gregor. It had been a little over two weeks since they'd parted ways, and every single day had been a reminder that she'd allowed fear to win. She hadn't wanted it to be goodbye, but she'd been too afraid to risk her heart again. Too afraid to believe in fate and the possibility that it had brought them both to Lake Lamont at the same time for a reason.

The pressing question was, what had been fate's goal? To help them loosen the grip of the past they both were clearly chained to? To remind them that life went on after heartbreak? To give them hope? What? Maybe this hadn't been the workings of fate at all, but instead a mere coincidence. Her gut told her differently.

Gregor had done something to her. To her mind. To her body. To her spirit. Something only he could undo, which meant she was destined to remain in a perpetual state of miserableness.

"Something's different about you, Zah."

Ava's words pulled Zahra from her thoughts. "What?"

"I don't know. Ever since you returned from Lake Lamont you've had this amazing glow."

Zahra hadn't gotten around to telling Ava about the time she'd spent with Gregor—or the fact that he'd been at Lake Lamont at all. Mainly because she knew exactly what would happen. Ava would make a mere flicker into a four-alarm blaze. She was trying to forget Gregor, not relive him over and over again with her sister.

"This is the glimmer of happiness produced by finishing my tenth novel," she said.

"Is it?"

Accusation dripped heavy in Ava's tone. This was what happened when your sister was also your best friend and could read you like the Sunday newspaper.

"Yes, it is," Zahra said, hoping to derail the topic.

"Okay," was all Ava said, then set her gaze straight ahead.

Ugh. She hated when her sister did that. Made her feel

guilty without actually accusing her of a crime. Zahra changed the subject before Ava had her singing like a canary. "Did I tell you how much I love your hair? That fiery co[per color looks amazing on you. So does the short cut."

Ava had made the big chop and gone natural a little over a year ago. Zahra had chickened out, not believing at the time that she had the dedication it took to maintain natural hair. But looking at how healthy and beautiful—not to mention curly—her sister's hair was had her reconsidering a chop of her own. She needed a change.

"Yes, you have told me. And your telling me again means you're deflecting. What are you hiding, big sis?"

Zahra debated for a moment whether or not to tell Ava but decided to. This was definitely BFF territory. But the confession came with a condition. "Don't blow what I'm about to tell you out of proportion, Ava. It happened. I don't regret it. It's done."

Ava stopped abruptly. "Oh. My. God. Zah, please don't tell me you took Braswell's trifling ass back."

"No. Hell, no. Why would you even think I'd do something so stupid?"

Ava blew a sigh of relief. "Good. That slick-talking serpent doesn't deserve you." She folded her arms across her chest. "So, who did you sleep with?"

Zahra's eyes widened. "Shh. You don't have to let the entire building know." Lowering her voice even more, she said, "And how do you know I slept with someone?"

"Call me psychic. Now I get why you've been zoning in and out. You're thinking about him, aren't you?"

When was she *not* thinking about him? They started to walk again. "I can't purge him from my system, which is absolutely insane. We only spent a week and a half together. Why is he in my every thought?" Zahra sighed her frustration.

"Wait. Back up. Who is *him* and…spent a week and a half together, where?"

Zahra bit at her lip, tasting the fruity lip gloss she wore. Getting her thoughts together, she spent the next several minutes telling Ava about Gregor and how he'd unexpectedly been at the lake house. About saving Waterspout—aka Brownie—their crossed pasts and their no-strings arrangement.

As feared, Ava ignited a wildfire. "You can't get him out of your head because he's a part of you and you're a part of him."

"No one's a part of anyone, Ava. We just slept together, damn."

"Once?"

"Once…ish. Several times. Okay, a lot. A whole lot."

Ava squealed. "You do know what this means, right? You absorbed each other every time you were intimate. You two are linked now. That's why you can't stop thinking about him."

One thing Zahra could say about her sister was that the woman certainly knew how to take things to the extreme. "I'm not looking to be linked to anyone," Zahra said. "Braswell and I swapped energies, but I never thought about him like this. Not even after we broke up."

Ava's face contorted into a ball of distress. "That was tainted energy, because he had a dark, ugly soul."

It was no secret Ava hadn't liked Braswell from the moment Zahra had brought him home to meet the family. Nor had her mother, whom he'd offended by hinting at a woman's place being in the kitchen. And definitely not her father, whom Braswell had disrespected by assuming he could call her father—his elder—by his first name without an invitation to do so.

"Is Gregor anything like what we see on television and on social media?"

Zahra compared the different versions of Gregor in her head. "He's nothing like the media portrays him. Heck, he's nothing like he portrays himself. He's gentle, kind, amazingly humble." And incredible in bed, but she kept that to herself. "I wanted to believe that I liked having him around because I felt sorry for him. Truthfully, I liked having him around because I like him." She tossed her head back in a groan. "God, I shouldn't like him, but I do."

"Why is liking him a problem?" Ava asked with genuine concern in her tone.

Zahra stopped walking again. "Why is it a problem? Are you kidding me? I'm fresh out of a bad relationship. I was cheated on. Gregor's an athlete. And not just any athlete. One of the most celebrated quarterbacks in history, which makes him a target for thirsty women. It would never work between us."

"Excuses, excuses, excuses. That's all I'm hearing. Everyone has had at least one or two bad relationships,

Zah. Everyone has been cheated on. And news flash, any man—or woman, for that matter—with money is a target, not just athletes and not just Gregor Carter."

Ava made valid points, but Zahra wasn't looking to be talked into Gregor; she needed to be talked out of him.

"There's something there, Zah. I've never seen you this enthralled with a man. Not even slimy Braswell."

"Yeah, well, it doesn't matter. We both agreed that our time together wouldn't extend beyond Lake Lamont. End of story."

"What is it you always say about love stories? That they don't end until there's a happily-ever-after, right?"

"Yeah, something like that," Zahra said.

"You haven't had your happily-ever-after, big sis, which means your love story isn't complete. You deserve a happy ending."

Zahra would agree.

"You know what I'm thinking?" Ava said.

Zahra laughed. "Usually not."

"We should have your palm read."

Great. Just what Zahra needed—someone predicting she was destined to spend her life alone. "I don't—"

Before she could finish her protest, Ava dragged her toward one of the booths inside the arena. A middle-aged woman with long, flowing chestnut-brown hair partially covered with a red-and-gold scarf motioned them in. Lady Castilla, the table banner read.

Zahra resisted when Ava pushed her forward.

"Don't be shy," the exotic-looking woman said. "Sit. I will not bite."

Lady Castilla spoke with an accent Zahra couldn't quite place—not that she was a linguistics expert. Was it authentic or simply part of the gimmick?

With reluctance, Zahra eased down into the velvet-covered, navy blue chair. The fancy piece seemed out of place among the other generic furniture—a red cloth-covered table, several folding chairs, and a smaller rustic-looking table holding flyers and business cards.

"I am Lady Castilla. What is your name?" she asked.

Shouldn't she have known it already? "Zahra. And this is my sister, Ava."

"Two beautiful names for two beautiful ladies. Nice to meet you both." Lady Castilla stretched her arms out. "Your hands, Zahra."

She slid them palms up toward her.

"Which is your dominant hand?" she asked.

"My right."

Lady Castilla studied her right palm. "You are very successful in your career. You're a creative." She glanced up. "What do you do?"

"I'm a writer and photographer."

"I see." Lady Castilla's attention fell back to Zahra's palms. "Hmm."

Hmm. Zahra shot a glance in Ava's direction, the cryptic *hmm* causing Zahra distress. Maybe she should have told Lady Castilla not to tell her anything bad she saw. *Wait.* She inwardly laughed at herself. Why was she stressing? It wasn't like she believed any of this crap.

"This is very interesting," Lady Castilla said, tracing the lines in Zahra's left hand with her index finger.

"Desire drives you, but when it comes to love your heart takes complete control."

Unfortunately, that was true. Oftentimes she used her heart instead of her head. One of the reasons she'd stayed with Braswell for far too long.

"You're deeply affectionate. Good-hearted. Loyal." Lady Castilla laughed softly. "But you can be stubborn."

"Mmm-hmm," Ava hummed.

When Zahra shot her sister a look, she shrugged and mouthed, *It's true.*

Lady Castilla continued. "You fall in love easily. And when you love, you love hard. But when love is lost, you feel the loss strongly, even allowing it to cripple you. You must move forward."

Zahra shifted slightly in her seat. Creepy. Still, she wasn't buying into any of this because this could be true for millions of people, not just her.

"Are you married?" Lady Castilla asked, not bothering to look up.

"No."

"When you do marry, it will be filled with passion and an abundance of love. You will have a long, happy and fruitful marriage. Four, no, five children."

Five kids. Now Zahra knew for sure the woman was crazy, and she'd heard enough. Reclaiming her hands, she said, "Thank you very much for the reading. How much do I owe you?"

"My treat," Ava said.

Lady Castilla gave a hearty laugh. "You can run, but you cannot hide from destiny, my child."

It sounded like a line from a horror movie.

The second Zahra walked away from Lady Castilla, she turned to Ava and said, "Can you believe that? I mean...*when you love, you love hard*," she mocked. "Who doesn't. And five kids? Ha!"

"I do recall Lady Castilla saying something about stubborn, too. She hit that one right on the head."

"I'm not stubborn." Zahra gave a playful pout.

Ava stopped and faced her. "Really?"

"Yes, really," Zahra countered.

A smirk curled Ava's pink painted lips. "Then call him."

Zahra eyed her sister for several seconds. "I can't, Ava." Her wounds were still fresh, and so were Gregor's. This just wasn't their time. Neither fate nor destiny would change that.

"The universe may not accept that," Ava said.

"It has to."

Ava threaded her arm through Zahra's and started to move again. "Believe it or not, you're somehow cosmically aligned with this man. Something tells me you couldn't deny him, even if you wanted to. And as hung up as you are over him, I guarantee he's experiencing the same inner turmoil over you."

Gregor Carter could have any woman in the world he wanted. Zahra seriously doubted he was sitting around pining away over her.

Chapter 13

Zahra's studio had been transformed from what was usually open space equipped with props and lighting equipment, to a backdrop of beautiful photographs and extravagantly dressed men and women in attendance to support a good cause.

She was thrilled with the number of people who'd shown up for her black-tie charity event, but far more impressed with the fact that they'd already raised several thousand dollars and the auction hadn't even started yet.

She gave Ava all the credit for that. Her sister knew how to work a room. It didn't hurt that most of the men in attendance had salivated over her most of the night. But who could blame them. The woman was gorgeous. The sweeping, formfitting dress she wore showed off her bodacious figure, sculpted legs—a dedication to the gym Zahra didn't possess. And as always, both her hair and makeup were on point, along with her sparkling personality.

Zahra loved Ava to pieces. Other than her parents, no one had her back like her sister. As if Ava could sense Zahra's eyes on her, she turned and waved what was appeared to be another check through the air.

Her sister angled her head, and Zahra's gaze followed, landing on the Honorable Eli Chandler, one of Mecklenburg County's most esteemed district court judges. Zahra was sure he'd added an extra zero just to impress Ava, who he'd shown interest in for the past several months. But his reputation as a ladies' man hadn't helped his cause.

Boisterous laughter drew Zahra's attention to a familiar face. *Nadine Trendal.* The brown-skinned, mature woman held the gold for being the life of any party, especially after several drinks. Zahra liked her. Considered old money, she was always gracious with her donations.

Chatter and laughter swirled around Zahra, bringing a smile to her face. She scanned the room. Everyone seemed to be having a good time mingling and appreciating the gorgeous photos scattered through the studio. Her breath hitched, and she dragged her eyes back to where they had been seconds earlier. *Gregor?*

"Champagne?"

Zahra sidestepped the young woman holding the silver tray of flutes and frantically swept the room. Nothing. Releasing the breath she hadn't realized she'd been strangling, she laughed at herself. Clearly, her mind was playing tricks on her. Her amusement ended there, though, because after a month, she still hadn't gotten over Gregor Carter.

Why couldn't she simply view him as just another moment in her past? She was determined to banish him from her thoughts, at least for the next two hours. Taking a glass from the tray, she downed it in one gulp. Hopefully, the sparkling wine would help.

"Everything okay?" Ava asked in a hushed tone, as she walked up beside Zahra.

Recharging her smile, Zahra faced her sister. "Yes. This is an amazing turnout tonight, right? And I see you have a not-so-secret admirer."

"Judge Chandler." Ava and the judge held each other's gazes from opposite sides of the room. "He's charming."

"Be careful," Zahra said, her big sister protectiveness rearing its head.

"I will. And you be careful with this," Ava said, passing Zahra a five-thousand-dollar check from the judge.

Zahra thanked Ava for all of her hard work. And by hard work she'd meant dazzling charms that had wrapped the single and married men around her finger tonight. When Ava sashayed away, Zahra escaped to her office to deposit the check along with the others in a lockbox.

Inside her tiny space, she kicked off the three-inch heels she wore to give her feet a break. While the open-toed, black, strappy shoes were gorgeous, they were not designed for comfort.

"Excuse me, miss. Has anyone told you how absolutely stunning you look?"

Zahra whipped around and gasped. "You're here." The sight of Gregor in what she was sure was a custom-tailored suit snatched her breath away. Her mind and body hadn't been playing tricks on her. The scorching heat of temptation burned through her. "What are you doing here?"

"I'm here for you."

He'd come for her? A twinge of excitement swelled her chest.

"Friends support friends, right?" he added.

She'd totally not expected that reason. Flashing an uneasy smile, she said, "Right. Thank you for coming. Friend." Gregor scrutinized her so attentively, it rattled her. "What is it?" she finally asked.

"That's not the only reason I'm here, Zahra."

"Okay," she said.

Gregor brushed past her and propped himself on the edge of her desk. She tried—unsuccessfully, of course—to ignore how sexy and powerful he seemed there. By the look on his face, something troubled him. Even though public commentary about him had significantly decreased, more fallout from the accident was her first thought.

"I…" He stopped and cleared his throat. "Something happened to me."

Zahra's brow furrowed, unease knotting her stomach. "What happened?"

"You. You happened. At Lake Lamont you became like molten lava in my soul. Then our time together was over." He paused. "I feel your absence, woman. With every breath. I know we—"

Feeling a rush of confidence, desire and need, Zahra crashed her mouth to Gregor's before he could finish his thought, kissing him with all the pent-up longing she'd harbored since they'd parted ways. Instantly, he responded to their connection, mirroring her hunger. One of his large hands rested behind her head as if to ensure her mouth didn't escape his. He had no cause for alarm. She wasn't going anywhere.

Gregor's free hand curled around her waist, pulling her even closer to him. His kisses never disappointed, but this one was defining and made a statement. More like a confession: *I've missed you.* Oh, she'd missed him, too.

Something about Gregor made her forget that she was usually methodical and cautious. When it came to him, there was no order, no vigilance and most noticeably, no fear. She wasn't sure whether that made her a fool or not.

Their mouths didn't part for a long time, but when they did, it was only for a millisecond, with Gregor crashing his mouth right back to hers. Every cell in her body was aware of him.

Aware of his touch.

Aware of his taste.

Aware of his scent.

Aware of his warmth.

And doubly aware of the hardness between his legs.

Her body relaxed against him, and he wrapped her in his arms. She was so comfortable and secure in them that it almost felt as if this was where she'd always belonged. His hold was both strong and gentle. And for the first time in a long time, she felt protected.

When their kiss ended a second time, their chests heaved up and down as if they'd run several miles to get to each other.

"I've been waiting on you," she said in a tiny voice, unsure if she'd actually meant for the words to come out.

"Sorry it took me so long," he said, pecking her gently. "I'm here now."

And while she was thrilled by his presence, she had concerns. "Are you sure you're ready to be here, Gregor? It would be remiss of me not to mention the fact that you're really fresh out of a relationship. And I'm—"

"You're not a rebound, Zahra, if that's what you're thinking. I know you feel it, too. This insanely powerful connection between us. Can you honestly tell me you don't?"

"If I said no, I'd be lying."

He smirked. "I know. I also know you have reservations and concerns. But we'll take it slow. I don't want to force this, Zahra. I want whatever this is happening between us to happen naturally. Are you okay with that?"

"I'm okay with that." She held his face between her

hands. "I want you. We have about ten minutes before Ava comes looking for me. Undress me."

Gregor released a tortured grunt. "There's nothing more I'd like to do than to strip you naked right here and now, but I want to do things differently this time." He kissed her palm. "I want to take sex out of the equation for now."

Zahra laughed, but stopped when Gregor didn't join in. "Wait, you're serious."

He nodded. "I am."

"Are you saying you want to old-fashion court me?"

He laughed. "An interesting way of putting it, but yes. Do you have a problem with that?"

Let's see. Did she have a problem with a man wanting to take the time to get to know *her*, not just her body? Hmm. That was a hard one. "No, I don't," she said.

Gregor kissed her hand again. "Good. Are you free on Saturday? I'd like to take you on a date."

Zahra wrapped her arms around Gregor's neck. "Well, I'll have to check my calendar, but something tells me I am."

"Where would you like to go?"

"Surprise me."

"Okay. I can do that."

His mouth covered hers, but their kiss was cut short when Ava entered the room. She released an audible gasp, followed by, "Holy shit."

Zahra broke away from Gregor's mouth and turned to face her sister. The woman wore sheer shock on her face, and her mouth hung wide open. Once her sister's face unfroze, Zahra made the introductions. Ava clearly couldn't contain her excitement, because she grinned so hard it looked as if the corners of her mouth would tear.

After several minutes of small talk, Ava excused himself. But, of course, she couldn't go quietly into the night. Stopping shy of the door, Ava snapped her fingers. "Oh, Zah, I almost forgot to tell you. Lady Castilla called to say congratulations." She smirked and was gone.

"Lady Castilla. That sounds exotic," Gregor said.

"She's..." Zahra stopped shy of revealing Lady Castilla's profession. No doubt he would think she was crazy. "...my old photography teacher." Zahra made a mental note to strangle Ava.

"Ah."

Gregor appeared satisfied with her answer. Before she was forced to make up any more tall tales, she took his hand. "Come with me. I want to show you something. But you have to promise you won't get upset."

Gregor wasn't usually into making promises he couldn't keep. But since he couldn't imagine anything Zahra had to show him would upset him, he agreed. "Are you sure you want to parade me through the studio? I don't want to disrupt your event."

"No one will recognize you with that beard and all of these curls."

When she ran her fingers through his hair, he realized just how much he'd missed her doing that.

"Tonight, you're just the average Joe."

She had no idea how refreshing that sounded. Moments later, he trailed her through the studio. As she'd predicted, no one recognized him. The handful of people they'd encountered paid little attention to him.

Coming to a stop, she said, "Close your eyes."

He looked at her with hesitation. For a man who trusted very few people, she had no idea the burden she was placing on him. She rested her hands on her hips, pulling his attention to the dress she wore—a formfitting, lacy black number that showed off just the right amount of cleavage.

"Come on. Shut them. I'm not going to take advantage of you."

Darn. Following her instructions, he let Zahra lead him a short distance; then she gave the order to open his eyes.

"Whoa," he said, massaging his beard.

Several framed, black-and-white shots of him, standing in the yard at the lake house, smoking his cigar, sat on easels. He remembered that moment well. It was the night after they'd made love for the first time through the fifth time. "It's me."

"Do you like them?"

Gregor moved closer for a better look. While none of the shots showed his face, they captured him in a way he couldn't explain. Zahra had a great eye. He didn't just like them. "I love them."

Zahra stood beside him. "I know you said no pictures, but there was just something about you at that moment. I couldn't resist. Your body is so beautiful, so commanding. It deserved capturing."

If she were trying to stroke his ego, mission accomplished. "Are they up for auction?"

"Initially, they were."

"Initially?"

"I couldn't bring myself to part with them. I didn't like the idea of you hanging on another woman's wall."

This made Gregor grin. "You wanted me all to yourself."

"I can't have you all to myself. You're Gregor freaking Carter." She wrapped her arms around his waist and rested her head against him. "I know I have to share you with the world, but with these, I get to appreciate something no one else can. Our memories at Lake Lamont." Zahra glanced up at him with tender eyes.

"There you are."

They both turned to see Ava. By her tone and the frantic look on her face, something was up. Obviously, Zahra sensed it, too, because she hurried over to her. He stayed back to give the women their privacy. Ava whispered something to Zahra that made her go stiff.

When she rejoined him, he could tell whatever news Ava had delivered wasn't good. He instantly felt the need to make whatever was wrong, right. "Is everything okay?"

"No. My ex just arrived."

She paused as if to gauge his reaction. He didn't have one. At least, not an outward one. Inwardly, he had questions. Why had she invited her ex? Hadn't she told him at the lake that they no longer associated? Had it been a lie?

He withdrew a little.

"Of all nights for him to pull one of his foolish stunts, he chooses tonight. He knows how important this event is to me."

Now he was confused because it sounded as if her ex had crashed the function. "You didn't invite him?"

"God, no," she said.

"Do you want me to handle it?"

Distress played on her face. "And risk drawing attention to yourself?" She shook her head. "No. I will handle this."

"Okay." But he couldn't promise he wouldn't intervene if he felt she needed him.

Curious for a glimpse, Gregor trailed Zahra to the main area. His gaze narrowed on the tall, brown-skinned man she approached. By the way her ex's mouth curled into a wide smile, he was overjoyed to see her.

Gregor's jaw clenched. Taking a glass off one of the passing trays, he tossed the liquid back. The dainty beverage did little to relax him as the scene unfolded in front of him. When the man leaned forward in an attempt to kiss Zahra, Gregor's chest tightened in anger. She pushed the creep away, then appeared to scold him. Good.

Gregor was about to walk away when Zahra's ex called for everyone's attention. Once he had it, the beaming man proceeded to get down on one knee.

What the...

Chapter 14

All Zahra could do was blink dumbly at Braswell down on one knee. In his hand was the gaudiest diamond ring she'd ever seen. This proved he'd never truly known her at all. For one, she'd never wear such a flashy piece of jewelry, even an engagement ring. For two, her ideal proposal was not in front of a room full of people. It also confirmed something else: Braswell Chesterfield had lost his damn mind.

Struggling to project an air of calm that she absolutely did not feel, she spoke through clenched teeth, "What do you think you're doing?"

"Winning you back," he said.

Braswell's expression teetered between uncertainty and hopefulness. Why, in a trillion years, had he believed this was a good idea? Had he assumed an audience would influence the outcome? If so, he was sorely mistaken.

Her gaze rose from the sparkly diamonds and settled on the sea of gleefully anticipating observers. They may have been touched by the moment, but she wasn't. Not one iota. A camera flashed, startling her. This was not a moment to be captured.

The first unmoved face Zahra connected with was Ava's, whose stunned look morphed to one of sentiment. The second was Gregor's. His inscrutable countenance gave little away. If she hadn't already intended to reject Braswell's ridiculous proposal, the way her heart swelled and stomach fluttered as she stared across the room at Gregor would have changed her mind. She just hoped this didn't change his about her.

Before she was forced to embarrass Braswell in front of all of these people, the fire alarm blared, shifting the focus inside the space. As would be expected, everyone lost interest in the proposal and focused more on saving themselves from whatever potential peril lurked.

As people filed out of the building, Zahra grabbed Braswell by his arm and dragged him toward the back of the building.

"What are you doing? We have to get out of here. The place could go up in flames at any second."

"There is no fire, Braswell, but there sure as hell are about to be some smoke and flames," a shaken Zahra said.

Immediately after the alarm sounded, Zahra had caught a glimpse of Ava moving away from the pull station. Like any great sister, Ava had gotten her out of a sticky situation. While she hated her guests had fallen victim to the diversion, Zahra was glad she'd been taken off the hot seat.

Immediately crossing the threshold of her office, she laid into Braswell, damning him for placing her into such an awkward position. Blasting him for trying to force her hand. Blaming him for ruining her event.

"I just want you back. When we were together, you always dropped marriage hints. I just thought that if I gave you what you wanted, you'd forgive me, and I'd get a second chance."

As usual, Braswell rattled off a hundred reasons why he'd done what he'd done, all of them in some way placing her at fault for his infidelity. All of them still not moving her one bit. He went on and on until she just couldn't take it anymore.

"Stop it! Just stop. I've moved on, Braswell. I'm seeing someone."

When his features hardened, Zahra knew the vulnerable-man routine had been a ruse. "Wow. That was quick. You didn't waste any time replacing me, did you?"

Zahra's face contorted into a ball of displeasure. "What did you think I was going to do, sit around and mourn you for the rest of my life?"

He slid his hands into his pockets and lowered his head briefly. "Who is he?"

"That's none of your business."

"Is he out there tonight?"

"Yes."

Zahra regretted her response instantly. All she needed was Braswell harassing every single man in attendance. And she definitely didn't need him and Gregor coming to blows over her. Truthfully, she doubted she needed to worry. Gregor was probably long gone. And who could blame him? No one wanted to deal with someone's crazy ex.

"I think you've caused enough damage for one night, Braswell. You should go."

He closed the distance between them, pasting on one of those smiles that, at one point, had the ability to make her panties slide right off. Thankfully, it no longer had an effect on her.

"You want to throw away everything we have, Z?" He trailed a finger down the side of her face.

Jerking her head away, she said, "*Had.* And for the record, you threw everything away the moment you *chose* to sleep with another woman."

"Dammit, Z, you know it meant nothing to me. She meant nothing to me."

"Apparently, neither did I. Goodbye, Braswell."

Lingering in silence for a long time, he finally moved away. Before leaving the room, he said, "He can't make you happy because he'll never be me."

She laughed. "See, that's where you're wrong. Knowing he'll never be you makes me extremely ecstatic."

Something dark and menacing flashed across his face before he continued out the room. Zahra wasn't sure what to make of the look. All she knew was she hadn't liked it.

The roar of sirens refocused her attention and alerted her to the presence of the fire department. A short time later, Zahra joined Ava and an extremely attractive fireman out front. After a quick sweep, the building was given the all clear.

"Are you okay?" Ava asked in a gentle voice, smoothing a hand up and down Zahra's back. "What that bastard did tonight was out of line."

Zahra massaged the nagging headache at her temple. "I just want to forget the last hour and revert back to how happy I was before Braswell arrived."

"Leslie and I can manage here if you need a moment," Ava said.

Zahra knew she could trust both Ava and Leslie—Zahra's part-time assistant—to handle things just as efficiently as she would. "You don't mind? I could use a moment to catch my breath." And prepare for the tons of questions she'd have to field.

"You know I've got your back. Always."

"Thank you." She paused, unsure about her next question. "Have you seen, Gregor?"

Ava's features softened. "No."

Zahra flashed a low-wattage smile, then headed to the back and out of one of the side doors to get some fresh air, using a tripod to prop it open. Hugging her arms around her waist for warmth and comfort, she closed her eyes and focused on the sounds of the night—

mostly the swoosh of cars buzzing by. Gregor's was probably one of them.

When the door banged closed behind her, her eyes flew open. Whipping around, she nearly stumbled over her own two feet. Large, warm hands shot up to brace her.

"Careful."

Zahra was sure astonishment showed on her face. "You're still here. After all of that commotion, I was sure you'd raced to your car and hightailed it out of here."

"And miss all of this excitement? It's not every day your girlfriend gets proposed to in front of you. Then fire trucks. I can't wait to see what else you have in store. You really know how to throw a party."

Zahra gave a dry laugh. "I'm glad you were entertained. I wasn't."

"Come here. I'm only messing with you," he said, kissing the top of her head. "So that was Braswell, huh?"

She grumbled, "Yes."

"I understand his addiction. You're one helluva drug, Zahra Hart. I imagine he's going through withdrawal."

He removed his coat and draped it over her shoulders. His scent—manly and fresh—saturated the expensive fabric, soothing her frayed nerves. While she would have preferred his arms around her, the coat was an acceptable substitute. "Are you addicted?"

All he offered was a cheeky grin. Zahra meshed her body against his, rested her head on his shoulder and closed her eyes. Gregor's strong arms encased her. She could stay like this forever.

"He left in an awful hurry. You're not wearing an engagement ring. Is it safe to assume you turned down his proposal?"

She reared her head back. "Of course, I did. Braswell's not the man I want in my life."

One side of his mouth lifted into a smile. "Being with me won't be easy, Zahra. It's not what you're used to. There'll always be media. There'll always be cameras. There'll always be rumors. It's going to take patience and a whole lot of trust. But I'm going to do my best to make you happy."

She knew he would.

Chapter 15

To Zahra, this day felt like it would never come, but it was finally Saturday and date night. Her *official* first date with Gregor. The way butterflies fluttered in her stomach, one would think it was prom night, and she had plans to lose her virginity.

In less than an hour, he would be ringing her doorbell, and she couldn't wait to see him. With his insane schedule—a trip to Indianapolis to finalize the new endorsement deal, a photo shoot for his menswear apparel line, and Thoroughbred obligations, they hadn't seen one another since her charity event the previous weekend.

Well, that was if you didn't include video chatting—and she didn't—because it wasn't the same as Gregor physically being there with her.

"Ow, Ava. It's too tight. It feels like my forehead is peeling back." Zahra lifted her hand to the bun her sister was fashioning on top of her head, but Ava swatted it away.

"Stay still, Zah. You're like an antsy five-year-old."

Zahra sighed. "You act like I'm about to walk down the aisle. We're just going to dinner *and*—" She paused, having no idea what came after the *and* because Gregor had refused to tell her. Truthfully, it didn't matter what he had in store. They would be together and that was enough for her.

"Well, I'm going to get you closer to the altar. Once he sees you, he'll be ready to propose."

Zahra groaned at Ava's mention of the word propose. "Please don't say that word. Flashbacks."

Every time she thought about the stunt Braswell had pulled at her studio, she seethed with anger. That alone should have soured her to men, but Gregor was the kind of sweet your body craved.

Ava cringed. "Sorry. And speaking of lowlife bastards, has he tried to contact you?"

"No, thank goodness. I think he's finally gotten the hint that we're *never* getting back together."

Ava pretended to spit. "Good riddance."

Zahra hoped.

"Do you think I'm being naive, Ava?"

She held Zahra's gaze through the mirror, a bemused look on her face. "About?"

"Gregor. We are from two totally different worlds and—"

"Stop right there." Ava moved around to face her. "Does Gregor strike you as the type of man who would invest the level of energy he's investing in you on a woman he's not interested in being with? The man came to claim you, for goodness' sakes. He could have simply chosen to go on with his life, but he wanted you to be a part of it. This is not a coincidence, Zah. It's destiny."

Maybe she was right.

Ava returned to tussling with Zahra's hair. "You really do like him, don't you?"

"Yeah, I do. I've never experienced a connection this strong, this intense with anyone. It thrills and scares me."

"Scares you? Why?"

"As crazy as it sounds, I'm already feeling something for Gregor, Ava. Not love, but something that suggests I am going to fall in love with him. I don't want to be hurt again."

Ava bent at the waist, wrapped her arms around Zahra's neck. "He's your one, big sis. I can feel it. And I have the sneaky suspicion that he does, too."

Gregor scrutinized himself in the mirror for the fourth time in the last twenty minutes. Why in the hell was he so nervous? It wasn't like he was about to walk down the aisle. A vision of Zahra all radiant in white filled his head. He shook the image away.

What the hell was that?

Had he really just visualized Zahra as his wife? More urgently, why hadn't the thought terrified the shit out of him? Marriage wasn't something that often bleeped on his radar. Which had been another source of tension in his and Selene's relationship. She'd wanted to be Mrs. Carter; he'd been content with her staying Ms. Hampton.

Zahra Carter. It had a nice ring to it.

"Slow down," he told the impeccably dressed man that stared back at him. "You're taking it slow, remember?" But Zahra made him want to move at the speed of light.

Gregor ran his hand over his clean-shaven face. While he'd chopped off the beard, he'd kept the curls. At least for now. He liked the way Zahra's hands felt running through them. They, too, would have to go once workouts started. It was hot enough under his helmet without the added mass further blocking air circulation.

Checking his watch, he gave himself one last once-over, then headed downstairs to the waiting sedan. There was one stop he needed to make before Zahra's, so he headed out a little early. He didn't want to chance being late for their first date.

Gregor slid in back of the Mercedes-Maybach and relaxed against the heated leather seat. *Damn.* Was it normal to be this anxious about seeing a woman? *No,* he answered quickly. But in his defense, Zahra wasn't just any woman. She was special. He'd realized it the first time he'd seen her. Okay, maybe not the first time. Definitely, the second time. Hell, he'd eventually realized it.

Special. He'd used that term plenty in the past, but this time he actually meant it. Zahra was the exception to the one rule he'd sworn to never break again: falling. A rule that had flown out the window before he'd ever left Lake Lamont. What was so different about Zahra? He didn't tax his brain trying to figure it out. Knowing in his gut was explanation enough.

Gregor engaged the massaging seat function, eased his head back against the rest and closed his eyes. The entrancing vibration nearly put him to sleep, and probably would have had the driver not announced they'd reached their destination. With all the traveling he'd done the past week, he was exhausted.

It took Gregor only several minutes to retrieve the gift he'd purchased for Zahra. He hoped she liked it. A short time later, he arrived at her townhome in historic West End. Tucking the gift-wrapped box under his arms, he moved to her door and rang the bell.

Ava answered and invited him inside. Gregor remembered Zahra telling him that her sister spent more time here than she did at her own place. Zahra had also confessed to enjoying her company. From what he gathered, the two were close. He wished he had siblings with whom to share the good and bad times. The closest he had to family were his teammates and Thad.

Scrutinizing his surroundings, Gregor nodded his approval. He favored open floor plans like this, too, and the high, vaulted ceiling. It made him feel less boxed in. Zahra's choice of vibrant colors—blues, greens, yellows—suited her personality. Colorful and cheery.

"Can I get you anything?" Ava asked.

"No, I'm good, but thanks."

"In that case…" She grabbed her purse off the counter. "Zah will be down shortly. Make yourself at home. I hope you two have a lovely evening. And it's nice seeing you again. I hope to see more of you."

"Thank you," he said. "It was nice seeing you again, too. And you definitely will."

Ava headed toward the door. Snapping her fingers, she

stopped and faced him. "Silly me, I almost forgot to tell you something." Her voice changed to a sinister pitch and the jovial expression morphed into a sneer when she said, "If you break my sister's heart, I'll come full-throttle for you."

Damn. "Um. Got it?"

She reverted back to the smiling, upbeat woman who'd welcomed him in. "Great. Tootles."

Gregor wasn't sure if he should be touched by Ava's dedication to her sister's happiness or fearful for his own safety. Conversely, she had said *if* he broke Zahra's heart. He definitely had no intentions of doing that. In theory, he was safe.

His eyes were still pinned to the front door when Zahra descended the stairs.

"Sorry for keeping you waiting," she said. "Ooo, you shaved your beard. Why? I liked it."

"It—" Zahra's appearance paralyzed him, causing his words to evaporate in his head. "Wow." Just when he thought she couldn't get any more beautiful.

If he had been a dog, his tongue would be wagging. Her hair was fashioned in a perfectly symmetrical bun on top of her head, exposing a neck that begged for his kisses. While she didn't need any at all, her face was lightly dusted with makeup. Not overdone, but just right. Her lips were glossy, yet bare of color.

Her lips were so tempting he had to fight the urge to dart across the room and crush his mouth to hers. His eyes drifted down the column of her neck and along her exposed shoulder. When he imagined peppering her soft skin with kisses, a shiver crept up his spine. The black and dark gray dress she wore clung as magnificently to her body as a priceless painting hung on the wall of a museum. And just like a curator would do, he planned to protect Zahra at all cost.

"You look absolutely amazing. I'll be the envy of every man."

She neared him, pressing her body against his. He hooked an arm around her waist.

"Since being envied is probably no different tonight than from any other day in the life and times of Gregor freaking Carter, I think you can handle it."

Yes, he could. He could handle it and her. *No sex, Carter. No sex.* The reminder didn't keep him from wanting the hell out of her right now. "I'm a lucky man."

Zahra smiled. "Kiss me, Mr. Lucky."

She didn't have to tell him twice.

The instant their mouths touched, they moaned in unison. As with each time her lips met his, a shock of awareness sparked through his entire body. His hand glided over the dip in the small of her back and came to rest on her butt, giving it a teasing squeeze. A tiny whimper slipped from her.

"You're trying to weaken my resolve, woman," he said against their joined mouths.

"I wouldn't dream of doing such a thing."

A second later, her hand snaked around to his crotch. His shaft blossomed in her grip. Allowing himself to enjoy several seconds of Zahra's stroking him, he pulled away from her hold and mouth. She donned a pouty face that made him laugh. Trapped in a fog of desire, he'd nearly forgotten he had a gift for her.

"I have something for you." He pointed to the medium-sized box on the table.

Zahra's eyes glowed with excitement, despite saying, "You didn't have to do that."

"I wanted to."

Retrieving the box, Zahra eased herself onto the sofa. After removing the bow, she lifted the top of the fancy enclosure. Pushing aside the blue filler, she gasped. He gave a modest smile when she glanced up at him. When he'd contemplated what to get her, he knew it had to be something meaningful. By the warmhearted expression on her face, mission accomplished.

She lifted the stuffed dog from the box.

"Do you like it?" he asked.

"I love it. It looks just like Waterspout—er, Brownie. I love it."

The way she hugged it to her chest, he believed her. "Come on, let's get out of here."

Fifteen minutes later, Gregor and Zahra were seated at the chef's table inside the bustling kitchen of The Duchovney Steakhouse. The way Zahra's eyes had lit up when the restaurant's executive chef came to personally welcome them gave him a feeling of triumph. He couldn't explain why her happiness was so important to him, but it was.

Honestly, he couldn't explain a lot of anything when it came to Zahra: why he thought about her constantly, why her touch uplifted him, why her smile ignited his soul. He'd never been that guy. The type to free-fall for a woman he barely knew. Yet, he was in full spiral.

"It smells amazing in here, Gregor," Zahra said. "The fresh bread, the spices. It's a sensory overload. Plus, we're sitting in the kitchen where all the magic happens. And we got a visit from Chef Norton. I follow him on social media," she whispered. "How did you manage to get reservations? They're booked for like the next eight months."

"I'm Gregor freaking Carter." He winked. "I know people."

While the prestigious Duchovney usually only offered one chef's table—that, coincidentally, had already been booked—a second had been placed to accommodate him and Zahra. He and his teammates were longtime supporters of the restaurant—putting them on the map, some would say—and it was where the team held the majority of their celebrations. So, when Gregor's assistant had called to secure reservations, it hadn't been a problem.

Another thing he liked about the place was their discretion. Gregor knew that they wouldn't walk out to a sea of flashing cameras due to one of the staff having alerted the media to his presence. Mark Duchovney always made sure their privacy was respected and had once fired an employee for trying to score a payday off several players on the team.

After a five-course meal fit for royalty, Gregor paid the check, thanked the kitchen staff for their hospitality, then led Zahra to the waiting car to take them to their next stop.

"So, what did you think?" he asked, threading his fingers in hers.

"My taste buds are still celebrating. That Parmesan and herb-crusted salmon was amazing."

Gregor laughed. "You're the only person I know who comes to one of the most renowned steakhouses on the East Coast and orders fish."

"I like fish."

"Yeah, but you could have gotten a forty-two-ounce tomahawk rib eye. I was paying, remember?"

"You're saying I should have taken advantage of the fact that you were paying and gotten something I didn't want just because it was expensive. Plus, what in the world would I have done with forty-two ounces of meat?"

A roguish grin spread across his face, an ungentlemanly-like image flashing in his head. Zahra leveled him with a playful scowl, and he laughed. "What?" he asked.

"Behave yourself."

"Yes, ma'am." He brought her hand to his mouth and kissed the back. "I just want you to have a great time tonight."

"My great time started the second you rang my doorbell. Everything that follows is just a bonus." She shifted slightly in her seat. "Gregor, I'm not with you because you can buy me hundred-dollar steaks. I can buy my own steak."

Curiosity got the best of him. "Why are you with me, Zahra?" It clearly wasn't for his money. And she wasn't a fame seeker. If rich and influential wasn't a draw, what was?

Straight-faced, she said, "Because you're just so damn good in bed."

Gregor barked a laugh. "Oh, you're only with me for *my* meat. I see how it is now."

She smirked. "Well, we both know that's not true, because you won't let me have any of your meat. And about that—"

Before she could launch a protest, Gregor latched his mouth to hers and kissed her senseless. The sweet wine they'd had at the restaurant still lingered on her tongue. He savored it just as much now as he had then. Even more so.

When their kiss ended, Zahra rested her hand on his cheek. "That's one of the reasons why I'm with you."

His brow furrowed. "Because I'm a good kisser?"

"Because you give me spontaneous kisses. You make me feel like a giddy, inexperienced schoolgirl, and I love it. I've never been kissed the way you kiss me. Completely. Thoroughly." She paused a minute. "It feels like you leave behind a piece of yourself every time our lips touch. I'm going to hold them safely and securely and keep collecting them until I can complete this puzzle known as Gregor Carter."

Had anyone ever said something so poetic to him? If they had, he couldn't recall it. "You think I'm a puzzle?"

"Yes. Sometimes, you look as if you want to share something with me. But just when I think it's coming, you falter."

"I've shared things with you."

"Surface things." She placed her hand over his heart.

"I want to hear the things you have locked away here. The things that truly make you who you are."

Feeling a smidge too vulnerable, Gregor looked away from Zahra's penetrating eyes. "Those things aren't pretty." Holding her gaze again, he said, "I don't want to scare you away."

She shook her head, the most sympathetic expression playing on her face. "You won't."

He eyed her in silence for a long moment. "Give me time?" It was more a question than a statement.

Leaning in, she kissed his temple, his cheek, a corner of his mouth, then pecked him on the lips. "I'll be right here when you're ready."

He was about to speak when Zahra's cell phone rang, startling her. "That's Ava's ringtone. I had better get it. She'll just keep calling until I do."

Gregor nodded his understanding, then slid his gaze out the window, focusing on the world zipping by. Admittedly, he'd never been an overly emotional person—another one of his ex's quips—but what Zahra had said overwhelmed him and had him feeling things he wasn't sure he was ready for.

"Ava. Esha? Is everything okay?"

When Zahra's body tensed beside him, it clued him in that something was wrong.

Chapter 16

The call from Ava's best friend, Esha, was the moment that had turned one of the best nights of Zahra's life into one of the worst. Though Esha had assured her Ava was okay, Zahra wouldn't be satisfied until she'd assessed things for herself, seen Ava with her own two eyes.

She rushed through the emergency-room doors of Carolinas Medical Center. For a Saturday night, it didn't appear all that congested. Her shoes clacked against the polished tile as she made her way to the reception desk.

Whispers swirled around them, and she noticed several sets of eyes staring past her, focusing on Gregor. Obviously, the lack of his beard made him recognizable, but no one approached for autographs or pictures. She did, however, notice several folks trying to use their phones on the sly to steal shots.

The women ogling him so intently didn't faze her. All she could focus on was getting to Ava. Approaching the desk, she gave the heavyset receptionist with purple hair her sister's name. The woman tapped on the keyboard, then provided her with a bay number. Purple Hair clicked the lock to the security door that separated the waiting area from the patient intake area, and Zahra rushed through.

Just as he had during the trip into the building, Gregor fell in step with her. She hated having to end their date night prematurely, but Ava needed her.

Or so she thought.

Laughter guided them to the location. When Zahra entered, Ava lay reclined in the bed, laughing at the handsome doctor who'd obviously told her a joke. Ava's blissful laughter calmed Zahra's frazzled nerves. All types of horrific thoughts had swirled inside her head on the drive here.

Other than an oximeter attached to her finger, no other machinery was connected to Ava. That had to be a good sign. No serious injuries. Esha was nowhere in sight. Had the woman left Ava there all alone? The thought frustrated Zahra.

"Sissy," Ava said, attempting to come up on her elbow. "Owww," she moaned, easing back down.

"Careful," Dr. Handsome said, flashing Ava a toothy grin.

"Yes, Doctor."

The brown-skinned, tall, slender man seemed completely enthralled with Ava, not giving them so much as a sideways glance. Aaron Culpepper, MD, the black stitching on his white coat read. Zahra reached Ava's bedside and took her hand into hers. "What happened, sweetie? Are you okay? Did you get hurt?" She shot questions off like missiles.

"I'm fine, Zah. I promise." She shifted her focus briefly to Dr. Handsome, who was grinning at her like a Cheshire cat. "I'm in good hands." Addressing Zahra again, she said, "I told Esha to tell you not to come."

Like that was supposed to stop her. "Where is Esha?" she asked a little too snappily.

"She went to the cafeteria."

So Esha hadn't abandoned her, after all. "Okay, so tell me, what happened?"

"Some idiot on his cell phone ran the red light. Thankfully, the sedan only hit the front end. A little more it would have T-boned me."

Zahra's gaze slid to Dr. Culpepper. "Is she going to be all right, Doctor?"

Dr. Culpepper's focus left Ava. "A bit sore for the next couple of days, but other than that, she'll be fine."

"See. I told you." Ava looked past Zahra. "I see you hiding back there, Gregor. Sorry for ruining your date."

Gregor took a step forward. "No harm, no foul. I'm just glad you're okay."

The smile on Dr. Culpepper's face dimmed when he eyed Gregor. By the slight wrinkle of his brow, he'd recognized him, too. But not in an I'm-a-Carolina-Thoroughbreds-fan kind of way, but more like a personal one. Gregor nodded at the man but hadn't reacted with familiarity. A beat later, Dr. Culpepper informed Ava a nurse would be in soon to discharge her, then excused himself from the room. Judging by his speedy escape, he definitely had some connection to Gregor. But how?

After a little more small talk, Ava insisted they leave and continue their date, assuring Zahra Esha would make sure she got home safely. Zahra wasn't having it. Asserting her big sister authority, she informed Ava that she would be the one making sure she got home unscathed.

Ava threatened to call security and have her removed from the premises. They all shared a hearty laugh. Eventually, Zahra surrendered. But under one condition—Ava called her the second she arrived home, just to put her mind at ease. Ava agreed.

Before Zahra reluctantly left, she hugged her sister as tight as she could without hurting her, said "I love you" a hundred times, ordered Ava to never scare her like this again and promised to allow Ava to tell their parents.

They bumped into Esha on their way out of the room. Zahra made sure the woman would, indeed, make sure Ava got home okay. Satisfied with her response, they said another round of goodbyes and continued out of the room.

In the hallway, Gregor turned Zahra to face him. He rested his hands on either side of her neck. "She's fine. Are you?"

Zahra appreciated Gregor's concern. "Yes. I'm just a little overprotective of the people I love."

Zahra kicked herself for using the term *love*. She didn't want Gregor to misinterpret what she was trying to say. Would he think she was hinting at being in love with him? *No*. Gregor was far more astute than that. She was just being paranoid.

"We all are," he said. "Your sister is just as protective over you. Trust me."

Zahra groaned. "Oh, God. What did she say? She threatened you, didn't she?"

Gregor smiled, then started moving again. Yep, she threatened him.

Zahra threaded her arm through his. "I won't be much fun for the rest of the night, Gregor. You should probably just take me home."

"Woman, do you actually think I'm going to let you be alone tonight?"

She'd hoped he'd say that. Spotting Dr. Culpepper at the nurses' station, Zahra wanted to thank him for tending to Ava, but when he spotted them, he took off in the opposite direction. Gregor was clearly oblivious to the man's odd behavior, but she wasn't. Then again, maybe she was the one misinterpreting the situation.

"Do you know him?" she asked.

"Know who, babe?"

"Ava's doctor. Dr. Culpepper."

Gregor looked baffled. "I don't think so. Why?"

"No reason."

Moving down the brightly lit corridor, Zahra noticed things she hadn't before. Like the framed photos of North Carolina landmarks that lined the walls, the multitude of beeps and chimes, intercom chatter and the heavy smell of disinfectant.

Zahra chuckled. "These shoes were definitely not made for a lot of walking," she said.

"I can carry you," Gregor offered.

"As tempting as that sounds, I think I'll pass." All she needed was pictures of Gregor carrying her through the halls of the hospital plastered on the front page of the morning paper. And speaking of media, she'd half expected a frenzy to be waiting for them as they left the hospital, looking to spin some ridiculous story. Luckily, there hadn't been.

The car waited for them when they exited the building. Zahra assumed they'd be staying the night at her place, but Gregor instructed the driver to take them to his.

"Are you okay going home with me?"

"Of course I am."

A soft smile hiked one side of his mouth. "Good."

He lifted her feet into his lap, removed the black four-inch heels she wore and began to massage her feet. She released a deep moan of satisfaction.

"You like that?" he asked.

Zahra responded in a drawn out yes.

The sedan pulled into the underground parking garage at Gregor's building a little after nine. Strapping back into her shoes, she exited the vehicle with him and took an elevator to the thirty-eighth floor. A short walk down an elegantly decorated hallway led them to Gregor's front door. Instead of using a key or the numbered pad, Gregor accessed the lock with his thumb-print. Stepping aside, he allowed Zahra to enter first. The second she walked into the foyer, motion-activated lights illuminated the impressive interior.

"Wow. Your place is…" Her words dried up. "Just wow."

The condo had to be at least six thousand square feet. The dramatic color scheme was dark, yet somehow welcoming. It suited Gregor. A modern design with an open floor layout made the place seem even larger. Walls of windows gave way to a breathtaking view of the city that she could get lost in for hours. The spotless kitchen was decked out in state-of-the-art everything.

Gregor took her coat and hung it in a closet near the front door, then removed his own. "Can I get you anything?" he asked.

Facing him, she said, "No, I'm fine."

"Yes, you are."

Gregor wrapped one arm around her waist and pulled her flush against his chest. The tiny peck he gave her only revved her up for more, but she warned her body to behave.

"Have I told you how amazing you look tonight?"

She shrugged one shoulder. "Once or twice. But can a woman really hear it too much?"

He chuckled. "You. Look. Amazing."

The kiss that followed was the kind she was used to receiving from him.

Deep.

Passionate.

Long-lasting.

Exhilarating.

The list could go on and on, but she chose to put her focus elsewhere. When Gregor pulled away, it took all her might not to follow his lips.

"Make yourself at home. I'll be right back."

Gregor climbed the floating staircase, eyeing her all the way to the top. When he moved out of sight, she took the opportunity to thoroughly scrutinize her surroundings. Something was missing here. After several sweeps of the room, it finally hit her. Photos. None of friends. None of family. None of himself. Nor were there any personal effects such as awards, trophies, degrees. Nothing. The space was sentimentally barren.

Moving toward the sofa, she changed her mind and veered, instead, out onto the massive balcony. The gust of cold air that greeted her made her shiver. She closed her eyes and inhaled a deep, cleansing breath.

"There you are. I walk away for five minutes and you disappear on me," Gregor said. He draped a throw over her shoulders, then wrapped his arms around her from behind, kissing the crook of her neck. "What are you doing out here?"

"Enjoying this magnificent view and thanking God for protecting my sister."

Gregor kissed the back of her head. "If you have a moment, say a prayer for me."

She rested her head back against him. "I haven't stopped praying for you since the first day we met. It felt like you needed it then. It feels like you need it now." Especially after seeing just how alone he seemed.

"No one's ever done that for me," he said.

"What? Said a prayer for you?"

"Yes."

"I'm sure they have, Gregor. You just don't know it." There had to be someone in his life who thought enough of him to lift him in prayer. There had to be. But if not, she had him covered.

"Yeah, maybe," he said, tightening his arms around her.

Silence descended on them for a brief moment.

"Gregor?"

"Mmm-hmm."

"You don't have any photos sitting around, not even of yourself. Why?" Gregor's body tensed slightly as if he'd been uncomfortable with the question. She considered withdrawing the query, but then decided against it. If they were to get to know one another, this was how they did it, by asking and answering questions.

"Before I went to live at The Cardinal House, I moved around a lot. From one foster home to another. I was never in one place long enough to settle in, make it mine. I guess that mentality is embedded in me."

"But this is your home." No one could snatch this one from him.

"I love this place, but it doesn't quite feel like home yet."

"How long have you lived here?"

"Three years."

Three years! Zahra screamed in her head. And the place still didn't feel like home to him? At that moment, she garnered a great deal of sympathy and compassion for Gregor. "It sounds like you only consider this place a temporary refuge."

"That's the perfect way of describing it," he said.

"We have to change that. When you walk through your front door, it should feel like you've entered your sanctuary. This should be one place that always brings you peace." She rotated in his arms to face him. "You have to establish your roots. I'll help you."

Chapter 17

Gregor left the field at the Thoroughbreds' practice facility and headed for the shower. Instead of taking a lavish vacation to some international location and spending insane amounts of money, as he usually did, he chose to use the off-season to get his ankle in tip-top shape. Definitely by OTAs. While the organized team activities were voluntary, he'd never missed participating. Thank God his ankle was pretty much there.

At the mention of God, he thought about Zahra and her admission to praying for him. How blessed was he to have a woman who remembered him in her prayers? He used the towel tucked inside his waistband to wipe away the sweat beads rolling down the back of his neck. Eighty-four was not typical for early April. That, along with the unforgiving midday sun beaming down, had nearly melted him during his outdoor drills.

Grabbing his cell phone, he smiled at the text message Zahra had sent him.

Miss u. Stay hydrated.

He thumbed a reply.

Miss u 2, baby. Coming over tonight?

Book club, remember?

She punctuated it with a sad and a happy face.

You're more than welcome to join us, if you like.

A grinning emoji followed.

Damn. He'd forgotten about that. Zahra had provided early copies of her upcoming release to the ladies, and they would be discussing the book tonight. Five women, wine and a book where the hero was loosely based on him? Nope, he would pass.

Since I haven't read the book, I would only be in the way.

Send.

That wasn't wholly true. Zahra had left a copy she'd been proofing at his place. He'd read a page, then a chapter, and then ten chapters. Before he'd known it, he'd finished the entire book in less than three hours. Afterward, he'd downloaded her entire audiobook library. His boys would clown him off the team if they knew he'd spent hours listening to—and thoroughly enjoying—her romance novels.

Zahra was talented. Like crazy talented. Her books had made him laugh, yell and once or twice fight tears, especially the one about the homeless female vet. Just like in real life, she had a way of scrambling your emotions in the books she wrote. Writing was her calling, and he experienced her passion for it on every page.

Gregor chuckled at the pouting GIF she sent back.

About to shower. Talk later, he typed. His thumb hovered over a heart sticker but reconsidered adding it. He pressed send.

Okay. Several lip images came through.

Before he could place the phone back in his bag, it vibrated. Swiping a finger across the screen made the call active. "What's up, Thad?"

"You just love giving me heart palpitations, don't you?"

"What did I do this time?" He'd kept his nose squeaky clean since the accident. Honestly, his low-key behavior had more to do with Zahra than anything else. She made him want to do better, be better. Plus, she wasn't the type of woman who would put up with his antics.

"Did you steal someone's fiancée?"

Steal someone's— Shit. He had to be referring to the incident at Zahra's event. How did Thad know about that? It was a silly question. The man was abreast of everything.

"And when were you going to tell me you're *dating* my wife's client?"

"I didn't realize I had to."

"G…" Thad released a heavy sigh. "We're barely arm's distance from the last media frenzy. We don't need any more bad press. Not right now. Not ever, would be nice, too. Tell me you didn't steal someone's future wife?"

The idea of Zahra being anyone's future anything, other than his, had an unpleasant effect on him. "No, I didn't," he grumbled into the phone. "Where are you even getting this BS from? Wait. Let me guess. One of those trash gossip sites."

"Does it matter? It's out there. We're trying to repair your image, remember? This doesn't help. Maybe you two should stay low-key for a while. Just until this blows over."

Was he kidding? Hide like some fugitive? "That's not going to happen, man." And he definitely wouldn't make Zahra feel as if she were some dirty little secret of his. "Her lunatic ex thought she'd take him back if he proposed in front of a room full of people. It didn't work."

"Do you think he's responsible for leaking the story? If so, I'll slap him with a defamation suit so fast his head will pop off his body." Thad slammed what sounded like an open hand against his desk.

Gregor washed a hand over his head. "It's a possibility. Or it just as easily could have been one of the dozens of attendees at the charity event who'd witnessed the fiasco." Which seemed more likely the case. "They could have seen pictures of Zahra and me online and jumped to conclusions. Who knows? But I'm not sweating it." And he doubted Zahra would either.

"Well, I am. And you're paying me good money to do so. Is this ex going to be a problem?"

"No," Gregor said with confidence. However, he couldn't see into the future. He didn't know what the man was capable of. But, by the same token, Zahra's ex didn't know what he was capable of either. And for Zahra, he could be capable of a whole lot.

"We'll see," Thad said. "We'll see."

Zahra popped open another bottle of moscato and carried it back into the living room where her Hartfelts—the name she'd given the ladies who made up her book club slash beta reader team—laughed and snacked on appetizers. Ava, who'd been one of her biggest supports since day one. Charity Chastain, Zahra's childhood friend. Moni Cox, her hairstylist. And Tameka Bell, her college roommate and very first beta reader. She loved when they all got together because it was a guaranteed awesome time.

Zahra refilled everyone's glass, set the bottle on the small table next to the sofa, then eased onto one of the oversize pillows on the floor, next to Ava.

Moni raised her hand as if she were about to say the Pledge of Allegiance. "I swear 'fore gawd, if a man did half the things in the bedroom the hero did to the heroine, I'd have all his babies, suck his toes, even shave his hairy balls if he asked me to."

The room exploded in laughter.

Ava tossed an olive at Moni. "You'd do those things if he offered you a steak dinner."

Another round of laughter filled the room.

Once things settled, Zahra said, "Okay, ladies, give me your honest opinions. Did *The Sweet Scent of Love* stink?"

For Zahra, this was the first in a long time that she actually loved every single word she'd placed on the page. Leona had thought so, too. Zahra felt she'd done the book justice and truly allowed the hero and heroine's love story to authentically shine.

"Z," Charity began, "I'm not sure what kind of love voodoo you worked on that keyboard, but I personally think this is the absolute best novel you've ever penned."

When everyone voiced their agreement, Zahra felt an overwhelming sense of relief. One thing she liked about this group is that no one sugarcoated anything. If they thought the book was garbage, they would have certainly told her, like they had with the last book.

With that book, each woman had agreed it lacked the usual connection her characters held. At the time, things had been rocky between her and Braswell, and that had clearly projected onto her writing. This book was different. She'd experienced something wonderful at Lake Lamont and she spilled every ounce of it onto the pages of *The Sweet Scent of Love*.

Chasity continued. "The chemistry between the hero and heroine leaped off the pages. The way he cherished her was mind-blowing. The simple things he did to make her happy were beautiful."

"Yesss," Ava said. "He was so in tune with her that it was magical to read. You made me want to fall in love."

Tameka chimed in with, "If a man adored me the way Gabriel adored Kimberly, I might consider remarrying."

"Nah," Ava and Tameka said in unison, then high-fived.

"Speaking of marriage—"

The doorbell rang, halting Charity and drawing all their attentions to the front door.

"Must be the food delivery," Zahra said. She pushed up from the floor. "I'll be right back."

Laughter flowed from the room as Zahra moved toward the door, snagging a pen off the counter to sign the receipt. When she opened the door, an instant smile swelled her cheeks.

"Gregor?" She pushed her brows together. "What are you doing here?"

He flashed one of those dazzling smiles. "You invited me, remember?"

Zahra placed a hand on her hip. "Yes, I did. But I do remember you declining."

He stepped forward, hooked one arm around her waist and pulled her flush against him. With his mouth inches from hers, he said, "I changed my mind. Is that okay?"

"Y-yes," she said, experiencing dizzying effects from his close proximity.

"Good."

His mouth covered hers, claiming it in a raw and hungry manner. Obviously, one of her girls must have peeped around and witnessed what was happening, because there was a gasp. Zahra and Gregor laughed into each other's mouths.

When the kiss ended, she took his hand. "Come meet the girls."

Inside the living room, Zahra made the introductions. Ava and Gregor greeted as if they were the best of buddies. Charity and Tameka were visibly stunned by his presence and did little more than stare, trancelike, at him. Who could blame them? The man was hypnotizing. And the pair of relaxed-fit jeans, and a sage-colored T-shirt that hugged his toned frame only added to his appeal. Moni's face glowed with appreciation.

"Ladies," Gregor said in a smooth tone. "Hope you don't mind me joining you."

"Not at all," Moni said, twirling a lock of her green hair around her finger.

Zahra laughed at Moni's harmless flirting.

Amused, she pointed to the pillow she previously occupied. "You can have my spot," she said. "I'll sit here." She pointed to the space beside him. As she lowered to the floor, Gregor grabbed her midsquat and directed her into his lap.

Sounds of endearment swirled around them.

"My lap's a lot softer than the floor, don't you think?"

For a brief moment, everyone in the room disappeared and it was only the two of them there. Zahra snapped out of her trance. "Um, where were we?" she said.

"We were about to discuss the proposal," Moni said.

The mention of a proposal made Zahra think about the mistruth floating around that Gregor was responsible for breaking up her engagement to Braswell. How ridiculous. She hated rumors. Especially ones about her. However, she hadn't poured much energy into it, because she knew the truth.

Moni cooed. "That scene was definitely one of my favorites. It was simple, yet so elegant and just what Kimberly had dreamed of. A man has to truly know a woman to get it so perfect."

"That was a great scene," Gregor said. "I never would have expected that from Gabriel. He didn't strike me as sentimental. At least at first. But I guess when a man cares for a woman the way he clearly cared for Kimberly, there are no limits to what he's willing to do for her."

Every set of eyes in the room landed on Gregor. Zahra's chin was nearly touching her chest.

His brows bunched. "What?"

"You...you read my book?"

He nodded. "You left it at my place. I was hooked on page one. You are truly gifted."

"You read my book," she repeated, still unable to believe he'd taken the time to do so. Braswell had never taken the time to read any of her books. She hadn't even been able to get him to listen to an excerpt.

"I've read all of your books," he said. "Actually, I've *listened* to all of your books."

All she could do was stare at him. *He's read all of my books.* Something in her heart pounded even stronger for him.

"Um, do you two need some privacy?" Ava asked.

Zahra tossed a chip at Ava. "Mind your business."

Within an hour, it felt as if Gregor had always been a part of their group. The women seemed to view him as an average Joe and not the star football player that he was. He truly could adapt to any situation. She valued the fact that he got along with her friends and Ava so well. What fascinated her was the fact that Gregor had been an extremely active participant, asking one thought-provoking question after another.

"Okay, Gregor, since we're talking about attraction, what drew you to Zahra?" Moni asked.

"Hey. We're discussing Gabriel and *Kimberly*, not *Gregor* or *Zahra*," Zahra said. "Next—"

Gregor cut into her protest. "Her confidence. Her compassion. Her ability to soften and tame an angry beast."

"Aww," the women said in unison.

He continued. "We were like oil and water when we first met. She was so damn ornery."

Zahra gasped, then pressed her fingers into her chest. "Me? I nicknamed you Mr. Crabby. You were an asshole when we first met."

Gregor chuckled and raised his hands in mock surrender. "Okay, okay. I'll admit I wasn't easy to get along with. Thank you for putting up with me." He leaned forward and stole a peck.

"Look at you two now. Like a perfectly blended soy iced chai tea latte," Ava said.

More laughter filled the room.

"Your turn, Zahra," Charity said. "What drew you to Gregor?"

A lazy smile curled Zahra's lips as she stared at Gregor. "Those eyes," she said. "What I saw in them."

Fine lines crawled across Gregor's forehead. "What did you see?" he asked.

"Gentleness. I knew you weren't the brute you pretended to be."

"God, you two are just too stinking cute," Moni said.

"Okay, enough about us. Let's get back to the book," Zahra said.

It was a little past eleven when Zahra said good-night to her girls. She stood on the porch, waving goodbye until they each were safely in their vehicles and on their way. When she returned inside, Gregor had retaken a seat on the oversize pillow. Zahra straddled his lap, wrapping her arms around his neck.

"I have to admit, you kind of impressed me tonight," she said.

"Did you think your man couldn't hold his own?"

"I never doubted you for one moment." She pecked his lips gently. "There are a lot of layers to you, Mr. Carter. I'm enjoying watching them slowly peel away."

"You make it easy," he said. "I'm comfortable with you. Like genuinely comfortable. It feels good."

"Thank you for coming tonight. I'm still stunned that you read the book."

"Hey, the hero is loosely based on me, right?"

"My characters are loosely—"

"Based on everyone you come in contact with," he said, finishing her thought.

Zahra laughed, still refusing to confess Gabriel was 99.9 percent influenced by Gregor. "Exactly." She sobered. "You have no idea how much your reading my books means to me."

"As your man, I should be one of your biggest supporters. Plus, I learned a lot."

"Like what?"

"For one, I discovered I really like romance novels. Yours, at least. And don't you dare ever repeat that. Especially to any of my boys. I have an image to uphold."

Zahra hadn't actually met any of Gregor's friends yet, but she was looking forward to being introduced to them and their significant others. From her shameless indulgence of reality television, Zahra knew how snooty and rude the wives or girlfriends of athletes could be. She hoped that wouldn't be the case. While she wanted to get along with them, she wouldn't allow herself to be disrespected.

"For two, the right woman can totally change a man's entire view on life. For three, romance novels can be the perfect escape. For four, you're a freak. Some of those bedroom scenes, just scandalous," he said in a voice filled with humor.

"I can't believe you just said that. My love scenes are tasteful. Scandalous. I'll show you scandalous." She fought him playfully.

"I give, I give," he said. "Seriously, though, I think it's beautiful how much Gabriel enjoyed making love to Kimberly, and the fact that he made it his priority to know every single inch of her body. What she liked." He dragged a finger along her arm. "What turned her on. Places she enjoyed being touched, teased."

"That was why she loved when he made love to her. He made her feel things no man ever had before." Her eyes lowered. "I wonder if he had been able to stop making love to her, would she have felt like—" she paused a moment, her gaze coming up to meet his "—like maybe she wasn't fulfilling him in the same way he was satisfying her?"

"I'm not—" Gregor stopped abruptly. "Wait, is that what you think?"

Zahra glanced away, not believing she'd allowed the words to travel beyond the safety of her head.

"Look at me, Zahra." When she did, he continued, "Is that what you think?"

Exhaling, she said, "I'm not sure what to think, Gregor. At week one, I was like okay. Week two, I was like hmm. We're at week four now, and I'm confused. At the lake, it felt like you couldn't get enough of me. Now, it's like you don't want me."

"Do you think I'm cheating on you?"

"No. Not once have I felt that way," she said without hesitation.

Gregor eyed her hard, possibly trying to decide whether or not to believe her. He could. If she'd thought for one minute that he had been unfaithful, they wouldn't be here.

"I love making love to you. Love it. Like really love it," Gregor said. "But for the first time in forever, sex hasn't felt like a priority for me. I love just being with you, Zahra. Talking. Laughing. Just being. But don't think for one second that you don't turn me all the way on. That I don't want you. Trust me, I do. Every single second we're together I want you. But I also want more than just your body. And that's what I was trying to show you. I'm—"

Zahra pressed her index finger to his lips. "Shh." She grabbed the hem of her shirt and pulled the material over her head. A second later, her bra followed. An exhilarating feeling washed over her when Gregor drew his bottom lip between his teeth.

Clinging to Gregor's dark, hungry gaze, she smoothed her hands over her breasts, further stimulating her already aching nipples. As she continued to run them down her rib cage, Gregor placed his hands over hers and glided along with her.

Her movement stopped at her waist. Drawing her hand from underneath Gregor's, she unfastened her jeans, then lowered the zipper. Gregor's eyes lowered. His manhood hardened and pressed into her pulsing clitoris.

"You've shown me that we're about more than just sex. Now show me how much you want me."

It was a challenge he eagerly and swiftly accepted. Before she could take her next breath, he had her flat on her back. She raised her hips to allow him to remove her bottoms. He didn't bother removing panties. Instead, he pushed them aside, lowered his head between her legs and worked potent black magic.

Gregor devoured her. She screamed his name, over and over again. Torn between wanting this sweet torture to last and needing it to end so that she could feel him inside her, she closed her eyes and rode the beautiful wave. Her body capsized when he curled two fingers inside her.

The powerful orgasm shattered her into a thousand tiny pieces. Her body still quivered when he removed his fingers, stood, undressed and sheathed himself. Returning to her, he removed her panties, then blanketed her body with his. His thick erection teased her opening, and she angled her hips to take him inside her.

He wouldn't allow it.

A whimper rolled from her throat. "I need you," she said. "Desperately."

Gregor's mouth lowered to her breast. He sucked one nipple between his lips, lapping and teasing it with his tongue, while he rolled the other between his thumb and forefinger. Kissing his way up her body, he glided his tongue across her bottom lip.

Zahra cried out when Gregor plunged deep inside her. His strokes were long and hard, giving her exactly what she'd craved for so long. Their bodies slapped together, filling the room with the sounds of untamed lovemaking.

Gregor withdrew long enough to flip Zahra onto her stomach and hike her hips. He entered her from behind. Securing a firm grip on her waist, he drove into her with speed, force, determination.

Heat pooled in her belly, signaling the onset of another orgasm. Her nails dug into the fibers of the carpet as she fought off the release. Unfortunately, neither of their bodies cooperated. Seconds after her body quaked, a growl tore from Gregor.

He collapsed on her, his damp chest resting against her back. The weight of him felt wonderful. His heavy breath tickled her shoulder. "That was amazing," she said.

"That was just the beginning," he said, kissing the back of her neck.

Her head shifted toward him. "What?"

"You said to show you how much I want you. I plan to do just that." He kissed her shoulder. "You should probably get some rest, baby. It's going to be a long night."

Chapter 18

Zahra eyed the calendar on her office desk in disbelief. Was it really the first day of May? Where in the heck had the time gone? Her focus shifted to the large red circle drawn around the twenty-sixth. Her parents' forty-second wedding anniversary. A warm sensation filled her chest thinking about how they were still so much in love and happy after all of these years.

"I was told I could find the most beautiful romance writer in the world inside this office. Is that true?"

Zahra glanced up, her lips curling into a wide smile. "Gregor. What are you doing here?"

She came from behind her desk. Once she was within arm's reach, he pulled her into him. God, she loved when he did that. Acted as if he could never be this close to her and not touch her. Instantly, her body relaxed against his as it always did.

"I was in the neighborhood and was hoping you were free for lunch."

"Just so happens, I am." Her noon appointment had canceled, freeing up her schedule until two. "In the neighborhood, huh?"

He flashed one of those killer smiles. "Okay, I may have exaggerated. I just wanted to see you. And…" His mouth moved within inches of hers. "I really needed to do this."

Gregor captured Zahra's mouth in the all-consuming manner she'd grown accustomed to. Their tongues engaged in a tantalizing battle. Gregor's hands snaked down her body and rested on her backside, giving it a gentle caress. She moaned softly into his mouth, their delicious exchange awakening her body. Why couldn't she control herself around him?

A minute or two later, Gregor groaned and pulled away. "Quit trying to seduce me, woman. I am not a piece of meat."

Zahra laughed. She loved his wacky sense of humor. "You are full of it. Let's go before you get me in trouble."

After overindulging at her favorite sushi restaurant, Zahra was all too willing when Gregor suggested they take a stroll through Freedom Park. She needed the energy the walk would give her because she had a long evening ahead of her.

All of the unsolicited publicity dating Gregor had garnered her had caused her studio bookings to triple.

She wasn't complaining. She was grateful for all of the new business.

"I love it here," she said as they moved along the trail. "It's even better being here with you," she added, bumping Gregor playfully.

"Keep on, you're going to make me feel special," he said.

"You are." She pulled her gaze away from him and eyed the water. Far more special than she'd ever dreamed he'd be. "Do you come here often?"

"Not often. Me and a couple of the guys run here sometimes. We mostly do Laurel Loop at Lake Norman Park. I like it because most of the trail is shaded. On occasion, we'll do Booty Loop in Myers Park."

"For the life of me, I don't understand why people run if no one is chasing them," Zahra said.

Gregor chuckled. "It helps me clear my mind. And helps me stay in shape during the off-season. I like to eat."

"Yes, you do." She recalled how he'd polished off her leftovers at the restaurant. "But with that chiseled body, no one would ever know it." She ironed a hand over his midsection and moaned.

"All right. You better quit before you start something."

Gregor draped his arm around her shoulders and pulled her close to him. She loved being close to him. It was hard to believe that the Gregor the public experienced and the one she'd gotten to know so well were one and the same. Shading her eyes, she said, "I wish I would have had the foresight to bring my sunglasses. It's bright out here."

Gregor stopped, removed his designer eyewear and slid them onto her face.

"Trust me. You don't want me wearing these. I've gone through about twenty pairs already this year. I'm not sure I can afford to replace these."

A roguish grin spread across his face. "If you break them, I can think of one or two ways to recoup the cost." His brows bounced twice.

"You're bad." She adjusted the glasses. "Ooo, I like these. How do I look?"

"Like a goddess."

When he winked at her, butterflies fluttered in her stomach. She was a grown-ass woman, so why did Gregor constantly make her feel like an inexperienced teenager in love with the star quarterback? Maybe because she was. Not the teenager part. The thought rattled her, so she pushed it aside for now.

"So, one of my boys is having a birthday party for his girl in a couple of weeks. What do you think?"

"What do I think about what?"

"About going with me?"

Whoa. He wanted her to meet his friends. That was a huge step for them both. "Are you asking if I'd like to accompany you to a star-studded affair to celebrate with your football buddies and their significant others?"

Gregor's brow furrowed as if she'd confused him. "I'm not sure about the star-studded part, but the rest sounds about right."

Zahra pressed a finger into her cheek and glanced

heavenward. "Hmm." A second later, she grinned. "I would love to attend with you, Mr. Carter."

"Good."

Gregor turned away and washed his hand over his lips, a troubled look on his face. Had he hoped she'd say no to his invitation? Was he apprehensive about her meeting his friends? Did he think she wouldn't fit in? A thousand questions pulsed through her head. *Ugh. Stop it, Zahra. You're being ridiculous.* If he hadn't wanted her to go, he wouldn't have extended the invitation. Right?

"Is there something else?" she asked.

"Hmm?"

"Was there something else you wanted to tell me?"

A tense beat of silence played between them before he said, "No. There's nothing else," then flashed a smile.

So why did her gut tell her there was? Quieting her instincts, she said, "I'll go under one condition."

Gregor stopped, then shifted to face her. His eyes narrowed in obvious curiosity. "What's the condition?"

"You have dinner with my parents and me at the end of the month. It's their anniversary."

Gregor's lips parted, then closed as if he reconsidered what he was about to say. His gaze slid away briefly. When he eyed her again, an uncertain look was on his face.

"I, um…" He rested his hands on his hips and dropped his head.

"You think it's too soon," she said as more of a statement than a question. If that was the case, she would understand. Never would she force him into an uncomfortable situation.

His head rose. "It's not that. I've never..." His words trailed. "I've never met a woman's parents before. No one has ever invited me to meet their parents."

Zahra was sure her face flashed utter confusion. "Really? Never?"

He shook his head.

"But you were with your ex, what, close to two years. You *never* met her parents? Ever?" How was that even possible?

"Her parents were extremely religious and didn't approve of some of her life choices. Namely, me. I was a bad boy and not good enough for their daughter, they thought."

"She gave up her family for you?" The thought of such a sacrifice was jarring to Zahra because she was so close to hers. The idea of being forced to choose was tormenting.

"No, nothing like that. I would have never stood between her and her family. Family is everything."

Zahra noted a hint of sadness in Gregor's eyes. He was right; family was everything. Maybe one day he'd get to know the joys and blessings of having one. Maybe she would give him that.

"She visited them," Gregor continued. "*I* was just never welcomed with her." He shrugged. "I respected her parents' position. That was their daughter. They were just doing what they felt was necessary."

"And your ex was okay with their judging you like that?"

He shrugged. "Apparently."

Wow. To think his ex's parents had labeled him without ever taking the time to get to know him. They'd blown the opportunity to know a kind, gentle man. Had his ex even stood up for him? Had she not loved him enough to ask her parents to get to know him before casting him aside like garbage?

Zahra threaded her arm through his and started moving again. "Don't worry. My parents won't judge you. They're going to love you." Just as much as she did.

God, she couldn't believe she'd just admitted that. Even to herself. She was in love with Gregor. *Wow.* She was in love with Gregor, she repeated as if the first time hadn't rattled her enough. *Okay. This was real.*

She was in love with Gregor. And it couldn't have felt more right.

Zahra's jaw had touched the floor when they'd entered the Sanctuary South Ballroom for the birthday bash close to two hours ago. The lavishly decorated room looked as if it had been snatched from the pages of a child's fairy-tale book. No expense had been spared transforming the space into an enchanted garden.

Flowers dangling from the ceiling. Makeshift grassy knolls. Sculpted topiaries everywhere. The scene was absolutely breathtaking. She'd desperately wanted to take a picture, but cameras and cell phones had been prohibited.

Honestly, she couldn't believe how much fun she was having at the birthday celebration. And to think she'd been nervous about attending. To her delight, everyone had turned out to be great. Well, almost everyone. There had been two wives who'd been dismissive. That was okay. Gregor hadn't seemed overly fond of their husbands anyway, so she doubted they'd be spending much time around either of them. Which was fine with her.

Gregor turned her in a spin, then pulled her to him, her back resting against his chest, his arms secured snuggly around her. They'd spent the past half hour on the dance floor. The good thing about being here was the fact that most of the attendees held some level of celebrity, so there were no awestruck fans wanting autographs or selfies. In this setting, she had Gregor all to herself.

"Are you having a good time?" he asked over the roar of the cover band, who'd performed everyone from Anthony Hamilton to Marvin Gaye.

"The best," she said in an equally elevated tone.

"Good," Gregor said, kissing the side of her neck. "Just so you know, the second we're home, that dress is coming off," he whispered close to her ear.

"Promises, promises."

Dancing through several more songs, Zahra excused herself to the restroom. She marveled at the marble-laden room. The theme had spilled over into the elegant space, with the ten or so mirrors draped in greenery and dotted with butterflies.

A check of her makeup reminded her of the spine-tingling kiss Gregor had given her before she'd left him on the dance floor. Touching her lips with two fingers, she smiled. Was this really her life? Was it truly possible that she could be this happy with someone?

Giving herself a once-over, she admired the dropped V-neck, sequined, champagne-colored party dress she wore. The one Gregor had promised to rip off her the second they got home. *Home.* It was the exact word he'd used. It had rolled off his tongue so effortlessly that she wasn't sure he'd even realized what he'd said. But hey, she'd spent so much time in his bed that his place felt like a second home.

She latched the stall door just as someone entered. Several someones, judging by the click-clack of heels against the floor.

"The nerve of him to bring his rebound to *my* cousin's birthday party. Who in the hell does he think he is? That wasn't cool. Not cool at all."

Uh-oh. Sounded like someone was upset. Zahra usually tended to her own business, but her ears perked to the fuming woman's rant. Someone attempted to speak but was cut off by her raging friend.

"And Janay. Smiling all in her face. If it wasn't for me, she wouldn't even be having this whack-ass adolescent birthday party. She'd still be back in Riegelwood, scrubbing pots and pans. Ungrateful heffa. *Family.* They're worse than foes sometimes."

From the sounds of it, someone here had really pissed her off, including Janay, whom the party was for.

"You know the only reason he brought her here is to make you jealous," one of the females said.

Zahra stilled, recognizing the voice as belonging to one of the women who'd given her the cold shoulder earlier.

"Yeah, he had to know you'd be here. You should have listened to me and brought your new boo. That would have messed him up for sure."

And that was the voice of Cold-shoulder-giver number two.

"He had to work," the ranter said. "He's always working," she grumbled. "But he has to be able to properly take care of me."

"Too bad he's working. Seeing you with that fine-ass Dr. Culpepper would have really done the trick," Cold-shoulder-giver number one said.

Dr. Culpepper? No way. It couldn't be the same doctor who'd treated Ava. She sneered. The one who'd made goo-goo eyes at her the entire time. *Bastard.* She knew something had felt off about him. Talk about a small world.

Zahra tried to steal a peek through the slit in the door for the identity of the third woman, but she couldn't see a dang thing. At least, without giving herself away. Obviously, the women had no idea anyone was there, because they spoke openly.

"It's obvious he still loves you or he wouldn't be trying to make you jealous. I mean, look at her. She doesn't hold a candle to you. And a man like Gregor doesn't date down. It's all a ploy."

Zahra's breath seized in her lungs. *Gregor?* Had she just said Gregor's name? Her Gregor? Zahra's head was fuzzy, so she wasn't sure who was speaking now.

"He loves you, girl. He's just pissed right now. And

you have to admit he has a right to be. That was some real shady shit you did to him, Selene."

Selene. The raging woman was Gregor's ex. Zahra pressed a hand to her midsection, feeling sick to her stomach.

"I did what I had to do. I gave him two great years, and he thought he could just kick me aside like that."

"Well, he did catch you screwing another man, sooo…" one of the women said.

"I had a moment of weakness. Anyway, forget Gregor. I'm on to bigger and better things. He can have that off-the-shelf cheap imitation of me. It's not like it's going to last. Gregor's not built for long-term. I know the only reason he was with me was because I was so damn good in the bedroom. I turned him out."

All three women laughed, and Zahra could hear them high-fiving each other.

"She can have my leftovers."

Zahra's hand rose to the door lock. She'd show that heffa off-the-shelf and set the record straight that she was no one's damn pawn in some type of game or— She froze, something occurring to her. What if she was?

What if they'd been right? Gregor had to know his ex would be here. Why hadn't he mentioned it? And why hadn't he told her Janay was his ex's cousin? Her stomach knotted. What if they were right?

The catty women chatted a while longer, assuring Selene how Zahra would never be a part of their clique. When they left the restroom, Zahra fell against the stall wall, the icy chill feeling good to her scorching flesh.

Her mind worked overtime to filter all she'd just heard. The air in the room grew thick. Almost too thick to breathe.

Angry tears rolled down her face, and she slapped them away. She had to get out of this building.

Gregor glanced up just in time to see Zahra rushing toward the exit. Where was she going? He didn't bother excusing himself from the group, he simply took off across the crowded room. On his way through the door, he caught a glimpse of Selene. When had she arrived? A sinking feeling washed over him. Was she why Zahra had fled the ballroom? His jaw tightened. If so, what in the hell had Selene said to her?

"Zahra," Gregor called to no avail. He ignored the handful of people mingling in the hallway, despite their obvious interest in him. "Zahra, stop!"

This time, she swung around to face him. His chest tightened at the sight of her red eyes. Had she been crying? "Baby, what's wrong?"

"How could you not tell me Janay was your ex's cousin? Or that there was a chance your ex would be here. I overheard her and her minions in the bathroom going on and on about me being just a tool for you. And that the only reason I'm here is to make her jealous. And how you're still in love with her. Are you, Gregor? Are you still in love with her?"

Zahra's voice cracked, and tears spilled down her cheeks. He reached for her, but she quickly backed away, then took off again. When Gregor reached her this time, he scooped her into his arms, headed through the first open door he saw, then kicked it closed with his foot, causing a loud thud.

Zahra's reaction was delayed—she was probably stunned by his actions. A millisecond later, she squirmed like an agitated fish trying to avoid hot grease.

"Let me down," she said.

He did as she demanded, and hoped she wouldn't try to go before hearing him out.

"Please leave me alone," she said, her eyes welling with tears. "I just want to go home."

"Not until we talk." At the moment, he didn't care how much of an asshole he was being. He just needed to straighten this mess out.

Zahra folded her arms across her chest and rolled her eyes. A single tear escaped down her cheek. To Gregor's surprise, she allowed him to wipe it away. "Let's sit and talk." She didn't pull back when he rested his hand on the small of her back and led her to a tiny round table. He took it as a good sign. Once she'd eased down into her chair, he positioned his directly in front of her, rested his elbows on his thighs and took both her hands into his. "Baby, I messed up. I should have been open and honest with you."

"Why weren't you?"

He lowered his head briefly. "I don't know."

"Was the invitation merely for show? When you invited me to come here with you, had you hoped I'd say no?"

God, where was she getting all of this? If there was

one thing he disliked about relationships, arguing was it. He was no good at it. Typically, he fled the scene for hours, then came back with some extravagant gift that would smooth things over. With Zahra, he hadn't had that urge. He wanted to talk things out with her, desperately needed to get them right. He couldn't lose her. "No, Zahra. No. I invited you here because I wanted you here with me."

"Were they right, Gregor? Am I only here to make your ex jealous?"

"Zahra, do you really believe that?" He regretted how snappy he'd sounded, but this was ridiculous. And it annoyed him that she would even make such an assumption in the first place. But in her defense, he understood.

"Honestly, I don't know what to believe." Zahra sighed, her tone softening. "I just need you to be honest with me, Gregor. Does any part of you still love her? I can't compete with the history you two share, and I won't try."

"Zahra, baby, I need you to believe in me. Not all the noise around us, but *me*. There are no pieces of me left to love her, Zahra, because every piece of me is too damn busy loving you."

Zahra gasped, her eyes wide with surprise. "Wh-what did you just say?"

This was definitely not how he'd imagined this moment, in a dusty conference room and fresh off an argument. Truthfully, he hadn't imagined any version of him being the first to confess his love. He knew he loved her, had known for a while. But like most men, he'd expected her to say the words first. Yet, here he was, hoping and praying that his love was something she wanted.

"I said I love you, Zahra Antoinette Hart. I'm in love with you."

A single sob escaped, and Zahra slapped her hand over her mouth.

"I don't want to lose you. Especially over this. Not over anything." He kissed her hands several times. "Zahra, I'd like you to accompany me to a birthday celebration. It's for my ex's cousin. My ex will probably be there, but that doesn't matter to me. Because, in a room filled with a thousand women, you're the only one I see, because I love you. I love you like I've never loved anyone. And I need you. Please don't leave me."

Never in a million years would he ever have imagined caring for one person enough to swallow both his ego and pride in the same gulp, and with no regret.

"You should have told me."

Guilt gnawed at him, but she was right. He should have told her. Guiding her from her chair and into his lap, he said, "I know. Forgive me?"

Zahra's eyes glistened with unshed tears, and her lips curved into a stiff smile. A second later, she cradled his face and kissed him gently. "I'm in love with you, too."

Chapter 19

Apparently, Gregor had mentioned to Abrim—a Thoroughbreds wide receiver and Janay's fiancé—what had happened at the birthday party. He'd obviously mentioned it to Janay, because a week later, Janay had called Zahra and profusely apologized. As if it were her fault her cousin was a wicked witch.

A couple of days after that, Janay had called to invite her to lunch. Initially, Zahra held a suspicion that Gregor had put her up to it. But as it turned out, Gregor had known nothing about the invitation. It had been all Janay.

Still, Janay was Selene's cousin, so Zahra had been apprehensive about coming. But, for whatever reason, she'd agreed. Maybe because of the conversation she'd overheard in the restroom the night of the party. Janay and Selene didn't appear to be all that close. At least, not anymore.

Zahra checked her watch. She'd arrived at the downtown bistro several minutes early to make sure they got a table before the lunchtime rush. Janay arrived a short time later. The generic T-shirt and jeans she wore surprised Zahra. She'd expected the woman to be draped in something designer from head to toe. Even the small shoulder bag she carried appeared off-the-shelf. Zahra grimaced at the same phrase Selene had used to label her.

With her flawless dark brown skin, height and thin, shapely figure, Janay could have easily been a model. The visibly excited woman crossed the semicrowded restaurant, arms outstretched, fingers splayed and wiggling. When she was close enough, they embraced like old friends.

After the episode at the party, Gregor had wanted to leave, but Zahra had insisted they stay. She refused to allow his bitter ex to ruin their night any more than she already had. Selfishly, Zahra had wanted the spiteful woman to get a good dose of her and Gregor together.

Zahra was glad they'd stayed because twenty minutes before the function ended, Abrim had gotten down on one knee and asked Janay to marry him. She had tackled him to the floor with a resounding yes. It had been one of the most beautiful and most hilarious proposals she'd ever witnessed. Not that she'd witnessed that many. The stunt Braswell had pulled at her studio flowed like dirty water into her head, causing a bad taste in her mouth.

Parting, they both slid into the booth. Janay gave her drink order to the young, freckled-faced blonde, choosing the same thing Zahra had ordered when she'd first arrived. When she moved away, Janay squealed, startling Zahra. "I'm so excited we're doing lunch," she said. "The first of many, I hope."

Janay flashed a hopeful expression, prompting Zahra to say, "Definitely. I'm glad you invited me."

"Can I be honest?" Janay asked.

"Absolutely." Zahra braced herself for whatever was to follow.

"I debated calling. I thought you might say no. You know, because of what happened at my party."

"Janay, what happened that night wasn't your fault. In fact, I hate Gregor even said anything about it at all."

"No, I'm glad he did. It needed addressing. I don't think I've ever seen Gregor so angry. I gave Selene a piece of my mind. As always, she played the victim." Janay sighed. "Anyway. We're not here to talk about her, are we?"

"No," Zahra said. *But why exactly are we here*, she wanted to ask but sipped her blackberry lemonade instead.

"I'm glad we met, Zahra. We clicked at my party." Janay flashed a hesitant expression. "At least, I think we did."

"So do I," Zahra said, garnering a beaming smile from her lunch companion.

"You seem down-to-earth and genuine. Most of the football wives and girlfriends walk around with their noses in the air like their shit doesn't stink," Janay said.

Zahra laughed hard, apparently prompting Janay to do the same.

Before either woman realized it, two hours had passed and neither of them seemed pressed to leave. They'd talked about a multitude of things, including Janay's wedding. It didn't surprise Zahra that Janay wanted a winter wonderland theme, falling snowflakes and all. And she had no doubt Abrim would make sure she had it.

"Gregor's different since you two have been together," Janay said out the blue.

"Really? How so?"

"He seems…more at peace. If that makes sense. Abrim noticed it, too. Since I've known Gregor, he's always been so tightly wound. Not anymore. Are you making him meditate or something? If so, where can I sign Abrim up?"

Zahra recalled what Selene had said in the restroom about her being the reason Janay was no longer scrubbing pots and pans. "Did Selene introduce you and Abrim?"

Janay barked a laugh. "That's what she'd have everyone believe. She invited me to Charlotte for a weekend. I nearly didn't come because I knew she was only inviting me to show off. We went to a nightspot where a lot of the players hung out. Abrim was there." A delicate smile touched Janay's lips. "The second our eyes met I felt this instant and insane connection to him. But I ignored it."

"Why?"

"He was a professional athlete. I didn't have time for games. But he was relentless in his pursuit. The rest, as they say, is history." Janay shrugged. "I guess Selene does deserve a little credit. If it hadn't been for her, I never would have come to Charlotte."

"It was the total opposite for Gregor and me."

Zahra attempted to give Janay the rundown of how she and Gregor met. To her surprise, Gregor had already given both her and Abrim the condensed version. To know that he'd shared their story with them warmed her heart.

"I wanted to strangle him," Zahra continued. "He was so obnoxious."

Janay snickered. "He said the same thing about you."

Zahra narrowed her eyes in a playful manner. "Oh, he did, did he?"

Janay slapped a hand over her mouth. Allowing it to fall, she said, "Don't tell him I told you that."

"I won't."

After another half hour of chatting, both women agreed it was time to go.

"Can I be honest?" Zahra said, flipping the script.

Obviously, Janay got the reference, because she grinned. "Absolutely."

"I almost canceled. You're Selene's cousin. I thought this would be an hour of you trying to milk me for information to carry back to her."

"I get it," Janay said. "But I'm definitely not a carrier pigeon for Selene. We're family, but we've never really been all that close. I hope you and I will be."

Zahra had a feeling they would.

Gregor wasn't sure which he should be more worried about, meeting Zahra's parents for the first time or her driving. For now, he settled on the driving because he wasn't sure they were going to make it to her parents' place in Lexington. He should have known the terror he was in for when she'd asked to drive, slid behind the wheel of the Mustang and tore out of the parking garage, leaving a cloud of white smoke behind.

If he clinched his butt cheeks any harder, he'd pull the red leather right off the seats. This wasn't the first time he'd ridden with her. However, this was the first time she'd displayed speed demon tendencies. And while he prayed every second since leaving his condo, there was no other place in the world he would rather have been than right here risking his life with her. That said a lot.

He'd finally found the one thing—person—who outweighed football for him. If he could, he would spend every waking moment with Zahra, with the only goal of trying to make her the happiest woman alive. Actually, the past couples of weeks kind of felt like they'd spent every waking moment together. With July quickly approaching—signaling the start of training camp—he'd wanted to spend as much time with her as he could since his availability would be drastically reduced and pretty much nonexistent in August.

"Babe, I can take over if you're tired." Gregor raised his voice over the whip of the wind.

"We're almost there. I'm good," she said.

"O-okay."

Gregor was sure I-85 still had lines, but they were buzzing down the interstate so fast, the white stripes blended with the road. "Babe, you should probably—" Before he could add "slow down," the chirp of sirens and flash of blue lights came from behind them.

"Uh-oh," Zahra said, signaling and pulling onto the shoulder.

While he didn't rejoice in the fact that she was probably about to get one hell of a ticket, he was thankful for the fact that she'd more than likely want him to drive the remainder of the way.

"Dang, dang, dang. I thought if you were only doing up to nine miles over the speed limit, they wouldn't pull you," she said.

Nine? Gregor stared openmouthed at her. Clearly, she hadn't paid attention to the speedometer. When he'd casually glanced at it, she'd been doing at least fifteen over the speed limit.

"Do you think he's going to ticket me?"

"Yep."

"*Gregor!* You were supposed to say no to make me feel better."

"Sorry. I'll pay the ticket for you. How's that?"

Zahra gave him an air kiss. "That's not necessary."

When the trooper exited his vehicle and moved toward them, Zahra plastered both hands to the steering wheel and sat ramrod straight.

"Act normal," she said, checking the rearview mirror.

Gregor reached for the glove box.

"What are you doing? Don't do that," she said out the corner of her mouth. "Do you want to get us shot?"

Damn. She had a point. He withdrew his hand and relaxed back against the seat, now feeling as tense as she looked.

"Afternoon, ma'am, sir," the trooper said, tipping his hat.

"Hello," Zahra said.

Gregor nodded.

"Ma'am, do you know how fast you were traveling?"

"I…um…seventy…two."

An unintended snicker escaped Gregor, prompting Zahra to give him the evil eye. The trooper's lips twitched as if he were attempting to hold back a laugh. "Eighty-seven, ma'am."

"Eighty-seven," Zahra said calmly, her posture slumping a bit. "Huh."

"May I see your license and registration, please," the trooper said.

"Um, sure."

While Zahra rummaged through the suitcase she called a purse, Gregor cautiously reached into the glove box, retrieved the registration and passed it to the trooper.

"I know I have it," Zahra said, still searching.

The man's gaze rose and settled on Gregor. There it was. Recognition. Sometimes, one of the privileges of being a well-known athlete was people made exceptions for you as well as for the ones around you. Zahra might just get off easy, after all.

"Caught a clip of you guys during OTAs last week," the trooper said, passing the card back. "Looking good."

"Thanks," Gregor said, accepting the registration.

"You two enjoy the rest of your afternoon. And slow down, ma'am," he said, tipping his hat again, then returning to his vehicle.

"What just happened?" Zahra asked, finally locating her license.

"Welcome to my world," Gregor said. "Now move out the way, woman. I'm driving."

A short time later, they pulled into a mile-long driveway lined with trees. They stopped in front of a two-story brick home, sitting on what had to be at least ten acres of the lushest, greenest land he'd ever seen. It was gorgeous. And peaceful. No honking horns. No roaring traffic. No hustle and bustle. All of which reminded him of Lake Lamont. *Where it all began.*

Parking next to a small white SUV hybrid, Gregor inhaled a deep breath. Why did it feel as if he were about to play the most intense game of his life? Because he was in a way.

A thousand questions flooded him. Had her parents already formed an opinion about him from the images they'd seen on TV? Would her mother like him? Would her father hate him because he was an athlete?

He hadn't realized that he'd been bouncing his leg

hard enough to shake the car until Zahra rested a hand on his thigh.

"You okay?" she asked.

Gregor huddled his thoughts, focused on the end zone and scoring the goal of a lifetime. "Perfect."

"Gregor freaking Carter nervous sounds like an oxymoron," she said.

"I'm not nervous. I'm…" His words dried up. "Okay, I'm a little nervous." But not for the reason she probably assumed.

Zahra rested a hand on the side of his face. "You have absolutely nothing to worry about. They're going to love you almost as much as I do," she said with a gentle smile.

Leaning over, he kissed her gently on the lips. He'd wanted more of her mouth but couldn't chance that her parents were watching from inside the home.

On the walk up to the house, Zahra explained that her father wasn't coping well with his recent retirement as CEO/EVP of an insurance company. That he'd dabbled in numerous hobbies, the most recent being making custom fishing lures. She pressed the bell and a short time later a petite, wrinkle-free, brown-skinned woman opened the door. This had to be Zahra's mother. Their resemblance was uncanny. Her shoulder-length hair pulled back into a ponytail was peppered with gray.

"Hi, Mom."

"Hi, sweetheart. I'm so glad you made it here safely. Come inside."

Inside the Hart home was just as welcoming as the

outside. The tantalizing aromas of onions, fresh bread and cinnamon greeted them the second they strolled through the door. Gregor's stomach instantly reacted, growling its desire to devour whatever was being prepared in the kitchen.

Zahra wrapped her arms around her mother in an affectionate embrace. When they parted, Zahra said, "I want you to meet someone. Mom, Gregor Carter. Gregor, my mom, Carolyn Hart."

Gregor stuck out his hand. "Mrs. Hart, it's a pleasure to finally meet you."

Carolyn swatted his hand. "Put that away and come over here and give me a hug."

She delivered the same amount of motherly warmth to him as she had to Zahra.

Pulling away, Carolyn said, "Welcome to our home. You're not a guest here." She patted his cheek. "You're family. You're welcomed to anything here."

"Thank you," he said, emotion swirling in his chest. He loved Mrs. Hart already.

"Where's Dad?" Zahra asked.

Carolyn rolled her eyes heavenward. "In his study working on those dang lures. We're going to blow through our retirement on his hobbies. Last month it was home-brewed beer. The month before that it was knife-making. Now lures. He doesn't even fish. If that man doesn't pick one and stick to it, I'm going to scream."

"Ava hasn't made it yet?" Zahra asked.

Carolyn put her hand on her tiny waist. "When have you known your sister to be on time?"

"Good point."

Excusing them, Zahra took Gregor's hand and led him down a hallway. The walls were smothered with pictures that seemed to catalog decades. He was drawn to the images, stopping to inspect several of them more thoroughly. The backstory Zahra provided on several of them made him laugh.

"Memories," he said absently.

Zahra ironed her hand up and down his back. "We'll make memories, too," she said.

Gregor couldn't resist pulling Zahra into his arms and kissing her hard. If one of her parents had walked out, he would have simply had to explain to them that their daughter always knew what to say and exactly when to say it. Pulling away, he stared into her eyes. "I love you, woman."

"I love you, man."

When they entered the large study, Zahra's father was bent over a desk, intricately working on something. Al Green poured from the speakers.

Zahra snuck up behind him and covered his eyes with her hands. "Guess who?"

"My heartbeat number two," her father said, dropping what he'd been working on to greet his daughter with a bear hug.

At full height, he towered over Zahra. The tall, solid man could have been a linebacker.

"Daddy, I'd like you to meet someone special," Zahra said.

When Mr. Hart's eyes settled on Gregor, his expression morphed from soft to stern. Gregor swallowed hard. *Uh-oh.*

"No introduction necessary. Gregor Carter. Best QB in Thoroughbreds' history. Don't ever let anyone tell you different." Mr. Hart offered his hand. "Montgomery Hart."

Some of Gregor's unease lessened. He shook his hand. "It's a pleasure to meet you, sir."

Mr. Hart folded his large arms over his chest and studied Gregor. "I've got one question for you, son."

Gregor was sure it had something to do with their blown chance at the Super Bowl. "Okay."

A second or two ticked by. "What in the hell are you doing in my house?"

That he hadn't expected. Gregor's eyes slid to Zahra, who surprisingly looked as if she waited for the answer, too. Refocusing on Mr. Hart, Gregor parted his lips to speak but was cut short by Mr. Hart's hearty laughter.

"I'm only messing with you."

When he clapped him on the back, Gregor released the breath he'd been strangling. Zahra snickered, obviously aware her father was pranking him.

"Welcome to our humble abode. Make yourself at home. Once you taste my Carolyn's cooking, you're going to want to stay forever. But you got to get the hell up outta here."

"Daddy."

"Okay, okay. I'll behave. Where's your sister?"

Before Zahra could respond, Ava strolled through the door, greeting everyone in her usual boisterous manner.

Zahra neared Gregor. "Will you be okay here for a moment? I need to chat with Ava."

"Everything okay?" Gregor asked.

She smiled. "Yes."

"Okay. Yeah. Sure. I'll be fine." He hoped.

A second later, the women were gone.

"Have a seat," Mr. Hart said, then moved to the small bar in the corner, removing two glasses. "You drink bourbon?"

"Yes, sir."

"Good." Mr. Hart filled two glasses and passed one to Gregor.

"Thank you," he said, accepting it.

Mr. Hart eased into one of the chairs adjacent to Gregor, crossed his ankle over his thigh and relaxed against the cushioned back. "I'm guessing Zahra left us here together to get to know each other. So, tell me something good."

This was his moment. The opportunity he'd prepped for ever since he'd known he'd be meeting Zahra's parents. He considered taking a sip from his glass but decided he didn't need it. All the courage he needed was housed in how much he loved Zahra. "I'd like permission to marry your daughter."

Chapter 20

Zahra glanced at Gregor in the driver's seat. When he regarded her, she flashed a lazy smile. Something was up with him, but she didn't know what. He hadn't spoken ten words since they'd left her parents' place almost an hour ago. In fact, she'd noticed a shift in his demeanor just after he and her father had emerged from the study.

Through dinner, he'd socialized but had seemed preoccupied with his own thoughts. Had her father offended him in some way? *Oh, Daddy, what did you say?*

Montgomery Hart was a fierce protector of his *heartbeats*—as he called his wife and daughters—so there was no telling what he'd put Gregor through. Well, Gregor hadn't run screaming out of the house, so that had to be a good sign. *Right?*

She hadn't sensed or felt any tension between the two. Not like there had been with Braswell and her father. That had been the longest and most uncomfortable two hours of her life. Maybe it wasn't anything her father had said at all. Maybe Gregor's shift had something to do with the phone call he'd taken in the bathroom.

She'd gone to check on him and heard chatter over the sound of running water. While she hadn't been able to hear what was being said, she'd asked him about it. He'd said it had been about football stuff. Specifically, the approaching start of minicamp.

She reached over and touched his arms. He flinched. "Hey. Everything okay?"

Gregor gave her a half smile. "Yes."

"Are *you* okay? You've been awfully quiet since we left my parents' place."

"I think I ate too much. Your mom can throw down in the kitchen. Now I see where you get it from."

Okay, now she knew something was wrong, because he hadn't come close to putting away the amount of food he usually consumed. At the time she'd chalked it up to him not wanting them to witness his ferocious appetite.

Moments later, they pulled into one of Gregor's parking spaces.

"Are you sure you're okay?" Zahra asked when he shifted the car into Park.

"Come here," he said, leaning into her. After placing a gentle kiss on her lips, he said, "Anytime I'm with you, I'm perfect."

He got out and came around to open her door. Hand

in hand, they moved toward the elevator. Inside, Gregor hugged her to his chest as they rode the metal box up in silence. Gregor's heartbeat thumped against her breast as if he'd climbed several flights of stairs.

When they reached his condo, Gregor stepped aside to allow her to enter, popping her butt as she walked by. "Ow," she said.

Zahra stopped dead in her tracks, gasping at the sight in front of her. Several vases of red roses were placed around the room. Thousands of fresh rose petals littered the floor. Hundreds of candles flickered. Turning, she said, "Gregor, what—"

Her purse fell from her grip. She slapped a hand over her mouth and stumbled back several steps. Her brain quickly processed Gregor down on one knee, holding a burgundy ring box that held the most beautiful diamond solitaire she'd ever seen. A thousand and one emotions swirled inside her. The most potent being shock. Utter and complete.

Gregor motioned her over, then captured her trembling hand. "Baby, I know we've only been together a short time, but it feels like you've been mine a lifetime. I've never been so comfortable with anyone in my life. I've never felt so connected to anyone in my life."

Zahra tried to speak, but nothing would come out.

"I never have to pretend with you. You love me just the way I am, flaws and all. I knew I would fall in love with you, Zahra. I just never could have imagined how much. Everything I never knew I needed, I've found in you. And I want to spend the rest of my life experiencing this level of happiness. Making beautiful memories with you. Building a life, a family with you. Insanely loving you. I want to grow old with you. So, Zahra Antoinette Hart, will you marry me?"

"Are you sure, Gregor? You seemed so tortured on the drive here. Are you sure this is what you really want?"

Gregor placed the ring box on the floor, stood and cradled her face between his hands. "I wasn't tortured. I was anxious. I needed everything to be perfect. You deserve flawless. I am sure, Zahra. A hundred and fifty percent. And that's exactly what I told your father earlier when I asked for your hand."

Stunned again, she said, "You asked Daddy for my hand?"

He gave her a sexy grin. "It was the gentlemanly thing to do. Plus, I know how much you love your father and would want his blessing."

She fell in love with him all over again.

"When I asked your father for your hand," he continued, "he asked me why I thought I deserved you." He paused. "I told him that I wasn't sure I do deserve you. And that nothing in my life had ever been easy, except for loving you."

Gregor continued schooling her on all of the beautiful things he'd said to her father, her heart swelling more and more with each declaration. By the time he was done, she was a blubbering mess.

"You brought me out of a dark place, Zahra, and I've been following your guiding light ever since. You're my strength, my serenity. Because of you, I believe in happily-ever-after. So…" He lowered himself to one knee again. "Will you marry me and make me the happiest man on this planet?"

Zahra nodded clumsily. "Yes."

Zahra wasn't sure what she'd been thinking when she'd asked Gregor if she could join him on his Saturday morning run. Actually, she did. She'd been thinking about the twenty pounds she wanted to lose before the wedding. Those pesky pounds didn't seem so relevant now, because she was sure she was about to die.

Winded, she asked, "How many miles have we gone?"

Gregor stopped, prompting her to do the same. When he turned, so did she.

"Well, we've made it across the street from the condo. So, point one miles, maybe?"

"Ha ha," she said at his glaring attempt at humor.

"You ready?" he asked, jogging in place.

"No." She rotated her ankle. "I think I have on the wrong type of shoes."

Zahra held her amusement when Gregor's eyes lowered to the pricey sneakers he'd purchased, specifically designed for running.

"Maybe you have them laced wrong."

See, that was one of the millions of reasons why she loved him. He chose to spare her feelings by not stating the obvious. That she was lazy. Zahra pointed over her shoulder. "I'm going to head back to check these laces." She tried not to react when Gregor attempted to harness his laughter.

"Okay, babe." He leaned in to give her a kiss.

"Get a room," came from a passing car.

They both laughed.

Pulling away, Gregor said, "Can you make it, or do I need to put you on my back and carry you?"

With animated anger, she jabbed her finger in the opposite direction of the condo. "Go!" He grinned, then took off. The sight of his strong legs as he pounded the pavement sent a shiver up her spine. Every inch of his body turned her on.

Zahra did a leisurely stroll back. This experience had taught her two things: losing twenty pounds by their March wedding date—eight months away—wasn't really all that important, and that she preferred cake over running.

Digging into the stylish fanny pack Gregor had clowned her about, she pushed aside the bottle of water, her cell phone, the pen and paper, and removed the dark chocolate and banana fruit bar. *One serving of fruit.* Healthy eating. She just might lose that twenty pounds, after all.

Before she could tear into the wrapper, her cell phone rang. Fishing it out, her brow furrowed. A line of zeroes was all that showed. Making the call active, she said, "Hello?" She repeated it when there wasn't a response. A second later, the line went dead.

Several minutes later, the phone rang a second time.

The same string of zeroes crossed the screen. This time her greeting was a bit harsher. "Hello! Who is this?"

"Good day, ma'am. I am Abayomi Adbu Awolowa," the caller said in accented English, "and I am calling to let you know you have won an all-expenses paid five days, four nights luxury vacation to any destination in the world."

"Really?" she said, entertaining the enthusiastic scammer.

"Oh, yes. Yes."

"Oh. My. God. I am *sooo* excited. You know what, Abayomi? I think I'd like to take you on vacation with me."

"Me, ma'am?" His words dripped with confusion.

"Absolutely. You sound like a very intelligent man. And you obviously have a job. Two things I'm looking for in a husband and father for my eight kids. How much money do you have in the bank, Abayomi?"

"Umm, not much, ma'am."

"That's okay. When you move to be with me, you can get a second and third job to take care of your new family. When will you be able to come and—"

Click.

"How rude," she said, then cracked up at her antics.

Stashing her phone, she breathed a sigh of relief. Her and Gregor's engagement had been plastered all over social media. For a brief moment, she thought Braswell had resurfaced. Thank God for huge favors.

Chapter 21

The first place Gregor headed after the official end of minicamp was Zahra's place. Not only because she'd prepared him a celebration dinner, but because he'd missed her like crazy the past three days. While the thought of climbing into his bed and sleeping for the next three weeks was alluring, the idea of falling asleep with his fiancée in his arms was far more appealing.

His fiancée. He had a fiancée. He was getting married. To the woman of his dreams. She was perfect. In every sense of the word. And he couldn't wait to make her his wife.

Arriving at her place, he lifted the single red rose he'd plucked from the bucket at the gas station, climbed out and made his way to her front porch. She'd been so fascinated with the keyless entry at his place, he'd had a similar device installed on her door. Before he could rest his thumb against the reader, the door swung open.

The smell of good cooking hit him instantly. Man, he couldn't wait to feast on a home-cooked meal. And Zahra. One look into Zahra's red eyes told him that something was up. When she turned and moved away, he followed, discarding the rose on the counter as he passed.

"Zahra, what's wrong?" His first thought was Selene. Word from Abrim was that she'd been livid over their engagement.

Several uncomfortable seconds passed before she faced him. Despite desperately trying not to get alarmed, the uncertainty and waiting for her to speak took a toll. "Zahra." When she flinched, he regretted the amount of forcefulness he'd placed in his tone. Resting his hands on her waist, he said, "Baby, you're making me really nervous," in a much softer tone.

"We…" Her eyes rose to him but fell again. "We need to talk. I need to tell you something."

A feeling of despair settled in his stomach, tying it into a thousand tiny knots. "What is it?" he asked, bracing for impact. Whatever it was wouldn't be good.

Unfortunately, his cell phone chimed, forcing him to wait seconds more to find out what was going on. "Shit." He fiddled, trying to get the phone out of his pocket. By the time he pulled the device out, it was a symphony of chimes, dings and swooshes. His eyes rose to Zahra's and hers slid away. When she blinked, a tear rolled down her cheek. The phone vibrated in his hand with Thad's name flashing across the screen.

Sending the call to voice mail, he stashed the phone back inside his pocket and steadied his gaze on a now trembling Zahra. "Tell me," he said.

"There's a—" Her voice hitched.

"A what, Zahra?"

"A—" She stopped abruptly. "Oh, God, I'm going to be sick."

When she took off toward the bathroom, Gregor started after her until his cell phone vibrated again. This time he answered, but in an impatient tone. "Hello."

"Now is probably not the best time to say I told you so, but I told you so. No statements from either you or Zahra. Let me handle this," Thad said.

He forced his brows together. "No statements? About what?" Obviously, everyone but him knew what was going on.

"The video," Thad said.

The video? "What video?" he asked.

Thad spent the next couple of minutes telling Gregor about the tape Zahra's ex had sold to one of the tabloids. A sex tape. Gregor dropped onto the sofa and stared at the bathroom door. "How—how recent is the tape?" The implication of his inquiry caused his temple to throb.

Thad sighed. "I don't know. The claim is that it's recent, but I don't know."

The bathroom door creaked. A second later, Zahra emerged. "I'll hit you back, Thad."

"If you love her, G, don't watch the video. There's no need."

"Yeah." Gregor ended the call, rested his elbows on

his thighs and passed the phone back and forth between his hands.

Zahra's voice was scratchy when she spoke. "I'm guessing you know."

He nodded. In a controlled tone, he said, "You were sleeping with the both of us?"

Zahra hurried across the room. "What? No. No. That video is almost three years old. A bad decision I made after too many drinks. I was mortified when I learned Braswell had recorded us. I demanded he destroy it. I thought he had."

Obviously, she did have a few skeletons in her closet. Gregor stared at her for a long, hard moment.

"You don't believe me," she said, a calmness to her voice.

He didn't respond because he wasn't sure what to believe. His heart and head were in a fierce battle. One was anchored in the present, reminding him how much he loved this woman and urging him to trust her. The other ushered him to the past, reminding him of the deception that lived there.

The dual arguments, myriad of emotions raging inside him and his throbbing head made it all too overwhelming. This was a conversation he couldn't have. Not now. Not when he could hardly breathe. Not when his thoughts crippled his brain. Not when he could barely focus.

He stood abruptly. "I'm gonna go. I need… I need to catch my breath."

"Gregor—"

"I'll call you later." He made haste to the door, flung it open and damn near ran to his vehicle. Sliding behind the seat, he gripped the steering wheel. A second later, he pounded it until his palm hurt. Tossing a glance toward the house, he saw that Zahra stood on the porch, her arms hugging her body. *Go to her*, a tiny voice said. He ignored it.

An hour later, he sat in front of his computer watching the video of Zahra and her ex, wishing he'd taken Thad's advice.

Unable to focus on the happy couple smiling in the images on her computer screen, Zahra pushed away from her desk. With a heavy sigh, she reclined in her chair and pinched her lids shut. God, she was exhausted. Because of that video, Gregor's reaction, her overactive brain, she hadn't gotten much sleep over the past several days.

If Braswell's goal for releasing the tape had been to turn her life upside down, he'd succeeded. Clients were canceling appointments left and right. The media wouldn't stop hounding her for interviews. She was humiliated beyond belief. Her parents and Ava stood by her, but she knew they'd been unsettled by the scandal. On top of all of this, she didn't have Gregor to comfort her.

Surprisingly, she hadn't heard from him since he'd left her place four days ago. *Four days*, she said to herself. Her eyes popped open and she eyed the ceiling, a tear rolling from the corner of her eye. Yes, she understood and respected his need to deal with this in his own way, but shutting her out of his life?

A tap sounded at her office door, drawing her away from the morbid thoughts. Ava pushed through a moment later. Her smile lit the room.

"Hey, sis. I was in the neighborhood and decided to stop by to see if you wanted to do lunch. My treat."

As much as Ava had been "in the neighborhood" lately, Zahra would have thought the woman was a stalker had she not known better, or the real reason for Ava's frequent visits. Zahra loved her sister for the support. While Zahra really hadn't had much of an appetite the past several days, she figured a little fresh air would be good for her.

Half an hour later, they sat on the patio of one of the pizza joints not far from the studio. Zahra pushed around the contents of her Greek salad with a fork. Typically, she'd have devoured the fresh lettuce mix by now.

"Not hungry?" Ava asked.

Zahra pushed the plate away. "No. I'm sorry."

"You have no reason to apologize. You want to talk about it?"

"No." Zahra rolled her eyes heavenward. "Yes. It's like he doesn't even care that he's hurting me. The man who asked me to spend my life with him." Her eyes lowered to the engagement ring she still wore. "He said he loved me, Ava. Yet, I call him, and he won't even answer the phone. If this is his way of ending things, why can't he just be a man about it and end them properly? Face-to-face."

"Are you *sure* you don't want me to pay him a visit?

I'll flood his condo, bleach his clothes and graffiti his walls," Ava said.

For the first time in days, Zahra actually laughed. "No."

Ava shrugged. "Let me know if you change your mind."

"Okay."

Ava shared how Dr. Slime-ball wouldn't stop calling her even after telling him she knew about him dating Selene, to which he'd replied they weren't serious. Zahra pretended to listen, but truthfully couldn't care less about anything dealing with Selene. For all she knew, she and Braswell had teamed up.

Too occupied with her own thoughts, Zahra's attention left Ava and settled on the engagement ring again. She twirled it around her finger. The night Gregor had slid it on her finger, she'd been so happy.

"He lied to me, Ava," Zahra said. Her eyes rose. "He said he loved me. But he lied. Daddy always said if you'll lie, you'll steal. He was right. Gregor stole my heart, then lied about always protecting it. He's a liar and a thief." And she deserved better.

Music boomed inside Eternity 704, but it did little to drown out Gregor's thoughts as he'd hoped. Relaxing on the sofa, he scanned the room. While he wasn't in the mood for the club scene, he'd needed to get out of the house. Every inch of the place reminded him of Zahra. Every picture that now hung on his walls. Every framed image she'd placed throughout the condo. She'd given him roots. They'd made memories. Memories he just couldn't handle right now. Hadn't been able to handle for the past several days.

He missed her. God knows he missed her. He'd wanted to call her a thousand times over the past week—the length of time he'd run from this situation. Each time he'd picked up the phone, he'd slammed it right back down.

Damn, why had he watched that video? Images of Zahra on the screen still haunted him. And no matter how hard he tried, he couldn't force them away.

His jaw clenched when he thought about Zahra's slimy ex. What kind of bastard took advantage of his own woman like that? His fist clenched so tight he felt his knuckles crack.

"You cool, man?"

Abrim's voice drew him from a volatile place. Gregor nodded, but it was a lie. He was far from all right.

"Number four? What up? What up? What up?"

Gregor glanced over his shoulder to see Rico, his usual harem of women and entourage in tow. Whenever Rico was this boisterous, he'd been drinking, which always led to complications.

"What's up, Rico?" Gregor and Abrim said in unison.

Gregor and Rico gave each other the Thoroughbred wrist bump.

"Glad to have you back on the scene," Rico said. He glanced in the direction he'd sent his woman. "I got you covered if you want to blow off some steam." He winked.

"I'm good," Gregor said.

"Yo. I watched the tape." Rico barked a laugh. "Old girl's got some skills."

Rico's words sparked a flame inside Gregor, but he kept his cool.

"Rico, chill, man," Abrim said.

Rico flashed his palms. "My bad." He smirked. "Is she really that flexible?"

Gregor was off the sofa before he even realized he was moving. Abrim grabbed him before he could get to Rico. The man's muscle, along with club security, converged on the VIP area.

"Calm down, man. You don't need the attention," Abrim whispered to him, still holding him back. "Pull it together, QB."

After several seconds, Gregor said, "I'm good. I'm good," he repeated, pushing Abrim away.

"Yo, what the hell is wrong with you, G?" Rico said. "I was just joking with you. That's what we do."

"You took it too far," Abrim said.

Gregor stuck out his hand. "My bad. I apologize," he said.

Rico seemed hesitant for a moment, but finally took the steps forward and grabbed Gregor's hand, pulling him into a manly hug. "We're brothers."

"You're right," Gregor said, clapping Rico on the back.

"I was out of line. I apologize, too," Rico said. "We good?"

"Yeah, we're good," Gregor said.

"All right, then," Rico said. "Sit down and let me buy you another drink."

Gregor checked his watch for effect. "Nah. I'm gonna head out."

"You sure?" Rico said. "The night is still young."

"Yeah. I'll check y'all later," he said, giving several wrist bumps before leaving the building.

Inside his vehicle, he tapped in a number. When a groggy greeting came from the opposite end, he said, "I need to see you."

An hour later, he arrived at Old School's place, a mammoth-sized, two-story white stone home located in the historic Myers Park neighborhood. Dr. Reed directed him to a room that reminded Gregor of Montgomery Hart's study. Wood furnishings, bookcases swelled with books and plenty of space. The only thing missing was a bar.

Gregor took a seat on the leather sofa, rested his elbows on his knees and interlocked his fingers. For several minutes, he said nothing at all and Dr. Reed didn't urge him. After a long while, he opened up. "You're a therapist. Tell me what's wrong with me. Tell me why I'm like this," he said, his voice cracking with emotion.

"Like what?" Dr. Reed said in the same calm tone he always used.

Gregor darted to his feet. "Screwed up! Why am I so damn screwed up? Help me," he said. "Please."

Chapter 22

Zahra wasn't sure how to react to Gregor showing up at her front door at three in the morning. Her first instinct had been to slam the door in his face, but he looked so damn pitiful she couldn't bring herself to do it.

"It's three in the morning, Gregor. What are you doing here?"

"I needed to talk to you," he said.

"Really? Well, I've needed to talk to you for the past week, but you've avoided me. Maybe you should leave, and I'll give you a call when *I'm* ready to talk." She attempted to close the door, but he stopped her.

"Zahra, please."

She allowed him inside, then led the way into the living room. "Make this quick. I'm tired." Which wasn't a lie. She'd finally dozed off, only to be awakened by the very person keeping her up at night. How ironic.

When Gregor motioned for her to have a seat, she folded her arms across her chest in a defiant manner. Mainly to hide the fact that she still wore his engagement ring. *Not for much longer.* "Say what you've come here to say," she said.

"I'm not good at apologies. I've never had to be. In the past, expensive gifts were all I needed to make things right."

"Your bribes won't work on me," she said.

"I know." He paused for a couple of seconds. "Are you sure I can't buy you a Bentley?" He gave a nervous laugh.

Stone-faced, Zahra said, "Are you sure you want to waste your extremely limited time here on jokes?" It was clear he was using humor to help him approach whatever he struggled to say, but she wasn't in a laughing mood.

"I…" He blew a heavy breath. "I needed time to—"

She gave a humorless laugh. "It's been a week." She shook her head. "I honestly didn't fault you for needing a day to get your thoughts together. *A day.* But one day passed. Two days passed. Three. Then an entire week. Not one single word from you, Gregor. Not a peep. Nothing."

"Zahra, I—"

She wanted to stop to give Gregor the opportunity to speak, but there was so much pent-up frustration inside her that she couldn't keep herself from continuing. "Did you ever consider that I needed you?"

"I—"

"No," she snapped. "You never once thought about me, only yourself. Only *your* suffering. You weren't the only one suffering, Gregor. It was my naked body going viral on the internet. It was me being called everything from a freak to a THOT. I was the one who was being absolutely humiliated in front of the world." When Gregor reached for her, she abruptly moved away. "Don't you dare touch me," she said through clenched teeth. "You no longer have that privilege."

"Okay," he said, barely audible.

Zahra's heart sank a bit when she noticed the raw and pure hurt in Gregor's eyes. He took a step back and slid his hands into his pockets. *Dammit. Stay strong.*

Unshed tears burned Zahra's eyes. "During all of *my* suffering, the only thing I wanted, the one thing I needed, was you. Whispering in my ear that, though this was bad, we would get through it because we had each other." A tear finally slid down her cheek. "I needed you, Gregor. I needed you," she repeated. "I needed my protector, my lover, my best friend. But you weren't there. So why are you here now?"

"To fight for you," he said without hesitation.

"You should have been fighting *with* me," Zahra said.

"You're right. I should have been by your side." He washed a hand over his head. "When I watched that tape, Zahra, it triggered something inside me."

The admission jarred her. He'd watched the tape? The idea made her stomach queasy.

"Something…" A pained looked distorted his features. "I was wrong, baby. The way I handled things. The way I shut you out. I was so wrong."

"Yeah, you were. You hurt me, Gregor. It was the one thing you'd promised to never do. And I trusted and believed you."

"I know." He lowered his head briefly. Meeting her eyes again, he said, "I don't like to talk about my past, but it's the only way for me to help you understand. My past molded me into who I am." He shrugged. "Good and bad. Before The Cardinal House, I'd never had anyone, Zahra. No one to talk to. No one to listen to my problems. No one to care. No one had my back but me."

Gregor's body language told her how difficult this was for him. The urge to comfort him grew intense. She fought it with all her might.

He continued. "When things happened that I couldn't handle, I'd shut down. It was what I knew. I would retreat into my shell like a turtle in hiding. And when I was there, it was always hard for me to come out. My ther—" Gregor stopped abruptly but continued a second later. "My therapist says it's a self-preservation mechanism."

Therapist. Wow. She was stunned he'd shared this with her. A part of her softened.

Gregor eyed her intently, like he expected her to have a negative reaction to him seeing a therapist? She wished more people—especially black men, who often carried the weight of two worlds on their shoulders—would seek the professional help they needed instead of holding so much inside. She thought no less of Gregor for seeking professional help.

"Why did you hesitate to share the fact that you're in therapy?"

"It's not something I go around advertising. Until this moment, I've never even admitted it to myself. I disguised it as talking to an old friend."

Zahra studied him for a long moment. "Is that all your therapist had to say? Nothing about ego? Pride? Stubbornness?"

"He may have mentioned something about pride being a catalyst for destruction."

"Sounds like a smart man."

Gregor closed the distance between them. "I'm not perfect, Zahra."

"I never needed you to be. Yet, it seems like you expect perfection from me."

"To me, you are as perfect as perfect can get. You're the closest I've ever gotten to perfection."

Zahra glanced away, wanting to pretend his words hadn't touched her, when they truly had.

Gregor placed a hand under her chin. This time she didn't pull away.

"You changed my life, Zahra. You believed in me when I didn't believe in myself. I love you, Zahra Antionette Hart. I. Love. You. And I've never been surer about anything in my life."

Nope, she refused to allow his words to penetrate her shell.

"For as long as I can remember, my looks, then my money, then my fame have been my blankets. You stripped that all away. All that was left was me. The real me. Gregor Denton Carter. You make me feel as if that's just enough. That I'm enough. Just me."

For someone who wasn't good at expressing himself, he was doing a damn good job of it. "How do I know, Gregor? How do I know that the next time we approach stormy weather, you won't shut down?" How could she live with such uncertainty?

"You can't know, Zahra. And I can't convince you. All I can do is ask you to believe in me again. I'm asking you to trust that I'll never again do anything to jeopardize us."

Zahra took several steps back, turned and lowered her head to her engagement ring. Behind her, Al Green's "Let's Stay Together" began to play. She turned. "Is this supposed to influence me?"

"In one of your books, you said the perfect song could soften a heart," he said.

Zahra cursed the tender sentiment that swirled inside her, turning her hardened heart to mush. "That was in reference to my characters and their love story."

"Baby, we are a love story. We're just waiting for our happily-ever-after." He captured and lifted her left hand, then eyed the diamond on her finger. "You still love me, Zahra, or you wouldn't be wearing your ring."

She never said she'd stopped loving him. "It's stuck," she said with mild humor in her tone.

"That means fate has spoken. You're stuck with me." He tossed his phone aside and cradled her face between his hands. "Being in this kind of love, Zahra, is like an emotional minefield for me. But I'll risk life and limb every single day just to be with you."

She swallowed the swell of emotion lodged in her throat.

"Stick with me, baby. Stick with me, and I swear I'll make you the happiest woman alive." Moments later, he lowered himself to one knee. "Zahra Antoinette Hart, will you find your way back to me? Will you forgive me? Will you love me? Will you spend your life with me? Will you make me whole again?"

"Yes," she said without hesitation, because she wanted to feel complete again, too.

Gregor's head dropped, and he exhaled heavily as if he'd been holding his breath. A second later, he came to his feet and snatched her into his arms and held her tight. "God answered my prayers," he whispered into the crook of her neck. "I'll love you for a lifetime."

She knew he would.

Epilogue

Eight months later...

Zahra didn't know what was up when her wedding planner directed her into a chair placed in the middle of the dance floor. Several seconds later, Gregor and all of his groomsmen appeared, forming a line in front of her.

"What's going on?" she asked no one in particular.

When Marvin Gaye's "Pride and Joy" started to play, Gregor stepped out from the formation and started to lip-sync the lyrics, his groomsmen serving as background singers. The room erupted in cheers. Zahra cupped her hands over her mouth in disbelief and smiled so wide her cheeks hurt.

These burly men, fresh off a Super Bowl win, moving in synced perfection, was a sight to see. Clearly, they'd had a great deal of choreography. But when?

When the song got to the line where Marvin sings he worked seven days a week to give his woman all his money, Gregor and the guys formed a circle around her, reached into their pockets, pulled out wads of cash and showered her with hundred-dollar bills.

The room went bonkers.

A couple of minutes later, the music faded, and Gregor extended his hands toward her. When she took his hands, he helped her to her feet, then pulled her into his arms. Their first dance song, Stevie Wonder's "Ribbon in the Sky," began to play. They swayed back and forth, staring deep into each other's eyes.

"That was beautiful," she said.

He kissed her gently. "You're beautiful." He kissed her again. "This is the second-best night of my life," he said.

"What was the first?" Zahra assumed it was signing his first NFL contract.

"Meeting you a second time." He shook his head. "I fall in love with you over and over again every second. How is that even possible? I owe Leona."

Zahra smiled as she recalled how Leona had confessed that the Lake Lamont mix-up had not been by error. Unbeknownst to her husband, Thad, she'd orchestrated the entire thing after overhearing him planning for Gregor's arrival at the house. Yeah, she owed her meddling agent, too.

"Mrs. Carter," Gregor said.

His words pulled her back to reality. "I love the sound of that," she said.

"So do I." He rested his forehead against hers. "No one has ever loved me the way you do. I wish you could read my mind, so you could see how much I love you."

"I don't need to read your mind. I already know how much you love me," she said.

"How?"

Zahra smiled. "You made me Zahra *freaking* Carter. And I'll wear the title like a badge of honor. This is our story, our happily-ever-after, and it's written with love."

* * * * *

**Soulful and sensual romance featuring
multicultural characters.**

Look for brand-new Kimani stories
in special 2-in-1 volumes.

Available October 15, 2019

His Christmas Gift & *Decadent Holiday Pleasures*
by Janice Sims and Pamela Yaye

Her Christmas Wish & *Designed by Love*
by Sherelle Green and Sheryl Lister

Christmas with the Billionaire & *A Tiara for Christmas*
by Niobia Bryant and Carolyn Hector

SPECIAL EXCERPT FROM

*Despite her family's billions, Samira Ansah is climbing
the corporate ladder on her own. She needs to buy
a lucrative property owned by bestselling author
Emerson Lance Millner. The sexy recluse isn't selling,
but when he assumes she's his new assistant, Samira plays
along to get closer. There's nothing fake about the sizzling
attraction between these two opposites. But revealing the
truth could close the book on their future...*

Read on for a sneak peek at
Christmas with the Billionaire,
the next exciting installment in the
Passion Grove series by Niobia Bryant!

She took another step closer. "Mr. Millner—"

"I'm sure Annalise explained to you that I need an assistant for the weekends only. Your main priority would be typing my handwritten book, updating my social media accounts and running errands," he said, turning to stride across the room to stand next to the lit fireplace.

"You write by hand?" she asked, unable to hide her amazement and forgetting the reason for her visit.

"Yes," he said, his voice deep.

"And you've finished your new book in the Mayhem series?" she asked.

"So, you're familiar with my books?" he asked, his attention locked on the crackling fire.

Samira wished she could see his face. She felt almost like he was hiding it from her intentionally. "Yes," she finally answered. "My favorite is *Vengeance*."

He grunted.

She eyed him. There was something so powerful but still sad about his stance. The way he moved. The way his stare was downcast. She was surprised at how strongly she needed to know what gave him such a demeanor. It, plus the dark interior of the home and neglected exterior, was all so mysterious—maybe even more so than one of his novels.

The man was an enigma. How could someone so abrupt and insolent write with such emotion and rhythm that she was forever transformed by his words? The two did not match.

"I assume since you're here you made Annalise's round of cuts," he said.

Annalise? As in Annalise Ray?

"Absolutely," she lied, completing winging this unexpected interaction.

"I like that you don't talk much."

She pressed her lips together.

"Do you want the job?" he asked, crossing his strong arms over his chest.

She didn't miss the way the thin material stretched with the move. "Wait. What?" she asked, forcing her attention from his fit form framed by the light of the fire and on to his words.

A billionaire heiress working as an author's weekend assistant. The thought actually made her smile.

The smile widened.

And maybe a better chance to get to know him and just what his reservations are about selling the land.

She contemplated all the pluses and minuses of the ruse. Some work related.

Samira eyed the fine lines of his taut body and her body instantly responded to him.

Some not.

"Yes or no?" he asked, his tone brusque.

Is this crazy? Am I?

"Yes, Mr. Millner, and thank you," she said.

Will this work?

"Good. Ms.…."

She opened her mouth but closed it as she almost supplied him her real name. He might very well know the Ansah name. "Samantha Aston," she lied, pulling the name out of the air.

Ding-dong.

She briefly looked over her shoulder to the front door at the sound of the doorbell.

"Your first duty is sending away all the other applicants," he said, turning and leaving the room with long strides.

What the hell have I gotten myself into?

Don't miss Christmas with the Billionaire
*by Niobia Bryant, available November 2019
wherever Harlequin® Kimani Romance™
books and ebooks are sold.*

Want to give in to temptation with
steamy tales of irresistible desire?

Check out **Harlequin® Presents®,
Harlequin® Desire** and
Harlequin® Kimani™ Romance books!

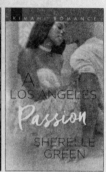

New books available every month!

CONNECT WITH US AT:

Facebook.com/groups/HarlequinConnection

Facebook.com/HarlequinBooks

Twitter.com/HarlequinBooks

Instagram.com/HarlequinBooks

Pinterest.com/HarlequinBooks

ReaderService.com

ⒽHARLEQUIN®

**ROMANCE WHEN
YOU NEED IT**

PGENRE2018

Looking for more satisfying love stories
with community and family at their core?

Check out **Harlequin® Special Edition**
and **Love Inspired®** books!

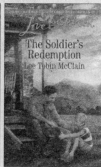

New books available every month!

CONNECT WITH US AT:

Facebook.com/groups/HarlequinConnection

Facebook.com/HarlequinBooks

Twitter.com/HarlequinBooks

Instagram.com/HarlequinBooks

Pinterest.com/HarlequinBooks

ReaderService.com

◆ HARLEQUIN®

**ROMANCE WHEN
YOU NEED IT**

HFGENRE2018

Rewar
love

Earn points on your purchase of new Harlequin books from participating retailers.

Turn your points into **FREE BOOKS** of your choice!

Join for FREE today at **www.HarlequinMyRewards.com.**

Harlequin My Rewards is a free program (no fees) without any commitments or obligations.